HEADLINES & HYDRAS

TERRA HAVEN CHRONICLES BOOK 2

REBECCA CHASTAIN

Copyright © 2021 by Rebecca Chastain
Cover design by Yocla Designs
Author photograph by Cody Watson

www.rebeccachastain.com

Mind Your Muse Books
PO Box 374
Rocklin, CA 95677

ISBN: 978-1-7344939-3-1

ALSO BY REBECCA CHASTAIN

NOVELS OF TERRA HAVEN

TERRA HAVEN CHRONICLES

Deadlines & Dryads (prequel)

Leads & Lynxes

Headlines & Hydras

Muckrakers & Minotaurs

GARGOYLE GUARDIAN CHRONICLES

Magic of the Gargoyles

Curse of the Gargoyles

Secret of the Gargoyles

Lured (newsletter exclusive)

THE MADISON FOX ADVENTURES

A Fistful of Evil

A Fistful of Fire

A Fistful of Flirtation (newsletter exclusive)

A Fistful of Frost

Madison Fox Novella Box Set

STAND ALONE

Tiny Glitches

Sign up for Rebecca's VIP List to receive newsletter-exclusive content.

ACKNOWLEDGMENTS

I'm grateful to all the people who helped shape this book into its final form, including:

My superb team of beta readers, Scott Ferguson, Sarah Gibson, Renea Kania, and Rebecca Moore, whose feedback improved this book in nuanced but vital ways;

My copyeditor, Carrie Andrews, and proofreader, Crystal Watanabe, for polishing the edges off my grammar;

Abigail King, who gave Yarra the perfect name;

And my husband, who made the appropriate and surprisingly helpful "hmm" and "uh-huh" contributions when I used him as a sounding board to work out plot tangles.

Constructive Elements

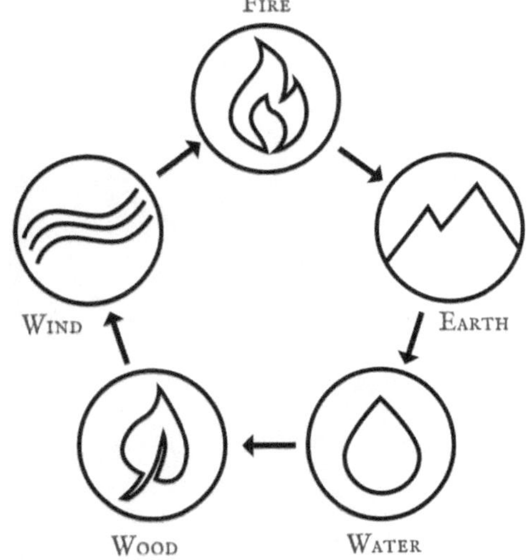

Destructive Elements

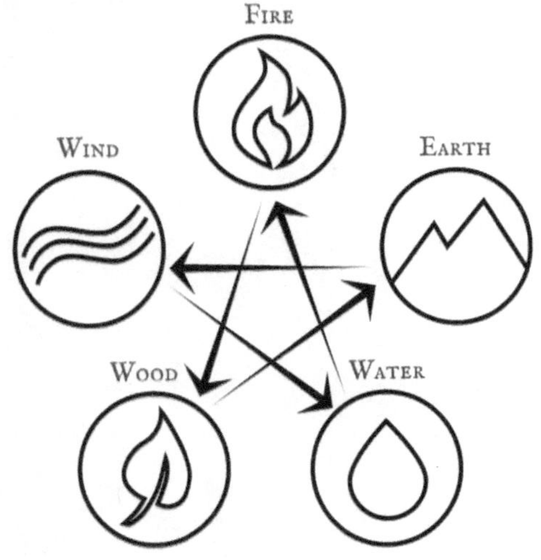

1

A rapid hammering jerked me awake. I seized a fistful of air element before my bleary vision cleared. *I shouldn't have let my guard down. It's too dangerous—*

The familiar sight of my apartment punctured my panic. I was home. Safe. My escape from Lunacy Labyrinth hadn't been a dream, though the horrors I had witnessed there haunted me in my nightmares.

Breathing deep, I released my magic and fought free of knotted, sweat-damp sheets. Pain flared through my thighs and biceps, and I bit down on a groan. After mending the cuts and scrapes I had received yesterday, the healers had claimed doing more—like soothing away the soreness of strained muscles—would have overtaxed my exhausted body. Allowing those muscles to relax overnight had only invited the stiffness to root deeper.

A fist pounded the balcony door again, hard enough to rattle the whole wall. "Are you awake?" Mika asked, her voice muffled through the door.

"I am now," I grumbled.

Normally I appreciated living on the second floor of a large Victorian house, renting a room connected to my best friend's by a balcony.

However, my best friend normally didn't wake me at dawn.

Grunting with each step, I hobbled to the door and opened it.

Mika burst into my room, haloed in morning sunshine. I shielded my eyes as I staggered back to my bed, slumping onto the edge. She followed, too fast for my tearing eyes to track. Her long strawberry-blond hair hung loose, still snarled from sleep, and she hadn't bothered to change out of her striped pajamas or put on shoes. Oliver trundled into the room on her heels, his sinuous dragon body casting a red glow across the ceiling as the sun refracted off his glossy carnelian scales. Despite the gargoyle's stubby legs, Oliver's head now cleared my bed, and I hoped he was close to done growing. If he got much bigger, he wouldn't fit in our tiny apartments.

"Is everything all right?" I asked before I spotted a copy of the *Terra Haven Chronicle* clutched in Mika's fist. My heart sank. I scooted back on the bed and drew my feet up in front of me, wishing I could crawl under the covers and avoid this conversation.

"Is this true?" Mika spread the paper open and waved toward the black-and-white print beneath a picture of a firebird. "Are you the Airstrong heiress?"

"I . . ." My thoughts scattered when Mika lifted her gaze to mine, the pain of betrayal glistening in unshed tears.

I hadn't wanted Mika to find out about my family like this. I hadn't wanted *anyone* to find out, period. I had chosen to leave behind my parents' world and their upper-crust lifestyle in favor of making my own way. With their blessing, if not their understanding, my parents had freed me from the expectation of assuming responsibility for their international shipping empire and allowed me to pursue my passion as a journalist. Doing so anonymously had been my decision. I had wanted to make sure I succeeded on my own merit, not because someone owed my parents a favor. It had taken years of scraping by before I landed a junior journalist position at the *Terra Haven Chronicle*. Now, just when I was starting to get noticed by the editor in chief, my nemesis, Nathan, had taken it upon himself to out me to the world in his front-page article.

"Your real name isn't even Kylie," Mika said, her voice soft. "It's Harriet, isn't it?"

I flinched. I hated my first name and loathed hearing Mika use it. It had been bad enough to see it printed in the paper. *Grayson daughter, Harriet, has been operating seemingly independent of her parents' business under the alias Kylie Grayson.* I would never forget the line—nor forgive Nathan for writing it. The article should have focused solely on the recovery of the missing firebirds and the destruction of Lunacy Labyrinth. However, my parents' shipping company, Airstrong, had been the business responsible for the fire-birds' transportation. Having the firebirds *discovered in the possession of the Airstrong heiress*—another deplorable quote from the article—had given Nathan the opening he needed to slander me to the world.

Keeping my voice neutral, I said, "Kylie is my preferred name. My full name is Harriet Kylie Grayson."

"You used an alias—"

"Not an *alias*," I said, hating that Mika was quoting Nathan.

The paper crinkled in her fist. "You lied to me about your name."

"I didn't lie—"

"Stop parsing words with me. You lied by omission." Her words landed between us, the vulnerability in her expression cracking and anger seeping out. "You let me believe you were someone you're not. What else have you been lying about?"

"Nothing. I swear." I leaned forward to stand, but she didn't give me enough room. "I wanted to tell you. I just ..."

"Let me guess. You couldn't find the right time in the last *half decade*." Mika spun away, pacing in the limited space, stepping over Oliver without seeming to notice the gargoyle. Confined by the tight room, she about-faced and bore down on me. I fumbled for the right words to make her understand, but her glare silenced me. Reversing course, she paced away from me again. Oliver hopped onto the love seat and curled his slender tail out of the way, his wide eyes tracking Mika. He reached a paw out to her when she stomped close but withdrew it when she didn't acknowledge him.

Golden light bounced across the walls as Quinn dropped from the roof to fill the doorway, worry etching his feline features. Sunlight slanted across the gargoyle's broad lion shoulders and glinted off his long wings. Quinn's citrine body sported an alarming number of clear quartz patches, a testament to all the injuries Mika had healed. Navigating the blood-magic ruins of Lunacy Labyrinth had been harder on Quinn than it had been on me, and I resolved not to complain about my own soreness.

Against my will, my gaze dipped to Quinn's everlasting seed. It hung from a cord around his neck, ugly and brown. Thanks to our adventures in Lunacy, it had evolved into its current shape, though maybe *devolved* was more appropriate. The original artistic ebony knot of a snake biting its own tail had transformed into a fist-size mess that resembled a muddy, half-melted, half-exploded pinecone. Staring at it made me woozy. Quinn had used his one question to ask the everlasting tree how he could best help me, which was why I tried not to let on how unnerving I found his seed's new shape. Especially since saving my life had been the catalyst of his seed's evolution, whereas initiating my seed's transformation had nearly killed us both, and its current shape pointed toward even greater danger.

A bundle of elements coasted through the open door, drawing my attention from Quinn's seed. The tight knot of magic curved in the ubiquitous lines of a message sphere, but the magical signature—the texture of structured fire and steady winds underlying the spell—was unmistakably my boss's. Expecting the sphere to settle into my message bowl, I nearly levitated when it dropped to pop in my face. Editor in Chief Dahlia Bearpaw's brusque voice spilled out, as loud as if she were standing in the room with us.

"Ms. Grayson. My office. Now. Don't make me wait."

My stomach flipped. Nothing good could follow that tone.

"Did she know?" Mika asked.

I shook my head.

"So it's not just me." With Quinn filling the balcony doorway, Mika's pacing space had become confined to a few steps, and she stopped to glower at me with her hands on her hips.

"I understand why you're mad," I began.

"Oh really? Please enlighten me, *Harriet*."

My teeth clenched, but I forced them apart. "I should have told you, but honestly . . . it wasn't important."

"It . . . it wasn't important?" she sputtered. Her hands

twisted the hem of her shirt, her eyes bright. "Because I'm a commoner and it doesn't matter what I think?"

"That's not it at all," I protested. "Mika, please—"

"What is all this to you?" She swept a hand to indicate the cramped apartment, with its secondhand furniture, faded curtains, overflowing hamper, and claustrophobic bathroom. Or maybe she included the entire low-income neighborhood beyond the curtains in her gesture. "Is this some sort of elitist rite of passage? See how long you can slum it? Now you'll return to your 'peers' and regale them with tales of living among the pitiable poor?"

My explanation withered on my tongue. I shoved to my feet and pointed at Mika. "*This* is the other reason I never said anything! I knew how judgmental you would be."

"I'm the one to blame for your lies? That's rich. Very full spectrum of you. I didn't ask you—"

The house's wards broke, the magic popping against my eardrums as it shattered. Something heavy crashed into the roof, rattling the whole house. I ducked, my hand flinging out to find Mika's.

The rafters creaked and popped. Breath held, I stared at the ceiling, straining to see through solid matter. Mika's fingers clamped a vise around mine. The Victorian's roof had endured extraordinary strain in the last half year from the weight of five growing gargoyles roosting nightly along its ridges, but their movements never made this kind of racket. These steps sounded wider, more scratchy, like a dragon or a—

"Harpy," I whispered, my muscles locking in a wave of terror. The stench of sunbaked feces and carrion oozed into the apartment, confirming my words.

Zipporah had found me.

Quinn whimpered. I jerked my gaze from the ceiling.

"Get inside," I hissed, frantically motioning him forward.

Mika backed up to give Quinn room to squeeze into the apartment, and I half fell over him in my rush to close the door behind him.

How had Zipporah figured out where I lived? Did she know I didn't have her payment? Was she here to collect anyway? The only item left on the bartering table was my life.

I rubbed sweaty palms down my cotton shorts and glanced around for inspiration—or for an escape. I didn't fool myself into thinking we were safe inside. The bay windows were cloaked by curtains, disguising our movements, but once Zipporah figured out where I was, those panes would be no barrier against her talons.

"What's going on?" Mika whispered.

The answer came from above. "Kylie Grayson, show yourself!"

"Where are Anya, Herbert, and Lydia?" I asked Mika, listing Quinn and Oliver's littermates, who also frequented our rooftop.

"They went to the park before dawn."

"So no one's up there?"

Mika shook her head, and I let out a tight breath.

"Why does a harpy know your name, Kylie? What are you mixed up in?"

I bit my lip, debating if we had time for an explanation. "I made a bad decision and—"

"Little girl, I can smell you inside," Zipporah called. "Come out, or *I'm coming in.*" She screeched the last words loud enough to echo through the neighborhood. If my landlady hadn't been woken by the house wards breaking, she was awake now—along with everyone else in a three-block radius.

"We can't let her find you," Quinn said.

"I think it's too late for that."

"She hasn't seen you yet." He nosed me toward the apartment's front door, which opened onto the upstairs hallway of the Victorian. In a few steps, I could be downstairs, protected by the bulk of the enormous house instead of one thin layer of rafters and shingles. But as much as I longed to flee, I didn't let him move me.

"Don't make me wait!" Zipporah shouted. "I'm not in a patient mood." Claws raked across the roof, the deafening swipe tearing apart shingles and timber. The pictures on my walls rattled and crashed to the floor. I flinched, eyes darting to the ceiling, expecting to see the harpy's claws puncture the roof. The wood held, but it wouldn't take much additional abuse before Zipporah burst through.

Grabbing Mika's shoulders, I gave her a shake so she would focus on me. "Go. Get downstairs and take Oliver and Quinn with you. Make sure everyone stays inside, even Josephine." I had a horrible vision of our middle-aged landlady rushing up to the roof with a broom and a handful of questionably legal repellent spells, thinking she could chase away a harpy as easily as she did the occasional gang member who thought to cause trouble on our street. Zipporah would flatten her without a second thought.

Mika allowed herself to be pushed a step before she firmed her stance. "What are you going to do? You can't go out there."

I couldn't stay inside either. Zipporah was fully capable of tearing the roof off a house, and even if I was all right with allowing the harpy to destroy my home—my *rented* home—there was nowhere I could hide that she couldn't find me. Running was out of the question, too. She was faster, had an aerial advantage, and could brush aside any spell I cast with depressing ease. But most important, I couldn't allow Zipporah near Mika or the gargoyles. I wouldn't be able to live with myself if they were hurt because of me.

"I'll get Grant," Quinn said.

Zipporah tore into the roof again, ripping a chunk free with an earsplitting screech of shattering boards. A shadow flashed past the drawn curtain; then the lumber hit the cobblestones below with a resounding clap.

"There's no time." I braced myself and eased open the balcony door.

The foul odor of excrement engulfed me, and I wavered. My debt to Zipporah was straightforward: I acquiesced to a favor of her choosing or I died. At the time I made the foolish bargain, my choices had been the same—owe her or die on the spot. I had envisioned all kinds of frightening requests Zipporah might make, but none came close to her horrifying demand that I bring her the Chiefmaker, a deadly, blood-magic artifact last seen inside Lunacy Labyrinth. She had even gone so far as to toss me into the hellacious ruins. Neither of us had expected me to survive. Yet here I was, empty-handed but alive.

How was I going to convince Zipporah not to kill me?

On watery legs, I crept onto the balcony and peered past the roof awning. The harpy filled the sky, her oily wings spread, every glob and crust of filth caking the undersides of her giant bird body intimately visible from this angle. She faced away from me, one clawed foot braced on the roof's peak while the other gouged a hole through the shingles.

I pulled a thick ward of earth and air around myself. The magic came easily, enhanced by Oliver and Quinn. The gargoyles' natural ability to boost the elements in others gave me twice my usual strength, and I added extra layers to my protective ward. It did little to reassure me. Zipporah had proven she could rip through my gargoyle-enhanced wards before, but I couldn't step outside without at least the illusion of protection. I glanced down at my thin cotton pajamas. I might as well be naked for all the protection they would afford, but I didn't dare take the time to change.

Quinn squeezed out onto the balcony behind me, and Oliver and Mika stood inside the threshold. Did they not understand how dangerous Zipporah was?

Stay back, I mouthed. I wouldn't try to stop Quinn—he knew the dangers, and it would take too long to convince him to stay behind—but for once I wished Mika was more of a coward. If she involved herself in this confrontation, she would only get hurt.

Giving Mika one last, stern glare, I vaulted onto the balcony railing, then up to the roof above Mika's room. The abrasive shingles bit into my bare feet and scraped my palms. I scrambled for the peak of the roof where my footing would be the most stable, every nerve in my body tensed in anticipation of being skewered. A dog barked several houses over, and I caught glimpses of shocked faces pressed to the windows of the nearby homes as hasty wards flashed into place.

Quinn sprang onto the railing, then surged up the roof after me, so close his half-spread wings brushed against my legs. I wanted to order him to fly away for his own safety, but his determined expression stopped me. Instead, I laid a grateful hand atop his shoulders and extended my ward to encompass him.

Mika and Oliver hunkered in the shadows just inside my apartment doorway. Mika mouthed something, but I couldn't read her lips.

Zipporah hopped in a tight circle, shaking the roof as

she turned to face me. I bent my knees for balance, hands splayed as if I could hold her at bay by sheer will.

"How disappointing. I thought you might try to run," she said before launching toward me. Torn shingles and ripped boards scattered into the air behind her. Snapping her wings wide, Zipporah closed the distance between us in a single flap, her talons splayed before her. I ducked beneath them, clutching the shingles with my fingertips. Her next flap cupped around me as she back-winged, drowning me in noxious fumes. I struggled to rise, stumbling when she added an elemental enhancement to the buffet of her wings.

Quinn caught me, a sturdy stone wing supporting me until I regained my balance. I glanced over my shoulder. The drop-off to the street two and a half stories below yawned behind Quinn's back foot, one meager misstep away.

Cackling, Zipporah landed, crowding me with her filthy body as she folded her wings loosely against her back. The movement thrust her flaccid human breasts toward me, the skin mottled with sun spots and puckered with permanent gooseflesh above the brown feathers of her abdomen. We were almost matched in height, but she effortlessly loomed.

"Here you are. Alive." Zipporah shoved her face into mine.

I fought against the instinct to retreat. I had nowhere to go. Instead, I squared my shoulders and lifted my chin, attempting to project courage and pretend my knees weren't quivering. Up close, Zipporah's features looked less human than ever. Grime crusted the wrinkles etched in her bald forehead, around her yellow eyes, and down her hollow cheeks. Spindly feathers matted the rounded crown of her leathery head, giving the impression of oily hair, and her nose jutted like a misplaced beak above her lipless mouth.

"Which makes me wonder," she hissed, revealing razor-edged teeth caked with gore, "where is my bloodstone? Where is the Chiefmaker?"

I choked on her exhale, my eyes watering at the olfactory assault.

"I was—" I coughed, struggling for a breath without actually inhaling. "I was unable to find it before the firebirds destroyed the ruins."

That wasn't precisely true, but even if the Chiefmaker hadn't been destroyed, I would never have handed it over to the harpy. The bloodstone had granted the user complete control over anyone with blood running through their veins. I had been helpless against it when it had been used against me, and when I had held it . . . The power the stone had offered would haunt my nightmares for years to come. If someone as immoral as Zipporah had gotten the Chiefmaker in her clutches, she could have wreaked unfathomable devastation.

Zipporah cocked her head left, then right, as if trying to decide if I was telling the truth—or perhaps to decide which piece of me to eat first. "Isn't that unfortunate for you. Or do I have to remind you of the consequence of coming back without my bloodstone?"

Ice crystallized down my spine. "I did my best. In fact"—I summoned the paltry argument I had pieced together last night in anticipation of this confrontation—"I searched as long as I could, until I was forced out when the ruins collapsed. I did everything you instructed."

Zipporah's eyes narrowed, her nostrils flaring and her wings flexing. Quinn's wing dug into my hip as I shrank away from her fury.

Licking my lips, I rushed to get the rest of my words out. "Beldame Zipporah, our deal was that I owed you a favor.

You called on that favor when you sent me into Lunacy Labyrinth. I went; therefore, I am no longer in your debt."

Zipporah's foot shot forward too fast to avoid, her steely talons knocking Quinn aside as if he weighed nothing. The gargoyle tumbled helplessly off the roof. I yelled his name, shoving a brace of air beneath him. It wasn't enough to stop his plummet, but it slowed him. Quinn's wings snapped open, and he flapped heavily to regain altitude. By then, it was too late: Zipporah's claws encased me.

Effortlessly, she crushed my ward. The broken elements snapped back into me. My vision tunneled, pain bowing my body. Zipporah squeezed, grinding my ribs together, robbing me of oxygen. Mika hurled a blade of earth magic at the harpy, but Zipporah shattered it with a negligent slice of wood, then used a punch of air to toss Mika and Oliver deeper into my apartment. A second later, the harpy's magic slammed the door shut and fused it in place.

Zipporah lifted me until I dangled inches above the rooftop. Lungs burning, I clutched her filthy toes, each larger than my thighs, straining to get free. I might as well have tried to straighten an oak's branches with my bare hands.

"Our deal was your life for a debt," Zipporah said. "I see no debt paid, which leaves only your life as payment."

Quinn dove from above, an arrow of golden quartz. Zipporah bludgeoned him with a club of air, and he tumbled into the ruined roof above my apartment.

"Don't hurt him," I wheezed. I would have begged Quinn to stand down if I could have projected my voice that far. Air scraped down my throat in painful rasps, coated in Zipporah's putrescence. Black flecks danced at the edges of my vision. "Give me another chance."

Zipporah tipped me, dangling me higher above the

sloped roof. If she dropped me, I wouldn't have time to catch myself before tumbling to the hard cobblestones far, far below. I stopped struggling and twisted to meet her rapacious gaze. The angle exposed my neck, and her hungry eyes sliced to my visible, pounding pulse.

"Please, one more chance. I won't let you down again," I babbled.

She relaxed her grip. I screamed as I dropped half a foot before she clutched her talons around me again.

"One more chance?" Zipporah unfurled a wing, exposing the bony digits that protruded from the alula like a deformed skeletal hand. Fanning the fingers, she drew a clawed tip through my hair, catching a snarl and cutting through it with a sharp tug. A clump of my pale hair drifted to the rooftop. Dread caused goose bumps to break across my scalp. I trembled helplessly as Zipporah drew the digit down the side of my face, scratching lightly into my jaw, then more heavily down my throat. An involuntary hiss escaped my lips at the white-hot pain that followed in the claw's wake.

"For all I know, you're lying to me about finding the Chiefmaker. I'm not inclined to be lenient."

"I'm not lying to you. I swear the Chiefmaker was destroyed."

"You sound awfully certain for a woman who claims she didn't find the bloodstone." Zipporah's cadaverous fingers squeezed my throat, and I fought not to swallow, afraid I would puncture myself if I did.

"The firebirds," I rasped.

"Yes, the firebirds," Zipporah agreed with a foul sigh that drew bile up the back of my constricted throat.

Sweat trickled down my temple. I wracked my brain for a spell—any spell—that I could use against the harpy.

Quinn and Oliver still boosted my magic, but it was no use. With their help, I might be able to fashion an elemental weapon powerful enough to hurt Zipporah, but I would never be able to complete an attack before she slit my throat.

"Few are stupid enough to disappoint me. No one has lived to do so twice," Zipporah said, stroking her bony claws down my neck again, lighter this time, the scratches chasing shivers down my body. She observed my reaction with unblinking eyes.

In my peripheral vision, Quinn struggled to stand, but Zipporah held him pinned to the mangled roof above my apartment with a sheet of air. She had used the trick on him before, and we both knew he wouldn't be escaping until she let him.

"I can be useful." I hated the words coming out of my mouth as much as I despised my pleading tone, but I had no choice if I wanted to live.

"We'll see about that." Zipporah dropped me.

I plummeted to the roof and slid. The drop-off rushed toward me, and I scrambled for purchase on the steep incline. Fiery pain flared in my hands, knees, and feet, but I managed to claw to a stop with my toes curled into the shingles inches from the edge. Heart pounding, I shoved to my hands and knees, craning my head to look up at Zipporah.

She remained at the peak of the roof, studying me indifferently. Shouts echoed from farther up the street, and Zipporah's head swiveled toward the commotion. Distaste twisted her expression. She hopped to the edge of the roof, shaking the house beneath her. I curled my toes and fingers into the rough shingles, wishing I had a solid handhold.

"I always collect my debts, and yours just got more expensive," she promised. "See you soon, Kylie Grayson."

The gusts of Zipporah's departure rocked me, but it was the full import of her words that caused my arms to collapse. I rolled to my side and stared blindly after the harpy.

One way or another, I had a feeling I wouldn't be free of my debt to her until I was dead.

2

Zipporah's spell caging Quinn broke. He launched from the gable above my room and landed heavily next to me, quartz claws scraping for purchase. Worry pinched his brows when he shoved his face into mine.

"I'm all right," I said. My scraped knees throbbed and pain spiked across my palms and the soles of my feet, but it could have been so much worse. "You?"

"I feel awful," he whispered. "I couldn't do anything."

"Neither could I." Wrapping an arm around his neck, I pulled him close and pressed my cheek against his.

Rapid footsteps pounded the cobblestones in front of the house. They slammed up the porch stairs, and the front door bounced off the wall with a slap that shook the house all the way to the roof. Alarm jolted through my tense muscles, and I braced my feet to stand. Quinn leapt to straddle me before I could rise, his wings flared wide in a citrine shield. We both gasped when Grant Monaghan blasted from the ground to the roof on a sheet of air scant wider than his feet. The speed of his ascent ruffled his thick dark hair and plastered the protective fabric of his FPD uniform to his muscular frame. His intense gaze flicked over me, quick and assessing, before he surveyed the rest of the scene, taking in Zipporah's retreating silhouette, the ravaged rafters above my apartment, and the talon-scored shingles along the ridge of this gable. Only then did he land, his thick-soled boots touching down lightly.

I had seen him fly before—no one became captain of a Federal Pentagon Defense squad without being exceptionally gifted with the elements—but I still had to stomp on my burst of envy. Even enhanced by two gargoyles, I wouldn't have been able to master that levitation spell, let alone make it look graceful.

"You sure know how to make an entrance," I said, craning my neck to study his battle-ready expression. A cocktail of embarrassment, relief, and excitement swirled in my gut when our gazes connected.

"Grant!" Quinn gently headbutted the captain, his grin revealing long citrine fangs. "You saved us!"

I belatedly put it together, realizing it must have been Grant and whoever had stormed through the front door that had scared Zipporah off, and bitterness tinged my gratitude. Grant's mere presence had done more to protect me than anything I had attempted. I had been useless.

Grant dropped to one knee, and Quinn scooted back, finally freeing me to sit all the way up.

"I was afraid I would arrive too late." Grant's words came out stiff as his gaze skimmed past the wet glob of harpy excrement plastering my cotton shorts to my hips and fixated on the blood dribbling down my knees.

I swallowed a groan. When we had last parted ways, I had been a bedraggled mess. I had promised myself that the next time I spoke with Grant, I would be wearing something sexy that enhanced my womanly curves, what little I had of them. My hair would be spelled to fall in waves around my face, and I wouldn't have a speck of dirt on me. In my imagined scenario, Grant wouldn't have been able to take his eyes off me because he would have been overwhelmed by his attraction to me, not because a combination of shabby pajamas, bloody smears, and fecal-flecked grime made me look and smell like a day-old corpse.

"How did you—" I started, but then answered my own question: "Mika." She must have sent word for him while I had been climbing onto the roof.

"We came as fast as we could," Grant said. His gaze flicked to the balcony below us, and I looked down in time to see Marcus Velasquez stride across the open walkway from Mika's apartment to mine.

Of course. Mika and Velasquez were dating, and it made sense that she would send her urgent message to him, not Grant. As the fire elemental in Grant's FPD squad, Velasquez was more than qualified to confront whatever dangers threatened Terra Haven citizens, harpies included. It was what the FPD did.

"If I had known Zipporah would find you this fast . . ." Grant stroked a callused finger across my temple, hooking a grubby hank of hair behind my ear.

My stomach somersaulted, and I held perfectly still, mesmerized by the emotions playing through his brown eyes.

"I should have known better." Grant shook his head. "When Zipporah is owed a debt, she's ruthless."

A gasp jerked my gaze from Grant's. Mika stood in the doorway to my apartment, her hair disheveled and her cheeks flushed with adrenaline, but her expression radiated pure betrayal when she met my eyes. Seeing it stabbed another knife of guilt into my gut. Not twenty minutes ago, I had sworn to Mika that I didn't have any other secrets, forgetting I hadn't yet told her about my loathsome debt.

Mika stalked back into my apartment before I could decide what to say. My spine deflated.

"Thank you for coming," I said, speaking to Grant's chest. "And for scaring Zipporah off."

"She's not gone for good."

"I know." I glanced bleakly at the ruined gable above my apartment. Zipporah had broken through the roof as easily as she had the house's wards. She had nearly killed Quinn. I was alive only because she had decided I was still of use to her. I dreaded what might happen the next time she showed up.

Quinn ducked his head, also apparently finding it easier to talk to the elemental patterns on Grant's shirt than to meet his eyes. "I tried to protect Kylie, but I was useless against Zipporah."

"That's not true," I said. "I would have fallen if not for you."

"But then she flicked me aside as if I were nothing. A fly. I fought with all my strength, but I couldn't break free once she pinned me down." Quinn turned anguished eyes on me.

I rubbed his shoulder soothingly, wishing for the thousandth time that I had never been so foolish as to make a deal with the harpy to begin with. "You were brave, and you were there for me when I needed you."

"Not everyone can stand toe-to-toe with a harpy, especially not one as strong as Zipporah," Grant said. "There's no shame in that."

Quinn didn't look like he agreed, and I knew exactly how he felt.

Grant turned my chin toward him, lifting it so I was

forced to meet his eyes. "Not everyone is a fighter, and that's all right, too."

I drew in a deep breath, wanting to protest, but I let the air out on a long sigh instead. He was right. I wasn't a fighter. I had never trained magically or physically to defend against or attack another being. But maybe I needed to if I was going to survive being in Zipporah's debt.

Abruptly tired of being on the roof, tired of wallowing in my own failings, and tired of circling through the same grim thoughts, I pushed to my feet. Grant straightened and helped me, supporting me when putting weight on my abraded soles made me wince. I examined my scraped palms. Blood oozed from several gashes, and bits of shingle were embedded in my flesh. Then I glanced at the drop to the railing and balcony below it.

Getting down was going to hurt.

"Allow me," Grant said. He gently tugged me against his chest, wrapping his arms around me.

Surprise stiffened my spine, but it took only a second for my arms to slide around Grant in return. The supple texture of his uniform encased a body that was anything but soft, and I relaxed against the hard pillar of his chest. Grant's arms tightened, caging me against his body; then he lifted me enough to slide a thin layer of wood- and earth-laced air beneath my feet. I gasped and clung tighter to him when he floated us down to the balcony, effortlessly balancing us atop the delicate platform until our soles connected with the worn wooden planks.

I expected him to release me immediately. He didn't. A tiny part of my brain analyzed what Grant's continued embrace might mean—that maybe his feelings for me were more than adrenaline-fueled impulses from our shared near-death encounters; he might genuinely care for me. The rest of me simply existed in the moment, enjoying the novelty of his strong arms wrapped around me. I was safe. Protected. I leaned into his embrace, pressing my face to his chest. He smelled delicious, like sun-warmed vanilla with a hint of sweat.

Unfortunately, I smelled a lot worse, and as much as I wished I could snuggle against Grant's chest for another hour—or maybe just another five minutes—a sense of urgency already prodded the back of my mind.

I straightened, and Grant dropped his arms. The scrapes on my knees and hands throbbed as if in protest. When I took a step back, sharp pain stabbed the balls of my feet.

"Thank you," I said.

"You need healing," Grant said.

"And a shower."

I limped into my apartment. I made it two steps before I slammed into Velasquez.

"Oof."

He shot a hand out to steady me, withdrawing it just as quickly when Grant's hands settled on my shoulders first.

I waited for Velasquez to back up. He wore the same gray uniform as Grant, though the collar of his long-sleeve shirt was embroidered with a red fire-element symbol rather than Grant's air symbol. I lifted my eyes to his face, forced to tilt my head back to do so. He stood a head taller than me, equally as tall as Grant and equally as imposing—especially with fury burning in his deep-blue eyes.

"What kind of imbecile shares her home address with a harpy?" Velasquez demanded.

I jerked as if he had slapped me. "I didn't. I don't know how she found me. She just showed up."

His hands flexed into fists, then relaxed. Leaning closer, Velasquez loomed over me in blatant intimidation. "Do you ever consider the people around you that you're putting in danger?"

His question ripped open the knot of guilt pulsing beneath my breastbone. My fingers fluttered to the phantom pain, and I swallowed hard. I had put Quinn's life at risk more than once, and now I had endangered Mika and Oliver, too. I wanted to protest that I would have prevented the incident if I could, that I had no control over Zipporah or where she went, but those were excuses.

"I'm sorry," I said, my voice breaking.

"You need to—"

"Velasquez." The warning in Grant's soft tone caused the fire elemental to clamp his mouth shut. Jaw clenched and nostrils flared, Velasquez stepped aside.

Mika stood behind him, her expression caught between worry and anger. White dust coated her hair and shoulders. My bed lay buried in broken plaster and splintered boards. More detritus coated the narrow love seat and table, spraying all the way to the front door of my one-room apartment. Rays of sunlight slanted through the ragged holes in the roof, illuminating shafts of fine dust hanging in the air. I took a hesitant step forward, double-checking Mika for injuries. A small cut bled on her knee, another on her forearm. I opened my mouth to apologize again, but Mika stopped me with a wave of her hand.

"No. Not now. I—" She glanced from Velasquez to Grant, both men taking up too much space. Anger tightened Velasquez's mouth, but Grant wore his familiar stern mask, not letting anyone see his emotions.

Quinn jumped to the balcony railing, then to the balcony, his wings tucked tight to his body. Abrasions dulled his shoulder and feathers where the friction of his escape attempts had worn away layers of his quartz body.

"I . . . I need to tend to Quinn," Mika finished, changing whatever she had originally planned to say when she spotted Quinn's wounds. She stepped around me, then squeezed past Grant and through the door.

I lifted a hand after her, but I remained silent. I wanted to explain myself, but now wasn't the time. Quinn needed medical attention, and I was loathe to have a heart-to-heart with Mika while Grant and Velasquez looked on.

Oliver followed Mika out, taking a moment to twine around Velasquez's leg before he departed. The narrow balcony wasn't big enough to fit both him and Quinn, so Oliver jumped to the railing. I monitored Quinn for signs of distress, but as always, Mika's healing touch appeared soothing, and his eyes closed.

"What is the meaning of this?"

I spun toward the front door, flinching when the movement stretched the cuts on the bottom of my feet. My landlady, Josephine Zuberrie, stood in the open doorway, her fists planted on her hips. Thin and small boned, with her usually tidy white hair hanging in a sloppy bun, the petite woman shouldn't have looked daunting, but both men jerked to attention, and my own spine straightened at her tone.

"Was this your doing?" Josephine demanded, pointing a finger at Grant and Velasquez. Ruddiness marred her pale cheeks, a sure sign of her temper. "Did you bring a harpy to my doorstep?"

I wanted to shrink behind Grant, but I forced myself to step forward.

"No. It was my fault."

Josephine's pale-blue eyes snapped to me. "You?"

"I didn't—"

"I was abundantly clear when you signed your lease,"

she said, not waiting for my explanation. "I don't care if you're an Airstrong Grayson or a nobody Grayson, the rules still apply to you."

I grimaced. Of course she had seen Nathan's article. "Yes, ma'am."

"I run a clean, safe house. It's right there in the contract: Any criminal activity and you're out on the street—no refunds, no delays, no excuses. I won't suffer that kind of drama under my roof."

My heart sank. She was going to evict me. "Josephine, I'm sorry. I—"

"Sorry won't fix my roof."

"I—"

She waved me silent, studying me with narrowed eyes, as if examining my soul. After an excruciating minute, she nodded. "This is your one *and only* pass, Kylie. If anything like this happens again, if you bring any violent or unscrupulous characters to this house again, that will be your last day under this roof. Is that clear?"

"Yes, ma'am." Relief enabled me to breathe. I had been leasing from Josephine for years, ever since I moved out on my own. I had shared countless meals with her and countless hours of gossip. I thought of her as a friend and a kindred spirit. It hurt to have our relationship reduced to a transactional agreement of tenant and landlady, but I understood her reasoning. She didn't deserve to have my problems dive-bomb her peaceful morning. Nor did she deserve to have her life and livelihood threatened by my enemies.

"Here. This nearly knocked me down on my way up." Josephine stepped aside, revealing a bubble of elements she held restrained in a net of air. Something rectangular and flat lay within the bubble. Josephine released her net, and the elements blasted across my tiny room, straight for me.

Grant and Velasquez tensed, but they must have discerned the specifics of the spell at the same time I did, and they didn't interfere when I plucked the envelope from the elemental cradle. At the recognition of my magical signature, the magic popped softly around my hand, and a smaller sphere zipped out the open door behind me, off to inform the sender that the package had reached its intended recipient.

I hadn't seen that style of elaborate, elementally personalized mail delivery since I had moved out of my parents' house. It was the sort of elemental excessiveness typical of high-society, full-spectrum pentacle potential individuals who could wield all five elements with the mastery and strength some of us could achieve with only one or two elements, if that. I couldn't fathom a reason for an FSPP to send mail to a lowly junior journalist residing in near poverty on the outskirts of the blight. This must be a mistake.

Three words graced the ivory envelope in exquisite cursive: *Harriet Kylie Grayson*. My gut hollowed out. I ripped open the envelope, and a thick sky-blue card fell out. The Kwan crest, an artful hibiscus flower, embossed the top, the petals inlaid in gold. The same elegant handwriting looped across the card's surface, short and to the point, though I read the words twice before they sank in.

"It's an invitation," I said, realizing everyone was staring at me. "For a solstice ceremony Persephone Kwan is hosting."

Not *a* solstice ceremony. *The* solstice ceremony. The Kwans were one of the oldest FSPP families in Terra Haven. It was no surprise they had seized the coveted privilege of hosting this year's solstice party for the upper echelon of society. It would be—according to upper-crust families—*the* event to attend this summer. Every full-spectrum family, family friend, and business partner would be in attendance. Seeing my name on the invitation sent a traitorous thrill through me, one chased by bittersweet melancholy. Nathan's article had cleared the presses less than twenty-four hours ago, and already forces were in play to drag me back into my old life. My treasured days of anonymity were well and truly dead. I closed my eyes, needing a moment to catch my breath and mourn the loss of the life I had so carefully constructed.

The shrill whistle of a teakettle pierced the silence. I jumped. Josephine gave her skirt a firm shake and pinned me with a final, weighted stare that promised a much longer discussion later. Then she spun on her heel and departed.

"The same Persephone Kwan who just got engaged to the insanely rich full-spectrum Luther Wetherill?" Mika asked, her voice high.

"Did she?" I asked, startled. "There's no accounting for taste."

"You say that like you know these people," Mika accused.

Because I did. Persephone was an old acquaintance of my mother's; Wetherill ran Capstone Transportation, a lucrative international shipping company that was Airstrong's top competitor. As a child, I had attended multiple gatherings at both households—I had once won a kid's pegasus race at one of Persephone's lavish parties, and when I was eight, I stole my first kiss in an alcove of Wetherill's hedge maze—but I took one look at Mika's suspicious expression and kept the memories to myself.

"This is just a formality," I said, tossing the invitation onto my dresser. Plaster particulates puffed into the air.

Mika straightened, having finished healing Quinn's injuries. "Did you know we had an heiress in our midst?" she asked Velasquez and Grant.

"I figured it out," Grant said. He squeezed around Velasquez and shut my apartment's front door.

"Before or after the upper class started sending Kylie invitations to their exclusive parties?"

"Yesterday," Velasquez said.

Mika's eyes widened. Velasquez had basically just admitted he'd had time to tell her my identity, if he had wanted. I respected his honesty and discretion, and Mika would, too, when she had a moment to calm down.

"I'm not going to their party," I said, redirecting her attention. The last place I wanted to go was a full-spectrum event where I would be surrounded by pretentious elitists.

"Of course you're not going," Mika said. "Because you're so famous and important that you can say no to an invitation from the head of the Kwan family to the most important ritual of the year." Sarcasm rasped through her words.

"It's not like that. It's complicated," I said.

"Why don't I save you the effort of trying to dumb it down for me." Fists clenched, Mika spun on her heel and stormed into her apartment, pausing only long enough for Oliver to scurry in after her before she slammed the door.

Quinn remained on the balcony, peering anxiously after Mika.

Velasquez leaned close to my ear, dropping his voice so it wouldn't carry beyond the two of us. "If you don't want people to think you're a self-centered, high-society brat, stop acting like one. Think about someone other than yourself for once."

Tears sprang unbidden to my eyes, and I locked my jaw, holding my eyelids wide so my tears wouldn't spill. I had made a mess of my relationship with my closest friend and gotten people I cared about hurt. I had also been attacked by a harpy in my own home and now teetered on the precipice of being evicted. And given Dahlia's terse message, my position at the *Terra Haven Chronicle* was just as tenuous. It wasn't even breakfast time yet. It was too much, and Velasquez's censure piled on top threatened to shatter me.

Velasquez held my stare for a long, painful moment, then stomped past me to Mika's apartment.

I jerked around. "I need a shower."

"You need healing," Grant said.

"Shower first." Grabbing the closest pair of clean pants and a shirt, I fled into the bathroom, keeping my back to Grant so he wouldn't see the trail of tears rolling down my cheeks.

3

The shower stung, reawakening every cut and scrape as if it were being inflicted anew by the water, and I allowed myself to cry. It helped, freeing my thoughts to focus on something other than self-chastisement. By the time I toweled off, I had a clear plan, and I hurried to dress.

My urgency stalled when I exited the bathroom and caught sight of Grant Monaghan, the sexiest and most intriguing man I had ever laid eyes on, sitting on my bed. If only he looked happy to be there. He perched on the edge, with his elbows braced on his knees, his square jaw resting atop his interlaced fingers, and his eyes focused farther away than the boards under his boots. He had swept all the debris to the side of my bed, leaving the rest of the room cleaner than it had been before the harpy's attack. He must have used a spell to eradicate the smears of dirt and offal that had transferred to his clothing from mine, because his uniform was once again pristine. Quinn sprawled at Grant's feet, his head on his paws, his eyes downcast. Both males looked up at my abrupt entrance, identical expressions of pity sliding across their disparate features.

"What do you know about thunderbirds?" I rushed to ask before either of them could speak.

"Is that what Zipporah wants? For you to do something with thunderbirds?" Grant asked.

"That would be convenient." Zipporah's first demand had led me to the firebirds. Maybe her next would link up with the thunderbirds.

"Kylie . . ."

"Hmm?"

"I'm not a fan of cryptic statements."

"What? Oh. Right. I need to show you."

"You need to sit and let me heal you."

"That can wait." I padded across the small room, trying not to wince when the throw rug tugged at the scrapes on the bottoms of my feet.

"No." Grant pointed to the coffee table in front of him. "Sit."

I arched an eyebrow at him and continued to the head of my bed. We were in *my* apartment, not on one of his missions. His authority as an FPD captain didn't supersede mine here. Besides, I preferred his look of glowering irritation to his earlier pitying expression.

I lifted my pillow and retrieved my everlasting seed and a firebird feather. A few days ago, along with thousands of other people, I had stood beneath the branches of an everlasting tree at the precise moment when it had bloomed. Like every other person there, I had whispered a question into the magical tree's canopy and received a seed in response. Legend—and firsthand accounts from older generations—said that if each person followed the clues of their seed, they would be led to the answer they sought, no matter the question.

I had asked the everlasting tree the question that burned in my heart and had guided my adult life: Where could I find the story of a lifetime?

On the surface, my question sounded shallow and fame-grabbing, but I knew better. I had chosen to be a journalist because I believed well-crafted articles could alter society and improve lives. The way I saw it, the story of a lifetime would be the pinnacle of positive change. It would be the story that helped the most people and did the most lasting good. I was ambitious enough to want to be the journalist who wrote such an important article, but more important, I wanted my everlasting seed's answer to leave the world changed for the better.

Unfortunately, I was no longer certain the everlasting tree had the same grandiose outcome in store for the world —or me.

The tree's first clue had been a seed shaped like a peach pit with the red-gold pattern of a firebird's feather in its grooved surface. Obtaining a firebird feather had nearly killed me. Chasing the new clue my seed had revealed last night might just finish me off.

"Here." I handed the seed and feather to Grant. While I showered, Grant had opened the curtains and windows and installed powerful wards to barricade each pane of glass and screen. It gave my apartment all the appeal of a prison cell, but I didn't comment. The wind whistling through the simi-larly warded rift in the ceiling proved I needed all the protection I could get.

I shut the balcony door, closed the windows, pulled the curtains tight, and fitted a tinted sheet of air over the harpy-made skylight. Grant watched me hobble around the room, a scowl stamped on his handsome features.

"It's easier to see in the dark," I explained, drawing his attention to the items in his hands.

I sat down on the low table in front of him, waiting for our eyes to adjust to the gloom. The red-gold vanes of the feather shone with their own soft, metallic light, casting a pale golden shimmer over Grant's hands. Quinn scooted closer, the soft light creating the illusion that his citrine chest and face were lit from within. Shadows danced across his everlasting seed, but not even the rosy illumination could improve its appearance.

I yanked my gaze from the dizzying depths of Quinn's seed, focusing once more on Grant. The feather's light softened his bold features, emphasizing the curve of his bottom lip and dancing like fire in his brown eyes. I glanced away when I realized I was staring.

We hadn't had time to talk after our harrowing escape from the demolished ruins of Lunacy Labyrinth. Grant had been pulled away by his duties as captain of an FPD squad, and I had been preoccupied with being healed and recuperating. It hadn't been the time to bring up our almost-kiss inside Lunacy, but the smoldering look he gave me in parting had held a scintillating promise—one I had fully intended to explore at the first opportunity. However, that had been before my everlasting seed evolved, before Nathan turned my world inside-out with his atrocious article, and before Zipporah tore apart my home and proved I had no haven she couldn't breach. Nothing and no one I held dear would be safe until I was free of her debt.

I cleared my throat and locked my gaze on the seed, refusing to notice how the cramped furniture arrangement forced me to sit with my knees between Grant's or the way his warm breath fanned across my temple.

"Hold the firebird feather close to the seed," I instructed.

Grant brought the seed and feather together. The gold and tan curves and crevices of the seed darkened, as if a shadow and not light were being held over it. Stormy blue-gray markings swept across the seed, ending in three navy lines zigzagging along the lower third. Only the edges lightened in a dusting of pale, silvery blue, as if a layer of frost sparkled along the seed's ridges.

My stomach chilled at the sight.

"It's a thunderbird feather," Grant said.

"Turn it over."

Grant flipped the seed with a finger. In bold navy against the seed's slate-blue ridges lay the stylized winged-A logo of my parents' business, Airstrong Shipping. The seed's message was impossible to misinterpret.

"My parents are in trouble."

"Yes, they are."

Quinn's gaze bounced between us, and he leaned closer, offering me silent support.

"Then you know something about the thunderbirds?" I asked.

"I was on my way to see you when Velasquez got Mika's summons," Grant said. "I wanted you to hear it from me."

"Hear what? Grant, I've been fretting about this half the night. Don't leave me in suspense."

Grant closed his fist around my seed, his expression somber in the warm light. "It's not just the firebirds that were stolen from Airstrong. There have been more thefts."

"When?"

"Earlier this month."

My mom had lied. Again. When the firebirds had gone

missing, she claimed Airstrong hadn't been responsible for their transportation. Furthermore, she had asserted that Airstrong had *never* lost a package. Not a single one.

Grant brushed the knuckles of my clenched fist with a callused finger. "I came to tell you because it's going to become public knowledge later this morning, and I thought you should hear it from a friend."

"Airstrong was transporting *thunderbirds*? Was it the lightning—"

"No. As far as I know, Airstrong has never touched a thunderbird." His brow pinched, Grant opened his palm and fanned the firebird feather across the top of my everlasting seed, contemplating the thunderbird markings as they darkened, then faded. I drummed my fingers on my knee.

"Then what? What did they lose?"

"Banned spells."

The blood drained from my head. I braced a hand against the table, ignoring the jab of pain in my palm. Losing any package could be disastrous to Airstrong's reputation. Losing illegal, banned spells was the kind of catastrophic mistake that could ruin a company.

"How do you know this is going to become public knowledge?" I asked, but my thoughts raced ahead, faster than Grant's answer. The only organization that could ship prohibited spells was the government, and they kept meticulous track of their property. The moment a spell had gone missing, an investigation would have been opened. If the theft had taken place almost a month earlier, and the FPD hadn't recovered the spells or discovered the thief's identity, the next step would be— "A press conference."

I sprang from the table and limped to the closest

window, throwing the curtain wide to let in light. "I need to talk to my mom."

"You need to let me heal you."

"I have to get—" My voice cut off with a squeak when Grant tightened a band of air around my hips and levitated me the short distance to the table.

"Sit," he ordered.

I sat, crossing my arms, then uncrossing them when the pressure stung my palms. Grant pushed the rest of the curtains open with flicks of air. A soft breeze swirled through the room, pulling out the residual harpy funk lingering in the air and replacing it with the scent of cinnamon rolls from downstairs.

"What types of banned spells?" I demanded.

Grant pulled a folded piece of paper from his pocket and handed it to me. Quinn shifted to read over my shoulder.

A single word spanned the top of the page, printed in tall block letters: **REWARD**. Beneath lay the chilling head-line: AIRSTRONG SHIPPING HEIST. A cluster of four simplistic sketches of seemingly random items took up the bulk of the page, each labeled: beguiling beads that looked like a pair of clip-on marquise-cut pearl earrings, a thief's key that resembled a rune-etched umbrella, a truth hex embedded in a six-pointed bone star that gave me chills, and a snare and slice that could have passed for an ornate tablecloth. All four spells received the classification of *lethal*. A bulleted list ran under the sketches, calling out the additional thefts of expensive—but in no way deadly—booster spells: two for strength, one for healing, and one for speed. Beneath the list, a succinct paragraph requested individuals contact the FPD or local guards with any information about the heist or missing spells. A generous reward amount domi-nated the bottom of the page, with a smaller, equally bold warning for individuals to avoid contact with the illegal spells.

"A reward poster?" I waved the paper at Grant. "What is the FPD thinking? This will shatter the public's trust in Airstrong. The fallout will be devastating." When the FPD announced to the world that Airstrong couldn't be trusted with its cargo, their clients would bolt. Shipments would dwindle. My parents wouldn't be able to afford to pay their employees. Their entire business would collapse.

"Investigator O'Hara is doing what he thinks is best to keep the citizens of Terra Haven safe. Airstrong will weather the storm."

"And if it doesn't? This could ruin my parents."

"There's a flaw in their company that's endangering the public. People have a right to know." Grant reached for my foot. I scooted it out of his reach.

"No, they don't. Not at the expense of my parents' livelihood."

"Would you feel the same if we were talking about anyone else's business?"

Of course not, and Grant knew it. If it had been Wetherill's company, Capstone, to blame for losing four banned spells, I would have been the first to submit an article to the *Chronicle*. Part of my responsibility as a journalist was to keep the public apprised of dangers so they could avoid them. But this was different.

"My parents are good people. They are responsible, conscientious business owners. They do everything in their power to protect their clients and their cargo."

"I'm sure they do." Grant seized my ankle. "It's best if you hold still while I heal you."

I glared at the top of his head and considered jerking my leg from his grip, but it would have been too childish.

Besides, I wasn't angry at Grant. Harpy aside, he hadn't needed to come here today. His actions were those of a friend, and I should have been thanking him for sparing me from being blindsided when news of the stolen spells hit the papers today. If I was going to be angry with anyone, it should be with my mom, who hadn't bothered to give me advance warning herself.

Grant lifted my right foot, wove a complex patch of fire, water, and air, and pressed the elements to my sole. The heat of a molten poker seared into my flesh. I screamed and tried to jerk away, but he held my foot stable.

"Are you doing that right?" I gasped. "I don't remember it hurting this badly after the spriggan."

"That was a bandage spell. I'm guessing you want to walk today, so I thought you might want to be fully healed. Am I wrong?" He lifted one eyebrow, his expression one of polite curiosity, as if he hadn't just fried my nerve endings.

I tugged my foot from his grip and feathered a finger across new, pink flesh where a rash of cuts had been moments before. The entire bottom of my foot throbbed in tandem with my pulse, but the pain had already begun to fade. Reluctantly, I lifted my opposite foot toward him.

"I admit healing is not my specialty," Grant said, applying his torturous magic to my left sole, "but I get the job done."

"Are you sure you're not melting my flesh away?" I asked through gritted teeth.

Quinn shifted closer, but he couldn't do anything to help—other than boost Grant's magic, and I didn't need strength added to this clumsy healing spell.

"Knees," Grant said.

I took my time rolling up my pants to expose the abrasions, stalling. "Why were prohibited spells being shipped in the first place? Why weren't they destroyed when they were originally confiscated?"

"The spells are symptoms of a bigger problem; we want the individuals responsible for making them. A division of our Yakama offices up north is devoted to dissecting the spells in a controlled environment to pinpoint the creators' signature patterns. Then they're destroyed."

"So miscreants know all they have to do is intercept these shipments to get their hands on powerful, inimical spells? You guys didn't think that might be a flaw in *your* system?" The last question came out on a gasp as Grant's magic seared the cuts on my knees. While I was still recovering, he grabbed my hands and healed my palms. I bit down on my bottom lip and blinked away tears of pain, not letting out my breath until I could exhale without whimpering.

"We ship dangerous items in dummy containers. These spells were stolen from boxes labeled as food. Not even the carriers knew what was really inside."

"Someone must have figured it out."

Grant sighed heavily in agreement.

I rubbed my palms together gingerly, then shook away the lingering pain. "Just so you know, I'm not coming to you for future healing. I thought it would be a lot more satisfying and far less painful when I finally discovered something you're not good at."

"Maybe you shouldn't take delight in others' inadequacies," Grant said, sitting back.

"Trust me, I took none in yours." I bent to unroll my pants, but not before I caught Grant's swift grin. My heart squeezed, kicking up my pulse. I took a deliberate, deep breath and mentally stuffed my hormones into a box. I could flirt with Grant once my parents' livelihood was no longer in danger.

"I know the spells were all banned for a reason," I said, bringing us back on topic, "but what else can you tell me about them?"

"Every one of them is lethal. If activated, the snare and slice will capture anyone who touches anything on its surface. Attempting to escape would then set off the spell's offensive elements. I've seen everything from building-dropping explosions to wire-sharp elemental blades embedded in snares. I don't know the specifics of this snare, only that it was classified as highly sophisticated and powerful. Same with the beguiling beads. They're not your run-of-the-mill mental manipulation spell. They're much more subtle. Whoever holds them can convince anyone to do anything. You can see the appeal to the criminal-minded."

I could see the appeal to the non-criminally minded. Who wouldn't enjoy having other people do whatever they said?

"The truth hex—"

"Let me guess," I interrupted. "It tells you the truth."

"About anything anyone says, yes."

"Truth-seeker spells aren't illegal."

"A truth hex only works when it's embedded inside a six-pointed star made of bone. The most common side effects of using it are crippling paranoia and insanity." He gave me a significant look.

"That sounds ominous and familiar." Everyone knew only five elements existed—air, water, wood, earth, and fire. However, the ancient society that had created Lunacy Labyrinth had believed blood made the sixth element, and they had performed human sacrifices to wield the forbidden magic. It had driven them insane, ratcheting their paranoia to catastrophic levels that ultimately destroyed their society. It sounded like the effects of the truth hex followed the same pattern.

"You can see why we like to track down the people who make them," Grant said.

I nodded. Anyone employing blood magic needed to be arrested and imprisoned—for their own safety as much as for the safety of those around them.

"What about the thief's key? I've never heard of that one."

"It's a fancy ward breaker designed to mimic a ward—or a series of wards—and destroy it without the ward's creator noticing. It's banned—and not simply illegal—because the key forces the person holding it to absorb the unraveled magic rather than releasing it into the ether. The stronger the ward, the more powerful the thief has to be to withstand the onslaught of elements. Most thieves don't use a key more than once or twice."

"Because they get caught?"

"Because they're suicide spells. If the user's lucky, the key will only cause them to burn out—permanently."

I tried to imagine anything I wanted badly enough to risk death or nullification, and came up blank.

I studied the crumpled reward poster in my lap. "Let me make sure I have this right. Someone stole beguiling beads that can make anyone do anything they want, a truth hex to know if anyone is lying to them, a thief's key to break through any ward, and a snare and slice to trap anyone who gets in their way, plus strength, speed, and healing boosters."

"That about sums it up," Grant said.

"Whoever the thief is, they're set up to do a lot of damage." Starting with demolishing the reputation and trust my parents had spent years cultivating among their clients. I rubbed my freshly healed palms over my face. "This is bad."

"Really bad," Grant agreed.

"But what does any of it have to do with thunderbirds?" Quinn asked.

"I don't know," I said. "And that scares me."

4

———

I yearned to rush straight to my mom, seed in hand, to offer whatever help I could in the investigation. However, Dahlia's curt message rang in my head. Between Zipporah's attack, cleaning up afterward, and talking with Grant, I had already made my boss wait over an hour. I didn't dare push it further.

Thankfully, Grant offered me a ride in his air sled, cutting my commute time in half. Velasquez opted to stay behind with Mika, and Quinn flew ahead. Neither Grant nor I spoke during the short trip, each of us consumed with our own thoughts. Mine bounced between fearing I was about to be fired and worrying about the breaking scandal poised to tear apart my parents' business. I wracked my brain for a way to convince Dahlia to make me the lead reporter on the story—if I still had a job. My everlasting seed had shown me the Airstrong logo, and my question had been for the story of a lifetime. Surely this time Dahlia would see I was destined to cover this incident. Would anyone else do the story justice? Would anyone else make sure my parents were seen as victims, not potential criminals? Would anyone else protect Airstrong's image?

I mentally growled at myself. My intentions lacked journalistic integrity, but the need to protect my parents weighed as heavily as the everlasting seed's promise. I couldn't separate them, and I couldn't deny either of them.

Perhaps that was the point. I had a unique perspective into the Airstrong thefts. I had worked in the warehouses as a child; I understood the business, from its daily operations to its nationwide marketing strategies; and I had one-of-a-kind access to and insight about the owners. I had advantages no other reporter could come close to attaining.

"You've got a scary look on your face," Grant said.

"I'm smiling. What's so scary about a smile?"

"It's the one that says you're hatching a reckless plan."

"You've categorized my smiles?"

"Not all of them, but I've seen that one often enough. Tell me you aren't going to interfere with the investigation."

"Interfere? No." Help along? Yes.

Grant jerked the air sled to a stop next to the sidewalk in front of the *Terra Haven Chronicle* and kicked the lever to drop the wheels. We landed with a brain-jarring jolt. Grant twisted to brace one hand on the front of the sled, the other on the seat back, caging me in.

"Have you considered that by dabbling in the investigation, you might tip off the thieves?" he asked, keeping his voice low enough that people on the sidewalk couldn't eavesdrop. "You could destroy the FPD's chance of solving this case."

"They've been investigating for a month. It seems like they could use the help. Isn't that exactly what today's press conference and the reward is all about?"

"You know as well as I do that the reward is to motivate

people to speak up if they know something. It's not a request for anyone to get involved in the investigation. You have a knack for ferreting out the most risky situation in a hundred-mile radius and stumbling in at the wrong time. If you pursue this on your own, you're liable to wind up in the thieves' den, expecting me to rescue you."

His assessment stung, but I hid it behind a snort. "Make up your mind: Am I going to mess everything up or break this case wide open?"

"Bumbling around until you hit a hornet's nest of trouble is not an investigative strategy."

"I see now why you made captain. It's your ability to motivate others, isn't it?" I patted his shoulder. I intended the gesture to be condescending, but my hand lingered a fraction too long on Grant's firm bicep. Recovering, I sprang from the sled and tugged my bag from the floorboards. "I'll keep your flattering feedback in mind. Thank you for the ride."

Quinn coasted from the rooftop to the sidewalk, and I waited for him to land before tossing Grant a wave.

"Kylie, hold up," Grant said. He jumped from the sled, stopping me before I reached the *Chronicle*'s door. "Here."

He dropped a small object into my palm. I glanced at it, then back at Grant.

"Your badge? I don't understand."

"The badge carries my magical signature and my blood."

I took a second look at the badge. Resting on a palm-size piece of supple leather lay a small copper disk inlaid with a silver pentagram and topped with the FPD logo. The metal gleamed in the sunlight, and the leather looked as if it had been polished this morning. Any bloodstains must have been under the pentagram.

"It will make an ideal tracker," Grant said.

My gaze snapped to his. "Tracker?"

"We got lucky this morning. But if Zipporah returns and abducts you when I'm not around, I'll be able to find you with this. From now until you're out of the harpy's debt, wear it. Discreetly. If you're seen flaunting an FPD badge, you'll be arrested."

Fear slithered through my gut. In my preoccupation with Airstrong's problems, I had completely forgotten my own. My fingers clutched Grant's badge, but having a tracker did little to ease my anxiety. I didn't want to wait for the harpy to abduct me and then discard me somewhere terrifying—again. I wanted to prevent Zipporah from getting her talons on me in the first place.

"I've got it! Arrest her!"

"Who?"

"Zipporah, of course. Hasn't she broken the law?"

"When?"

"When?! How about this morning, when she shredded my roof?"

"Accidental damage while she spoke with a servant."

"A *what*?"

"When you agreed to be in her debt, you made a verbal pact. Since you agreed to owe her a favor, essentially you agreed to open-ended servitude."

"I did no such thing!"

"In the eyes of the court, you did."

"That's preposterous!" I double-checked Grant's expression to see if he was teasing me in some awful way. He wasn't. "Then what about when she abducted me and threw me into Lunacy? That had to be illegal."

"She transported a servant to a new location. If she had breached a ward, that would have been grounds for detaining her, but the ward was down."

"Even though I didn't want to be transported?"

"Would refusing have broken your contract with Zipporah?"

"No. Maybe." I blew out a frustrated breath. "Why does it feel like you're defending her?"

"Tossing Zipporah in prison for a few days or months isn't the answer to your problem. You need to clear your debt. Let's stay focused on that."

"I'll put it on the list, right after 'find out who is sabotaging Airstrong' and before 'chase down thunderbirds.'" I shoved the badge-turned-tracker into my pocket.

"Leave the investigation to the professionals. I can't always be on hand to rescue you."

"I didn't ask you to be," I shot back.

"Right. I'm beginning to think you search out dangerous situations just to have an excuse to spend more time with me."

"Of all the egotistical—"

"There are easier ways to get a man's attention," Grant continued, talking over me. "You could, say, ask him out for a meal."

"What? That's . . . I don't . . . Are you . . . ?"

My sputtering died when Grant dropped a featherlight kiss on my slack lips. Then he hopped into his air sled, tossed me a mock salute, and, grinning, zipped into traffic.

I gave myself a shake. A blush flooded my cheeks when I realized I had been standing on one foot, the other arrested in the air.

"Very dignified," I muttered. "Like a fat, wingless flamingo."

"He's probably right," Quinn said.

"You think he wants me to ask him . . ." *On a date?* I

couldn't finish the sentence out loud, afraid I might jinx myself.

"You might need him to rescue you."

Quinn's morose tone as much as his words yanked me from my daydream.

"I think you and I can handle just about anything together," I said, squatting to look him in the eye.

"Except Zipporah."

I scrunched up my face. "Not head-on like this morning. We need to figure a way out of this debt that doesn't involve more bloodshed or violence, and I can't do that without your help."

"And maybe Grant's?"

"If necessary, but I would rather do it on our own. Grant has the entire city to keep safe. We should be able to handle one harpy."

If I was being honest, I didn't want to rely on Grant because I didn't want him to see me as weak and needy. I would much rather . . . Well, I would much rather go out for a meal with him.

"Speaking of helping ourselves, let's sneak up to the roof before I report in," I said.

A raised wooden platform covered half of the *Chronicle*'s wide, flat roof, secured in place by massive bolts. The planks were gouged and scraped by the claws of gryphons and the hooves of pegasi. The paper's resident gryphon, Bright Fang, was absent, likely out with her rider, Raquel, and some lucky journalist on an exciting assignment. I checked the skies for any Pegasus Express deliveries headed our way, but the air lanes were clear.

Satisfied we were alone, I strode to a corner of the roof where I would be hidden from anyone looking out the windows of adjacent buildings; then I crafted a rumor scout. I wasn't a warrior like Grant. I wouldn't be able to nullify a dangerous felon wielding lethal spells. I wasn't a skilled businesswoman like my mom, with in-depth knowledge of her company's operations and its possible flaws. But I *was* a journalist. Gathering information and piecing together facts were my specialties. Maybe if I treated the Airstrong heist as if it were an article I was researching, I could help my parents save their company.

I keyed the first rumor scout to the phrase *truth hex*, then released it. The bundle of elements shot across the roof and zipped down the wide boulevard. I regarded my departing proprietary spell with a fond smile. Rumor scouts were a combination of a standard recording sphere, a homing spell, and a magic-signature-tuned ward melded into one, with a few extra tweaks to boot. To my knowledge, I was the only person who had ever devised such a spell, and they had proved invaluable in the past.

I assembled and released four more rumor scouts for *truth hex* and an equal number for every other stolen spell, plus a dozen for *Airstrong, Charlotte Grayson, Owen Grayson*, and a handful for *Zipporah*. Quinn suggested searching out mentions of Investigator O'Hara, booster spells, and other thefts in Terra Haven, and I sent those rumor scouts winging away, too. Finally, light-headed from the elemental exertion but optimistic, I hustled inside. The scouts would circulate the city for the next five hours. If they encountered someone saying their specified phrase, the recording portion of the spell would activate, and the scout would record every sound in the vicinity for the next minute. Then it would beeline to my apartment message bowl to await my return. If a scout didn't encounter its phrase, the spell would gradually weaken and dissolve.

My rumor scouts weren't foolproof, but with any luck, they would generate some fresh leads.

———

A SKELETON CREW POPULATED THE WRITER'S BULLPEN. THE vacancy surprised me until I remembered today was the summer solstice. Between getting trapped in Lunacy Labyrinth and fighting off Zipporah this morning, I had forgotten about the day's festivities. I needed to get home in time to meet up with Mika to—

My heart sank. Mika wouldn't want to go anywhere with me today, especially not to a celebratory event.

Battling the urge to slump, I trudged across the bullpen. Frosty glances and censorious glares tracked my progress, and my footsteps faltered. Several writers in the room looked like they would happily trip me into the nearest pile of road apples, if given the opportunity. Because I hadn't told them my real identity? I hadn't given their reactions much thought, but from their scowls, I should have.

Dahlia stalked out of her office, spotted me, and stopped in her tracks. Disapproval etched the tanned lines of the editor in chief's face as she studied me. After an interminable second, she turned her back on me, but not before beckoning me into her office with a crook of her finger.

"Maybe you should wait here," I whispered to Quinn.

"Are you sure?"

No. "Yes."

Quinn took a seat next to an empty desk, his eyes crinkled with worry. I ran my hands down my hips, hoping the sweat on my palms would smooth the wrinkles out of my lightweight pants. Before leaving my apartment, I had changed into my best business attire, hoping it would bolster my confidence. Given the rush of nerves that one glare from my boss had sent quaking through my body, I might as well have worn my ruined pajamas.

Holding in a sigh, I squared my shoulders and strode into Dahlia's office.

"Close the door behind you," she said.

It shut with a soft *snick*. Tension climbed my shoulders. Dahlia settled behind her desk, but my feet took root in the middle of the room.

"How did you end up in Lunacy Labyrinth, Kylie?" Dahlia's hickory-colored eyes studied me dispassionately, making me squirm.

"Wrong place at the wrong time. I was following up on the missing firebirds—"

"After I told you not to?"

"I can't ignore my everlasting seed." When I had shown Dahlia my seed and told her I was chasing the story of a life-time, I had expected her full support. Instead, she forbade me from spending time on what she deemed a "dead-end" story. Arguing with her had gotten me demoted to the business section, writing filler articles. It wouldn't help my case to point out that same stolen-firebird story had made the front page of the paper the next day. "I tracked down a lead on the firebirds in my free time after I finished my assigned interview," I continued, keeping my explanation intention-ally vague. Confessing to Zipporah's role in my unautho-rized adventure wouldn't win me any points with my boss. The harpy was my problem to deal with and had nothing to do with my job. Taking a deep breath, I rushed to finish, "In the process, I got trapped inside Lunacy Labyrinth with the FPD, escaped with the firebirds, and the rest you know."

"*Do* I know everything?" Dahlia asked. "You don't have a story to pitch me about your time in Lunacy?"

A thrill of excitement jolted my spine, but I did my best not to let it show. Any story about Lunacy would be novel enough to receive prime placement in the paper, and I wanted to jump at the chance. However, yesterday's front-page article had already supplied the pertinent details of the recovered stolen firebirds and Lunacy's destruction. Anything else I might add would either be self-aggrandizing or read like a glorification of the barbaric blood-magic ruins. It was better that the story died with the labyrinth.

Reluctantly, I shook my head. "What happened in Lunacy isn't really news, and Nathan covered everything else."

"He did, didn't he? A few facts more than you would have included, too, I daresay." No anger laced her tone. No emotion of any kind leaked out.

"True, but not because I— I didn't *want* to lie." With Dahlia's dispassionate gaze locked on me, the articulate explanation I had rehearsed came out stilted. "I didn't tell you my full name because I wanted to be certain I got this job on my own. My merit. My sweat and skills. Not because of who my parents are."

"That sounds noble."

"It's the truth."

"Did you happen to notice every other person at this paper got where they're at by their hard work and nothing else?"

"Yes, but I also noticed none of them come from upper-society families." Perhaps I shouldn't have pushed the point, but I needed Dahlia to see my reasoning. I had wanted to become a reporter badly enough to walk away from everything my parents had planned for me. I had cut ties with the kind of lifestyle most people would trade five years of their lives to possess. "This isn't a game to me. Changing my identity was integral to my goal. I want to be a journalist."

"Why?"

I sensed Dahlia expected a neat, distilled answer, but this was my dream and my passion, and it wasn't so easily summarized. "I want to make a difference. To write about what really matters. To help shape the opinions and beliefs of the people of Terra Haven. To make people's lives safer and better. Writing is fun, and I'm good at it. Chasing down stories is even more intoxicating. I enjoy putting the pieces of an investigation together. I like how a story can be written from a dozen different angles, and I really like being the person who gets to decide which way will be best—with my editor's help, of course."

"We can't forget about those editors, can we?" Dahlia asked, her tone dry.

"That's not how I meant—"

She shook her head, waving me to silence. "Sit down. You're giving me a neck cramp."

I perched on the lip of the chair in front of her desk, setting my bag on my lap.

"I hired you because of every reason you just listed," she said. "I would like to think I would have done the same even if I had known to call you Harriet instead of Kylie."

"Please don't. I mean, I prefer Kylie."

"I don't appreciate finding out the way I did."

"I'm sorry. But did the *Chronicle* have to print my real identity in such an awful, almost slanderous fashion?"

"It might not have, if you had been honest with me. Which is exactly what I expect going forward: complete honesty."

"Of course." Did that mean I still had a job?

Dahlia scrutinized my expression, hers giving me no

clue to her thoughts. Her fingers thrummed the hard surface of her desk; then, finally, she spoke. "I understand you're a friend of the Kwan family. Ms. Kwan sent word this morning that she would like you to attend the solstice ceremony at her estate."

My stomach somersaulted. I had attended enough full-spectrum events in my youth to know they were vain affairs populated by extravagantly wealthy people with copious elemental powers and a pathological need to impress each other. However, their obsessive one-upmanship led to inspiring ritualistic displays actually worth writing about. As assignments went, it could have been worse.

Unfortunately, Dahlia hadn't finished.

"It appears Ms. Kwan has an up-and-coming author, Adelaide Flemming, staying with her. Flemming is releasing a history book, and Ms. Kwan requested you interview her today. I believe you were already sent an invitation to the event, so you're all set."

"This isn't about the ritual? Persephone wants me to interview a debut author?" I asked hollowly. More important, Dahlia wanted me to waste the solstice interviewing some no-name writer?

"Yes."

"But ..."

This was the kind of story I would have pegged for a gossip rag like the *Full Spectrum Gazette*, not the *Chronicle*. I knew how this worked. The "author" would be someone's niece or daughter grasping at fame, and Persephone was playing the benevolent mentor, opening doors with her title and wealth. The book had likely gotten picked up by a publisher for the same reason, not because it had any substance or value to society. I couldn't believe Dahlia wanted to promote such drivel to the *Chronicle*'s readers. But since she did, why did I have to be the one to write it? If I took this assignment, I would be pigeonholed into the role of a society writer—one of their own at the beck and call of the collective FSPP. I shuddered at the thought. If all I were allowed to report on were the antics of full spectrums, I would be miserable. Who was dating who and seen at which party was not news; no matter which way you penned it, it was soulless fluff. I couldn't—I *wouldn't*—let all my efforts to distinguish myself be swept away with one assignment.

Of course, I couldn't say *that*. Instead, I wracked my brain for a diplomatic way to tell my boss no.

"I had hoped to talk to you about covering the thefts at Airstrong," I said, trying not to sound too eager. "I understand the FPD will be holding a press conference this morning to inform the public, and I'm in a unique position to address this story from all sides—the public's, the FPD's, and Airstrong's."

"By Airstrong, you mean your parents."

I saw the warning in Dahlia's expression, but I couldn't let it go. "Yes, and they aren't going to open up to just any reporter. I have an advantage here—"

"You have a conflict of interest."

"I have a strong motivation—"

"And a stronger bias. No. I already assigned that story to an impartial, *senior* journalist with more experience handling criminal investigations. And he doesn't need your help."

I bit my lip to keep my protests from spilling out. I *needed* to be assigned the Airstrong story. My everlasting seed said as much, though I knew better than to use that argument with Dahlia. I could tell from her tone that nothing I said would change her mind. Feeling like my stomach was lined with burrs, I let the argument drop.

My boss was one of the most savvy women I knew. This had to be a test—or a punishment. On the day my parents' company would be eviscerated in the press, she was feeding me into the jaws of the high-society elite, forcing me to socialize with people who loved nothing more than to revel in other's misfortunes. All so I could waste my time coddling some full-spectrum woman-child.

It wasn't fair.

Dahlia's hard gaze never wavered as I carefully selected my next words.

"Is there a reason Flemming can't meet me in Terra Haven?" Just the possibility of getting interviewed by the city's most prominent newspaper would have most new authors camped out in the lobby. Of course, I was thinking about normal people, not full spectrums who were used to everyone catering to them.

"A reason aside from the fact that I assigned you *this* interview at *this* time and location?" Dahlia asked. "Ms. Flemming is only available today. Tomorrow she is holding a signing at the Live and Learn Bookstore. I trust you agree it makes more sense to tell our readers about the event in advance." The ice in Dahlia's tone should have frozen me to my seat.

I nodded, clamping my lips together to prevent myself from blurting out further protests. I had burned through all my goodwill with my boss. Another verbal misstep might be my last.

"It seems your social standing did us both a favor," Dahlia said dryly. "Without your family contacts, the *Chronicle* would not be getting this exclusive scoop."

I mentally winced at the phrase *family contacts*, but it

was the word *scoop* that my thoughts stuttered over. Dahlia had to be kidding. For there to be a scoop, the story had to be of interest to more than one person. Did anyone other than Persephone know—or care—who this debut author was?

"This isn't a punishment. This is an opportunity for you to work on a variety of stories and expand the reach and impact of this paper."

I nodded. This was a filler piece with all the trappings of being important.

"Or we can talk about alternative employment options." Dahlia's fingertips drummed against her desk.

I jerked my attention from the floor and smoothed my expression.

"Good," she said, as if I had spoken. "I already informed the transportation department to prep a carpet for you. Don't waste this opportunity, Kylie."

"I won't. Thank you."

With a bitter taste in my mouth, I trudged out of her office. Even though Dahlia had called me Kylie, I had just accepted my first assignment as Harriet Grayson.

The contemptuous expressions of the writers in the bullpen made it clear they had heard every word of my conversation with Dahlia. My cheeks heated. By this afternoon, there wouldn't be a writer on staff who didn't know I had gotten a special assignment based on who my parents were and not my skill.

Quinn rose, a frown furrowing his brow. "We're not going to celebrate the solstice with Mika?"

"No."

Resentment simmered in my muscles, stilting my stride as I marched for the door . . . until I spotted the bastard who had forced me into this untenable situation.

Senior journalist Nathan Aspell.

With his slicked-back black hair and slimy demeanor, he looked the part of a snake oil salesman. Dark stubble outlined his narrow jaw, and heavy-framed glasses rode his nose. He paused halfway out of the mail room and clutched the doorknob as if he were considering scurrying back inside to hide.

You're not escaping me, cockroach.

I barreled across the room. Nathan's gaze darted behind him, then to our riveted coworkers. Hugging a stack of papers to his chest like a shield, he swaggered into the bullpen. I slammed to a halt in front of him.

"Oh, hey, Kylie—I mean, Harriet. You're in early." Nathan drew himself up to his full height, using his extra two inches to talk down to me.

"How dare you."

"You're going to need to be more specific," Nathan said, exaggerating his confusion.

"Don't play the idiot, Nathan. You do it too convincingly."

His lips twisted, but I plowed on before he formulated a rebuttal.

"Was your latest article another example of your famous senior journalist wisdom? Let me guess: It was a magnanimous lesson to show little junior me how to manipulate slander until it resembles facts. Very clever, Nathan, and masterfully executed."

"I did no such thing!" His protest projected across the room as if he were an actor onstage—fitting, since we had a rapt audience.

"You insinuated I had something to do with the stolen firebirds, as if I were a criminal."

"The firebirds were stolen from Airstrong, your parents' company, and you were conveniently on hand to retrieve them. I didn't *insinuate*; I reported."

"You slapped together correlating facts and ran with them without doing any deeper research." Fury quavered through my words. "It was the kind of sloppy, sensationalist reporting I would have expected of a gossip columnist—especially the part where you took my private life and smeared it across the front page."

"Wow. Don't you think a lot of yourself." He glanced around in practiced disbelief. "I only mentioned you. It's not like I wasted column space on who you're sleeping with or where he works."

It was such an obvious bait that it caught me flat-footed. Did Nathan think such a juvenile taunt would goad me into blurting out something rash and embarrassing? Even more absurd, did he think he could use my relationship with Grant as blackmail? If I hadn't been so furious, it might have been laughable.

Nathan had disliked me since I wrote my first front-page article. He had tried to stifle my successes, warning me to slow down and develop my skills before I dared to write stories that outshone his. He didn't believe a junior journalist should be competing with him for the top articles, never mind that I had discovered each headline-grabbing story on my own. When his poisonous mind games didn't work and I continued to submit front-page pieces, he tried to steal them from me. Allowing his personal bias to poison his latest article was a whole new low. His jealousy was the reason he had twisted my quiet life into a scandal. It was why he had exposed my identity in the paper, where I couldn't defend myself, rather than confronting me directly. He had wanted to see me humiliated, humbled, and ostracized by my peers.

It was working, too. Worse, he had succeeded in hamstringing my career, and for that, I would never, ever forgive him.

"You should have checked with me first," I said.

"Before printing your name in the paper? Why would I?"

"Because that's not who I am."

"You mean who you were *pretending* not to be. I don't know why you're so mad, Harry."

My molars squeaked as they ground together, and a malicious spark lit Nathan's eyes when he realized the nickname got under my skin.

"I told the truth, *Harry*. That's what quality journalism does. If you didn't know that, you shouldn't be working here. Which reminds me." He lifted the pages he held high, displaying them to our audience. I caught a familiar flash of four images beneath the giant *REWARD* header. My stomach sank.

"I just came from the FPD press conference, and it was quite informative. They even had handouts." Nathan sauntered around the room, disseminating the damning flyers to everyone present before posting the remaining copies to the bulletin board. All but one.

Brushing past Quinn, Nathan returned to hand the last flyer to me. If he heard Quinn's low growl, Nathan did a good job of pretending otherwise.

"It looks like your family has been trying to cover up a lot more than a pair of mishandled firebirds." He rattled the paper obnoxiously in my face.

I ripped it from his grasp, rage pulsing red through my vision. Around me, the journalists erupted into a flurry of whispers, but their words couldn't penetrate the roaring in my ears.

Punching the smirk off Nathan's face would have been satisfying, but it wouldn't win me any goodwill from Dahlia. Nor would entertaining my second-favorite fantasy of barging into Dahlia's office and demanding she fire Nathan. Not only would that feed into the self-centered heiress stereotype, but it would also go nowhere. As much as it galled me to admit it, Nathan was right: He had technically done nothing wrong.

Nathan gave me a saccharine smile. "As you can see, the

truth *always* comes out. Now, Harry, if you'd like to leave a comment for my article, keep it short. This story is big, and I've got a lot of information to cover." He tossed me a wink, then sauntered into Dahlia's office and shut the door.

———

A GENTLE BREEZE CLEARED THE LINGERING DUST CLOUD raised by a convoy of cerberi-drawn chariots. I released a frustrated sigh and brandished my dirt-repellent ward for the twentieth time. Inhaling the clean scents of drying weeds, warm leaves, and sunshine-soaked pine bark, I lifted my hair from my neck and fanned myself. My flying carpet skimmed along, six feet above the ground, steady but mind-numbingly slow. Circling high above on languid currents, Quinn effortlessly kept pace.

Despite having left Terra Haven's city limits over an hour ago, I continued to be haunted by Nathan's smug expression. How could Dahlia have assigned him to cover the Airstrong thefts? The article should have been mine. It was my parents in trouble and my seed that pointed the way to the story of a lifetime. If I had a conflict of interest, so did Nathan—as he had clearly demonstrated by allowing his competitiveness to taint his last article. At least I had motivation to pursue the thief, whereas Nathan would likely look no further than the ready-made scandal the FPD had handed him. His obnoxious remark about me giving him a quote only reinforced my suspicion.

Yet Dahlia had chosen him.

A pony-size bundle of elements blasted over my head. I ducked and clutched the carpet to prevent myself from falling. Before I finished righting myself, the magic disappeared beyond the treetops.

"Cursed full spectrums," I groused, shoving my hair out of my face. A plethora of FSPP families kept country estates here, tucked amid Gypsum Valley's private forests, and the sky had been full of similar communication spells flung here and there for the last half hour. A certain amount of elemental showmanship was expected when full spectrums lived near each other, but the solstice gathering had exacerbated today's magical activity to an obnoxious level.

I jammed a heap of air and earth through the carpet's propulsion spell, trying to coerce more speed from it, but the carpet continued at the same sluggish clip. The spell woven into the sturdy fabric wouldn't allow it to outpace a loping horse. What was plenty fast for the streets of Terra Haven felt like crawling in the countryside. I was forced to hug the edge of the road or risk being run over by full-spectrum conveyances. FSPPs were all fully capable of propelling aircraft straight across the treetops to Persephone's front door, but etiquette dictated they take the road. Plus, full spectrums had a pathological need to show off, and none would deny themselves a grand entrance at the front gates. I had dodged being trampled by a fleet of specialty-breed horses with uncanny stamina and miniature pegasus wings, clung by my fingernails to my bucking carpet as it was buffeted by the winds of a coterie of wyvern-drawn floating chaises, and driven into the weeds by a low-flying hippogryph team pulling an elaborate floating castle-like bus that could have housed the entire *Chronicle* staff. When I wasn't cocooning myself in wards to stave off being drowned in dust, I was clinging to shields to protect myself from being blasted by wind-flung detritus. It was exhausting.

I shifted from one numb butt cheek to the other. The carpet's unyielding surface had been designed for durability, with little regard given to a traveler's backside. When I spotted the low stone sign denoting the edge of the Kwan property, I might have cheered if I hadn't known that Persephone's estate lay miles farther up the road. I strained for a glimpse of the mansion, but all I could see were trees, trees, and more trees.

And a game trail.

I deactivated the propulsion spell and coasted to a stop, surveying the well-worn deer path. Enormous oaks and slender pines cast heavy shade over the narrow trail, but despite the plethora of trunks, I could see quite far into the woods. Even without the trail to follow, I would be able to navigate the nominal undergrowth reasonably well on my slender carpet.

I contemplated my options. I could continue on the road, spend another hour atop the carpet, arrive fatigued from repeatedly casting wards, and, worst of all, enter through the main gates, where I would be forced to disembark next to full-spectrum guests in their fancy attire and be subjected to the crush of gossip-rag journalists invited to froth over the spectacle. Or I could take a shortcut through the forest, shave a half hour off my travel time, slip into the estate through a side entrance, conduct my interview, and be on my way before the midday ritual.

Gathering a bundle of fire and air, I shot a signal into the sky. Quinn spotted it and dove to meet me.

"Could you see the party from up there?" I asked once he had landed.

"It's impossible to miss. Persephone invited a *lot* of people. Did you see the squadron of gryphons? They had bronze armor on their chests and talons. I wonder if they know Fang. And the black swans that passed you twenty minutes ago? They were larger than me! Did you see the people inside their carriage all wearing feather cloaks?" Quinn's eyes glowed with excitement, and he pranced in place.

I couldn't help but smile. From afar, full spectrums and their ostentatious displays of wealth and power were rather enjoyable to witness. Hopefully his enthusiasm wouldn't wane once he got a closer look.

"The swans were pretty," I agreed. "Which direction is the estate?"

Quinn pointed to the exact position I had mentally mapped.

"Perfect. I'm taking this shortcut." I indicated the shaded path. "I used to play in these woods as a kid, and I think I can find my way easily enough. Do you think you can track me from the air?"

Quinn squinted at the trail, the trees, and the sky, then nodded. I waited until he was airborne before steering the carpet off the road and powering through the trees. Quinn's golden body shone like a winged sun above the forest canopy, and when I waved, he waved back. Assured we wouldn't become separated, I added a boost to the propulsion spell and focused on dodging trunks and low-hanging branches.

The road quickly fell out of sight. When I heard the muffled thunder of hooves pounding past, I pictured the plume of dust billowing behind the animals and allowed myself a smug smile.

It had been years since I had been to the Kwans' woods, though at one time, they had been as familiar as my backyard. My mom visited Persephone often in my youth, and I had been given free run of the expansive grounds. A pang of nostalgia pinched my chest when I passed a spiky outcropping of granite that I used to pretend was a fortress. From the top of the rocks, I had been able to spot a gnarled pine that had been struck by lightning. In my childhood fantasies, it was a murderous giant, and I had built elemental barricades to block it. Of course, my preteen magic consisted mostly of artistic flares of wind and water—fire having been forbidden when I was alone.

I hadn't thought about those games in a long time. When Airstrong expanded from a small in-town delivery service to a nationwide transportation company, our visits to Persephone's country home became less frequent. Finally, the business necessitated a move to the East Coast. Even though I had returned to Terra Haven when I made my break from my parents' company, it had been years since I visited the Kwan estate or talked to Persephone.

The carpet jounced over a boulder hidden in the forest floor, breaking my reverie. I raised the carpet to squeeze between two pine saplings, my speed slowing to a crawl. The forest had grown increasingly dense, and when the game trail veered south, forcing me to abandon it, I had to test the limits of the carpet's levitation to float over knots of manzanita bushes. The nominal shock absorption built into the spell stretched thin, and the slightest undulations in the ground caused the carpet's surface to wobble and bounce.

In my youth, the underbrush had been moderated and new tree growth monitored and cultivated. This—the waist-high manzanitas, pockets of brambles, and dense thickets of young pines—gave the appearance of a forest left untended by a wood elemental for a decade or more.

Circling a vine-choked oak, I peered through the fractured sunlight. I should have been close to the manicured lawns and floral gardens surrounding the house, but all I saw were more trees and shrubs. Had I drifted off course? Halting the carpet, I checked the sky for Quinn, but I couldn't locate his bright form through the pinholes in the foliage.

The skin on the nape of my neck tingled. I froze. The chorus of bird calls died; the small creatures rustling through the dried leaves beneath the trees stilled. Even the drone and chirps of insects ceased. A lazy wind stirred the high branches, but the forest around me remained caught between inhale and exhale. Unease knotted between my shoulder blades.

The first scratch sounded like two branches squeaking together. The next was unmistakably made by claws. They scrabbled against wood in short, sharp bursts followed by ominous silence—first on my left, then on my right. A husky chatter whispered from the shadows. Goose bumps chased shivers down my arms. I held my breath, squinting into the gloom.

Claws skittered across a thick branch above me, and I jerked to look. A small leaden object plummeted toward me. I caught a flash of beetle-black claws and a bushy tail before I flung a crude ward over my head. The creature slammed into the elements, but I still ducked reflexively. As it scrambled for purchase on the slick barrier, I got my first good look at my attacker.

It was a squirrel in size and shape, with a long fluffy tail and liquid-black eyes. Instead of coarse gray hair, it possessed tufts of mottled green fur. Canines longer than a house cat's nipped at my magic, bloodlust shining in the creature's beady eyes. Finally, it lost its fight with gravity and slid from my ward to the forest below. As it fell, its body turned transparent, all except its four feet.

It can't be. I clutched the edge of the carpet, leaning as far as I dared to keep the black paws in sight. My heart hammered in my chest. *Please, let it be something other than—*

The mutant squirrel landed on a slender manzanita branch, a spray of blue-gray leaves swaying through the space where the squirrel's body should have existed. Blood drained from my head. The black feet, disappearing body, and rodent shape: I was staring at a sciurid poltergeist—a spook squirrel—one of the most deadly varmints to infest the forests.

And they hunted in packs.

6

The spook squirrel launched from the manzanita and landed on an oak trunk. Its disembodied feet raced around the tree and disappeared. I spun to check behind me, then above, searching for its packmates. Sciurids were intelligent and bloodthirsty, and once they locked sights on their prey, they didn't let up until they had bled it dry. A small colony could bring down a wolf or a wild boar—or a lone human.

A rough cough sounded from my left. A hoarse chatter answered it from above. I tightened my grip on the elements. Spooks were small, but they had one terrifying advantage: Their claws could cut through any magical defense. It might take more than one attempt, but once they pinpointed the exact elemental combination of my ward, they would shatter it.

I fumbled for the propulsion spell, and the carpet jerked into motion. A shadow sprang from my left and crashed into my ward. The elements burst, the broken filaments snapping sharply against my mental pathways. I swung wildly.

My forearm collided with a small hard shape. My vision cleared in time to see a spook squirrel tumble to the ground.

A tingle across my scalp warned me seconds before two carnivorous squirrels dropped to my shoulders. I ducked and rolled. Claws raked my back in twin tracks of fire, and I lost my grip on the rug and fell. The forest floor slammed into me with the gentleness of a steam locomotive, stealing my breath and making the trees spin. My bag slapped the ground inches from my head.

Black sparkles clouded my vision. For a long, suspended second, I existed in a vacuum of pain. Then my lungs expanded, my throat made a terrifying sound like a reverse scream, and I sucked in a massive breath. The musky aroma of decomposition and moist dirt suffocated me. Coughing, I struggled to my elbows before movement in my periphery stilled me.

Seizing the elements, I created a glowball larger than my head and shoved it straight up. The golden light played across the maze of tree trunks, illuminating the encroaching horde of varmint poltergeists before they ghosted. A set of bodiless feet bounded from one trunk to the next in an uncanny collection before scuttling out of sight. Claws scraped. More disembodied paws scurried closer.

Terror pumped energy through me, shattering my dazed thoughts. I wrestled another ward into shape, this one rigid with wood element and knotted with fibers of air. It paled in comparison to the strength of my first ward, but it should hold off the next sciurid's attack, at least until the colony figured out I had changed up my magic.

A single spook squirrel flickered into visibility, clinging upside down on a nearby pine. Thrumming a foot against the bark, it rasped out a rhythmic cackle. Another spook higher in the tree took up the chant, then another farther away.

I tensed, ready to leap to my feet and bolt. It didn't matter which direction so long as it was *away*. The carpet had drifted up against a tree trunk, but I dismissed it. It would be too slow and clumsy with all the obstacles. So would I, I realized, surveying the forest floor in dismay. I couldn't run ten feet without getting snared in a bramble. I would have to make the carpet work.

A spook leapt for me, long nails scratching down my ward. I kicked out, breaking my elemental barrier before the sciurid did it for me. The spook morphed into a poltergeist a second before my boot made contact, but I managed to catch its hind feet in the blow. Those, at least, it couldn't dematerialize. The spook hurtled through the air, twisting to land on its feet at the base of a tree.

I constructed a fresh ward in time to repel four additional sciurids—only one of which I saw coming. The eerie scrabble and pops of their claws churned around me. I scuttled across the loamy floor, squeezing my back against a trunk. My breaths came in ragged pants, and I quivered from suppressing the instinct to flee. The moment I ran, the spooks would swarm. I could thwart one or two at a time, but I couldn't hold them off if they attacked en masse.

Claws slashed at my face. I threw an arm up to protect myself even as I dropped my ward and hit the miniature monster with a clap of air. The spook squirrel slammed into a low-hanging branch. A legion of disembodied feet converged on me.

That was stupid. I should have let the ward protect me. Opening myself to the attack like that had been reckless . . .

But it could work.

If I hoped to survive, I couldn't rely solely on cycling

wards. The spooks would wear me out long before I escaped or found help. As much as my stomach roiled at the thought, I had to kill them first. They were trying to murder me. I couldn't afford to be queasy about taking lives. But the weapons I knew how to create wouldn't work on poltergeists. Elemental blades would pass right through their ghostly bodies, and fireballs were more likely to spark a wildfire in this overgrown forest than incinerate the spooks. I would have to rely on air, my reflexes, and my wits.

I wove a heavy sheet of air against the underside of a new ward, stretching it to coat the thin protective bubble. Holding a glowball, ward, and air spell taxed my concentration, but it was worth it a breath later when a trio of sciurids clawed apart my ward. I flung the backlashing elements from me even as the simple wind spell beneath the ward exploded, flinging the spook squirrels into the air. Two landed unharmed. The third smashed into a tree trunk and floundered, falling into the dense underbrush. A flurry of spooks dove after it, all invisible except for their feet. High-pitched squealing sliced through the forest, followed by the sickening squelches of rending flesh as the spooks devoured their fallen packmate.

Stomach churning, I surged to my feet, snapping another ward into place. With a punch of air, I shot the glowball skyward. The flaming sphere scorched the branches it blasted past and burned a perfect circle through the leaves high above. Quinn swooped down to hover above the smoking gap. His bright eyes took in my dirt-caked clothing and fearful expression.

"Hang on, I'm coming!"

Folding his wings, Quinn plummeted like the enormous bundle of quartz he was, crashing through the delicate upper canopy. Twigs and leaves pelted my ward. The spook squirrels scattered, but I couldn't tear my eyes from Quinn. Uncurling, he slammed into a thick oak branch. It cracked and shuddered as he ran down its length before leaping to the next-lowest branch. My heart lodged in my throat. He didn't have space to unfurl his wings. If he lost his balance, the fall would cripple him. Only his innate gargoyle agility enabled him to maintain some semblance of control over his descent.

He plunged the last twenty feet with his wings partially extended, snapping saplings beneath his weight. His haphazard path landed him yards from me, and he hit the ground running. I met him halfway. Broken branches and torn bark rained down behind me.

"You're bleeding!" Quinn said. "What happened?"

I followed his gaze to my shoulder, surprised to see my blouse soaked with blood. "We need to get out of here."

On cue, the eerie scratch and squeak of little clawed feet tightened around us. The sciurids might have been frightened by Quinn falling from the sky, but they hadn't retreated far. A spook high above coughed its hoarse warning, drumming on a tree branch. Several more took up the call.

"What's wrong with those squirrels?" Quinn asked. A sciurid skulked horizontally around a pine's thick trunk to glare at us, then phased out of sight. "Did that squirrel just *disappear*?"

"They're sciurid poltergeists—spook squirrels. A distant cousin of the creatures you're familiar with. Technically, nothing's wrong with them, except they're carnivorous and they've gotten a taste of my blood."

Quinn moaned.

"Come on, I need to get the carpet." I scooped up my bag and jogged to the floating carpet, cinching a wind-layered ward around myself. It would have been a waste of energy to expand my ward to include Quinn. The spook squirrels couldn't harm him, but leaving him unprotected made me feel like a terrible friend.

I deactivated the carpet's levitation spell, but before I could climb atop it, five spooks sprang for me. I dove for the forest floor. Four sciurids hit the top of the ward, slid off the slick surface, and sprinted up the nearest trees. The last landed suspended by the ward above my calf. Quinn swiped it aside—or tried to. His paw slid through the spook's insubstantial body. A millisecond later, the spook punctured my protective barrier. Displaced magic slapped my brain, making my head ring, but the wind spell worked, launching the rodent poltergeist into the bushes.

"What just happened?" Quinn gave me a bewildered look, his toes dug into the soil, his ears flattened against his skull. "Did it break your ward? And why did my foot pass through it?"

"Welcome to the fun of sciurids. They can phase every part of themselves except their feet out of the physical world."

"Why not their feet?"

"I think it's what anchors them. Without solid feet, they can't morph back to eat their prey. They'd be stuck as full poltergeists and starve. At least it gives me something to work with. How close are we to the estate?"

"On foot? Maybe ten minutes." Quinn swung his head back and forth. "Less if we had a path."

This "shortcut" had turned into a nightmare. At least once I reached the estate, the Kwan wards would thwart the sciurids.

Where *were* the property wards? This whole forest should have been a safe haven. How had Persephone allowed her grounds to become infested with an entire scourge of sciurids?

Crawling onto the carpet, I dropped my bag into my lap and built another wind-and-ward combo spell. Despite Quinn's enhancement, the elements dragged through my grasp, and it took extra precious seconds to finalize the spells. I didn't relish keeping this up for ten more minutes.

I activated the levitation spell, then fumbled to control my ward as the elements quivered in my grasp, split in too many directions. When I regained control, I nudged the carpet into motion, only to realize I had lost all sense of direction.

"Do you think you can lead us?" I asked Quinn. The scrabble of claws grew closer. Ignoring the headache pulsing to life behind my eyes, I drew deeper on Quinn's enhancement.

"This way." The trees were packed too tight for Quinn to take flight. Instead, he leapt over a downed log and bounded into a blackberry-choked hollow. His stone body broke a path through the thorny vines that otherwise would have thwarted me. I floundered to keep up, dizzy from juggling too many spells.

Our chaotic dash ended less than a minute later when we came face-to-face with a twelve-foot-tall wall of brambles. Quinn lifted a paw to shove through the gnarled mass, but I stopped him with a shout.

"Look, it's warded."

Thick cables of fire, air, and water interlaced the unnaturally thick growth. Finally, I had found the Kwans' property ward. It wasn't a nuanced spell designed to recognize invited guests or friends of the family, either. It was a combat-zone ward.

"This is . . ." Quinn trailed off, craning his neck to take in the towering barbed wall.

"Excessive?" I asked.

"Scary."

"That too." If not for the murderous varmints on our trail, the ward would have been the type of curious anomaly to get my story senses tingling. Instead, the blockade sent a frisson of dread down my spine.

"We're going to have to backtra—"

The sciurids mobbed me. A dozen slammed into my ward, nails and fangs scraping my magic. I dropped the spell before it could snap and lobbed spooks into the trees. The next wave attacked on their heels. Creating wind-blast spell after wind-blast spell, I repelled them. For every spook I flung into the forest, five more took its place, their numbers never diminishing.

"I'll find another way." Quinn dodged around me, disappearing into the forest.

The carpet bumped against a tree and stalled. I fought it into motion, but it cost me: A spook landed on my crossed leg, slicing a long cut through fabric and flesh before I could swat it away. Two more clung to the edge of the carpet. They tumbled to the forest floor with my next air blast.

I shoved the carpet after Quinn. Twenty feet later, we hit the bramble wall again. Sweat dripped down my hairline. The spooks were small and their attacks limited, but at the rate I was burning through energy and how easily they slipped through the slightest gap in my defenses, I didn't stand a chance of escaping. They would wear me down first.

"How bad would it be to go through the ward?" Quinn asked.

I launched a berserker spook into the brambles. Its body flashed invisible, sparing it from being impaled on the massive thorns. Its disembodied feet scrambled for a grip, but it hit the ward first. Fire flashed white-hot, incinerating the tiny terror. The ward rippled as if a pebble had been tossed into it. Then the water in the spell extinguished the smoldering brambles, and the ward went dormant again. An acrid, burnt odor permeated the air.

"What if this ward goes all the way around the estate?" Quinn asked after a stunned pause.

It probably did—except for the public entrance. The entrance I should have taken.

I searched the trees for a convenient branch extending over the ward. None grew close on our side, and the trees on the opposite side were too far away. Maybe if we tracked the bramble wall, we would eventually get lucky, but it wasn't a gamble I could take.

"We have to go back."

I tried not to let my weariness bleed into my tone. Even with Quinn's enhancement, my elemental reflexes were slowing. I wasn't sure I could make it back to the road, but I had to try.

Quinn shook his head. "You have to go over."

"I can't." The carpet's levitation spell didn't extend that high, and I didn't have the skill or strength to alter it.

"You can if I boost you."

"I'm already using everything I can of your boost." Gritting my teeth, I punted the next wave of spooks. Two struck the bramble wall and died, their magic no match for the lethal ward. The rest landed unharmed and sprinted back into the fray. I should have tried to skewer them all on the ward, but that level of precision required more concentration than I could muster.

"Not my elemental boost." Quinn muscled a stump out of the ground and rolled it closer to the deadly ward. He jumped on top of it and turned sideways. Dropping one wing to the ground, he lifted the other, angling it toward the top of the bramble wall. "Use me as a ramp."

"I can't leave you behind."

"You have to. The spooks can't follow you to the other side."

I swiped sweat from my brow and studied the trees. Even if the sciurids climbed high enough to jump over the lethal barricade, they had nowhere to land on the other side. They would either impale themselves on the thorny brambles, incinerate on the ward, or splat on the ground.

Of course, if I took Quinn up on his proposition, I could be the one going splat on the other side. The carpet's levitation spell wasn't designed to cushion a drop; it might collapse under the pressure. If the ward didn't cremate me first.

I gathered air element for another pulse but bungled the simple spell. A spook ripped through my loose hair and scratched down my arm. I batted it aside with a weak flick of air. I would never survive the half-hour trip back to the road. Quinn's plan had to work.

"I'll find a place to get airborne once you're clear," Quinn said, eyeing the dense woods. He held the awkward position motionlessly. He was normally so animated that I tended to forget he was a gargoyle and as comfortable holding a statue-like position for hours as he was with soaring above the streets of Terra Haven.

"Let me get a running start."

I clung to the edges of the carpet, fighting off a battery of attacks as I maneuvered to give myself the longest straight line the forest would allow. My magic choppy, I powered the levitation spell higher between air blasts. The carpet rocked alarmingly as it rose to its full height, putting me even with the tip of Quinn's raised wing. The bramble wall rose even higher. This would be perilously close. If I had any other option, I wouldn't attempt it.

"Ready?" I asked.

"Ready."

I wanted to cross my fingers for luck, but prudence kept my fists clamped to the carpet's edges. Blocking out the chitters and barks of the carnivorous poltergeists, I locked a lightweight ward around myself. Then I channeled all my remaining elemental energy into the carpet's propulsion spell.

The carpet jolted forward. Claws splayed, a spook leapt for my neck, missing by inches before careening off the carpet. Trees flashed past, and I reached Quinn before the carpet had gained full speed. I hunched forward. The carpet shot up the ramp of Quinn's lowered wing, bucked as it transitioned across his horizontal back, then blasted up his raised wing.

I sailed past the tip of Quinn's wing, and the carpet went weightless beneath me. Nothing but momentum held me suspended. The bramble wall filled my vision, too close, too high. Digging deep, I shoved every last drop of my magic into the levitation spell. The carpet hiccupped and scraped across the top of the thorny wall, bouncing higher just as the ward surged to life. Heat bathed my legs. Then the carpet cleared the last of the towering brambles, tipped forward, and plummeted.

7

The carpet dropped out from beneath me, and only my white-knuckled grip on its edges kept me centered above it. A scream climbed my throat as the ground accelerated toward me. Frantically, I stacked dense air beneath the leading edge of the carpet, leveling it but not slowing my free fall. Less than a foot above the ground, the levitation spell finally engaged with a powerful jolt. The carpet ripped from my grip and I fell. Momentum sent me tumbling through the air before I slammed into a tree trunk.

Groaning, I stared up at green leaves and patches of blue sky, relearning how to breathe. Spook squirrels heckled me from their treetop perches, drumming their feet in agitation, but none dared attempt to cross the barrier.

"Kylie! *Kylie!*"

"I made it." The words came out a croak. I couldn't see Quinn through the dense bramble wall, though the rustle and sway of a cluster of saplings gave away his position. Shoving my hair out of my face, I shouted, "I'm fine."

It was mostly true. The deeper breath awakened bruises

across my ribs, and my head ached, but it could have been much worse.

Belatedly, I checked my surroundings. *This* was how I remembered the Kwan estate: large oaks spaced so their canopies barely overlapped and the forest floor beneath them clear of undergrowth all the way to the sunny lawns that sprawled around the house. I could even track a massive shadow accelerating across the sloped grass, bee-lining in my direction.

"Oh no." I staggered to my feet, clumsily gathering the elements. Zipporah had found me. I should have stayed on the other side of the wall with the spook squirrels. At least there the trees grew too close together for the harpy to land. I searched for somewhere to hide, but the well-groomed forest offered no inspiration.

When the creature swooped into sight, my breath caught. I couldn't make out more than its shape with it backlit by the sun and obscured by the trees' shadows, but it wasn't the harpy. It was flatter, shaped like the round top of a dining table with wings.

"What? What is it, Kylie? What's happening?"

"Something's approaching. I'm not sure what." I remained poised on the balls of my feet, vacillating between running and climbing a tree. I finally wrangled the elements into a basic ward, but it hung flimsily in the grip of my over-worked mental muscles.

The creature sped closer, rising and falling like an alba-tross above the ocean, its graceful sweeps taking it to the base of the oaks' lowest branches, then back toward the forest floor. It never flapped once. Sunlight swept across its back on a downward glide, revealing the mottled red, orange, and yellow of glossy quartz jasper.

My breath whooshed out, and my knees wobbled with relief. "It's a gargoyle!" I called to Quinn.

"Really?" Twigs snapped, and the brush around Quinn creaked. Above him, the spook squirrels quieted, ghosting to invisibility.

The unknown gargoyle banked and dropped to the ground a dozen feet away. A flurry of leaves and dirt gusted into the air, and I shielded my eyes in the crook of my elbow, too tired to use the elements to deflect the debris. When I lowered my arm, I looked into the face of a giant sea turtle. Deep red-orange patches decorated her cheeks and slender finlike feet; pale yellow gleamed down the underside of her chin, neck, and shoulders; and enormous albatross wings folded tight to her back, the flaxen and burnt-umber hues of the feathers blending in with the jasper patchwork of her shell. She rivaled Quinn in size, but her bright eyes spoke of decades more life experience.

"You should not be here," she said. "The ward can cause grievous harm."

"I know. I would have gone around if I'd had the chance. Sciurid poltergeists had me surrounded." I glanced over the thorny barrier at the trees. The spooks had faded into the forest, likely in search of easier prey.

"Why were you trespassing?"

I swung back around. "I thought we could take a shortcut."

"We?"

"My friend Quinn and me. Can you help him? He's trapped on the other side. There isn't enough room for him to stretch his wings to get the lift he needs to fly over."

"I could break through," Quinn suggested.

"No!" I flung a hand out to stop him, forgetting he couldn't see me through the thorny barricade. "Unless—" I turned to the sea turtle gargoyle. "Will the ward allow a gargoyle to pass through?"

"Your friend is the gargoyle I sensed?" The sea turtle's wings arched from her back, and her awkward legs flexed, lifting her six inches off the ground. "My name is Yarra," she called through the brambles. "Are you in search of a home, Quinn?"

I read surprise in Quinn's pause before he responded. "No, I'm here to assist Kylie with her story. She's a journalist."

Yarra craned her neck to study my face, and I felt compelled to say, "We have an invitation." I would hate to give the impression that I was the type of journalist to crash a full-spectrum event.

"How big is your friend?" Yarra asked.

"He's a lion with eagle wings. About so big." I stretched my arms to mime Quinn's approximate size, wincing when the extension pulled at the cuts on my arms and back.

"He should be compact enough," Yarra said before instructing Quinn to make his way east to a stream, where he would be able to crawl beneath the baleful wall. "Once you're on this side, you'll have no problem flying."

"Thank you! Don't go anywhere." Limbs cracked and popped as Quinn rushed off. We both remained quiet, listening to the sounds of his progress until they faded beneath the chirps of sparrows and finches that had come out of hiding after the spook squirrels' retreat.

I shifted on my feet, conscious of how I towered over Yarra. Would it be patronizing to crouch or was it rude to remain standing? Deciding on the latter, I lowered myself gingerly to sit in front of the gargoyle. Her gaze shifted to study me.

"My name is Kylie Grayson. Um, Harriet Kylie Grayson. I

used to come here with my mom when I was young, years ago." I scoured my mind for a memory of Yarra, coming up with a vague image of a sea turtle profile protruding from the corner of the Kwan mansion's roof. We had never interacted, but at the time, I had been more interested in exploring the grounds than conversing with anyone.

"Yes, we had more visitors then," Yarra said, a touch of emotion I couldn't identify in her voice.

A flash of refracted golden light preceded Quinn as he flew into view, following the top of the bramble wall. When he spotted us, he dove, landing fast and prancing to my side. Once he was satisfied I wasn't grievously injured, he turned his curious gaze toward Yarra.

The transformation in the elderly gargoyle was startling. Her long wings lifted in an excited V, and she smiled so wide that her chubby cheeks pushed her eyes almost closed. I rocked in place when a second elemental boost expanded my magical reach. The only other gargoyles who had enhanced the elements for me were Quinn's siblings. I wanted to express my gratitude to Yarra for the honor, but she was fixated on Quinn.

"I didn't realize you were *the* Quinn, friend of Guardian Mika!" Yarra said.

She knew of Mika? Way out here? I checked Quinn's expression, but he didn't appear surprised. He didn't question Yarra giving Mika the title of "guardian" rather than "healer," either. Instead, he puffed out his chest and acknowledged Yarra's comment with a regal nod.

"You were one of the first Mika healed." Yarra's wings dropped at this, folding back to her sides.

"I was," Quinn said somberly.

I laid a hand on his shoulder. Horrific torture had nearly ended his life when he was a cub. Mika had performed a miracle in saving him, and afterward, I spent countless hours lying on the roof with Quinn while he recuperated. Back then, he had been small enough to curl up in my lap. Now he was almost full grown and—lately—more likely to be the one keeping me company while I recuperated from an injurious ordeal.

"Your sister was the one to locate Guardian Mika," Yarra continued, nodding to herself. "She made a great discovery that day. I am honored to have you as guests. Will the guardian be joining us?"

"Not today," Quinn said. Yarra's smile drooped, and he added, "I'll tell her we spoke. Or you could come by the house and meet her."

Yarra glanced between me and Quinn. "I couldn't. Really? Maybe. It's been so long . . ."

I plucked a twig from my knotted hair, wincing when sap pulled out several strands by the roots. Chancing aggravating my headache, I gathered a modest dose of air and water and wove the familiar spell of an elemental bath. A whirlwind of dirt, leaves, and twigs spun from my body when I unleashed the spell, forming an impressive pile at my feet. I couldn't do anything about my torn clothing, and I didn't want to waste energy extracting the dried blood from the fabric, but at least I was clean.

"Are you sure you're fine?" Quinn asked.

I glanced up from my shoulder, where I had pulled apart the ripped edges of my shirt to view the jagged scratch beneath it. The wound had stopped bleeding, but it needed medical attention, if only for a good sterilization. Who knew what sort of nastiness lurked on the claws of varmint poltergeists.

"Nothing a shower and a change of clothes won't fix

once we get back to Terra Haven," I said, not wanting Quinn to worry.

"What's that around your neck?" Yarra asked Quinn.

He lifted a paw as if to cover his mutated seed, then dropped it back to the loamy soil. "It's an everlasting seed."

"Really?" Yarra shuffled closer, twisting her head to examine the seed. "It looks . . . Well, I don't want to be rude."

"It's all right. I know it's ugly, but it's supposed to tell me how to help Kylie."

"So you know what it means?"

Quinn shook his head.

"I was going to say it looks like an inverse of the elements."

I peered at Quinn's seed, but the mud-colored deformity hadn't altered shape. Yarra was either being polite or gargoyles viewed the elements differently than I did.

"More like the antithesis of beauty," Quinn grumbled.

I retrieved my fallen bag and the carpet from where it had coasted to a stop. The gargoyles trailed after me, Yarra much more awkwardly than Quinn. Her fins hadn't been designed for casual strolling. She didn't complain, though.

"Can you feel the way the elements are flourishing, Quinn?" Yarra breathed deep, a smile curving her round cheeks. "It's good to have so many people on the grounds again. It feels like old times."

I wondered how far in the past Yarra was referencing. Persephone was an only child, and her parents had died young. For a gargoyle used to having an entire family of full spectrums to enhance, I could understand how Yarra might have been lonely. However, since I couldn't imagine being happy to have a single full-spectrum family in residence, let alone an entire party's worth, I kept my mouth shut.

Miraculously, the carpet's spells had survived the abuse of the fall, so after I got my bag and myself situated atop the rigid surface, we set out for the estate. Yarra led the way, as graceful in the air as she was clumsy on the ground. She swept in and out of the trees on her long wings, never seeming to need to flap, and Quinn dipped and dove around her, chatty and carefree.

I wished I could share their good spirits. More than ever, I wanted to point the carpet toward Terra Haven and let it carry me home. My body ached, and I feared my vanity was going to take a worse beating. Wearing plain trousers and a blouse to a high-society event would have been humbling enough, and that was before the spooks refashioned my once-professional apparel into rags. Even if I could muster the energy to do something attractive with my wind-tangled hair, it wouldn't help.

I imagined the spoiled child-author I was supposed to interview sticking her snooty nose in the air and refusing to talk to me in my deplorable state. A smile tugged at my lips. Maybe this would work in my favor. If full-spectrum snobs decided I was too far beneath their high-society holiness to associate with, they might never insist Dahlia send me on one of their fluff-piece assignments again.

A girl could dream.

The tree line broke against an unyielding, rectangular lawn wider than Terra Haven's main boulevards. Eyes watering in the harsh sunlight, I surveyed the expansive geometric gardens lined with low square hedges and bordered with wide gravel walkways. Strategically placed fountains and shallow ponds populated with tropical fish softened the rigid lines of the manicured grounds. The whole effect was breathtaking, if smaller than I remembered. It must have been the exaggeration of memory and time that had made the gardens seem to stretch for miles when I was a kid.

The mansion, however, was larger than I recalled. It sprawled in an endless repetition of glistening windows and blinding marble columns. With its white-on-cream color scheme and exacting lines, it had all the appeal of a boarding school: attractive to look at, but I wouldn't want to live there.

We had the grounds to ourselves, though judging by the chaotic array of carriages, air conveyances, and animals lining the long driveway to the east, we wouldn't for long. At least this part of my plan had worked; I had successfully avoided the crush at the entrance and all the photographers and gossip reporters lurking there. It almost made my near-death shortcut worth it.

I angled for the section of the house with the largest chimney—the kitchen. Yarra soared up to the roof, tossing me a cheerful wave when I powered down the carpet. Quinn landed next to me.

The sun baked my scalp and sweat stung the scratches on my back by the time I rolled the carpet and tucked it under an arm. Lifting my chin and assuming my best expression of full-spectrum arrogance, I marched through the back door of the kitchen as if I owned the place. A wall of heat and sound hit me, but I kept my steps measured as I navigated the frantic environment. Quinn slowed, his head swinging to take in the chefs at a bank of stoves shouting orders to their underlings; the servers hustling out with platters of bite-size appetizers and glasses of wine; and the whirlwind of elements zinging through the air, warming platters, chilling wine, and carrying messages between staff members. Had I been a decade younger, I would have hidden out here, sneaking food and trading the snide company of the party guests for the honest interactions of the staff. I envied my younger self.

No one in the kitchen blinked at the sight of a wounded woman strolling through in ripped clothing, a gargoyle in her wake. Anyone working in the household of a full-spectrum family learned not to ask questions about the guests. The FSPP might treat gossip like a sport among themselves, but they didn't tolerate it in their staff.

I ducked into the first bathroom I spotted, grateful its closet-like size forced Quinn to wait outside while I washed my wounds. Scrubbing soap and water into the puffy red sciurid scratches brought fresh tears to my eyes, and by the time I finished rinsing off, I had run out of curses, and my breaths were choppy. I dried with a gentle air spell, pleased when using the elements didn't ignite a new headache.

Dressed once more, I slung my bag over my shoulder and artfully arranged my hair so it covered the worst of the bloodstained rips in my shirt. I couldn't do anything about my pants. Before I exited the bathroom, I shoved the rolled-up flying carpet into an empty cupboard under the sink. It would be easy enough to retrieve it and slip out through the kitchen after I finished my interview. Besides, I couldn't walk around the party with a carpet under my arm.

"Let's see what we have in store for us," I said, directing Quinn away from the stream of servers and up a set of stairs in search of the mezzanine overlooking the massive ballroom. From there, it would be easier to plot my approach and minimize my interaction with party guests. Not that I was hiding. Just exercising prudence.

The stairs led to an unfamiliar hallway. Undeterred, I strode down the worn carpet runner, peering into the side rooms. The first room lay empty. Utterly and completely empty.

"That's odd."

The next room contained a smattering of furniture, all of it draped in dusty drop cloths. My steps slowed, my gaze snagging on the grime coating the bottom panes of the windows. The rooms on the opposite side of the hall looked worse. Drooping wallpaper exposed cracked plaster and the raw boards behind them, ashes lay inches deep in the fireplaces, and nails dotted the walls where pictures had once hung, their size and shape defined by faint ashy shadows. Broken furniture lay abandoned in one room, piled against the wall along with a cracked door and a jumble of threadbare rugs.

"What is it?" Quinn asked.

"I'm not sure." First the forest had been neglected. No, not just neglected. Abandoned. Persephone had let the outer reaches of her property go feral, providing a nurturing habitat for deadly predators like the spook squirrels. The military-grade bramble ward was the only reason the grounds closer to the estate weren't similarly overrun. Now this?

"I think Persephone might be in financial trouble," I said.

"Why are you whispering?"

"Because." Because the financial downfall of a full-spectrum family was not something discussed openly, especially not within the walls of said family's home.

Voices echoed down the hallway, and I jumped. Motioning to Quinn, I jogged silently back the way we had come. The gargoyle's footsteps weren't as soft as mine, but we managed to reach the top of the stairs without anyone rushing our way and demanding to know why we were snooping. I glanced over my shoulder, spotting two servants in red-and-gray Kwan uniforms rounding the far end of the hallway. Ducking my head, I scurried down the steps, Quinn on my heels.

"Why are we running?" Quinn hissed.

"Because— Oof!" I smacked into a woman in scarlet, then grabbed her arms to prevent her from slamming into the wall. "I'm so sorry. I—"

"Charlotte?"

I blinked, surprised to be mistaken for my mom.

"Of course not. My mistake, Harriet," the other woman said, correcting herself. "You look so much like your mom. And, wow, you're all grown up. The last time I saw you, you were what? Thirteen?"

"Fourteen." Now that I got a better look at her, I recognized Persephone Kwan. She hadn't changed much—her ebony hair still hung in glossy waves, her porcelain skin remained flawless, and her eyes were as dark and unlined as ever—but the last time I had seen her, she had been several inches taller than me. Now, not only was she shorter than me, but she was also smaller, more delicate, almost fragile. It took a moment for my brain to process being the bigger person.

"Thank you for extending an invitation to me, Ms. Kwan," I said, recovering my manners.

"Don't 'Ms. Kwan' me, Harriet. You've known me for too long. Call me Persephone."

"I prefer Kylie these days. And this is Quinn."

Quinn stepped forward, and Persephone twitched, as if she hadn't noticed him standing behind me.

"It's an honor to meet you," Quinn said.

"Likewise. I'm surprised to find you back here. Both of you. How did I miss your arrival?"

"We got a little lost," I said, sidestepping the question.

"This place is a lot larger than I remember. And so different."

Persephone's gaze flicked to the staircase behind me, her expression tightening. "You know how it is. Out with the old, in with the new. We're always changing something around here."

Of course. I had forgotten one of high society's treasured tenets: always find new ways to flaunt wealth. I had assumed the disrepair and vacancy of the upstairs rooms indicated a downturn in the Kwans' finances, but a massive redecoration project made more sense.

"How *did* you end up by the kitchen?" Persephone asked.

"That's where we came in," Quinn said.

"By way of a shortcut through the forest," I added, curious what Persephone would say about the state of her property. "I don't think we saved much time, though. I got lost out there, too. And then I ran into the ward."

"That bothersome thing." Persephone waved a dismissive hand, as if every estate was ringed with a lethal bramble barrier set to incinerate trespassers. "But you're a strong elemental. I'm sure it didn't give you trouble."

"I got around it. Thankfully, the sciurid poltergeists couldn't." I allowed my lingering outrage to seep into my tone. I should have been safe while inside her property's borders. Having to defend my life and sustaining injuries while on Kwan land—not to mention nearly being annihilated by the very ward that was supposed to protect Persephone's estate and guests—was an insult many wouldn't forget or forgive.

Persephone's hands lifted to cover her bow mouth, her eyes widening. "Spook squirrels? In my forest? Luther told me I was taking things too far, but I thought he was just being a doting fiancé."

Her genuine shock was mollifying, and her phrasing caught me off guard. "That's right. You got engaged to Wetherill." The words blurted out before my brain caught up. I added a hasty "Congratulations," and I clamped my mouth shut before *What do you see in that slimeball?* could spill out.

"I'm a lucky, lucky woman." Persephone smiled, a flush of happiness brightening her cheeks. If I hadn't witnessed it, I would have said it was impossible for the thought of Luther Wetherill to inspire such a besotted expression. "I could go on and on about Luther, but I'm sure you've heard it all. Besides"—Persephone turned to Quinn—"this must be terribly boring for you. Why don't you head up to the roof? Yarra is up there. She's our resident gargoyle, and I know she would love your company."

"We met—" Quinn looked as if he wanted to say more, but Persephone cut him off.

"Wonderful! She doesn't get many gargoyle visitors. Then again, who does? It's such a treat that you're here. Please, Quinn, go speak with her."

I shared a look with Quinn and shrugged, seeing no harm in him spending more time with Yarra. I would be safe at the party—or at least I would be safe from anything Quinn could save me from. Neither of us had any defenses against general snobbishness or full-spectrum emotional machinations.

Wishing I could accompany Quinn, I made myself turn toward Persephone after he departed.

"Into the storm we go," Persephone said with a smile. She hooked her arm through mine, and I couldn't contain a hiss of pain when she clamped down on one of the spook squirrel scratches. Persephone released me instantly, only to grab me by both shoulders, her gaze scanning down my body. "You're hurt!"

"It's nothing. Just a few cuts."

Persephone poked a finger through a rip in my blouse's sleeve, gently shifting the fabric aside to examine the wound beneath it. I made a feeble attempt to bat her hand aside, but she was already circling me, plucking at the torn back of my blouse.

"This won't do," she announced. "Come, come. You need to let me make this up to you."

Persephone took my hand, and I allowed myself to be dragged down a narrow hallway until she released me in a modest room furnished with a sewing machine, a padded bench, and too many mirrors.

"I gave my seamstress the day off. It seemed like a good idea at the time, but now . . ." Persephone opened a door to a closet twice as large as the seamstress's workspace, every inch of it filled with bolts of cloth. A small row of completed outfits hung on a rack in the back. "I think I have a dress in here that will look wonderful on you. I wore it as a teen . . ."

"What I'm wearing is fine," I protested, wanting her charity about as much as I wanted to wear a twenty-year-old dress.

Persephone's mouth twisted. "Maybe it was when you left Terra Haven, but now it's a tad . . . distressed." She strode deeper into the closet.

I eyed the door to the hallway, contemplating my escape. Was there a polite way to say *My ripped shirt is better than your castoffs*? Deciding that arguing with her would only make me look like an idiot, I raised my voice and asked, "What did you mean when you said Wetherill—I mean, Luther—said you were taking things too far?"

"Hmm? Oh, yes, the party." Persephone returned, a

cobalt-blue dress in hand. "I wanted the solstice gathering to have real dramatic flair, so I let the estate's wards relax. Well, actually, I broke them down a bit, but don't tell Luther. It's all about the show, right? I can't tell you how many of these element-renewing ceremonies I've participated in where the host spent all their energy getting their estate spells perfect before we showed up. It's such a letdown. You can't tell the ritual has done a thing in that pristine environment. I mean, of course it helps balance the elements for miles around, but when there's an immediate difference to see, it makes everyone feel like they've actually done some good. That's so much better for everyone, don't you think?"

I clicked my mouth shut, nodding mechanically. She had let her property become run down because she wanted the solstice ritual to be more theatrically pleasing? Sure, that made sense . . . if you were an FSPP. If anyone could afford to put showmanship before safety, it was a full spectrum. I tried to imagine Josephine applying the same logic and had to shake my head. My landlady would sooner invite termites to feast on the support beams of the Victorian than she would allow her wards to become lax for any reason.

"Here, put this on," Persephone ordered.

Since I couldn't think of an acceptable reason not to, I shrugged out of my blouse. Persephone hissed in sympathy.

"Did you get all those scratches from the awful spook squirrels?" she asked.

"And tree branches. The forest was really overgrown." Several years' growth couldn't be explained away by intentionally lax wards. I paused before unbuttoning my pants, letting the question dangle, unasked.

Persephone's free hand fluttered toward her forehead, and she sighed heavily. "It's on the list, trust me. I've had my hands full upgrading this old house. The interior needs to be modernized in a major way, and I'm afraid I've been so focused in here that I let the forest get a bit wild. That's the next project. Or rather, the next, *next* project. First I'm overseeing the installation of a pool beneath the east wing."

A pool? I kept my eye roll to myself and unclipped Grant's badge from the waist of my pants while Persephone wasn't looking. I hesitated with it in my hand, unsure where to attach it to the dress. Even if I secured it to the inside of the bodice, the clip would still be visible. Attaching it to the hem would be risky and make it too easy to lose. I glanced down at my remaining apparel. Feeling silly, I clipped the badge to the waistband of my underwear and grabbed the dress from Persephone before she noticed. While she prattled on about her spring-fed swimming oasis, its heated rocks and waterfall, and all manner of other ostentatious features that only a full spectrum would deem "necessary," I squeezed myself into her old dress. Persephone finally wound down when I turned to examine myself in the mirror.

I couldn't take a deep breath, my ribs constricted by a tight bodice that squeezed my modest chest flat. An explosion of coarse black lace frothed around my clavicle and dripped down my biceps, ending at the bend in my elbows and leaving the cuts on my forearms exposed. The skirt was draped in a fluff of cobalt pleats, the hem line hitting five inches above my ankles. More black lace fringed the hem, though not quite enough to meet my brown boots.

"Stunning," Persephone said.

"That's a word for it." I looked stunningly washed out, my pale skin and white-blond hair giving me the appearance of a ghost who got caught in a rotting, mold-spewing blueberry. *Be gracious,* I reprimanded myself. The fabric was finer than anything in my closet, it wasn't ripped, and it covered the cuts on my leg. The garment's style might be out of date, but it was more in line with the dress code of this event than my slacks had been.

I tugged my hair into a bun. It minimized the ghost vibe. Now I only looked sickly.

Maybe I would look better once I wasn't standing next to Persephone. Styled in the latest fashion, her silk dress shimmered crimson from its fitted bodice and flat front to the modest bustle and train flowing behind her. Charcoal accents trimmed the cap sleeves and square-cut neckline, and intricate embroidered orchids adorned the hem in matching gray thread. A fancy braid contained the top half of Persephone's hair, but the bottom half hung in thick curls over one shoulder. With pearl earrings framing her face and a small broach at her throat, she looked every inch a high-society woman, whereas I looked like a girl playing dress-up in another woman's clothing. Which was depressingly close to the truth.

"Really, this is too much," I hedged.

"Nonsense." Persephone scooped up my clothes and tossed them atop the fireplace's ashes. "I fear I've left my guests alone too long. Let's go mingle, Harriet—I mean Kylie. Oh, that's going to take some getting used to."

I cast one last glance at my ruined clothing, then at myself in the mirror. Crouching, I retrieved my satchel. It clashed horribly with the dress.

I'm here for work. I'm not trying to impress anyone, I reminded myself.

Looping the bag's strap over my shoulder, I shuffled after Persephone, more motivated than ever to wrap up this assignment in record time.

8

Persephone set a quick pace toward the party, forcing me to jog to keep up.

"About Ms. Flemming and the interview—" I began.

"You're going to love her. But don't jump right into work. You've been away from society for so long." Persephone patted my shoulder, as if her statement merited sympathy. "Take some time to enjoy yourself first. Get reacquainted. I'm sure you've missed so much."

Missed wasn't the right word. *Avoided* was more accurate, but I didn't correct her.

The murmur of the crowd filtered down the hallway, and the louder it got, the more it amplified my nerves. I smoothed a hand down my borrowed gown, reminding myself I had survived much worse than a crowd of aristocratic busybodies. I had fought off a rampaging spriggan. I had navigated to the heart of Lunacy Labyrinth and returned alive. I would not allow myself to be intimidated by the snobs of high society.

Even if I wore a dress two decades out of date and two sizes too small.

We reached the wide-open double doors of the massive pentagon-shaped ballroom, and for a brief moment, I forgot my trepidation. Five floor-to-ceiling animated murals of pure illusion adorned the walls, one for each element. I gaped at the legion of wyverns frolicking among clouds that covered the far wall only to have my gaze snagged by the silent stampede of two-story-tall wild mustangs on the next wall. Color-changing glowballs studded the rafters as if suspended from invisible chandeliers, bathing the entire room and its occupants with a flattering glow. I breathed deep, savoring the heady aroma of roses circulating on discreet elemental currents and marveled that I could hear the enchanting melody of a violin quartet tucked out of sight.

If not for magical assistance, the music would have been drowned out by the chatter of a hundred voices. Full-spectrum elites packed the expansive floor in a collage of elaborate, elementally enhanced outfits. Color-changing fabric appeared to be in fashion this season. No less than five men and two women in my line of sight wore garments that ebbed through the color spectrum. However, the extravagant material paled next to the mind-bending outfits of masterful illusionists, who transformed their bodies into glass sculptures, walking oil paintings, and bizarre animal-human amalgamations, like the woman who appeared to stand on ostrich legs. I wished Quinn had opted to stay with me. He would have been awestruck by the whole affair. *I* was awestruck, and I had known what to expect.

"Oh good, no one burned the place down." With a cheerful laugh, Persephone wrapped her hand around my back and propelled me into the crush of guests.

Curious faces turned in our direction, and judgmental eyes scanned my hideous ensemble. Heat rose to my cheeks. Plastering on a smile, I pretended I didn't see the smirks directed my way.

"I have just the person you should meet," Persephone said, scanning the crowd.

"I really should get to work." The only thing worse than attending a full-spectrum party was being paraded around it by the host. Surveying the room, I cataloged faces I hadn't seen in years, attempting to anticipate who she might call over. "I have a deadli— Mom?" The question blurted out when I spied a familiar tall figure halfway across the room.

As if sensing my gaze, my mom turned. Her eyes widened in surprise when she spotted me, and she excused herself from a conversation to head in my direction. In typical Charlotte fashion, my mom had selected an understated gown. Next to its simplistic lines and subtle ivory and khaki stripes, the other guests' lavish costumes looked gaudy. Even her subdued gold-and-wood jewelry proclaimed she didn't need to compete or make a fuss to be respected. She traversed the packed floor with her head held high and an ease in her gait that wasn't matched by the turmoil in her sky-blue eyes.

I curled my toes in my boots, quelling the urge to rush across the room and bombard her with a thousand questions. This wasn't the place to ask them. The last thing my mom needed was for me to make a scene in front of the entire local population of full spectrums.

"Kylie? What are you doing here?" she asked when she reached my side. Her tone held the right amount of curiosity and joy to project the image of a pleasantly surprised mom, but her grip on my fingers conveyed her concern.

"My dear friend, I invited her, of course," Persephone said.

My mom pulled her gaze from me. "I'm sorry, Persephone. That was rude of me. I'm just shocked to see my daughter."

Probably about as astonished as I was to see her. With Airstrong's thefts announced in today's paper, I hadn't expected my mom to have time for social calls, let alone for a countryside solstice ritual.

A flurry of conversations swelled in my mom's wake. Despite staring at the three of us with open speculation, few bothered with the courtesy of erecting soundproof wards as they blatantly gossiped. My eyes narrowed before I caught myself and smoothed my expression. I had forgotten how much this world revolved around appearances. Like any pack of predators, if full spectrums sensed a weakness, they would pounce. With Airstrong's reputation on the line, my mom couldn't be anywhere *but* here today, letting her presence speak to her confidence in her company.

"I'm delighted you made it, Charlotte. I wasn't sure if you would after I heard about Airstrong's troubles," Persephone said, right on cue. "I want to let you know you have my support. I'm sure all this will blow over, but it must be dreadful right now. Thefts! Right under your nose. You must be furious."

"Among other things." My mom smiled serenely, as if the potential destruction of her livelihood didn't trouble her. "The FPD knows what it's doing, and I'm confident they'll apprehend the thief. In the meantime, Airstrong will continue to operate as normal. And speaking of shipping..." My mom flashed a dimple. "Congratulations on your engagement to the enemy."

Persephone laughed. "I like to think of it as marrying

into the industry. My fiancé and I were discussing your plight this morning. Luther is quite distraught about Airstrong's troubles."

I bet he was. It must have been positively anxiety-inducing to contemplate all the business that would rush his way once Airstrong's clients heard about the thefts and panicked.

"He's around here somewhere, and I know he wants to speak with you," Persephone continued, oblivious to the wry look my mom and I shared behind her back. "You, too, Harr— Kylie. Well, *everyone* wants to converse with Kylie. Your escapades are all anyone's talking about." Persephone beamed as if she were awarding me with a prize.

Fresh dread twisted my intestines. She was right: People were studying me with more curiosity than I could attribute to my atrocious attire. I had expected to be ignored and dismissed. My elemental powers, career, and monetary means all fell short of the criteria by which full spectrums judged a person's worth. In their eyes, I was a member of the hired help, on hand to immortalize their importance but otherwise not to be seen or heard. Or so I had thought.

"Kylie, dear, what happened to you? You look like you got into a fight." My mom gently swept aside the ugly black lace of my dress's sleeves for a better view of the spook squirrel scratches. The puffy redness around the wounds had diminished since I had washed them, but the jagged scrapes remained garish against my pale skin.

"I think she looks amazing, considering she just survived Lunacy Labyrinth," Persephone said.

"Indeed. At least that's what I read in the newspaper."

My mom's cool tone speared guilt through my gut. I should have sent her a message the moment I had returned to Terra Haven. If not right away, then definitely once I had read about my own adventures in the *Chronicle*. No parent wanted to hear that their daughter had spent the night inside blood-magic ruins, especially not through a biased secondhand account. But I had been so busy being angry at Nathan for revealing my true name that I hadn't thought about my mom—or how she might react to my identity being exposed so publicly.

"Persephone, will you excuse us?" I asked. "We have some catching up to do."

Persephone glanced between us, her eyebrows lifting in surprise. "You haven't given your mom a personal account of your adventures yet?"

I shook my head.

She bit her lip, as if she were contemplating how to shoehorn herself into that conversation, but good manners won out. "I'll leave you to it." She gave us each a fond farewell pat on the arm and walked away, barely making it two steps before a jewel-encrusted couple pulled her into a discussion about the latest pegasi races.

My mom and I pivoted in unison, putting our backs to the room and anyone who might mistake the moment as an invitation to approach. Taking my hand, my mom led me to a secluded corner, stopping beside a potted feathery palm. She tapped the elements and built a soundproof ward around us. Etiquette dictated the ward remain clear, so we weren't obscured to the other guests. The bubble was delicate enough to be broken by a touch but thick enough that a shout wouldn't be heard by someone on the other side. Like so many aspects of FSPP etiquette, the spell showcased power while maintaining a veneer of civility. I couldn't say which evoked a stronger sense of childhood nostalgia: being encased in a soundproof ward with my mother or the spell's underlying notes of uplifting air and stabilizing wood that denoted my mom's magical signature.

"This is the last place I expected to find you," my mom said.

"I'm on assignment, a fluff piece." Her tone had been teasing, her curiosity undisguised beneath it, but her choice of words ignited the hurt feelings I had been nursing since this morning. My words tumbled out too fast. "Why did I have to hear about the thefts from someone else? First the firebirds, now this. If the FPD hadn't published the reward information, would you ever have told me?"

"You chose to leave the business, Kylie. That means you lost certain privileges."

"Like being trusted? I'm still family, Mom. Why did you try to hide this from me?"

She sighed and tucked a wayward strand of hair behind my ear. "I was trying to protect you, but when you announced your full name in the *Chronicle*, you took away that option. Whatever possessed you to do that now, of all times?"

"I didn't. A coworker made the discovery and ran my name without my permission." My lips curled at classifying Nathan as a *coworker*.

"Problems at work?"

"Just general small-mindedness. Nothing I can't handle." I shrugged stiff shoulders, not wanting to get sidetracked.

"You won't be able to pull your disappearing act twice, not now that you're here."

"I'm well aware of that." I gritted my teeth.

"I'm sorry, Kylie."

Her genuine sympathy smoothed the sharp edges from my bitterness, and the rigidity seeped from my spine. "Thanks, Mom."

"I know how little you like playing high-society politics."

"That doesn't mean I'm not good at it." I gave her a small smile, acknowledging the lessons she had drilled into me as a child. Drawing my shoulders back, I mentally donned the persona of Harriet Grayson, Airstrong heiress, and surveyed the room. "So what's the company line and what aren't you telling the public? All I know is what the reward poster said. And, of course, that the FPD has the absurd notion that Airstrong might have been in on the thefts."

"Your source got it mostly right. The FPD finished ruling out all Airstrong employees yesterday."

"Why don't you sound more pleased?"

"Because Investigator O'Hara now believes only two people could have pulled off the thefts: me and your dad."

"What?!" I gaped at my mom. She smiled back, her expression radiating benign contentment rather than the outrage her statement demanded.

"Facial cues, darling."

Reminded of our audience of gossip-hungry full spectrums, I attempted to school my features.

"Try not to look so pained, dear," my mom said.

I stopped pretending to smile.

"That's better."

"Why are you and Dad suspects?" My voice sounded strangled, but at least I didn't shout.

"It's a moot point. The FPD's not going public with their preposterous theory. You don't need to worry."

Worry? No, this tasted more like panic. "Mom . . ."

"O'Hara claims I'm the only connection between all the stolen items—or rather, me and Terra Haven. He's suspicious of your dad by proxy. I have reminded the investigator that each stolen item was replaced with an object of its exact weight, and the thefts weren't discovered until the packages were opened by their recipients, which means the culprit could have made the exchange anywhere along the shipping route. But O'Hara is fixated on the fact that each theft occurred from shipments that funneled through Terra Haven when I was in town."

"Everything goes through Terra Haven." The city was a hub for most shipping routes.

"So I've mentioned."

My thoughts spun through this new information. If all the items had been stolen in the same manner, it implied a single thief or, at least, a single team. The thefts hadn't been committed based on a whim or opportunity. They had been premeditated. According to Grant, the banned spells had been shipped in disguised crates. Not only had the thief known which crates to burgle, but he had also known the exact items he would find in each shipment. Both facts pointed to someone with insider knowledge. As the owners of the company, my parents would have been privy to all those details, but that didn't make them criminals. They would never do anything to jeopardize their company.

"What about Airstrong's reputation? Your reputation?" I asked. "You've always said that without the trust of your clients, you wouldn't have a business. O'Hara had to know releasing news of the thefts could destroy Airstrong."

"I believe that's the point," my mom said wearily. "O'Hara assumed your father and I would call him off, stop the press conference, and confess rather than watch our company's reputation go up in cinders."

"But you're innocent. You have nothing to confess."

"Indeed." My mom made a moue. "But one way or another, it was going to come out. Maybe it needed to. We've been operating with our hands tied, trying to hide our manhunt from our own staff. This gives us more freedom, and if we're lucky, it will flush out the real thieves."

"And if you're not lucky?"

Her shoulders hitched. "Now you understand why I didn't want you involved in any of this."

"No, I don't. If not for Grant this morning, I would have found out from—" My fingers fisted around the strap of my bag. "That doesn't matter. You should have told me. I can help."

"This morning? Who is Grant? Why does that name sound familiar?"

I could tell from the forced lightness of my mom's tone that she was trying to change the subject—or her honed maternal senses had detected something in my voice that caused her to latch on to Grant's name. Ever since I had assumed my new identity, it had become imperative to avoid interactions between my parents and boyfriends—or in Grant's case, between my parents and a man I had almost kissed and who I hoped was boyfriend material. *Ugh.* Unfortunately, my secretiveness had only spurred my mom's tenacious attempts to ferret out anyone I might be interested in.

"Stick with me, Mom. This is important. I need to tell you about my seed."

She glanced over my shoulder and groaned. "Here too? Since when does the FPD attend full-spectrum solstice rituals? Shouldn't they be somewhere their skills might be needed?"

I pivoted, expecting to catch my first glimpse of Investigator O'Hara. Instead, I saw Grant. My stomach somersaulted. He wore a dress uniform, white to represent his element, with silvery elemental patterns spilling down his broad chest and across his flat abdomen. The spell-laced thread split to spiral down the outer seam of his white pants, ending at the hems above black boots. I doubted the delicate spells provided much protection or enhancement, but they turned the simplistic outfit into a study of power. Or maybe that was just Grant. He prowled through the room, trading nods with myriad guests but not slowing, his eyes perpetually scanning the crowd, as if he were expecting danger even here.

Seradon meandered in his wake. The FPD earth elemental wore a dress uniform similar to Grant's, though hers was a buttery khaki several shades darker than my mom's dress. She also studied her surroundings, but she appeared more interested in locating servers than ferreting out trouble. In the time it took Grant to cross the ballroom, she acquired a flute of sparkling wine and nibbled her way through three different appetizers.

"Does he think I'll be intimidated by that glare?" my mom asked. "Come. Walk with me, Kylie."

"Hang on. I think he's coming over here to talk to us." From the look on his face, Grant wasn't going to let us escape that easily. I had no desire to play the world's slowest game of chase through the ballroom, either. Better to see what he had to say. Besides, the sight of Grant in his white uniform had arrested important parts of my brain, and I wasn't sure I could walk at that moment without tripping over my own feet.

"I've had my fill of the FPD lately," my mom snapped.

"Facial cues," I murmured.

She shot me a dour squint before sliding her benign smile back into place. Dropping her ward, she faced Grant.

He crowded into my personal space, forcing me to kink my neck to meet his eyes. I had gotten better at seeing through his captain's mask, but today I couldn't decipher the emotion in his stern gaze.

"You said you were turning down this invitation."

"Dahlia had other plans." I peered around Grant, looking for Seradon. She had changed course to trail after a server carrying a fruit platter. "Is something going on? You didn't mention attending, either."

"I noticed you took an unconventional route here."

I noticed that wasn't an answer, I wanted to say, but his knowledge of my detour surprised me. Was he spying on— The tracker. I had forgotten about it again, and my hand lifted reflexively to cover his badge, which now pressed intimately against my hip.

"I took a shortcut."

"Emphasis on *cut*?" Grant's gaze lingered on the long scratches on my arm.

"Was that a joke, Captain?" I didn't want to talk about the spook squirrels or my cuts. Grant might decide to inflict his healing on me, and I didn't relish another dose of his crude spell work today.

Turning my body to include my mom in the conversation, I said, "Can I introduce you to my mom, Charlotte Grayson? Mom, this is Captain Grant Monaghan."

My mom snapped a soundproof ward around the three of us so fast, I jumped. The inner air crackled with discordant elements, and this time, I found nothing soothing about the swirling currents of her magical signature.

"Mom?"

She ignored me to glare at Grant. "You had better hope for your sake and the sake of the entire Federal Pentagon Defense that you aren't planning on *using* my daughter to further this investigation."

"The FPD will use whatever resources it deems necessary to recover the missing spells," Grant said, unruffled by the growing pressure of my mom's magic or the icy fury of her tone.

Sweat broke out along my scalp as my mom's magic constricted around me, and I blurted out the first words that popped into my head. "What about if I used Grant? Would you both be all right with that?"

Grant snorted, a barely there smile curving the corners of his lips. My mom glanced between us, then allowed the elements to drain from the air until only her ward remained.

What in the splintered elements had she been thinking?

"Grant is a friend," I said firmly. "He's the reason I survived Lunacy Labyrinth. Whatever you think of him, Mom, you've got it wrong."

My mom smoothed her fingers down the front of her dress and tugged her lips into a sweet smile, but her eyes remained sharp with accusation. "A friend," she repeated, not quite making it a question. Her gaze dropped to study my hand resting on Grant's forearm. When had *that* happened? I hastily clasped my hands in front of me, then switched to resting them on the strap of my bag, not wanting to look like I was begging.

My mom took her time finishing her perusal of Grant before finally meeting his eyes and giving him a regal nod. "Forgive me, Captain. This investigation has me on edge."

I thought he deserved a more heartfelt apology, but Grant dipped his head as if it had been enough.

Eager to change the subject, I blurted out, "Where's Dad? Why isn't he here with you?"

"He's been remanded to the East Coast offices, all travel forbidden. Just like O'Hara has put a ban on my movements. I'm supposed to be restricted to Terra Haven until my name is cleared, but the investigator so generously allowed me to attend this party." She sounded about as pleased as a person chewing glass.

The thought of my mom having to get permission from anyone to attend a party boggled my mind. This investigation had to end, and the sooner the better.

"I think I can help you, Mom. My everlasting seed—" My mom started to protest, but I overrode her. "My seed has the Airstrong logo on it now."

Her eyes darted from me to Grant.

"It's all right. He's seen it. I'd show you, too, but . . ." I waggled my fingers at the milling room of high society's finest, many of whom had made a point of roaming past our small group and more than a few who appeared to be trying to read our lips. "The seed has a thunderbird feather on one side and the logo on the other."

"A thunderbird feather?" A small furrow appeared in my mom's brow. "I don't think you're interpreting your seed correctly. We've had no problem with thunderbirds. We never ship them, and none of our routes go close to thunderbird territories. They're too dangerous. Besides, wasn't your question for the everlasting tree about the story of a lifetime? I appreciate the sentiment, Kylie, but the last thing Airstrong needs is another big splashy story, especially after today."

"Maybe it is," I countered, ignoring the stab of pain at her lack of faith in me. "Maybe I'm supposed to help track down the thief and write a story that restores Airstrong's reputation."

"Are you sure that's not wishful thinking? You didn't ask the tree for the story that would do the most good; you asked for the *biggest* story." My mom gave my hand a comforting squeeze, but it did little to soften the gut punch of her words.

I had never considered that the story of a lifetime would be anything but a good one. In my mind, the best stories were the ones that made the largest positive impact on its readership. But what if the everlasting tree didn't know that? What if my mom was right, and the everlasting tree had given me a seed that would lead to a horrific catastrophe? One with Airstrong and my parents at its epicenter?

9

____

"I can't ignore my seed. I won't," I said, finding my tongue. "But I swear I would never publish an article that harmed you or Dad or Airstrong."

My mom's expression tightened. "What do you expect to find that the FPD cannot? Splinters, Kylie! You barely escaped Lunacy Labyrinth yesterday. I don't want you throwing yourself into danger, not on my behalf, and not on your father's. I forbid it."

My jaw dropped. She *forbade* it? As if I were a five-year-old asking to play with a feral cerberus?

My mom waved a hand as if erasing her words from the air. "That was too far, but I still think you should drop this," she said.

"I can't."

"Can't or won't?"

Grant cleared his throat. "I've only known your daughter a short time, but she's never dropped a story after she's sunk her teeth into it."

I shot him the glare his unflattering metaphor deserved. It didn't deter him.

"She also has an infuriating knack for landing herself smack in the middle of whatever hailstorm she's hunting down. If her seed has anything to do with the thieves targeting Airstrong, she'll find them."

"That 'infuriating knack' is called journalistic skill," I said.

"Is that why you're here, Captain?" my mom asked, ignoring me. "Are you following Kylie around, hoping she'll lead you to the thief?"

Grant's jaw flexed, emotion threatening to break his stoic mask. A protest in Grant's defense leapt to the tip of my tongue, but I hesitated, wanting to hear his response.

My mom flinched as if she had been jabbed by an invisible finger, and her ward disintegrated before Grant spoke.

"Pardon me," Persephone said, slipping an arm around my mom's shoulder and giving her an apologetic pat. "That was unavoidable, I'm afraid."

My eyebrows lifted in shock at Persephone's presumption, but my mom managed a pinched-lip smile. It didn't reach her eyes.

"We can't have the three of you huddled in the corner all day," Persephone continued, her voice low and her expression excessively cheerful, reminding me of the roomful of onlookers. "Captain Monaghan, I'm honored you chose to attend our little solstice ritual. I can't recall ever seeing you at one of these before."

She couldn't? I had assumed Grant's presence fell under the purview of his job. As captain of Terra Haven's Federal Pentagon Defense squad, he presumably had to make appearances at all kinds of high-society functions. Full spectrums expected preferential treatment, and nothing reaffirmed their lofty status like having the most powerful warrior in the district partake in their gatherings and relate personal updates about the welfare and safety of their home city. However, if this was the first year Grant had attended a high-society summer solstice ritual, could my mom have been right? Was Grant here only because of me? Did he hope my *journalistic skills* would unearth a clue the FPD had missed about the thieves?

Or was he here for a more personal reason: because he was worried about my safety?

I hoped it was the former. I would prefer Grant choosing to stick close to me because he wanted to help me clear my mom's name rather than because he thought I would be in need of rescuing.

Naturally, Grant's expression gave me no clue as to what he was thinking.

"How do you know my good friend Charlotte?" Persephone asked.

"We just met," Grant said.

Silence hung a beat too long before Persephone realized he wasn't going to add anything else.

"Well, Charlotte and I go way back, don't we?" Persephone squeezed my mom, then released her. She transferred her grip to Grant's forearm, spreading a smile between us. "Which is why I know Charlotte won't object to me stealing you away. I have someone you'll want to meet, Captain. Please excuse us."

Grant tipped his head in a polite nod to my mom and me; then he docilely allowed Persephone to lead him away. She gripped his arm as if they were old friends, talking animatedly.

"Did Harriet explain why the property's wards are so relaxed, Captain? I admit I have a flair for the dramatic."

A scowl darkened Grant's features. Unfortunately, the

crowd swallowed them before I could hear his response. I hoped he gave Persephone the lecture she deserved.

"Is there anything you want to tell me about your captain?" my mom asked.

Alarm pinged down my spine. I jerked my gaze from the last spot I had seen Grant and strove to look innocently puzzled by my mom's question.

"What do you mean?" I stilled my fingers when they wanted to fidget.

"For starters, what was he doing with you this morning?"

The insinuation of her question heated my cheeks, and I fumbled for an answer. I didn't need to add to my mom's worries by telling her about Zipporah, and saying Grant had come to warn me about Airstrong's troubles would only fuel her theory that Grant was using me to further his investigation. However, I wasn't ready to explain my relationship with Grant, either—at least not until I understood what it was first.

"One of his squad members is dating Mika." That sounded plausible—mainly because it was true—and if I could have gotten it out without clearing my throat, it might have appeased my mom's curiosity.

"How long has your captain known your real identity?"

"Awhile." He had made the connection sometime after I departed for the everlasting tree, and he had been a real grump about being deceived. Apparently, he had expected me to confess my life history to him the first time we met.

"Longer than a month?" my mom asked.

I shook my head, deciphering her implication. "No. He figured it out after the thefts started at Airstrong." Grant wouldn't stoop to pretending to like a woman to further an investigation. He had too much integrity. Besides, I had been the one pursuing Grant, not the other way around. Not that I was going to share *that* with my mom.

"You didn't tell him?"

"He's a smart man, Mom. I didn't need to. Are you hungry? I'm famished. Where did all the servers disappear to?"

My mom burst into a hearty laugh. "We need to work on your subtlety, dear. Perhaps on your wardrobe, too."

I grimaced and plucked at the fabric of my skirt. "This wasn't my choice. What I arrived in didn't meet with Persephone's approval. She insisted I wear this gown. I believe she wore it as a teen."

"Thank the high winds." My mom wiped pretend sweat from her brow. "I was afraid you had completely lost your sense of taste. Or maybe that you were suffering from color blindness."

"It's not that bad, is it?"

"It was nice of you to placate Persephone."

Not exactly the answer I had hoped for.

By unspoken consent, we began to circulate the room. I scanned the occupants, doing my best not to make eye contact and invite unwanted conversations. I tried even harder not to fixate on Grant. He appeared to be the center of attention among a sizable group of men and women, though he wasn't talking much. Persephone beamed at everyone in the circle, laughing occasionally.

Never once releasing Grant's arm.

"Persephone seems off today, don't you think?" my mom asked. "She's been acting like we're reunited sisters. I've missed her, but it's been years since we had a real friendship. We both got too busy and drifted apart long ago."

"Maybe she's lonely," I offered, thinking of Yarra.

"Maybe the stress of the event is making her exaggerate.

She seems quite comfortable with your captain, doesn't she?"

Too comfortable for my liking. Honestly, it wasn't *that* loud in here. She didn't need to lean so closely to him to be heard. Was her bosom actually resting on his forearm or did it just look that way from across the room? And why didn't Grant step away and put some distance between them?

I snagged a glass from a nearby server's tray, peeking at Grant over the rim when I took a sip. Fruit juice spiked with alcohol caught in the back of my throat when Grant tilted his head to listen to something Persephone said, a smile playing across his lips. Coughing, I jerked my eyes to my feet and concentrated on breathing without choking.

"Too bad she tied herself to Wetherill. They make an attractive couple, don't you think?" my mom asked, idly rubbing my back.

I shot her a flat look. She pretended not to notice.

"Quite striking, actually," she said. "Especially with him in that uniform. It really emphasizes how large he is. And tall. The way Persephone's clinging to him, his height must be making her dizzy."

Don't look. Don't look.

"And he's so much closer to her in age."

"He's not that old."

A hint of a smile dimpled my mom's cheek. I mentally groaned. I needed to escape before I embarrassed myself further.

"I should get to work." I made a point of glancing around the room, purposely avoiding looking in Grant's direction.

"Right. Your fluff piece."

I winced. "You haven't met anyone named Adelaide Flemming, have you?"

"Not yet. Do you know what she looks like?"

I shook my head.

Now that I thought about it, I couldn't remember any full-spectrum family with the last name Flemming. Either someone new had moved up in the social ranks, or I could rule out Adelaide being the niece or daughter of someone powerful. Which left mistress or girlfriend. Oh joy.

"Well, once you're done, come find me, Kylie. I believe there are a few details about the past couple of days you've neglected to tell me."

"'Neglected'? No, I'm certain it was intentional."

"So there *is* something I should know about your captain."

"He's not *my*—" I cut myself off. Rolling my eyes, I kissed my mom on the cheek. "It was nice to see you, Mom. Please leave Grant alone."

I escaped into the crowd, my mom's soft laughter floating behind me.

Persephone paraded Grant to the next group of people. If I didn't know better, I would have sworn their clothing had been sewn together or perhaps that the spells in their garments had malfunctioned and fused with each other.

Grant greeted an attractive blonde, bowing slightly over their clasped hands. She simpered, a move that thrust her chest closer to Grant's face, and he said something that made her giggle. My fingernails dug crescents into my palms. I had never given much thought to the social side of Grant's professional life. Since when had he learned how to be charming? Where was the gruff captain who glared at everyone and everything?

A vise of air seized my shoulders and hauled me sideways. I stumbled, fetching up against a short man in a pink-and-maroon-striped silk vest. The pressure of the air band slackened, allowing me to straighten, and I found myself staring into the hawk-nosed face of Crispin Derwingson.

"Harriet, it's such a pleasure to see you," he said, steadying me with a familiar hand on my waist.

I stepped away from him, spine stiffening when the band of air kept me from going farther. Using powers on another in public, especially for something so demeaning as herding a person from afar, was rude no matter what a person's social standing. It was the kind of action a parent might take with a child. Had we been anywhere else, I would have retaliated with something sharp and painful, but mindful of how my actions might reflect on my mom, I lifted my chin and gave Crispin a tight smile.

"I was catching my friends up on the recent events of Terra Haven, and your name keeps popping up," Crispin said. "I thought, why not hear it from the source?"

I scanned the faces of his friends. Like Crispin, the men and women clustered around him were all roughly the same age as me, though they were so coiffed, primped, spell-saturated, and stuffy they could have been twice my age. Unlike Crispin, whom I'd had the displeasure of having taken riding lessons alongside, I knew none of them.

"Is it true you were inside Chicomoztoc?" asked a woman with curly red hair, mangling the pronunciation of the formal name for Lunacy Labyrinth.

"Tell us, what was Lunacy like?" a stocky man asked. He wrapped an arm around the redhead's waist and leaned close to whisper across her ear, "I heard it was full of dead bodies and the bones of madmen."

The redhead shivered dramatically and tittered. My expression flattened, and I didn't bother to correct it. What sort of nitwits flirted over the subject of death?

The stocky man's gaze slid down my body, assessing me

the way he might have inspected a horse he planned to purchase. "There's a rumor that anyone who enters comes out crazy," he said.

Malicious delight sparked through the eyes of everyone in the group, and the redhead snickered. I squashed the urge to start dancing and yelling maniacally to scare them away. It took even more control to rein in the scathing sarcasm on the tip of my tongue. Both might be temporarily satisfying, but my mom had taught me long ago that nothing could be gained by antagonizing imbeciles.

"Lunacy was about what you would expect of a place made by blood magic," I said, my tone and expression bland. "It was deadly and a bit sad. Now, if you'll excuse me..."

I turned to go, but the band of air squeezed tighter around me, restraining me. My temper flared. Meeting Crispin's eyes, I shattered his magic with a spade of earth. He flinched as the backlash of magic recoiled into him.

"Try that again, and I won't be so gentle," I snapped.

"Whoa, we're all friends here, Harriet." He raised his hands in an exaggerated pacifying gesture. "No need to get violent. I was merely excited to hear more."

My hands trembled as I stalked away. Snaring me like that hadn't been an enthusiastic social misstep. It had been the calculated tactic of a remorseless, full-spectrum bully flexing his power to provoke me into revealing my own elemental strength. The vulgar display had toed the line of illegal harassment, and not one of his friends had protested.

It reminded me of so many instances from my childhood —memories I had buried deep when I had left this lifestyle behind. I resented having them dredged up now, too. This wasn't what I signed up for when I took a job at the *Chronicle*, and when I returned to Terra Haven, I would tell

Dahlia as much. If she wanted someone to cover fluff-piece interviews at full-spectrum events, she would have to assign someone from the society pages.

A frigid breeze dispersed the humid atmosphere of the ballroom, the rush of ice-frosted air element circling me before spinning outward to subtly nudge people aside. Luther Wetherill, owner of Capstone Transportation and Airstrong's main competitor, stepped into the gap. I stifled a groan.

"Harriet Kylie Grayson, what a surprise." Bedecked in a tailored crushed-velvet suit more appropriate for a snowy winter day, Wetherill should have been a sweaty mess. Instead, hypnotic spirals of mist evaporated from his outfit, permeating his general vicinity with a pleasant chill. I couldn't tell if the suit had been spelled to keep the garment at near-freezing temperatures or if Wetherill was maintaining the spell himself. The former would be astronomically expensive; the latter would require an absurd amount of elemental strength and stamina. Either way, the outfit broadcasted Wetherill's wealth and power without him having to say a word. Standing next to him in Persephone's frumpy dress almost seemed like an insult.

As much as I yearned to slink away, I forced a smile and rooted my feet in place. Of all the people at this gathering, Wetherill had the most reasons to be invested in amplifying the troubles afflicting my parents' business. I couldn't afford to show the slightest weakness in front of him.

"Mr. Wetherill. Congratu—"

"I had almost forgotten about you, as had most people," he steamrolled over me, his affable smile never faltering despite his rude words. "That was an ingenious scheme, slipping you into a spot at the *Chronicle*. I'll have to congratulate Charlotte. And you living anonymously? Very daring."

So much for his engagement to Persephone softening his ruthless nature. This was the classic Luther Wetherill I remembered from my childhood, always ready with an insult framed as a compliment. He excelled at putting people on the defensive without giving them a solid target at which to retaliate.

Determined not to play along, I adopted a vapid smile and said, "It was, wasn't it? I so enjoyed not having people know who I was." Maybe the truth would trip him up.

"You timed your return to society well."

I hadn't had a choice in the matter, and he knew it. Nathan may have printed my name in the paper, but I suspected it had been Wetherill who had been the one to confirm my identity, just as he had been quick to provide Nathan with a damning quote to cast further blame on my parents for the theft of the firebirds.

"You couldn't expect me to stay away from all *this*, could you?" I asked, gesturing to include the whole party and taking care not to grind my teeth.

"Indeed. Right when Airstrong needed a boost to its publicity, there you were, miraculously in possession of the firebirds Airstrong lost." He raised his wineglass in salute. "Quite a feat."

I made a noncommittal sound and bowed my head fractionally, pretending to accept his praise at face value and to be oblivious to his insinuation that my parents or I had orchestrated the loss and recovery of the firebirds to boost business.

"Hopefully your heroic return to the business will be enough to save it. How many banned spells did the FPD report were stolen from Airstrong? Six?"

We both knew only four illegal spells had been taken, but I didn't correct him, recognizing yet another attempt to draw me into a defensive position. Instead, I allowed my expression to twist in confusion. "I'm not sure what you mean. Maybe you were misinformed: I'm not returning to Airstrong."

Wetherill's laugh came a beat delayed. Obviously, that hadn't been the response he had expected.

"Of course not," he agreed, then winked. "And good thinking. If you keep your distance now, you should be able to rehabilitate the company's image in a year or two."

"Can you improve something that's already perfect?"

Wetherill laughed again, and this time it reached his eyes. "Your loyalty is admirable, Harriet. Every parent should be so lucky."

If he weren't so insulting, I might have been amused that he assumed I cared what he thought. What did Persephone see in him? Was it his looks? He wasn't ugly—at least not physically. He kept his prematurely graying beard neat, and he possessed a full head of curly brown hair. His slate-blue eyes were attractive. If I wasn't comparing him to Grant, I would have described Wetherill as moderately fit. He was old for my taste, but not necessarily for Persephone. Or was their relationship a manufactured arrangement between two powerful families plotting to merge their wealth and status?

I masked a shudder. In so many ways, I appreciated the open-mindedness of my parents, but never more so than when it came to their views on marriage—mainly that it should be done for love, not political advancement.

"Oops, I believe your fiancée just signaled me," I lied, determining I had stomached enough duplicitous and disparaging snipes about my parents, my character, and my career to satisfy the unspoken etiquette of high society. "Excuse me."

I tucked my bag tight to my side and strode toward Persephone's last location. My path took me around a group of men in their late twenties, and they turned in unison to stare down their noses at me.

"Aren't all the gossipmongers supposed to be corralled out front?" the largest man asked loudly. "Looks like one escaped."

His companions guffawed.

Slowing, I raked my eyes over the group. "And here I thought all the asses were supposed to be in the stables."

Someone snorted with ill-suppressed laughter, and I turned to see Seradon intercept a server carrying a platter of tiny chocolate desserts. She deftly scooped several delicacies from the tray, then faced the man who had insulted me, her smile sharpening into something predatory. As one, the men turned tail and scurried away.

"Hopefully they can see themselves to their stalls," Seradon said. She grinned around a mouthful of chocolate. "I should have known I would find my favorite reporter here."

"Because of the stupid firebird article?"

She gave me a puzzled frown. "What does that have to do with anything?"

"It outed me as Harriet Grayson."

"Oh, right. No. You being Kylie is what makes everything make sense."

"You've lost me."

"Why else would the captain have a sudden change of heart about attending this event? He *never* comes to these functions if he can avoid them."

"Mmm, yes, clearly it was all about me." I cut my gaze toward the man in question, who was currently surrounded by a flock of glamorous socialites. Persephone remained glued to his arm, directing the conversation.

Seradon shifted to follow my line of sight and shook her head. "Ah, the uniform. Normally Monaghan's bubbly personality drives off the bulk of them, but those whites tend to blind young women. At least, that's my theory. So, what happened to you?"

"This little gem?" I tore my gaze from Grant and lifted a hand to my chest, batting my eyelashes and glancing away coyly, as if she had given me an embarrassing compliment. "It's borrowed."

"I meant the cuts on your arms. Are you talking about the dress? Because whoever loaned it to you must not like you very much."

"There were extenuating circumstances."

"If you say so. I don't— Oh, sand and stones," Seradon hissed, shoving me two steps to the right behind a woman cloaked in a waterfall illusion. "Don't look now, but Lidio Cardea is headed this way. He's going to want to lecture me for hours about how improving the fertilizer in the city's gardens will reduce crime."

"Really? How?"

"Stick around if you want to find out. I'm going to investigate that server's platter. Whistle or something if he follows me."

I watched with bemusement as Seradon skulked through the crowd, blending in surprisingly well with the brightly clad full spectrums. Lidio scowled after her, then turned his attention to me. When he resumed his march across the floor, a twinge of alarm loosened my knees. I hustled toward Persephone, only to draw up short. She and Grant had disappeared. Dang it, I couldn't take my eyes off him for a second.

Off *her*, I silently corrected myself. I couldn't take my eyes off *her*.

Aurelia Lonsdale planted herself in front of me, a false smile puckering the wrinkles around her thin lips. Curse my hesitation. I knew better than to be caught flat-footed at one of these parties.

"Harriet Grayson, it's been forever since we've seen you," she said.

"It really has, but I'm on my way—"

"We must catch up." Aurelia gestured to two middle-aged women who swooped in to flank me, cutting off my escape. Both were small and plump and appeared huggable, but I wasn't deceived. "You remember Melody and Darva."

"Of course." I had gone to school with their children. Darva's son had been a bully; Melody's an introvert who spent too much time playing with fire. Aurelia's daughter had once dyed my hair lime green as a prank, and it had taken three days and a dozen spells to fix it.

"You've grown into such a pretty woman," Darva said, her gaze sweeping down my dress with ill-concealed distaste.

"I hadn't realized you were living in Terra Haven these days," Melody said.

"She's been working at some paper," Darva said.

"How interesting. I have a nephew who penned a few editorials. He's a very bright boy. Of course, now he's a governor."

"Who did he marry?" Aurelia asked.

"Wasn't it a hippogryph trainer?" Darva asked.

Melody's lips pinched. "Lauren is a hippogryph breeder, and one of the most prestigious in the nation."

Maybe if I backed away slowly, they wouldn't notice.

"It's so fortunate for your parents that you're living in our city, Harriet," Aurelia said, her attention snapping to me when I shifted my weight. "And quite impressive what you did at those ghastly ruins. Who would have thought we had blood-magic users in our midst?"

The other women shivered dramatically. I refrained from rolling my eyes. She made it sound as if blood magic had been wielded by someone she knew rather than by criminals so far removed from her they might as well have been on a different continent.

"It was nice of your parents to give you time after you finished school to do some journaling," Melody said.

"I am a journal*ist* and—"

"Isn't it pleasant to have hobbies?" Darva's head bobbed as she beamed in encouragement.

"But when it mattered," Melody barreled on, "you were right there to help your parents. It speaks highly of your upbringing."

"Oh, yes, that dreadful business with the firebirds," Darva said, patting the swell of her cleavage, which threatened to spill over the top of her zebra-patterned dress. "Charlotte was smart to dispatch you after them. It really showed Airstrong's dedication to their clients."

This again? At least they weren't implying that my mom had arranged the theft, too. Only that she was cavalier enough with my life to send me after a pair of blood-magic madmen to retrieve dangerous magical birds as a means of saving face. Should I be more or less insulted?

"My mom had no part in—" I started to protest, wanting to squash the ridiculous assumption once and for all, but Darva overrode me.

"So tell us, what are you going to do about the other thefts at Airstrong?"

The three women squeezed so close, I could count their

pores. I opened my mouth and, when no one interrupted, managed to get out a full sentence. "We're working with the FPD to find the culprit and see them brought to justice."

All three women's faces fell.

"Certainly. The FPD is a wonderful resource," Aurelia murmured.

I wished I could have seen Grant's expression at being demoted to a *resource*.

"But what are *you* doing, Harriet?" Darva asked.

"Yes, you made such a splash in your return to Airstrong." Aurelia gave me a pinched smile. "We all expect big things from you."

I held in my sigh. I should have realized everyone would assume my presence meant I was resuming my place at my parents' side, training to take over their company when they retired. It probably would never occur to any full spectrum that I might prefer to be a lowly reporter rather than take charge of a nationwide company.

The trio of women stared at me, none speaking, and I realized they expected an answer to Darva's question.

I leaned closer and whispered, "Between you and me?"

All three nodded.

"The thief is in for a *very* bad day very soon." I added a wink for good measure.

Darva, Melody, and Aurelia exchanged knowing looks, as if I had said something profound. I used the lull in their interrogation to excuse myself. As I expected, the women promptly dispersed, each angling for a different group of people. I didn't need a rumor scout to tell me I was the topic of conversation on their lips.

I hoped I had made the right call. Full spectrums were all about perception, and as long as I mimicked my mom and projected confidence, the vultures would believe

Airstrong had the thefts under control and was running business as normal. It shouldn't hurt to hint that the FPD was close to arresting someone. It happened to be true— even if they had their sights on the wrong person.

My petty delight in outwitting the gossipy women withered. I didn't have time to waste fielding inane questions at a stuffy party. I needed to find whoever was behind the thefts, figure out what they had to do with thunderbirds, and clear my mom's name.

But first I needed to track down Persephone so I could get my blasted interview over with already.

10

I tapped my toe, contemplating the closed door of the Kwan family library, where Persephone had said I would find Adelaide Flemming. It had taken ten minutes of creatively dodging through the crush of guests before I had tracked Persephone down—surprisingly alone, without Grant affixed to her side—and I had been quick to bolt once I had the information I needed.

Now I hesitated with my hand on the doorknob, for the first time questioning Adelaide's isolated location. No one walking down this secluded hallway would suspect another guest was hidden behind this closed door. Had Persephone shut the mistress in her library to keep her away from the rest of the partygoers? Or had closing the door been Adelaide's decision? Would I get an eyeful of something I could never unsee if I opened the door?

Glancing over my shoulder to make sure no one was watching, I pressed my ear to the wood panel. No sounds emanated from within.

Easing the door open, I peeked in. The library had been cozily furnished with soft couches, a wooden desk, and warm lamps. Bookcases lined three walls, and windows spanned the fourth, opening out onto a small stone courtyard. For a second, I thought the room was empty; then I spotted a figure crouched in front of the farthest bookcase.

Clearing my throat, I strode into the room. The woman didn't look up, giving me a moment to study her profile. Dark-skinned, with thick curly black hair, she was two decades older than I had anticipated. She wore a soft yellow skirt and checkered blouse, both made of fine linen but no fancier than the items in my closet. Definitely not more expensive. Her outfit also wasn't what a man or woman might purchase for a mistress or even for a guest attending today's ritual.

I readjusted my assumption. Maybe Adelaide wasn't someone's mistress. Maybe she was a child's beloved tutor or a distant cousin of modest means.

"Hello, I'm Kylie Grayson from the *Terra Haven Chronicle*. Are you Adelaide Flemming?"

"Yes. Nice to meet you," Adelaide said, tossing me a smile over her shoulder before turning back to the bookcase.

"Is now a good time for our interview?"

"Sure."

I waited. Adelaide's fingers traced book spines. She selected a book, set it at her feet, and resumed her perusal. I crossed my arms, then uncrossed them when the sleeves' stiff lace pressed into the spook squirrel scratches. Adelaide moved on to the next shelf.

Strangling my irritation, I selected a chair and pulled out my notebook, a pen, and my camera. I assembled the camera's tripod after deciding which chair would place the self-important debut author in the best light. Finally, Adelaide deigned to leave off her browsing. She set two slim leather-bound volumes on top of a stack of books collected at the edge of the desk. Then she shook the dust from her skirt and situated herself in the chair I designated. She held still while I took her picture, spine piston straight. It was only when I took my seat that she spoke.

"I'm sorry I made you come all the way out here, Kylie. I made a deal with my publisher: I would take a semester away from my students to go on their publicity tour, but only if they guaranteed me access to this."

"The Terra Haven full-spectrum solstice ritual?" I asked, confused. If she had wanted to hobnob with high society, what was she doing tucked away in this little room?

Adelaide burst into laughter. "No, *this*." She pointed to the stack of old books atop the desk and then at the rest of the room. "Or rather, personal libraries like this. If you can count on full spectrums for anything, it's that they will hoard and protect rare objects. In this room alone, I found five out-of-print books that I spent the last two years searching for in public libraries. Ms. Kwan has been kind enough to let me borrow anything I want, so I don't have to spend the entire night trying to cram all this information into my memory. Anyway, I only had today to gather my treasures before they shuffle me off to Terra Haven for my talk tomorrow. I didn't want to lose any time here. Oh, don't I sound full of myself? What I'm trying to say is I'm glad you could come to me. I hope it wasn't any trouble."

"None at all," I murmured, and officially let go of every last assumption I had entertained about Adelaide. Not only was she obviously intelligent, but she also seemed genuinely enchanted by the books and not at all concerned that she was missing the chance to mingle with the upper crust of society. In fact, she seemed downright relatable. How often had I lamented interruptions when I was chasing down a story? Interruptions much like this party . . . "I know exactly how you feel."

A loud bang in the courtyard made us both jump. I leapt to my feet in time to see Quinn trot a few steps after landing and tuck his wings to his back. He squinted at the windows along our side of the building. I waved to draw his attention and used a bar of air to slide the nearest window open. Quinn settled his paws on the window frame and stuck his head into the library.

"Kylie! Fang is here!"

"Really?" I hadn't considered that Raquel and her gryphon, Fang, would be here. I wondered if they had brought the *Chronicle*'s society reporter. Maybe I could catch a ride back to Terra Haven with them. It would make for a much quicker—and safer—trip. "Here, come in. You're just in time for the interview."

Quinn hoisted himself up until he perched on the window ledge, all four feet clustered tightly together. The wood creaked and popped beneath his solid-quartz body. I hastily shoved aside a delicate chaise lounge to give Quinn somewhere to stand. He flowed to the floor with a lion's natural grace, clenching his wings to his body so they didn't knock into the furniture. Adelaide stared with unabashed curiosity.

"Quinn, this is Adelaide Flemming, our interviewee," I said. Quinn gave Adelaide a toothy smile. "Adelaide, this is Quinn, my partner."

"A gargoyle partner?"

"Mostly I help with investigative work. And protection."

Adelaide raised her eyebrows at his addendum. Not wanting the interview to get sidetracked, I blurted out my first question. "You mentioned being away from your students. Where do you teach?"

I was embarrassed to admit how little I knew about Adelaide, not having put any effort into—or had any time for—background research on her. Fortunately, Adelaide didn't seem to notice, and she spoke while allowing me to direct us back to our seats. Quinn sat on his haunches next to my chair, and I rested a hand on his mane, glad to have him back by my side. As if we had been conducting interviews together for years, Quinn and I drew all the key information about tomorrow's event out of Adelaide as well as several anecdotal stories and personal facts to flesh out the article. The more I learned about the woman, the more I liked her. She taught history at the prestigious Peale and Callister University up north, had once apprenticed in the FPD's records office, and now raised shangyang rain birds after learning they had been instrumental to the survival of a foreign city several centuries earlier.

"If the shangyangs hadn't brought rain, the city would have been reclaimed by the desert. The subsequent rulers never would have come into power, and the shape of foreign politics would be completely different. Besides, the birds are cute, and they do this little dance that collects and condenses the moisture from the air. I haven't had to hand-water my garden in years." Adelaide chuckled, then waved aside her words. "I'm digressing, but my shangyangs are part of the reason I wrote *Critical Moments in History*. Events like that, when a unique incident alters the course of history, those are the moments I'm interested in."

"The birds were more important than the full-spectrum rulers who came after them?" I quirked a skeptical eyebrow.

"I'm sure they would disagree, but for the sake of my book's thesis, yes. You would be amazed how seldom full spectrums have an impact on keystone events. They tend to come after, influencing the shape of society or building on the cataclysmic event. They're rarely the spark of the kinds of fundamental changes I discuss."

I found myself smiling. Despite having let go of my preconceived notions about Adelaide, I had still expected her book to deal with prominent full-spectrum families. The wealthy and powerful tended to be remembered at the center of history. This, however, sounded infinitely more interesting.

"Gargoyles, on the other hand, crop up more than once at these critical moments," Adelaide continued. "Take your city as a small-scale example. People credit the railroad for putting Terra Haven on the map, but it's far more complex than that. This town shared many similar characteristics with nearby villages two hundred years ago: fertile soil, multiple trade routes, a diverse group of people and magical talents, strong leaders, and loyal allies. But Terra Haven would never have taken root, let alone become the metropolis it is today, without gargoyles. When the first gargoyle settled among the people of this region, she strengthened the magic of the local inhabitants. Once that happened, Terra Haven's success became inevitable while the other villages faded to ghost towns. More gargoyles followed the first, which encouraged more people of power and means to settle in the area, bringing with them their elemental purifying rituals like the one we're participating in today to stabilize the region. It was only after a thriving community existed here that the railroad took notice and laid down tracks, not the other way around. The FSPP families in the area can take credit for the modernization and growth of the town, but ultimately, their actions mattered far less than the gargoyles."

"I had no idea my ancestors were so important," Quinn said.

"Sadly, not much is known at all about your ancestors. In all my research, I couldn't even unearth Terra Haven's first gargoyle's name. Everything I read about her was second-hand information." Adelaide sat up straight, hands fluttering excitedly in Quinn's direction. "But you! A literary gargoyle! You're just what we need. You could write a history from a gargoyle's perspective—or a history *about* gargoyles. It would go a long way to filling in the knowledge gaps in our culture."

"Me?" Quinn raised a paw to his chest, half covering the blob of his distorted everlasting seed. "You want *me* to write an article?"

"I was thinking more along the lines of a book." Adelaide's eyes shone. "Or a series of books."

"Really?" Quinn looked poleaxed.

"I would love to read those books," I said.

"I won't lie: It'll be hard work," Adelaide cautioned. "I spent six years gathering information for *Critical Moments* and another year writing it. But if telling gargoyles' stories is a compelling idea for you, you'll find every minute of it worthwhile."

My mind spun with ideas for possible leads and topics, but I held my tongue, watching Quinn mull the idea over.

"Oh!" Adelaide lifted a finger in the air. "I almost forgot I'm supposed to talk about the part our host plays in my book."

"Persephone is in your book?"

"Well, her ancestors and their Aurora Isle are. It was quite the destination in its heyday, but I'm most interested in one unique event there that reshaped—"

Something heavy struck the roof, rattling the mansion to the foundation. I jumped and grabbed the elements. Quinn sprang to his feet, his wings half unfurled, knocking over a small table. The crash barely registered above the pounding of my heart.

"That's not another gargoyle friend, is it?" Adelaide asked, her brown eyes wide.

I shook my head. The roof quaked under a rhythmic pounding, and books shimmied on their shelves. Sharp scrapes and cracks echoed in the courtyard.

I swallowed hard. It couldn't be. Not here . . .

The first whiff of rot filtered through the open window.

"Kylie Grayson, show yourself!"

My stomach dove for my toes. Shrieked at that ear-piercing decibel, my name had been almost incomprehensible, but I couldn't mistake her voice. Zipporah had found me.

The harpy dropped into the stone courtyard, landing hard enough to rattle the paintings hanging beside the door. Her foul musk gushed through the open window. I clamped my elbow over my nose, fighting the urge to gag. Adelaide grabbed the nearest book and buried her nose in the open pages, her eyes huge above the rim of its cover.

"Oh, how fancy," Zipporah said, strutting to a bronze tulip fountain decorating the corner of the courtyard. With a negligent clip of wood element, she capsized it. The basin hit the cobblestones with a deafening gong. Water splashed Zipporah's filthy feathers and sloshed across the courtyard. Squatting, she dunked her nether region into the pool of water, then gave herself a vigorous shake. Clods of sodden fecal matter and offal splattered the walls and windows. Vomit crept up my throat, and I swallowed convulsively.

Damn Persephone and her idiotic flair for the dramatic. As host, it was her responsibility to ensure the safety of her guests. First she had allowed the spook squirrels onto her property, and now a harpy? This was what came from full-spectrum hubris.

"Come out, come out, wherever you are, my tiny heiress morsel."

Fear frizzled down my nerve endings. She said *heiress*, not *journalist*. She knew who I was. Worse, the murderous harpy knew who my parents were.

I jumped when a tight ward of earth and wood sprang up around me. Adelaide grabbed my hand and tugged. I rocked in place; I couldn't remember how to work my feet.

"Quiet now," Adelaide whispered. "We'll slip out to the hall and make a run for the ballroom."

I blinked at her, understanding her logic but hesitating nonetheless. The ballroom currently housed the most powerful collection of full spectrums in all of Terra Haven. Their combined powers could bring down a hundred harpies. But would anyone step up to help me? For all their elemental strength, full spectrums weren't known for altruistic acts. And even if they were willing to help me, hiding behind their collective skirts didn't sit well with me.

"Harriet Kylie Grayson, you owe me." Zipporah's magically amplified voice penetrated the room and walls, likely carrying all the way to the borders of Persephone's property. I clamped my hands over my ears as the echoes vibrated through the library's cozy confines.

Footsteps pounded down the hallway, coming closer, and an unexpected—and unwanted—flush of embarrassment churned beneath my fear. Now every person at the gathering, every single judgmental member of high society, knew I had messed up. If they had thought my position as a journalist was demeaning, making a deal with a harpy screamed of desperation. I hated that any part of me, no matter how small, cared what these people thought of me.

Even more, I hated that my mom would suffer by association. This couldn't have come at a worse time for her and Airstrong.

Out in the courtyard, Zipporah's head cocked in our direction, and she hopped in a tight circle to face the library. Tilting her head back and forth, she examined the windows. With sunlight glinting off their surfaces, she likely saw only her own reflection. Hopefully.

"Make way!" Persephone's voice rang above the commotion in the hallway. "I will handle this. Everyone, return to the ballroom. We don't need a crowd. Grant, don't let Charlotte past you."

Adelaide attempted to pull me toward the door again, but I planted my feet and clung to the back of the chair. Grant wouldn't be able to stop my mom, not if she thought I was in danger. No matter what, I couldn't let her near Zipporah. My mom might possess minor elemental superiority to me in air and wood, but she was no more equipped to fight a harpy than I was—probably less so.

"Come on," Adelaide hissed.

"I can't." I shared a look with Quinn. He had shrunk against my vacated chair, hiding his bright body in its shadow. Anxiety pulled his brow into tight wrinkles, but he had positioned himself to leap toward the courtyard, not the hallway. "You go. Both of you."

"Not without you," Quinn whispered.

"Get the sand out of your feet, child," Adelaide snapped.

I shook off her attempt to move me and grabbed the historian by her shoulders, forcing her to focus on my face. "You need to hurry before the harpy sees you," I said.

Her jaw jutted stubbornly, but I didn't give her a chance to argue.

"This isn't your fight." I kept my voice calm, projecting as much authority as possible while not raising my voice above a whisper. "I know what I'm doing. I'm a journalist, remember?"

Surprisingly, the argument worked. Adelaide gave me a sharp nod, restructured her ward around just herself, and tiptoed toward the door.

Zipporah's claws scraped against the cobblestones as she strutted toward the open window. I dropped to a crouch next to Quinn, reaching a hand out to his wing for reassurance. Hiding wasn't a long-term option, but I needed a plan before I revealed my location.

"I can smell you, Grayson girl. Don't make me come in." Zipporah gouged her talons into the wall beside the window and tugged. Wood and plaster tore free with a thunderous snap. On the inside, a painting bounced from its hook and crashed to the floor. "Last chance, Kylie-Harriet." Zipporah raised a grimy foot to punch through the damaged wall.

"Stop!" The word burst from me before I thought better of it. Zipporah had already torn apart one house today. I couldn't afford to pay for repairs—*more* repairs—to Persephone's house, too. More important, the longer I delayed my confrontation with Zipporah, the more likely my mom would burst in and attempt to intercede.

Praying I wasn't making a fatal mistake, I straightened and took a deep breath. "I'm coming out."

I crossed the room on quivering knees, wishing Grant would sprint through the door and scare off Zipporah.

He didn't.

I glanced over my shoulder. Adelaide had closed the door behind her, but I could hear the murmur of voices on the other side. Persephone, I thought. Her words were too indistinct to decipher. Was she formulating a plan to assist me or reassuring her guests that they didn't need to get involved? I didn't hear Grant's deep baritone and hoped it meant he was stashing my mom somewhere safe.

I crouched in front of the open window. Zipporah bent forward, the flaps of her breasts dangling obscenely close to my head. Her sharp face pressed even closer, her carrion breath making my eyes water.

"About time, little heiress." She shuffled back a half step, talons screeching against the stones.

Quinn pressed tight enough to my thigh that I could feel the ridges of his mane through the thin fabric of my borrowed dress. "Be careful," he whispered.

Hiking my skirt up to my knees, I folded in half and straddled the window's threshold. The moment my foot touched down in the courtyard, I straightened. My trailing foot caught the windowsill, and I stumbled. Zipporah fanned out a wing, caging me against the wall, and I wobbled in place, drowning in the harpy's putrescence. Against all instinct, I refrained from forming a ward. Zipporah had proven again and again that she could demolish any protective barrier I created, and she had used the backlash against me more than once, too. But standing elementally naked before her only emphasized my impotence. Zipporah had the upper hand in every sense of the word, and she knew it.

"Did you think you could hide from me?" she asked.

"What do you want?" Maybe I could get her to issue her demands quickly and be on her way. *Before* my mom did something foolish, like attempt to rescue me. I would never forgive myself if I got my mom snared in Zipporah's clutches, too.

"From you? So much. So very, very much, little heiress." Zipporah cooed the words, but she didn't appear to be paying attention to them. Her head canted to and fro as she peered into the windows around us.

I tried to use her distraction to make room for Quinn to jump into the courtyard, but Zipporah curled her wing tighter around me.

"Are you smarter than you look?" she mused. Her head swiveled past her shoulder, then snapped back around. Piercing golden eyes drilled into me. "Did you try to set a trap for me?"

"What? No! I—"

Zipporah slapped a thick band of air across my mouth, cutting off my words. Faster than I could track, she swiped her talons around my torso and yanked me across the cobblestones. I lost my footing, and the rough stone scraped patches of agony into my knees. I screamed—or tried to. No oxygen made it past Zipporah's elemental gag.

Panic swelled in my chest. I tore at the gag with claws of earth element. The world tipped, slamming me into the ground. Zipporah leapt from the courtyard with an awkward one-footed hop. The cobblestones rushed toward my face, then snapped away a second before impact. I flopped like a rag doll in her grip as we lurched skyward, past the roof, then higher.

Black dots framed my vision as Quinn burst through the window and speared after me. A ward sprang into existence across the top of the courtyard. It wasn't Zipporah's making, either. Persephone had arrived, finally, her actions too late to help, now only a hindrance. Quinn slammed into the ward, flailed to right himself, then frantically battered the elemental barrier with his quartz paws.

Grant raced into view in his blindingly white uniform. What had taken him so long? He raised one arm to shield his eyes against the downdraft of Quinn's frenzied efforts, then spun to gesture to Persephone. Her hands waved in an agitated response, her long black hair whipping in the wind. My mom shoved past her, the worry of her upturned face the last thing I saw before my vision tunneled. Fire licked up my throat. My lungs demanded oxygen.

Desperately, I drew in every last drop of elemental boost Quinn provided. More power than I expected gushed into me. I had forgotten about Yarra, and I sobbed my gratitude as I ripped through Zipporah's air gag. My need to breathe overpowered my gut's attempt to vomit as I gulped sewage-flavored oxygen. Bile sloshed up my throat, and coughing and gagging, I watched through watery eyes as the Kwan estate disappeared into a fold in the countryside.

Zipporah's gnarled toes, each as thick as my thigh, circled my body, grinding my elbow into my ribs. Her talons gouged my back in rhythm with the beating of her wings, driving pain through my spine. I flopped horizontally in Zipporah's embrace, the front of my body smashed against the harpy's feces-caked underbelly. It hurt my neck to crane my face toward the ground flashing past beneath us, but the alternative was too heinous to tolerate.

I considered fighting free of Zipporah's grip, but if I succeeded, I would never survive the drop. I had been in this situation before, and the only option was to bide my time and pray she didn't let go before she landed.

The last time Zipporah had abducted me, she had dumped me in the heart of Lunacy Labyrinth. She'd had her heart set on the bloodstone enshrined at the center of the ancient ruins, but she hadn't wanted to risk the perilous labyrinth herself. If she needed me now, I could only assume it was to serve as her disposable minion again. Any place too deadly for a harpy to risk was certain death for me.

My survival of Lunacy had been a fluke. I wouldn't get that lucky twice.

My grip on the elements slackened, and I scrambled to gather magic. It came in as a trickle. We had passed beyond Quinn's and Yarra's reach. I was on my own.

11

The green tops of the dense forest around the Kwan estate gave way to rolling yellow hills dotted with large oaks. Time and the stench cauterized my fear and dulled my thoughts. With glazed eyes, I watched enormous full-spectrum estates flash past, slate roofs and secluded pools glistening in the sun. No one tried to stop Zipporah. No one likely even saw us fly over. All the residents of these expensive homes were at Persephone's. Not that they would have done much more than defend their homes even if they *had* witnessed our flight—as they had proved by doing absolutely nothing to assist me when I was abducted from right under their noses.

Useless. Every last one of them.

Except Grant.

Zipporah tucked her wings. I lurched in her grip, my neck snapping; then we were in free fall. I screamed, fresh panic flooding my numbed limbs. The ground rushed up at us, the yellow hill crystallizing into scattered oaks, then individual dried weeds and an alarming number of sharp boulders. Zipporah's wings snapped open, and the ground veered left, far too close. Her grip on me went slack, and I screamed again as I fell the final few feet.

I hit hard, the impact jarring my entire body. Skidding helplessly across the rocky soil, I crashed to a stop, half on my back, my legs twisted sideways. Pain radiated from too many places to individuate, and I took that as a good sign. If something were broken, the pain would stand out. Unless multiple bones were broken.

The blue sky stretched above me, the sun almost directly overhead. I blinked, fighting the urge to close my eyes against the glare. I needed to stand up, find some cover. I couldn't afford to be in such a vulnerable position when Zipporah landed. If only I could remember how to work my limbs.

A sheet of air slammed down on top of me, the condensed element heavy as a printing press. I strained to move. My fingers twitched. Everywhere else remained pinned flat, including my lungs. Breathing shallowly, I gathered earth element to cut through the harpy's magic but gave up before I had finished constructing my magical weapon. Zipporah's power with air far outstripped my strength with any other element, especially without Quinn's boost. Trying to fight her now would only be a waste of energy.

Zipporah landed next to my arm, kicking up dirt and small pebbles. I squinted and fought against a cough I didn't have the lung capacity to indulge. She shifted from foot to foot, raising puffs of dust. I couldn't turn my head to check, but it felt as if she were inches from cutting off my trapped fingers. If she did, she would break the elements holding me, but it would be too late for my hand. If she wanted, she could eviscerate me with a single lash of her foot. I wouldn't be able to do a single thing to stop her.

Zipporah tipped forward, angling her face close to mine. Her head blocked out the sun, and the light shining through the short feathers adorning her scalp gave her an oily halo. I blinked her into focus, instantly regretting it.

"You claimed to be a hatchling journalist." Spittle flew from her mouth, spraying the solid air holding me in place. Her wings flexed, the bony claws at the alulae stroking the air.

Sweat rolled down my temples. If possible, I would have shrunk away from the harpy's feral expression. I had seen Zipporah when she was scheming. I had experience with being treated like her plaything. This was different. She wasn't playing; she was furious.

"I *am* a journalist," I croaked.

"You're an heiress. You tried to cheat me, little liar. Did you think you would get away with it?" She formed a pincher of air, seized my head, and bashed it into the ground. Pain cleaved my skull. "The Chiefmaker wouldn't have been enough to cancel your debt, even if you *had* retrieved it from Lunacy." Zipporah beat my head against the ground again.

My debt to the harpy could only be repaid by a favor equal to the value of my life. I wanted to protest that a journalist's life was worth as much as an heiress's, but the logic seemed flawed, and I couldn't pinpoint why with my head ringing.

"You owe me more, so much more." Zipporah snapped her gore-stained teeth inches from my nose.

When she lifted my head for a third pounding, my terror spiked to a new level. Maybe this wasn't about collecting her debt. Maybe Zipporah just wanted to kill me. I fumbled for the elements, but they slipped through my grasp. My heart pounded erratically, my vision blurring. Words. I needed to speak up, to convince her to keep me alive. But when I opened my mouth, nothing but a pained whimper came out.

A lion's roar split the air seconds before a golden blur shot through the sky behind Zipporah's head. The harpy jerked upright, flapping sideways. Her attention slipped, and the air binding me fractured. I rolled away from her. Shoving to my feet, I ran for the nearest oak tree, hobbled by the skirt knotted around my calves.

"Quinn!" The elements hung as flimsy as wet paper in my grasp. I needed his enhancement.

A club of earth smashed into my temple. A gong reverberated inside my skull. My knees folded, and I pitched forward, instinct preventing me from face-planting. Panting, I crawled on hands and knees until I faced Zipporah, dropping a weak defensive ward over my huddled body, for all the good it would do me. What was stopping Quinn from boosting me? Was he hurt?

Quinn flashed through the trees farther up the slope, and another club of earth spun across the hillside, heading straight for him.

"Watch out!"

Quinn ducked out of sight behind the bend in the hill. I looked frantically for an escape. I couldn't outrun the harpy. The open countryside didn't provide any convenient cover, unless I counted the scattered oaks, and Zipporah wouldn't let me out of her sight long enough to hide behind one.

The harpy pivoted to face me, wings hunched past her ears like a vulture's. I had managed to put twenty feet between us, but she closed it in three swift hops. Behind her, Quinn crested the rise of the hill and soared along the slope, keeping his distance. *Still* he didn't boost me. I cowered beneath my pathetic ward and made a last-ditch effort to reason with the enraged harpy. Zipporah was a barterer, and there had to be something she wanted more than to kill me. Plus, every second I stalled increased my chances of being rescued. My hand dipped to my hip, grazing Grant's badge where I had clipped it to my underwear. Miraculously, it was still attached.

"Please. Just tell me what you want, and I'll get it for you."

Zipporah stalked another step closer, putting her within striking distance. I shrank back on my heels.

"You will bring me the banned spells Airstrong lost."

"That's impossible," I blurted. "I don't know where they are. No one does. The FPD has been hunting for the spells for weeks. How am I supposed to find them when they can't?"

"Are you saying you're not sufficiently motivated?"

Zipporah punched through my ward. I flung myself backward, out of reach, even as my magic exploded. Wind blasted outward in every direction, lambasting Zipporah with dust and dead weeds. What had sent spook squirrels flying barely rocked the harpy, though she did pause in surprise. I used her hesitation to scramble ten feet away before locking a fresh ward around myself, lining the inside with another blast of air.

Words vomited from my mouth, piling on top of each other. "I may be an heiress, but it's an empty title. Really, I'm just a journalist. How am I supposed to find stolen spells? Where would I look? And even if I found them, handing them over to you would be breaking the law. The FPD would find out, and they would arrest me. Not just me. What about you? If I agree to your request, the FPD would track the spells right to you. Then you would be in trouble, too."

"Your mistake is thinking I'm making a request." Zipporah stalked closer, fisting her feet with each step, her talons gouging divots into the hard soil. "You owe *me*. Stop thinking about the FPD. Your only concern is *me* and what I'll do to you if you don't bring me those spells."

She lashed out, demolishing my ward again. I dove sideways and rolled, evading the snap of her talons by inches but releasing the ward's broken magic too slowly. The backlash sliced into my brain. Through slitted eyes, I watched Zipporah scrape a talon through the crater my broken ward had created.

"This is getting tiresome," she said.

Exhausting seemed more apt. I staggered to my feet, wiping sweat-matted hair from my face. Blood dripped, warm and sticky, off my right ring finger, but I couldn't pinpoint the cut. I couldn't feel most of my body, the pains distant and unimportant in the face of Zipporah's wrath. Pulling elements along battered mental pathways, I erected another feeble ward.

"I can't give the spells to you. Please. There has to be another way to meet my debt."

Of all the things Zipporah could have asked of me, I couldn't think of anything worse than the missing lethal spells. It wasn't the unknown location of the spells that daunted me; I was already determined to hunt them down to clear my mom's name. It wasn't simply how dangerous the spells were, either, though that was part of it. It was what Zipporah would do with the spells. She could trap people in the snare and slice or break into warded vaults for even more rare and lethal items. She would be unstoppable with the beguiling beads. She wouldn't need to barter for anything; she could simply make people believe they wanted to do whatever she asked. If I handed them over to her, she could keep me enslaved to her forever, and I would never realize what she was doing. Even if all she did was sell the spells, that would put them back into public circulation, where they could harm an untold number of people before the FPD tracked them down and confiscated them again. I couldn't have that on my conscience.

Those should have been reasons enough, but they weren't. The truth was if she had demanded I retrieve items stolen from someone—anyone—else, I might have caved. But Zipporah wanted me to betray my parents. If I miraculously found the stolen spells and handed them over to Zipporah without being caught by the FPD, I would be dooming my mom and dad to take the fall for the thefts. Their names would never be cleared. Their reputations would be incinerated. Their business would implode. They would be arrested. Imprisoned. All so I could save my own skin. I would never be able to look them or myself in the eye again.

"You made a bargain. The terms are set. You'll bring me those banned spells."

"Never." The word came out soft, a protest issuing from my gut instead of my brain.

Zipporah's eyes widened. "Oh, you foolish child."

When she annihilated my ward, I was ready. Instead of a blast of air, arrows of condensed earth element shot into Zipporah's chest. Blood blossomed from a half dozen nicks in her leathery skin. Zipporah shrieked with fury.

"You're going to pay for that, you wretched girl!"

I sprinted for the nearest tree. Zipporah slashed out a wing, clipping my shins. My legs buckled. Sharp rocks cut into my knees, but all I could feel was the weight of the harpy looming behind me, poised to strike.

Quinn flashed over the treetops, his enhancement

flooding into me. *Finally.* I yanked the elements into a dome above me just in time to block Zipporah's strike. This time, my boosted ward quaked but held.

Zipporah battered at the elemental barrier with the razor-sharp feathers along the ridge of her wings, her small clawed hands bent toward me as if she intended to wrap the bony digits around my throat and strangle me. Spewing spittle, she shrieked incoherent insults, but it was the rage burning in her eyes that made my legs tremble. If she got through my ward this time, she would eviscerate me.

When her physical assault failed, Zipporah blasted me with a hurricane of wind. The colossal elemental attack pulverized my ward and earthen blades, then slammed into me. My arms and legs windmilled against empty air before I crashed down hard on my side, tumbling out of control until I fetched up against a sharp boulder.

Coughing, I grabbed for the elements. Pain spiked through my skull, and magic sifted through my mental fingers. I tried again, reaching simultaneously for Quinn's enhancement, but it had disappeared. The elements slithered from my grip.

Terror constricted my breathing. The earth tipped and spun when I surged to my feet, and I planted a hand on the boulder for balance. I couldn't afford to faint now. I had to stay strong until Grant arrived.

What was taking him so long?

I blinked darkness from the edges of my vision and scanned the rolling hills. I couldn't remember which direction we had come from, but it didn't matter; Zipporah, Quinn, and I were the only three souls out here.

Seething, Zipporah flung a lethal spear of air at my chest. I floundered for the elements and my coordination, too slow on both accounts.

The spear decelerated, bubbling and knotting. I gaped at the mutating magic even as I lurched out of its wobbling path. The massive chunk of air struck the ground several feet behind me, flinging rock shrapnel in all directions. I ducked and covered my head with my hands.

"Kylie, quick!"

Quinn's enhancement unfurled inside me, stabilizing the elements. I grabbed a fistful of magic and formed a hasty ward out of air and earth. Quinn's boost evaporated the second I finished anchoring the ward, and I staggered to hold the elements together unsupported.

What was going on? Why couldn't Quinn maintain his connection with me? What had Zipporah done to me? To him?

Zipporah spun away from me to fling a net of water and wood at Quinn.

"Duck, Quinn!" I cried.

Quinn swerved aside, but the net had already begun to deform, the elements folding and twisting. Abruptly, the spell boomeranged back toward Zipporah, engulfing her and crushing her wings to her sides. Water and earth mutated into wood and fire, and a single spark lit the spell. In seconds, an inferno engulfed the harpy.

I ran.

It wasn't just Quinn. Something was wrong with Zipporah's magic, too. Would I be affected next?

Tripping and stumbling, I sprinted to the relative safety of the nearest large oak trunk. The massive tree could have hidden me twice over, and I hugged close to its rough bark as I peeked at the burning harpy.

Zipporah stood in a patch of scorched earth, her tail feathers smoldering. The caustic stench of burning hair and feces permeated the air, overpowering the general harpy putrescence that my nose had long since grown numb to. Unfortunately, Zipporah appeared unharmed. Blotchy red patches suffused her cheeks and chest, a product of her anger rather than burns.

"It's time for you to die, rock brain," Zipporah growled.

My fingernails gouged the tree's bark. Did she think Quinn was responsible for her misfiring magic? How?

The harpy flung an elemental spear, this one thicker than my body, at Quinn's vulnerable flank. Quinn dove between a trio of oaks. The tip of his wing clipped a branch, and he careened toward the rocky soil, recovering inches from the ground. Weariness etched his face as he laboriously regained altitude. The spear tracked his erratic flight, then kinked in half and smashed into a towering oak. The tree shuddered. A heavy *crack* reverberated across the landscape, followed by the chaotic drumbeat of tearing wood. The four-hundred-year-old tree split, both halves crashing to the ground in a synchronous boom that rattled rocks loose from the hillside and vibrated the ground beneath my feet.

Oh crap. If one of those spears hit Quinn, it would do more than knock him from the sky. It would shear off a limb.

The moment I cobbled enough magic together to form a blade, I hurled it at Zipporah. It bounced off her backside, stopped either by her grime-coated feathers or by a shield. I grabbed more magic, unheeding of the liquid fire burning through my synapses. This time I dropped an elemental blade from above. It sliced Zipporah's scalp before she shattered it with a twist of air. A rivulet of blood trickled down her temple, but neither the cut nor the act of destroying my blade had distracted the harpy.

Another deadly spear chased Quinn down the slope. He

cut to the left. The spear followed. He dove right, and the spear twisted course, gaining on him. I threw a magic blade at Zipporah's neck, but it hit a ward and disintegrated. Quinn about-faced on heavy wings, climbing the slope toward us, the harpy's deadly magic closing in. Finally, it mutated. The tip of the elemental weapon halted as if it had slammed into a wall. The rest of the magic telescoped on the tip. With a thunderclap, the spell exploded. A wall of air blasted across the landscape, flattening weeds and trees, pushing dirt and Quinn ahead of it. I spun and crouched behind the massive oak, hands over my head. The gale slapped the tree. Twigs and sharp flecks of weeds and rocks pelted me, and the tree's branches groaned. Then the wind pushed past. I spun around the tree in time to see Quinn regain control and dive out of sight around the curve of the hill.

Zipporah pivoted to face me. Fury pulled her features into a terrifying mask. Blood oozed from a dozen cuts on her chest, and more ran into her left eyebrow.

"You *will* bring me the spells I want, and so much more." Zipporah stalked toward my hiding spot, wings hunched high.

My heart hammered in my ears. I fisted my skirt and prepared to run for my life.

A high-pitched whistle pierced the air, shrieking closer. Zipporah's eyes widened. With an undignified squawk, she flung herself skyward. A pentagram of raw elements blasted through the trees, whipping past me almost too fast to track. It sheared through the bottom of Zipporah's long wing feathers before burying itself into the hillside. Dirt exploded ten feet high.

Grant.

I would have recognized his magical signature even if it hadn't been as bright and bold as a lightning strike.

Zipporah battered the upper branches of the tree I hid under, her massive body distorted by the oak's leaves. "You can't hide behind your gargoyle and captain forever, Harriet Kylie Grayson. I'm going to make you pay and pay. You're going to be in my debt forever, heiress." With a foul explosion of wet feces, she jetted away.

I staggered clear of the grotesque downfall, my eyes locked on her retreating form and my ears ringing with the truth of her words.

Quinn wobbled through the air and plowed into the ground beside me. I collapsed to my knees and wrapped him in a tight hug. He folded his stone wings around me, blocking out the world.

"That was dreadful." Quinn's breaths came in ragged gasps, his chest heaving.

"But we survived." I buried my face in his sun-heated neck and breathed in the clean, earthy scent of him. We didn't pull apart until someone yelled my name.

Grant sped across the hillside, crouched atop a slender flying carpet, as if he expected to leap straight into battle. Raw elements crackled around his fingertips, and his granite expression promised violence. I had never seen a more beautiful sight.

When he spotted us beneath the oak tree, he changed course, jumping to the ground before the carpet came to a complete stop. Standing above us, his brilliant white uniform lending grandeur to his already impressive frame, he looked like a hero out of a legend.

"I've got Kylie and Quinn," he said into a message sphere. His gaze raked over me, his jaw muscle bouncing as he cataloged my injuries. Quinn received a quicker assessment. "They're safe."

The elemental bubble rocketed into the sky. Seconds later, a sharp, high-pitched eagle's cry rang across the hills. A rhythmic wing beat filled the air as Fang surged overhead. The huge gryphon flew past so fast I only had time to glimpse Raquel hugged tight to her neck, Seradon crouched behind her. The earth elemental deftly caught Grant's message bubble and tossed back a thumbs-up in response.

The oaks danced in the downdraft, releasing a flurry of leaves to join the billowing dust swirling in the gryphon's wake. I covered my mouth and nose with my elbow. Zipporah was already a speck on the horizon. She would be no match for a gryphon and those two women. If she had harbored any plans of circling back and resuming her attacks, they would dissuade her.

Grant scowled at our surroundings. It looked like a herd of drunken donkeys had plowed the hillside. Patches of soil furrowed by Zipporah's thick talons hopscotched down the hill interspersed with shallow craters from my exploding wards. The split oak lay in shambles to one side of the battleground, and flattened weeds defined the massive radius of Zipporah's shock wave. A patch of charred grass smoldered to our left, the acrid stench of burned feathers and harpy filth lingering in the air.

It was a miracle I had survived. I couldn't have done it without Quinn. Fortunately, he had suffered little more than scratches. I wished I could say the same about myself.

Grant dropped to his knees in front of me, heedless of his pristine uniform. Something savage glimmered in his eyes, and I froze, my lips parted but my words forgotten.

With a featherlight touch, he traced one blunt finger down the side of my face, brushing aside a snarl of dirty hair. Then he cupped my cheek in his callused palm. I drew in a shallow breath, mesmerized by the tenderness of his touch so at odds with his fierce expression.

He lifted his other hand to cradle my face, his scowl dropping to my mouth. Ever so gently, as if he thought I would crumble beneath his touch, Grant brushed his lips across mine. My breath hitched. Velvet heat cascaded down my nerve endings, sparking pleasure and soothing away pain. Grant returned for a second soft kiss, then another when I tilted my face up to him.

I had dreamed of this moment, envisioning it a dozen different ways, and none had included Grant treating me like porcelain. Steadying myself on his forearm, I ran the fingers of my free hand through his hair from his temple to the nape of his neck. The short strands tickled, and I curled my fingertips to trace my nails lightly back up his scalp. Grant released a gruff, appreciative sound, and his lips opened beneath mine. I darted my tongue over his bottom lip. His fingers spasmed, and he bent me backward for a deeper kiss. I cheered, the celebration a throaty moan as it escaped my throat. Grant tasted of sunshine and chocolate, and I wanted to consume every bite.

He must have eaten one of the miniature cakes at Persephone's party, I thought. Then I lost myself to the firm pressure of his lips and the zing of joy ricocheting through my bloodstream. When he swept his tongue over my upper lip a final time before sitting back on his heels, I released a ragged exhale.

Grant brushed his thumb back and forth along the side of my neck, each stroke chasing tingles across the sensitized skin. My eyes fluttered open, taking in Grant's hungry expression through my lashes. All too quickly, the passion in his eyes bled to concern, and his touch gentled again.

Reluctantly, I relaxed my grip and let my hands drop to my lap. A rock gouged painfully into my knee, and I shifted, brushing a shoulder against Quinn's. Embarrassment and guilt cut through the last of my post-kiss euphoria. How could I have forgotten Quinn's existence, especially when I was practically leaning on him? However, the goofy grin on his face mollified my chagrin. I rested a hand on his folded wing, silently thanking him for his support.

"Was that the standard rescue protocol after saving someone from a harpy attack?" I asked, afraid if we let this silence go on much longer, it would become awkward.

"Only if the woman is a pesky journalist with more courage than is healthy for her." Grant's words held no sting, and he gifted me with a rare smile. His thumb continued to stroke my neck.

"I've been wanting to do that for a long time." My confession came out husky.

"Me too," Grant said.

The tightness in my chest unwound, and I didn't try to contain my grin.

"Of course, if I had gotten a better whiff of you first, I might have waited," Grant said.

"Hey!"

"You really do stink," Quinn chimed in.

"Getting you cleaned up isn't going to feel good, either." Grant's gaze swept over me, his expression hardening.

"Honestly, I don't feel that great right now."

Grant helped me to my feet. Somewhere during the fight, I had lost my left boot, and the sole of my foot was bruised and abraded. I didn't examine the rest of my body too closely. Dirt and less identifiable grime coated me from head to toe, and I didn't need to see how bad my injuries were. I couldn't avoid noticing the damage the dress had sustained, though. Holes punctured the skirt's ruffles. Rips pockmarked the back of the tourniquet-like bodice—an unexpected improvement that enabled me to take full breaths. Half the skirt had separated from the bodice and drooped to expose a filthy, blood-smeared patch of my hip.

"Hold still." Grant formed a cleaning spell, the weave of elements stronger and more complex than my go-to dirt-remover spell. He set it spinning, then eased it down my body.

My hair lifted on the elemental breeze, tugged as if a full-scalp brush were going through it all at once. Flecks of pungent substances better left unexamined collected in a neat pile by my feet. Quinn wisely backed up. Fire bit into my scalp, and I flinched. Grant grabbed my shoulders and held me in place.

"Steady. We need to disinfect your wounds."

Gritting my teeth, I latched on to his wrists for balance as agony spiraled down my back, arms, sides, and hips. By the time the spell seared across the bottom of my bare foot, I was gnawing on my bottom lip to hold in whimpers.

Grant scooped me into his arms, carrying me carefully to the shade of a tree upwind of the dislodged filth. Trying to be discreet, I brushed tears from the corners of my eyes. Blood from a scratch on my forearm smeared across Grant's chest, and I cursed.

"Put me down. I'm bleeding on your uniform."

Instead of setting me on my feet, Grant sank to the ground. He rested his back against the oak and cradled me against his chest, anchoring me with a hand on my hip. I gave up the pretense of trying to escape when my wiggles only incited pain. Relaxing, I rested my cheek against

Grant's chest. I wanted to ask what we were waiting for, but since I suspected he was giving me a breather before he inflicted his torturous healing on me, I kept quiet.

"I should never have left your side." Grant spoke the words over the top of my head, his chest vibrating against my ear.

"Neither of us thought Zipporah would show up at Persephone's."

"That's no excuse."

"Fortunately you planned for this possibility." I patted the tracker clipped at my hip. I tried to keep the bleakness from my voice. Grant had saved my life this time, but Zipporah would return to torment me, expecting me to deliver the impossible—then do it again and again, until she finally declared my debt squared away. If that ever happened.

If she didn't kill me first.

Quinn joined us after retrieving my missing boot. He dropped the shoe beside me, then lowered himself gingerly to his stomach, his wings lightly fanned out to rest on the ground on either side of him.

"Are you hurt?" I had been certain his injuries were minor, but what if I had missed something?

"Just a headache."

Since when did Quinn get headaches? "Does it have to do with what you were doing to Zipporah? That *was* you, right? That's why I was never affected?"

Quinn started to nod, then grasped his forehead with a paw, his expression sickly. I shared a concerned glance with Grant. Neither of us had Mika's skill with quartz-tuned earth magic. If Quinn was suffering internal injuries, we wouldn't be able to do anything.

"How did you get her magic to mess up like that?" I

asked while calculating how to position Quinn on Grant's flying carpet and how quickly Grant would be able to rush Quinn to Terra Haven.

Grant leaned forward fractionally. "Mess up how?"

"Everything the harpy threw at us kept warping," I explained. Quinn no longer looked as if he was going to vomit—something I wasn't sure gargoyles could do—but his expression remained pinched with pain. "Her air spears knotted on themselves, and the net she tried to use on Quinn backfired and burst into flames around her despite being made of water and earth. If her magic hadn't malfunctioned, I would be much worse off." *Or I would be dead.*

"You did that?" Grant asked.

Quinn dipped his nose as if he was about to nod, then stilled. "You know how I enhance people's link with the elements?"

"Of course," I said.

"It usually feels good."

"And keeps you healthy." Mika had explained the symbiotic relationship gargoyles shared with those they enhanced. It was why they gravitated toward full-spectrum households. Gargoyles needed to amplify sizable quantities of all five elements to maintain their well-being, an endeavor made easier when living with people who wielded all the elements equally. To this day, Quinn's brother Oliver required occasional trips to the city library to get a balanced dose of the elements from the crowds—something he didn't get from Mika, who worked mostly with earth. Quinn did the same, though he preferred the *Chronicle* to the library. Lately, between our trip to the everlasting tree and the time we had spent with Grant's squad, he hadn't needed to supplement his elemental diet by enhancing anyone else.

Except right now, he looked far from healthy.

"But do you know *how* I do it?" Quinn asked.

I shook my head, realizing I had never contemplated the mechanics behind his—and all gargoyles'—ability.

"It's pretty simple, really. I start by collecting, folding, and collapsing the elements into a more efficient stream."

"Folding and collapsing the elements? Like with a spell?" I struggled to imagine what that would look like.

"No, it only works on raw elements."

"Nothing about that sounds simple." I tilted my head to check with Grant.

"I wouldn't even know where to begin," he said.

"Well, normally I do that, then link with the person I want to enhance. With Zipporah, I tried doing the opposite."

"Explain," Grant ordered.

"Instead of making the elements more harmonious, I distorted them when I linked with her." A fine tremor shivered through him. "Her magical signature was...disturbing. But I was able to warp the elements as she used them. It hurt, but it was worth it."

I climbed out of Grant's arms and sat beside him so I could reach Quinn. Running my fingers over Quinn's pinched brow, I did my best to soothe his headache. A massage wouldn't work with his quartz body, but he leaned into my touch, allowing me to smooth the crinkles from his forehead.

I didn't deserve Quinn as a companion. He had been nothing but a wonderful friend to me, and I repaid him by dragging him into one dangerous situation after another. Somehow, I had to make this all up to him.

After a prolonged silence, in which Quinn melted into my touch, resting his heavy head on my thigh, I finally asked, "What made you think to do that?"

"What Yarra said about my seed being an inverse of the elements. When I distorted the elements, this is what it looked like to me." He lifted his head to pat the everlasting seed he wore around his neck. His eyes widened, and he surged back on his haunches, hooking a claw through the leather thong to pull it over his head. "It changed!"

I helped him untangle himself, then held up the seed for us to examine. Gone was the mutated brown mess that had made me nauseous. In its place was the seed's newest evolution, a soft green metallic disc as large as my hand. Coppery lines crisscrossed its surface, and the hole for the leather cord sat off center. When I shifted the seed for Quinn to admire, the silvery shine on the opposite side caught my eye. Flipping it revealed a circular mirror. If I didn't know better, I never would have guessed the disc had originally grown from a tree.

"It's pretty," Quinn said, amazement making his words breathy. A slow smile pulled his feline lips wide.

I grinned back. For the first time, his seed wasn't frightening. It had to be a good sign.

"I did the right thing," Quinn said. "I helped you."

"You saved my life." *Again.* As much as I hated that it was becoming a habit, I was immeasurably grateful, too.

"Any idea what this new form means?" Grant asked. He hefted the seed in his palm, testing its weight. If one of us were to wear it, it would give us a neckache, but the weight would be no problem for Quinn.

"Not a clue," Quinn said, but his smile didn't lessen as I draped the cord around his neck once more.

A small craft rattled over the rocky hillside, flying on a levitation spell never meant to travel anything but a smooth city road. Even before Grant sent an arrow of light to guide it to our location, I recognized the aerodynamic lines of an

Airstrong courier cart. The bright blue winged-A logo painted on the front was my second clue. My mom sat in the driver's seat, fists clenched around the rudder shaft. The craft might have been fast for a delivery driver, but judging by my mom's anguished expression, it was far too slow for a woman tracking down her abducted daughter.

I started to rise, but Grant rested a hand on my shoulder, standing in my stead. He asserted a single finger of pressure, but it was more than enough to immobilize me. Perhaps remaining seated was the smart idea. Besides, even small shifts ignited fresh pain in my scratched back. I didn't relish the torment that would come with standing, and passing out in front of my mom wouldn't reassure her.

The moment the cart lurched to a stop, my mom launched out. Sweat plastered the elegant folds of her khaki bodice to her chest, and her hair had slipped from its smooth coil to flow in a tangled mess down her back. Naked relief flashed across her face when she spotted me in Grant's shadow, and my heart squeezed. I wished I could have spared her the last horrible, anxious hour of her life.

She flung herself to her knees beside me, her hands fluttering over me without actually touching me. "Are you all right? What happened? Why did that harpy attack you? What's going on, Kylie? I want answers. Now."

I captured one of her hands in mine. "I'm fine. Grant scared the harpy away."

She shot Grant a sharp look. He had moved aside to give us room, donning his expressionless captain's mask once more. It was hard to believe he was the same man who had kissed me so tenderly minutes earlier.

"Thank you, Captain," my mom said.

She's thanking him for saving you, not for kissing you, I told myself, but that didn't keep my cheeks from reddening.

Grant accepted my mom's gratitude with a nod before he glanced away to scan the skies. A silver flare of light ignited above his palm and shot upward through the branches. "Seradon's coming." He domed a ward over the four of us, cutting off the nominal breeze. Quinn sighed with relief. He must have been boosting Grant. After the painful experience of distorting Zipporah's magic, using his powers in the correct manner appeared to be soothing.

"Who is Seradon?" my mom demanded.

"The earth elemental in Grant's squad." The heavy flap of wings reached my ears at last. "That will be Raquel with her, flying the gryphon."

My mom looked like she wanted to ask more questions, but Fang descended on the clearing. The swift beats of her wings drowned out all but the gryphon's piercing cry of recognition when she spotted Quinn. A small dust storm studded with filthy harpy feathers, pebbles, twigs, and weeds pelted Grant's ward. Outside our protective bubble, Seradon and Raquel climbed down from the gryphon's back, chasing away the worst of the dust with pulses of air.

I tugged my mom's hand. She was uncharacteristically speechless as she took in the women, the gryphon, Grant, and finally Quinn, but I could see questions forming behind her bright blue eyes. I couldn't put off explaining everything to her much longer, but first I had something more important to do.

"Mom, this is Quinn, the most wonderful gargoyle you'll ever meet. Quinn, this is my mom, Charlotte."

My mom sat back on her heels to be eye level with Quinn. "I've heard a lot about you, Quinn, including how you've been there every time my daughter needs you. I'm indebted to you and forever grateful that you offered your protection to my impulsive and reckless daughter."

An admonishment for me even as she complimented Quinn; my mom was regaining her equilibrium with remarkable speed.

"Kylie's not reckless, Madam Charlotte Mom."

My mom laughed. "You can call me Charlotte. And I noticed you didn't claim Kylie's not impulsive."

"A good journalist needs to be ready for anything," Quinn said.

My mom arched an eyebrow at me. "I see you are well suited to each other."

Grant dropped his ward. A light haze hung in the air, but everything else had settled. Seradon and Raquel joined us, slapping dust from their clothes. Creases ringed their eyes from flying goggles, but otherwise they looked like they had partaken in a leisurely flight, not a high-speed chase. I considered getting up, but since I couldn't work up the energy to put my boot back on, I remained seated.

"We lost Zipporah near Stipple Rock," Seradon reported to Grant. "I don't know which was more impressive: her speed or that she was able to mask her scent trail from Fang."

"What would you have done if you caught her?" I asked.

Seradon ran a hand through her short tousled hair, shooting Grant a questioning look.

"Once we knew you were safe, the goal was only to chase her away," he said.

"Because she hasn't done anything illegal." My words came out stilted.

Grant's jaw muscle clenched, but he nodded.

I shouldn't have felt betrayed, but a scared, bloodthirsty part of me wished Grant would overlook the law and destroy Zipporah for daring to harm me.

"Nothing illegal?" My mom's tone could have frozen fire.

"That harpy abducted my daughter. Look at her. She looks like she was trampled by a centaur herd and picked over by vultures."

I winced. I had plenty of cuts and scrapes, and the dress lent a sickly pallor to my skin, but my ego wished she had picked a gentler description. I had been a wimp earlier, when I should have asked Grant to heal me. I would have happily endured the torture if I had known my mom was coming.

"What if you hadn't been there when Kylie was taken?" My mom pushed into Grant's personal space. Anger flushed her cheeks and snapped in her blue eyes. She didn't seem to notice or care that she was a foot shorter than him or that she had to crane her head to glare at him. "How can you say that dreadful creature hasn't done anything illegal? I thought you were supposed to protect the citizens of Terra Haven from attacks like that. I thought you and my daughter were . . ."

I bit my lip, wondering how she finished the sentence in her head.

"Your daughter's safety is my paramount concern," Grant said.

Seradon settled back on her heels, and if I didn't know better, I would say amusement lurked in her brown eyes as she watched her captain and my mom square off. Quinn appeared equally rapt. Only Raquel seemed to share my discomfort. The gryphon rider inspected the seams of her gloves as if searching for writing in the needlework, performing her fastidious examination without moving enough to draw anyone's attention.

My mom drew a deep breath, but I cut her off before she could launch into another diatribe.

"Mom, Grant hasn't done anything wrong. I have." My

throat wanted to close around my confession, and my words came out strangled. But as much as I wanted to put it off, my mom deserved an explanation. "I made a deal with Zipporah, and now I owe her a debt."

The fight drained from my mom's posture. She knelt beside me, her crystalline eyes bouncing back and forth between mine. "When? Why? Why didn't you come to me or your dad?"

"It wasn't like that. It was more"—I studied my fingernails, then forced my gaze back to my mom's—"impulsive and reckless."

Shame made my spine want to curl in on itself, but I held myself rigid and didn't look away from my mom's penetrating gaze as I explained how I had followed Grant up to Zipporah's nest after he had told me not to, and how I had promised the harpy an open-ended debt like a brainless simpleton.

My mom remained silent when I finished, studying me. Acid churned in my stomach as I waited for her compassionate expression to turn to scorn and disappointment. Instead, she reached for me, resting her cool fingers against the side of my face.

"We all make some bad deals. We'll figure this out."

My breath escaped with a ragged hitch. I held in a sob, and my mom brushed a rivulet of tears from my cheek before turning to the others.

"Who here has the best healing skills? My daughter has suffered long enough, and I want to hug her without hurting her."

I snorted, swiping my cheeks with the heel of my hand. I let my watery vision graze the others' faces, searching for condemnation. Seradon looked oddly pleased, Grant stoic, and Raquel unsurprised by my confession. She must have already heard about my story from Seradon.

"I know a thing or two about healing," Raquel said. "I'll need to link—"

"Done." My mom thrust a collection of balanced elements toward Raquel.

Grant and Seradon silently offered their magic, and Raquel linked with them. She tripped, legs unsteady as she settled beside me. Having experienced the headiness of linking with Grant and the members of his squad before, I understood her disequilibrium. It was a lot of power to have at one's fingertips, made all the more potent by Quinn's boost.

Raquel crossed her legs and took a deep breath. "Where is the worst injury?"

"My back."

She shifted to look, sucking in a sympathetic breath. "This is going to sting."

I closed my eyes, opening them only long enough to identify my mom when she clutched my hands. I gasped when the first tendrils of Raquel's magic delved beneath my skin, knitting broken flesh. Then I locked my lips together, resolved to bear the pain silently.

"Hang in there, Kylie. That harpy did a number on you."

Raquel must have had healing training in her past, because while her spells hurt, they weren't nearly as bad as Grant's cruder methods. Nevertheless, by the time she finished knitting the flayed skin on my back, sweat dripped liberally from my chin, and my breath came in choppy gasps.

"Just a few more," Raquel murmured.

I nodded. The motion set off a spinning in my head, and I opened my eyes to stare at my mom's hands locked in mine. I clung to her with a white-knuckled grip that must have been painful, but she didn't say a word. I tried to relax, but my fingers convulsed tighter when pain flickered and faded in the gashes on my knees. The wounds closed, growing new, puffy red skin. Raquel moved to the scrapes on my arms and then my foot before she finally sat back and wiped the sweat from her face.

Soreness pervaded my body, the underlying tenderness remaining even though the cuts were sealed. Raquel had done good work, too, and I didn't think I would have any new scars.

"Thank you." The words felt inadequate.

My mom echoed them, then pulled me into a tight hug. I returned it limply. Raquel looked on with a wan smile, her body slumped with exhaustion.

"You're one tough woman, Kylie," she said. "You'd make a good candidate for a gryphon rider."

I checked on Fang, who lay snoozing in the sun, curled up like a bus-size house cat. "I think I've got enough on my plate right now."

"Let's get you home," my mom said, starting to rise.

"That sounds good, but…I haven't told you everything."

"Zipporah's demands?" Grant guessed.

I nodded.

"She had *demands*?" My mom planted her hands on her hips. "Brutalizing you wasn't enough for her?"

"She wants the stolen banned spells."

Seradon broke the silence with an impressive string of curses that would have done her squadmate Winnigan proud.

"When she figured out who I am, she decided my life was worth more, and the first payment she expects is those spells."

"The first." Grant's growl was more accusation than question.

My mom shoved to her feet, studied her hands a moment, then lifted her gaze to Grant's. "My daughter trusts you, Captain, so I must." Taking a deep breath, she turned back to me. "We'll find those stolen spells, and when we do, we'll hand them over to the harpy and convince her to clear your debt."

"Investigator O'Hara would never allow that," Seradon said.

"He will if he doesn't know about it." My mom lifted her chin in silent challenge.

"Even if we said nothing, he would find out. Then you would be charged as an accomplice of the theft."

"So be it," my mom said.

I shook my head. "Now who's being impulsive and reckless? I can't let you do that for me, Mom. I won't." I struggled to my feet, refusing my mom's outstretched hand. My attempt to appear strong failed when I had to brace myself against Quinn's shoulder to remain upright. The fight had sapped most of my strength, and the accelerated healing had stolen the rest. I yearned for water and a soft bed. Even a hard bed. Maybe a nice comfy slab of granite. So long as I could get horizontal and close my eyes, I would be happy. But I couldn't rest just yet.

"Even if you had the spells in your possession," I told my mom, firming my voice, "I wouldn't take them. I certainly wouldn't hand anything that dangerous to Zipporah." I had no idea how I would get out of the harpy's latest demands, but it certainly wouldn't be by throwing my mom to the wolves. "I made this mess, and I'll fix it."

Somehow.

13

___

My mom relented the argument, most likely because I looked as if I would faint, not because she was done pressing her point. She was all for scooping me into her courier cart and whisking me to her house in Terra Haven, but no matter how delightful that sounded, I wasn't done for the day.

"I have to go to the *Chronicle*," I informed her.

"Work? After the day you've had?"

"I'm on a deadline."

My mom crossed her arms.

"Actually, I need to return to Persephone's, collect my camera and interview notes, *then* go to the *Chronicle*." My stomach knotted at the thought of returning to the hive of full spectrums. I didn't have the energy to fend off their questions or deal with their gossip.

"I can take you. I should get going anyway." Raquel pointed to the sun, which had slid past its zenith more than an hour ago. "The solstice ritual is over, and I need to transport Lucas back to headquarters, but I can fit another passenger on Fang."

I had forgotten that the *Chronicle*'s society journalist had been the reason for Raquel's presence at Persephone's party. I didn't relish a ride back with Lucas, but at least Fang's saddle made in-flight conversation all but impossible.

"Are you determined to do this?" my mom asked.

"I didn't plan to impress anyone at the party today, but I also didn't expect to bring shame to the Grayson name. At least if I get my article turned in, today won't be a complete failure."

"I don't give a hippogryph's hind hoof what those fools think."

I believed my mom, but unfortunately, the opinions of those "fools" could mean the difference between her business recovering or going under.

"I'm sor—"

"No. Don't apologize. This isn't your fault." My mom didn't give me space to argue. "Before I left, I grabbed your bag and supplies. It was all I could think to do after the captain tore out of there. They're in my cart. Come, I'll take you to work."

"Kylie rides with me," Grant said, his voice loaded with FPD authority.

I frowned at him, then at Seradon. I expected to see amusement on her face, but her expression was as serious as Grant's.

"Zipporah knows who you are—who you both are," she said. "She knows you're vulnerable. And she's not above returning to toy with you."

"Kylie cut her several times. It made her really mad."

Everyone turned to look at Quinn, then back at me. I swallowed my sigh. After keeping quiet for so long, Quinn had chosen a poor time to chime in.

"Defensive wards," I explained. "They worked well on the spook squirrels. I figured why not try them on a harpy."

"Defensive wards?" my mom echoed softly.

"Spook squirrels?" Grant's gaze scraped down my arms, but Raquel had healed the squirrels' scratches along with the rest of my injuries. I tried to compose a succinct explanation of my encounter with the sciurids, but my gaze snagged on the way Grant's scowl tightened his lips and emphasized the rigidity of his jaw. Maybe it would be easier to distract him with a kiss.

I clamped my lips shut before the thought tumbled out, thankful exhaustion hadn't demolished *all* my mental filters.

"It's safer for Grant to accompany Kylie," Seradon said. "I'll return with you, if you don't mind, Charlotte. Besides, it looks like Grant and Kylie have some talking to do."

"My carpet is faster." Grant made the statement sound like an order.

"Or we could go as a group," my mom suggested.

Grant continued to glare at me, and I allowed myself a sigh. When Grant had suggested I travel with him, my first thought had been that he might want to indulge in more kissing. Now it looked as if he would rather pick a fight.

"I have my deadline. I'll go with Grant." The words came out flat. Whatever argument Grant had brewing behind his scowl, I preferred to have it outside of my mom's hearing range.

"Are you sure?" My mom brushed a lock of hair off my face.

"The sooner I get back, the sooner I can write up this piece and crawl into bed."

My mom quirked an eyebrow, and I regretted my choice of words. I wanted to protest that I was too tired to even think of doing anything . . . interesting . . . with Grant tonight, but I *had* just been contemplating kissing him. A hot blush crept up my cheeks—one I pretended didn't exist.

"Do you want me to help you change?" my mom asked.

"Persephone threw my clothes away. This is all I have." I plucked at the ragged skirt. "It's still decent enough for the bullpen." I was already going to be gossip fodder among the writers for the foreseeable future. I might as well give them something to talk about.

My mom studied my mulish expression. "I want you to message me the moment you're in the city, and again when you make it home."

"Yes, Mom." It occurred to me that she viewed my home as a safe haven where Zipporah couldn't reach me. I decided not to disabuse her of the notion, and I narrowed my eyes at Grant, attempting to convey the same to him. His expression didn't change.

"This is my cue to depart. Stay out of trouble, Kylie." Raquel tossed a wave to everyone and jogged to Fang. Seradon followed her.

I stroked Quinn's forehead to get his attention. "Are you up for the flight? If not, I don't think there's room on the carpet, but you can hitch a ride on Mom's cart."

"I can fly. It's not that far. Besides, boosting Grant will help me feel better, and you'll need me if Zipporah returns."

Raquel delayed her departure for a private chat with Seradon, one that involved a lingering handshake and some heavy eye contact. I caught Seradon's eye when she jogged back to our group, and she winked. Before I could decide if we were good enough friends for me to pester her about her love life, the moment passed, and Grant herded us toward my mom's courier cart.

After accepting my bag and a final hug from my mom, I clambered onto Grant's flying carpet. It floated only two feet off the ground, but between my abused dress and clumsy appendages, it took me three tries to get settled. More than one rip in the skirt tore further when I crossed my legs and dropped my bag onto my lap. Grant folded himself into the space behind me, his shins pressed against my backside. Nothing about our positioning was intimate, but with my mom observing us, the whole situation gained an awkward air.

"I bet you have a lot of questions," Seradon said to my mom after Fang departed, making conversation audible once more. "Let me see if I can guess the first one: I've known Grant for almost a decade, and he's been a model captain since he got the promotion."

My mom looked surprised, then speculative, as she climbed into the courier cart after Seradon.

"He's currently not dating and hasn't for several months..." Seradon continued, her voice fading as she powered the vehicle into motion and steered it toward the nearest road.

I dropped my head in my hands. Maybe I *should* have flown with my mom.

"She's got all the subtlety of a minotaur," Grant grumbled.

He activated the carpet and steered us downhill, taking a more direct route across the rough terrain. Designed for battle, the carpet possessed a more sophisticated levitation spell than my mom's cart, and it gently undulated over the boulders hidden among the weeds, absorbing and smoothing out the smaller bumps in the hillside that would have been jarring inside the cart or even on the *Chronicle*'s carpet—

The carpet that was still tucked inside a cabinet in one of Persephone's bathrooms. After today, Persephone had probably banned me from her estate. I would have to send a courier to pick up the carpet if I couldn't convince her to ship it back to the *Chronicle*. I shook my head. That was a problem for future me, when my brain didn't feel like pulped paper.

Quinn loped beside us for several strides, then leapt into the air. With easy, quick beats, he ascended, catching an updraft and soaring higher in wide circles. My heart lifted with him, relieved to see him moving with his normal grace. If his head still hurt, boosting Grant was helping, just as he had said.

"Why didn't you wait for me?" Grant asked, his words clipped.

My mom's cart had flown out of sight, and I had allowed my spine to relax, but it snapped straight at Grant's tone.

"When?"

"Before you flung yourself into the harpy's talons."

I strained to peer at Grant over my shoulder. His tone might have been mild, but his displeased glower had transformed into a full-blown thunderous snarl.

"I . . . I didn't fling myself," I sputtered, confused as much by his anger as by his accusation. "I couldn't let her tear Persephone's house apart."

"Why not?"

"It's expensive!"

"That's her problem for letting her wards lapse. It doesn't excuse your foolishness."

I jerked to face forward and crossed my arms. "Zipporah could have injured someone. I couldn't stand around waiting for that to happen."

"No one there was helpless."

"What about my mom? She would have tried to intervene. I couldn't let her get hurt." At the time, it had seemed imperative to avoid an interaction between my mom and Zipporah, but now my reasoning sounded flimsy. My mom was smart. She would have formulated a better plan than throwing her body in front of mine like a melodramatic actress, as I had envisioned. In truth, I had panicked, and it had nearly cost me my life. My mom was right: I had been impulsive and reckless. When would I learn?

The carpet veered right. I tilted and flailed for balance. Grant gripped my shoulders, steadying me. He didn't let go when I stabilized, either. Grumbling under his breath, he stretched his legs out on either side of me and scooted me back against him. Then he dropped his arms around me, gently caging me in and resting his hands atop the bag in my lap. The carpet never slowed.

I kept my spine stiff, steeling myself against his next argument.

Grant sighed, brushing his thumbs across my knuckles. "Relax."

"I—"

"I was being a jerk. I'm done."

My mouth fell open. Had he just apologized? I twisted to check his expression. Grant channeled a punch of power into the propulsion spell, and the carpet jumped forward, knocking me back against him before I caught more than a glimpse of his compressed mouth. When I tried to lean forward, his arms tightened around me, holding me in place.

I smiled to myself. He *had* just apologized.

We swerved around a shallow spring and bounced onto a narrow road minutes later. Grant pushed the carpet to greater speed, and we blasted down the smooth lane. I allowed myself to rest against his firm chest, my head cradled against his shoulder. When we banked around a steep turn, Grant's arms held me steady. My eyelids drifted closed.

"What about the spook squirrels?" he asked softly.

I yawned. "Another of Persephone's lapses. Her forest is lousy with them." I yawned again. "Or it was. The ritual probably cleared them out."

Wind played through my hair and swept the worst of the summer heat from my skin. A hypnotic dance of light and shadows flickered across my eyelids, fuzzing my thoughts. It didn't take much longer for the steady rhythm of Grant's chest rising and falling to lull me to sleep.

I woke in the heavy shade of a stately pine. I still lay propped against Grant's chest and atop the carpet, but we had stopped. Swiping my bottom lip to check for drool, I sat up.

"Where's Quinn?"

"He flew ahead to rest. He's waiting for you at the *Chronicle*."

"Why are we stopped?"

"I didn't think you'd want to fly through the city like that." He gestured to my legs, which were sprawled inelegantly akimbo, the skirt hiked up above my knees. From his position, Grant couldn't see more than my calves, but anyone from the opposite side would have quite the view. Blushing, I tried to tug the skirt into shape, ripping a new hole near my knee. Reluctantly, I stood. Every muscle in my body protested, but my legs held. I shook out the skirt. Tufts of indigo threads floated away in the breeze. Patches of fabric hung like open windows to reveal glimpses of my knees and shins. I poked a finger through the hole at my hip.

"I look like a cerberus's chew toy."

"I hope that wasn't a favorite dress." Grant climbed to his feet and stretched.

"Not even if I were color blind. It's Persephone's. She insisted."

"Huh."

"I didn't have time to change into something more . . ." I waved a hand at him, meaning to indicate his tailored attire. My words died as I took him in. His pristine outfit looked like a fashionable butcher's uniform. Had all that blood been mine? No wonder standing had made me dizzy.

I tripped when I took a step, fetching up against Grant. I braced a hand on his chest and steadied myself. He quirked an eyebrow at me.

"Are you certain you need to go straight to the *Chronicle*?"

I paced away from him, willing my limbs to cooperate. With the return of blood flow, my coordination improved, and I circled the carpet before responding. "Is that your not-so-subtle way of telling me I look like crap?"

"You've been through an ordeal today. Plus the healing. You need more rest than a half-hour nap."

He hadn't denied my accusation, but I didn't press the issue. Did I really want to hear him tell me I looked awful? "I need to get this story turned in. If I don't do it now, I'll miss my deadline."

"You should at least get something to eat."

"No argument there." My stomach growled as backup.

I climbed back onto the carpet, taking care to arrange the skirt modestly over my legs, and Grant resumed his place behind me, caging me in place with his legs and arms. I had been too tired to appreciate the intimacy of the position earlier, but now it was all I could think about. I shifted, tucking my hair to one side so it didn't slap Grant in the face. The movement pressed me up against the curve of his bicep, and when I scooted in the opposite direction, my hip brushed the inside of his thigh. The heat of Grant's chest radiated against my back. A flush that had nothing to do with the summer sun climbed my neck, and sweat broke out along my hairline.

"Here we go." Grant leaned forward, steadying me as the carpet accelerated. I relaxed against him and relished in feeling both delicate and protected, safe in Grant's solid embrace. He threaded our fingers together and tightened his arms around me. I closed my eyes. Every torment I had endured today had been worth it for this moment.

All too soon, we cruised through the city gates and stopped at the first sandwich vendor Grant spotted. We had to rearrange ourselves into cross-legged positions to eat on the carpet, and as happy as my stomach was to receive food, I would have postponed the meal hours longer if it meant I could have remained in Grant's arms.

We both finished eating before we reached the *Chronicle*, but neither of us made a move to resume our earlier position. What had felt natural and secure when we were traversing the countryside seemed improper in the bustling streets of downtown.

Wadding up the empty sandwich paper, I scooted to the edge of the carpet and stood when Grant stopped in front of the *Chronicle*. It was the same place he had dropped me off after scaring Zipporah off my roof. Had that been only this morning?

My dress wilted around my body, ripped lace fluttering as I turned. Grant adjusted the carpet's levitation until he floated eye level with me. My lips tingled with the memory of our earlier kiss. It had obviously been a spur-of-the-moment impulse for Grant, but that didn't exclude future kissing, right? For instance, now would be a perfect moment. Was he waiting for me to instigate it? I took a step forward and—

"If Zipporah returns to your house, send me a message right away and stay out of sight. Whatever you do, don't go anywhere without my tracker."

"Of course." I fussed with the strap of my bag to hide the disappointment on my face. "Thank you for the ride."

"My pleasure."

My eyes darted to Grant's, and my stomach went weightless when I spotted his affectionate smile. With a mock salute, he navigated into traffic. I didn't allow my exhaustion to slouch my spine until he disappeared around the corner.

Quinn coasted down from the roof to join me, blinking sleepily.

"How are you feeling?" I asked.

"Better."

"Maybe you should head home anyway and have Mika take a look at you."

He shook his head. "We have an article to finish."

I held the door open for him, then paused on the thresh-old. Squeezing my eyes shut, I made a last-ditch effort to force my dress to improve by sheer willpower. When I opened my eyes, it still resembled a half-digested plum. Sighing, I plodded up the steps after Quinn.

The bullpen bustled with the frantic crack of typewriter keys, the flutter of paper, and the bluster of animated conversations as everyone rushed to get their articles completed for the evening deadline. I ducked my head when I reached the landing and hurried toward the junior journalist table.

"Look, everyone, *the* Harriet Grayson has deigned to join

us." Hannah's high voice cut through the hubbub before I made it two steps.

All activity in the bullpen ground to a halt. Bracing myself, I pivoted to face a sea of silent, judgmental faces.

Hannah stood for a better view from the far side of the room. "Is that what you think poor people wear? Rags? You're taking it a bit far, *Harriet*."

"Oh, honey." Even though Rudy was less than five feet away, he made a show of putting on his glasses and studying me. When he spoke again, his tone dripped with patronizing sweetness. "It looks like you're out of your depth. Maybe it's time to run back to your parents and leave writing articles to the professionals."

Snickers spread through the room. It was the kind of comment I would have expected from Nathan, but he wasn't even present. I clenched my teeth and strove to keep my face neutral. Maybe if I let everyone vent their derision, they would let it go.

"Don't be so rude, everyone," Gina said. I had barely exchanged ten words with the sports journalist, and her intervention surprised me. My burst of gratitude withered with her next comment. "An heiress is in our midst. The proper response is to bow."

Several writers tossed rude gestures in her direction—and mine. My fingernails bit into my bag's strap, an unwelcome flush heating my cheeks.

"Are you sure you want to associate with us commoners?" Jorge asked. The copyeditor tucked his pencil behind his ear and propped a boot on the edge of his desk. "Because, you know"—he dropped his voice to a stage whisper—"who your parents are doesn't impress us."

"Oooh," several people said, as if I were a child being sent to the school headmaster. Just as many rolled their eyes, though, and one wadded-up ball of paper smacked the side of Jorge's head. He chuckled and tossed me a wink. Tension bled from my shoulders. I turned to look for an available typewriter when Sheldon's words stopped me cold.

"I think she's lost," the politics writer said. "The offices of the *Full Spectrum Gazette* are on the other side of the river."

My lip twitched in an involuntary sneer. The *Full Spectrum Gazette* dealt exclusively with the lives and events of the rich and powerful—every party, every marriage contract, every business deal, and every public outing, all photographed and written about in the fawning prose of devoted classism. The paper was infamous for catering to the nepotism of full-spectrum elite and hiring young socialites who wanted to play at being journalists. Nothing in the *Gazette's* pages qualified as real news worthy of real journalism. It was exactly the kind of paper I would have been expected to work at if I hadn't kept my identity a secret.

"I don't know about the rest of you, but I had to work *hard* for this position," Sheldon said. "What do you want to bet that Mommy and Daddy got their little heiress this position?" Ugly grumbles circled the room.

"At least we know how Harriet gets all the good assignments," Rafi said.

Fury boiled through my bloodstream, hazing my vision. *This* was the reason I had hidden my true identity. I hated the assumption that my accomplishments had been handed to me, that my successes were due to favoritism. Rafi and I were both junior journalists, hired within a month of each other. In that time, I had written multiple front-page articles, and he had toiled in mediocrity. I had also worked longer hours and in more dangerous conditions. Rafi was the first person out the door in the evening, late on assignments, and lazy with his descriptors.

"It should have been me who was sent to the everlasting tree," Rafi grumbled. "I don't have rich parents to pay my way."

"I have actual talent. It should have been me," someone else asserted.

Exhaustion warped my anger to tears, and I blinked to prevent them from falling. In that moment, I hated each and every person in the bullpen. I hated those who stayed silent almost as much as those whose harsh words landed like slaps. I hated their bigoted attitudes and self-righteousness. But most of all, I hated Nathan for exposing me and stripping me of the respect of my peers with a few petty lines in his article.

Quinn drew himself up, wings lifting, his chest expanding. Any second, he would leap to my defense, and I couldn't explain to him how that would probably do more damage than good. Instead, I rested my hand on his forehead and shook my head.

"It's not worth it."

"Enough already. You all sound like whiny schoolchildren, not professional journalists," Audrey said. The senior journalist didn't raise her voice. She didn't even look up from her notes, but her words cut through the room. "If you have a problem with how our boss doles out assignments, you should take it up with her."

"I couldn't have said it better."

Every head in the room whipped toward Dahlia Bearpaw. The editor in chief stood in the doorway of her office, arms crossed, surveying her employees with hard eyes.

"Have I underestimated everyone's workload? Maybe I should double your assignments."

The bullpen burst into action. Chair legs scraped, pens

scratched papers, typewriters clacked and pinged, and heads dipped toward desks, everyone suddenly too busy to look up. Dahlia's gaze zeroed in on my attire, but she didn't say anything. With one last glance around the room, she disappeared into her office.

A hand clamped down on my wrist, yanking me around. Lucas shoved into my face, the journalist's short, wiry body jostling mine. The telltale imprint of flying goggles circled his slitted eyes, and his hair was a snarled mess from his flight back from Persephone's. I checked behind him, looking for Raquel, but Lucas jerked my arm again, and I snapped my glare to his.

"Don't think this means you can steal my job," he hissed. "I fought my way into this position, and I won't let a spoiled brat like you tear me out of it. I don't care who your connections are."

His position? Lucas wrote for the society section. He had the misfortune of being immersed in all things full spectrum. If anything, I pitied him.

"I would never—"

"Save it, heiress." His fingers squeezed tighter, grinding my tendons together. "You're not getting special treatment this time, especially not while you're indebted to that harpy."

My stomach flipped. Of course he would know about Zipporah. He had been at the party. If my peers had been harsh now, what would happen when they learned about my deal with the notorious harpy? Or when Dahlia did? Obviously Lucas hadn't had a chance to tell anyone in the bullpen yet, but it was only a matter of time.

Lucas jabbed a finger at my chest. "If you somehow manage to skirt the consequences of *that* and infringe on my territory, I'll see you ruined."

Spittle landed on my chin, and I wiped it away with my free hand. Then I smiled. It spread across my cheeks unbidden, cold and foreign, born out of the absurdity that this small man thought his threat could frighten me on the same day Zipporah had nearly killed me—twice.

He released my wrist and backed away, waiting until he was out of arm's reach to hiss "*Ruined*" one more time.

The noise level in the bullpen dipped as I strode to the junior journalist table, though no one openly stared or commented. Quinn stalked at my side, his snapping tail cracking against table legs.

Unlike more seasoned writers, who each had earned a personal desk, junior journalists worked at a table crowded with older-model typewriters, stacks of paper, and a hodge-podge pile of pens and pencils. I selected an open typewriter and scooted the neighboring chair out of the way to make room for Quinn to sit beside me. Pulling elements through my bond with Quinn, I crafted a soundproof ward around the two of us. The spell built sluggishly, and when it sealed closed, I had to brace a hand against the table to stay upright. One sandwich and a short nap hadn't gone far toward restoring my depleted reserves.

Some might consider the ward rude—myself among them, if the circumstances were different—but it was no less discourteous than the comments muttered by Rafi on the other side of the table. Drawing heavily on Quinn's boost, I layered a distortion illusion into the spell, feeling the need to block out the world.

I collapsed into a hard wooden chair and slumped against the desk, bracing my forehead against my hands. A pocket of blissful quiet settled around Quinn and me.

"Why did they say those things?" Quinn asked.

"They're upset." I sank into the darkness behind my

eyelids. Would it be so terrible to miss a deadline? I could slip out and be home in less than a half hour. Crawling under the covers and not emerging for a full twenty-four hours sounded heavenly.

"Because you didn't tell them your real name?"

I scrubbed my hands over my face and let go of the unrealistic fantasy. "Partially. They're probably jealous, too. They think I have more money than them and that it's made my life easier. Maybe they're right. And you heard that some of them are bitter because they assume I was handed this job because of who my parents are, instead of earning it like they did."

"But that's wrong."

"I know, but I don't think anything I could say would change their minds. At least not right now." I mentally walled off my hurt feelings and the echo of their insults. "The best thing we can do is focus on what's important: finishing our assignment."

I read through my notes, but the words disappeared behind mental flashes of my peers' scornful expressions. Were they still whispering about me on the other side of the ward? Were they lingering, waiting for my ward to drop so they could harass me further?

I ran a finger over the tear in the paper at the end of my notes. My pen must have made the rip when Zipporah had landed on Persephone's roof. Had I thrown my journal aside or set it down? I couldn't remember. I had been so afraid, but Adelaide had been surprisingly levelheaded. Maybe I should have gone with her and hidden deeper inside the house, like Grant had said. If I had, I would have avoided the terrifying abduction, the battle, and so much pain.

Using a light touch, I prodded my ribs. Raquel hadn't healed the bruises left from Zipporah's crushing grip or soothed the muscle-deep soreness in my back. She hadn't addressed the ache in my head from repeated elemental backlash—an ache that had risen to a dull pounding since I had erected my soundproof ward. I was incredibly grateful for everything Raquel had done and hoped I would have the opportunity to repay her, but if I hadn't been so foolish as to step into the courtyard with Zipporah, I never would have needed her healing in the first place.

I would still be indebted to Zipporah, though. The harpy would still expect me to retrieve the stolen, deadly spells. My debt to Zipporah would still have been exposed to the world, and my name would still be linked to the notorious harpy. Even if I had retreated with Adelaide to the ballroom, it wouldn't have freed me from my impossible bind. I couldn't decide if that was more or less depressing than realizing nothing I had done today had bettered my situation.

I shoved back from the table, needing to move, but my own ward brought me up short. With a frustrated growl, I jerked the chair back into place.

"Can I help?" Quinn asked.

"I just need to focus." Normally, I didn't have a problem tuning out the rest of the world to write, but despite the ward, the world kept seeping into my thoughts.

Quinn arched his neck to skim my notes. "I wish we had gotten a copy of Adelaide's book."

"Me too. I bet her talk tomorrow will be fascinating."

"Then we should make sure a lot of people attend."

I smiled at Quinn's use of *we*. For the first time since entering the bullpen, I felt a kernel of my usual story-writing excitement.

"I couldn't agree more."

I outlined the article with Quinn looking on and adding his ideas. Once I started typing, the words came easily. I included the pertinent event information but made sure to infuse the article with my fascination for Adelaide and the unique way she perceived the world. If I did my job right, others would be too curious *not* to attend Adelaide's talk.

"Do you think I should try writing about the history of gargoyles like Adelaide suggested?" Quinn asked when I had put the finishing touches on the article.

"You're considering it?" I pivoted in my seat to give Quinn my full attention. "I think it's a wonderful idea."

"But how would I do it?"

"You could start with your own experiences, but you'll need to interview other gargoyles, and I can help you scour the library for other resources. Once you see what you have to work with, you can decide how you want to publish. A book would be great, but a serial in a monthly journal might be fun, too."

"I meant physically." Quinn lifted a quartz paw. "I can write in sand with my whole foot, but stories have to be written on paper. I can't hold a pen." He curled his toes, sharp stone claws curving toward citrine pads. "If I tried to use a typewriter, I'd break it."

I took his paw in mine, running my fingers over the rough patches on his toes. Even if he had the dexterity to use his toes like fingers, he wouldn't be able to press individual keys on a machine made for a human. "We'll figure something out. Maybe I can be your typist, and you can dictate to me."

"Maybe." He retracted his paw.

"Come on. Let's go home."

I packed my bag, then steeled myself and dropped the ward. A small, egotistical part of me expected a crowd of writers to be standing outside my protective bubble, twiddling their thumbs while waiting for their next opportunity to ridicule me. Instead, the room was virtually empty, with only a handful of editors still at their desks. None bothered to throw anything worse than a distracted frown in my direction.

I breathed a sigh of relief, turned in my article, and left, head high. No matter what anyone said about me, I knew I had earned my place at the *Chronicle*—today as much, if not more, than any day prior.

14

The aroma of spice muffins followed by the growling of my stomach woke me the next morning. I opened my eyes and contemplated the ragged holes in the ceiling. Scattered beams of light shone through, exposing patches of blue sky. The pile of splintered wood and crumbled plaster still lay mounded next to my bed where Grant had shoved it yesterday. I tried to look on the bright side: It was summer. At least I didn't have to worry about rain or cold weather.

Blinking away the afterimage of spotty sunlight, I crawled to the end of my bed and peered over the edge.

"Good morning," I said when I saw Quinn was awake.

He yawned, stood, and stretched, his wings spanning nearly the entire length of my small room. "Good morning."

"How did your check-in with Mika go last night?" I peeked through the open balcony door, ashamed at my relief when I saw Mika's apartment was vacant. I wasn't up for another ugly early-morning confrontation.

"I felt fine. Mostly we talked about Yarra. I hope she comes to visit."

Caught up in my own problems, I had forgotten the Kwan estate gargoyle had mentioned wanting to drop by. I considered the peaked roof of the Victorian—and the holes above my own room—and wondered if Yarra would be able to roost on such a sloped surface. If she came, Mika would work something out to make her comfortable, but it wouldn't be the first time the Victorian had proven an inconvenient place to live. I had yet to broach with her my idea of the two of us, Quinn, and Mika's cadre of gargoyles finding a more suitable house. Given the current state of our relationship, the likelihood of Mika moving anywhere with me right now was pretty abysmal.

"Wow! Look at the message bowl," Quinn said.

Returned rumor scouts were stacked in a gravity-defying column high above the rim of the bowl. By the size of the pile, every single scout I had released yesterday before Dahlia sent me on my assignment had returned with information.

Excited, I grabbed my notebook, then selected the top scout and activated it. A stranger's voice spilled out, refined and masculine.

"—reckon it's those blight ruffians behind it. No one up to any good would mess with a snare and slice."

"Prohibited spells are just what that cesspool needs to escalate their barbarity," a second male voice agreed. "The guards should roust that whole district and drive them out of the city. We shouldn't have to—"

The elements holding the recorded words unraveled before I could disband them. Undeterred, I activated the next scout.

"—have it coming," a woman's voice declared. "It's a classic case of full spectrums thinking common folk should clean up their problems. As if *I* should risk my life for their table scraps. If—"

I slashed a knife of earth through the scout, destroying it. I needed facts, not prejudices. With a tinge of reluctance, I queued up the next rumor scout.

"—and a thief's key? It's got to be a marketing stunt, like those firebirds. Sure, Airstrong 'lost' those spells, and when their daughter 'finds' them, she'll get her name and picture splashed in the paper again."

"Nathan didn't bother to include my picture," I retorted to the empty air, trying not to let the stranger's aspersions bother me.

"—are in cahoots?" The gossipy tones of an elderly woman burst from the next scout. "They attacked the Kwans' solstice ritual. I heard they tried to kill Ms. Kwan herself. I can't believe anyone would team up with a harpy, but that Grayson girl seems shady, hiding like she did—"

Her words hit like a sucker punch. If people were talking about my involvement with Zipporah, that could only mean the papers had picked up the story. I should have expected it. Zipporah's dramatic arrival and my abduction had probably been the most exciting thing to happen at a full-spectrum event in years.

"I don't think these are going to be helpful."

Quinn nodded, his ears drooping. Unfortunately, the possibility that one scout might hold a nugget of useful information meant we had to listen to them all. Together, we suffered through dozens of snippets of hearsay and conjecture. When the last scout ran out of recorded conversation, I flopped back, worn out by the casual ugliness of people's assumptions. So much for my patented spell ferreting out new leads.

Quinn peered into the message bowl. "One more. Is that from Dahlia?"

"Yep." I had saved it for last, afraid it might contain another full-spectrum assignment.

"Are you going to listen to it?"

"Yes."

"Today?"

I shot Quinn an arch look, then finally activated the message.

"You and I need to talk. Now."

Acid churned in my stomach. I hadn't realized my boss could sound so cold.

Hobbling and groaning from the stiffness in my muscles, I yanked on a pair of clean pants and a nice blouse, used the elements to tug my hair into a smooth ponytail, splashed water on my face, cleaned my teeth, and then hopped toward the door, putting a shoe on with each step. Paper crunched under my heel before I could pull the door open. Stepping back, I bumped into Quinn. He shifted aside, and I knelt, holding the paper so he could read over my shoulder.

"Well, isn't that nice." It was an invoice in Josephine's neat handwriting, itemizing the repair costs for the damaged roof. The sum totaled more than three times my monthly rent—far more than I had in savings and more than I could save out of a year's worth of wages. Stuffing the invoice into my bag, I mentally added figuring out how to pay Josephine back to my to-do list. To the *bottom* of my to-do list. Too many more important concerns vied for my attention first.

I skulked into the communal kitchen, only crossing the threshold when I was certain it was vacant. Forgoing the spice muffins, since Josephine probably hadn't intended to offer any to her least favorite tenant, I grabbed an apple.

"Is that you?" Quinn pointed with a wing tip to the dining table, where an array of newspapers had been meticulously laid out. Stomach sinking, I crossed the room to examine them.

My younger self stared back at me from the cover of the *Daily Elemental.* I lifted the gossip paper for a better look. The picture had been taken years earlier, when I was in my midteens, given my hairstyle. Beside it, a photo twice as large and ten times as grainy showed a harpy-shaped blob carrying a woman-shaped smudge in her talons. The headline read, AIRSTRONG HEIRESS CAUGHT IN HARPY'S CLUTCHES. I stopped reading after the first paragraph proclaimed I was working with Zipporah and that together we had stolen the illegal spells from Airstrong.

"That's me," I confirmed, setting the paper down with numb fingers.

The *Full Spectrum Gazette* lay beside it, featuring a much clearer photo of me. A detached part of my brain calculated the photographer's location—likely on a balcony or upper floor. They would have had to be high up to catch the fear-stricken expression on my face as Zipporah abducted me in her crushing grip. A smaller photo ran below it, showing Zipporah's full body framed against an empty sky. A scandalous amount of my inner thighs was visible as I dangled below her. Bold letters announced AIRSTRONG LOSES ANOTHER PRIZED ASSET.

My fingers shook as I unfolded the paper. The article spanned the entire front page, with key phrases printed in large font. I skimmed it, amazed at the tale they had concocted. According to the *Gazette*, Zipporah had snatched me for a ransom, one my mom had been only too eager to pay. They included a small photo of my mom sprinting to her courier cart, my satchel clutched to her chest. If the caption was to be believed, the bag was stuffed with cash.

Quinn stood with his front paws on the table, reading the *Daily Elemental*. "How can they print this? It's not true."

"It doesn't have to be. The staff at these papers might call themselves journalists, but there's nothing factual about what they print."

"Don't their readers want the truth?"

"Some people just want an entertaining story. And some people actually believe this." A spike of anger pierced my daze. I crumpled the *Full Spectrum Gazette* into a wad. Then I did the same to the *Daily Elemental*. I told myself to walk away, but I couldn't stop my eyes from jumping to the next paper. DEATH SHIPPED FOR FREE: BLACK MARKET CABAL EXPOSED AT AIRSTRONG read the *Critical Informer*'s headline. The paper had printed two pictures across the front page, one of a stern-faced middle-aged man I assumed to be Investigator O'Hara and the other of my mom, her mouth pinched and chin tilted high in defiance. Both shots were in profile and framed so it looked like they were caught mid-argument with each other. The title had been designed to inflame the public's opinion against my parents and Airstrong, and my mom's haughty expression backed it up. The *Informer* also included the same dated picture of me that the *Daily Elemental* had used, only this time it hadn't been cropped, and my mom was shown standing beside me. Both of us were dressed in our finest gowns, jewels glinting in our ears and at our throats. It had been a winter wedding, I recalled, and one of the last high-society events I had attended.

"They claim my parents and I are dealing in banned spells," I said after skimming the text. "I am, apparently, the mastermind of the whole thing. And . . . yes, they also accuse Investigator O'Hara of being my puppet. According to their 'sources,' I've been plotting this for at least a year, and O'Hara has been helping me."

Quinn growled. "It's wrong and mean."

"It's classic shock journalism. They throw the truth out the window in lieu of printing whatever will sell the most copies. It's worse than giving column space to rumors." I shredded the page, then crumpled the rest of the paper for good measure.

"If I ever see reporters from those papers, I won't give them an elemental boost. In fact, I'll make sure *no* gargoyle ever does."

Quinn's vehemence pleased me, but I tried not to let it show. He had a big heart, and I didn't want to see it diminished on my account.

"You know it's not personal, right?" I straightened a sheet of the *Critical Informer* I hadn't shredded and scanned the page. "Look at this nonsense: They're claiming the mayor has a secret basilisk army holed up beneath Focal Park and the local centaur tribes are hiding a portal that leads to the future. And that's only in this edition."

"They're intentionally misleading their readers. How can they claim to be a newspaper?"

I couldn't help but smile. Quinn had to be the first gargoyle in history to care about the ethics of journalism, and it made me proud to have him working with me. "Most people are smart enough to know they're liars."

I shoved aside the rest of the slanderous papers, not letting my eyes linger on any long enough to read headlines or examine the pictures. Instead, I picked up the *Terra Haven Chronicle*. Sensible people looked to the *Chronicle* for facts, and it would be the *Chronicle* that shaped public opinion.

I groaned. "That's the image they went with?"

"What is it?"

I angled the paper so Quinn could see the bold reprint of the reward poster taking up half the top fold. The headline—STOLEN BANNED SPELLS BELIEVED TO BE CIRCULATING IN TERRA HAVEN—sat beside it in big, accusatory letters. Seeing Nathan's name in the byline beneath it tightened the knots in my stomach. His article outlined the FPD press conference with his usual uninspired but factual style, then included extraneous facts about Airstrong's quick rise to a national company, a smattering of quotes from full-spectrum clients, all indicating they would be taking their future business elsewhere, and a brief statement that my parents had refused to answer questions.

It was diabolical in its simplicity. From the thinly veiled accusation that Airstrong's success had been handed to my parents and not earned, to the curated selection of negative quotes to the insinuation of my parents' guilt in their lack of response to his questions, Nathan had done a remarkable job of painting my parents as untrustworthy, moneygrubbing, morally ambiguous business owners without actually stating it.

"He's making it personal." I slammed down the paper. Nathan didn't like me, so he was taking it out on my parents and using the most popular newspaper in the city as his platform. Worse, he had been clever enough to stop short of open defamation. I had nothing to go to Dahlia with and no concrete reason to demand a more impartial journalist be put on the story.

I wanted to scream and rail and maybe hit something, but none of that would do anything besides delay my meeting with my boss. Grinding my teeth, I wadded up the *Chronicle* and tossed into in the empty fireplace.

"Let's go."

We ran into Josephine on the porch. Her white hair was affixed in a neat bun this morning, and her expression was pinched in concentration. Vines of wood and earth magic flowed up the porch posts. I recognized the protective intent of the spell, if not the specific weave. The complexity of it rivaled that of a full spectrum's house ward, and my landlady would never have been able to pull it off without the help of Quinn's siblings. They ranged around her, Lydia perched on the porch railing, Anya at Josephine's feet, and Herbert curled up on a chair cushion. Like Quinn, they were all close to full grown, though he was the largest. Anya's blue-and-green panther body was sleeker, more predatory compared to Quinn's robust frame. Lydia's agate swan body rivaled Anya's in size, and her enormous lion's paws no longer looked too large for her. Next to the others, Herbert could have been mistaken for a hatchling, his armadillo body true to the flesh-and-blood animal's size, but his elemental boost was no less substantial than any other gargoyle's.

"Good morning," I said, the words tight. Those papers hadn't arranged themselves on the dining table. Josephine had wanted me to see them.

"About time." My landlady shot me a sharp look, one that took in my appearance from head to toe. "Glad to see you're still alive. Now get rid of your fan club. This is a respectable neighborhood, and I won't stand for lookie-loos loitering on my sidewalk. See that they don't come back, too, or I'll summon the city guard."

My fan club? I surveyed the sidewalk. A sandy-haired man with pale skin and a bold nose stood at the base of the walkway, peering curiously in our direction. A plump gray-haired woman straightened from where she had been leaning on the mailbox, watching me expectantly. I didn't recognize either of them, but I wasn't going to argue with Josephine. Not when her gruff demeanor and minor concession to worrying about me suggested she might be getting closer to forgiving me.

I waved farewell to the gargoyles and trotted down the steps.

"Harriet Kylie Grayson?" the man asked when I reached the bottom.

My footsteps slowed. When I spotted a press badge clipped to his belt, I stopped in my tracks. Quinn bumped into me from behind, and I stumbled closer to the sidewalk.

"Xavier Hawkings, *Daily Elemental*. I was hoping to talk to you about your parents."

"I have nothing to say to you." I forced my feet to step over the invisible property line and onto the public sidewalk. Quinn stuck tight to my side.

"How often does your mom transport illegal spells?" Xavier asked.

"You'll have to take that up with Airstrong." I dodged around him, keeping a hand on Quinn's back.

"Don't be like that, Harriet. I just want to ask you a few questions."

Before I could escape, the gray-haired woman planted herself in my path, flashing her press badge too fast for me to read it. "Jen Honfleur of *Gossip Today*. Our readers are dying to find out why you're hiding from your family. Are you ashamed of them?"

"What? That's preposterous!" The words blurted out before I thought better of it. Of course it was preposterous, considering the source.

"Did you have a falling-out?" Jen pressed.

"Were you disinherited?" Xavier asked.

"Of course not. Excuse me." I cut around the pair, and they spun to keep up. Ahead, two women trotted out of the shadow of a tree, recording spheres racing ahead of them. A fifth person jogged up behind us. Three men across the street broke into a run to intercept us. I traded a worried glance with Quinn and picked up my pace.

"Why do you always travel with a gargoyle? Are you making a fashion statement?" a brainless newcomer asked.

"Or is it a bodyguard?"

"Why didn't it stop the harpy from taking you?"

I glared, appalled by their tactless ignorance. A flock of elemental recording spheres jockeyed for position above me, swarming in a claustrophobic mass. I pushed through them, curling one hand around the strap of my satchel and anchoring the other to Quinn's wing. The reporters jostled me, their questions hammering one on top of the next.

"What debt do you owe the harpy? Did you pay up yesterday?"

"How long have you been working with Zipporah?"

"I'm not—" A recording sphere thrust itself into my face, the elemental lines wrapping around my startled exhale. I shoved the bubble of magic aside with a brush of air and clamped my mouth shut.

"You were spotted cozied up with Captain Grant Monaghan yesterday. What's the nature of your relationship?"

I twisted my head, searching for a way out. The mob squeezed around me, making me fight for every step. We had barely reached the street corner, and it was another three blocks to the air bus stop. I tried not to let my panic show.

"Can we expect an engagement announcement soon?"

"Does your lover know you consort with harpies?"

How had they twisted a shared carpet ride into a romantic affair and potential marriage in less than five seconds?

"Is the captain in league with the harpy?"

"What do your parents think?"

"Do your parents owe the harpy, too?"

"Have you ever used a banned spell?"

"Are you pregnant?"

"What's your next publicity stunt going to be?"

"Is the harpy working for you?"

I was using my elbows with unabashed vigor and had nearly fought clear of the vultures when a man's patronizing voice brought me up short.

"Come on, Harriet, you're a journalist, too. Give us something we can work with."

I whipped around, my lips curled in contempt. "How dare you lump us into the same group. True journalists don't resort to these vulgar antics, and they don't commit casual character assassinations for profit. They report facts."

A camera whipped into my line of sight and snapped a picture.

"Then give us some facts. How long have your parents been stealing from Airstrong's shipments?"

"My parents are blameless. They had nothing to do with the thefts."

"How can you know? Are you secretly working with them?"

"I know my parents. They're smart and honorable. They wouldn't mess with prohibited spells, and they wouldn't steal from their own company. If you want to find the stolen spells and collect the reward, you should look elsewhere."

"Do your parents suspect you're behind the thefts? You owe the harpy. Is this your way of repaying her?"

The question chased ice through my veins. If only they knew how close they had come to the truth. I raked the entire pack of lowlifes with a scathing glare, making sure my disdain came through loud and clear. "You all disgust me. Do any of you possess a shred of journalistic integrity? Rather than ruining the reputations of my parents and Airstrong with your wild speculations, how about you do your actual jobs and investigate?"

"Tell us how, Harriet," someone in the back goaded.

"Yes, please, heiress. I've been a reporter for three decades, but I want to hear all the wisdom you've accumulated in the *months* you've been at the almighty *Chronicle*."

Anger and frustration heated my face. Quinn growled, flaring his wings protectively around me. The hecklers skittered backward, clearing a bubble of space. Through the gap, I spied the air bus rounding the corner and slowing to pick up passengers.

"I'm not going to answer any more questions. Leave me alone and stay away from my home."

For half a second, silence reigned.

"So is that a yes about the harpy working with your parents?"

"Is you dad in hiding?"

"Does your mom have him trapped inside the snare and slice?"

Swallowing my pride, I bolted for the air bus. Quinn snapped his wings wide, momentarily thwarting the reporters. They circled around him, but I had gained the lead I needed. With their footsteps pounding behind me, I sprinted for the bus, hardly slowing when I leapt onto its running board. Quinn landed on the bus's roof. The driver peered around me, then activated the propulsion spell, pulling away from the curb.

Gasping for breath, I swayed down the center aisle, staring out the back window at the stymied reporters. I expected them to look disappointed or frustrated. Instead, they appeared energized, and they scattered with more smiles than frowns on their faces.

Apparently I had given them exactly the reaction they had wanted, and I dreaded finding out what they would do with it.

Quinn and I walked in silence from the bus stop to the *Terra Haven Chronicle*. The pedestrian traffic parted around us, making way more room for Quinn than for me. My thoughts caromed from the journalists' taunts to my upcoming meeting with Dahlia, and I alternated between clenching my teeth and releasing deep sighs. Every time I attempted to focus on my most important problem—finding and exposing the Airstrong thief—my imagination leapt forward to my next empty-handed encounter with Zipporah. Whether I found the illegal spells or not, I wouldn't hand them over to the harpy, which meant I needed to come up with a brilliant alternative plan to appease her and . . . That's when my mind went blank before restarting the whole vicious cycle.

"More reporters?" Quinn asked, interrupting a vision of Zipporah dropping me atop sharp rocks from a hundred feet up.

I squinted at two men and one woman leaning against the brick wall of the *Chronicle*. Each carried a notebook, one had a camera, and all three of them perked up when they spotted us.

"Crap. Not here, too."

Recording spheres sprang into existence in front of each reporter and shot toward us. The hyenas chased after them.

"Let's make a run for it." The advancing journalists were between us and the door, but if we could make it across the threshold, they wouldn't follow us.

"I'll meet you inside in a few minutes. I'm going to let the local gargoyles know not to offer enhancements to these meanies."

My eyebrows lifted at the word *meanies*. It was the closest I had heard Quinn come to insulting someone. "All right."

Quinn took off, his ascent intentionally shallow to force the reporters to duck. Nevertheless, they hardly slowed.

"Harriet, how much longer are you going to pretend to work for the *Chronicle*?"

Pretend? Could you be more insulting?

"Will you take over Airstrong if your parents are arrested?"

There won't be an Airstrong if it comes to that.

"What happened with the harpy yesterday?"

What do you think happens when a harpy snatches up a person and carries her to a remote location? That we shared a picnic?

The three of them attempted to box me in, but after the mob outside my house, their pitiful efforts couldn't cage me. I pushed past them and yanked open the door to the *Chronicle*, biting off a knee-jerk apology when the door smacked into someone's elbow. Their questions hammered through the closing gap of the door, and I rushed up the stairs, pretending to be deaf.

I paused on the landing to collect myself, then marched

into the bullpen with my head held high, determined not to react to any hecklers. Keeping my expression neutral, I ran my eyes over the entire room. Only half the desks were occupied this early, with more journalists trickling in behind me. A few people returned my look with unfriendly glares, but no one voiced any insults.

A foot shot out from behind a desk, tripping me.

"Careful, there," Nathan said. He rose, his "helping" hand preventing me from going around him. Scorn twisted his lips into a sneer, but his eyes shone bright. He was enjoying himself.

"I don't know how I missed it at first. You have *high-society brat* written all over you." Nathan kept his voice low enough not to carry to Dahlia's office, but that didn't prevent the writers around us from hearing.

"Funny. I never mistook you for anything other than an insecure jerk." I shook free of his grip.

"We have a word for people like you. For the kind of person who, when they can't steal front-page bylines still makes sure they get press—no matter the cost." Nathan leaned close, but his voice didn't lower. "Fame whore."

I jerked away from him. Nathan pursued me, thrusting a paper in my face. I recognized the stylized font of the *Chronicle*'s society-section letterhead swirling across the top of the page, but the picture beneath it cleaved my tongue to the roof of my mouth. The photo had been taken right outside Persephone's courtyard, capturing the moment when I had stood in front of Zipporah, hand outstretched, worry clouding my face. The angle gave the impression that we were having a reasonable conversation. Nothing about the image suggested that seconds later Zipporah would attack.

Solstice Renewal Ritual Interrupted by Interloper read the headline, leaving it unclear if the interloper in question was the harpy or me. I checked the byline. Lucas Abner. How had the *Chronicle*'s society journalist gotten to the courtyard? He should have been relegated to the press room on the other side of the mansion. More important, what had the weasel printed about me?

I reached for the paper, but Nathan snatched it away.

"You were sent to the Kwan estate for a simple interview, not to make a spectacle. How do you explain this, *Harry*?"

My fingernails sank into the meat of my palms, but I wrangled my expression into a condescending smile. "To you? I don't."

"Doesn't matter. With this"—he rattled the paper—"you can kiss being Dahlia's favorite good-bye. Your days of having everything handed to you are over."

I didn't take the bait. Instead, I rolled my eyes and stalked past Nathan, his ugly laugh tightening a knot between my shoulder blades.

Taking a centering breath, I knocked on the frame of Dahlia's open door. The morning sun outlined my boss's wiry frame and spiky hair. She stood at the window, drinking from a steaming mug, and the scent of herbal tea permeated the office. When she turned from her perusal of the street to assess me, I wished I could read her thoughts, but her expression gave nothing away.

"Come in. Shut the door."

I did, then took the seat she indicated at a round table beside her desk and settled my bag on my lap. Dahlia pulled a chair close and set her mug on the table in front of her.

"Tell me about the harpy," she said.

My fingers traced a seam on my bag, and I forced them to still. The quickest way through this conversation would be to stick to the facts.

"Her name is Zipporah. I'm indebted to her. It happened while I was working on the dryad story."

"That long ago? You didn't mention making a deal with her when you turned in that article."

"No." At the time, I hadn't realized how terrible my deal had been. "I didn't want it to impact my work. And I won't let it."

"I'd say it's too late for that." Dahlia held up a hand when I opened my mouth to protest. "Raquel told me about healing you and how extensive your wounds were. She also told me how insistent you were to return and write your article afterward. I appreciate your dedication to the job. The article you wrote was everything I wanted."

I sat up straighter. "Thank you. It was a pleasure to interview Ms. Flemming."

"Imagine that. Using your connections wasn't a detriment to your writing."

I tried to accept my boss's *I told you so* with grace, which meant swallowing my argument that Adelaide had been a special case. The historian was nothing like the standard high-society partygoer. Then again, the editor in chief had probably known that when she had sent me on the assignment.

Dahlia took a sip of her tea, studying me over the rim of the mug. "Were you able to pay off the harpy?"

"Not yet."

"That troubles me, Kylie. You have a lot of complications in your life right now." She gave her head a small shake, as if arguing with herself. "If it were only your family troubles to consider, we wouldn't be having this conversation. But I can't have an employee who essentially has another boss."

"It's not like that," I blurted out.

"How can I trust that the harpy won't ask you to write something false for the paper?"

"I don't think she cares what gets printed." Probably not the best argument, but it was the truth.

Dahlia snorted. "You're likely right, but can you guarantee that you can dedicate your full attention to the assignments you're given?"

"Of course!"

"The way you did with yesterday's interview? How many future assignments will the harpy tear you away from? You were able to write up a decent account of your talk yesterday, but what if you aren't able to complete future assignments because you're pulled away? I count on my writers to deliver articles. I can't run a paper with empty columns."

I studied the grain of the wooden table, my thoughts darting, searching for the right words to convince Dahlia she could rely on me.

"Even if you could guarantee the harpy wouldn't interrupt future assignments, your reputation has been poisoned," Dahlia said. "Our readers trust us because we present unbiased news. If they believed our staff was under the influence of anyone, especially a notorious harpy, the paper would lose credibility. Which is why I took your name off the article you submitted yesterday."

My gaze flew to Dahlia's. I had been so distracted this morning, I hadn't checked to see where my article had run in the paper. It had never occurred to me that I might need to check to see if I had been given credit. I wanted to protest, but I couldn't find my voice. I could barely breathe around the tightness in my chest.

"I'm relieving you of your position until you settle your debt with the harpy. This is only a suspension. I hope you see this as the opportunity I mean it to be. Take the time to get your life on track, to sort out your identity issues, and to help your parents. The *Chronicle* will be here for you when you return." For all the compassion in Dahlia's tone and expression, I read the resolve in her eyes. She had made up her mind and wouldn't be persuaded otherwise.

I stood, a soft ringing accompanying the hollow thump of my heartbeat against my eardrums. Dahlia stopped me with a gentle touch on my forearm.

"Stay safe, Kylie."

I nodded, unable to speak. Flexing my jaw to hold back tears of frustration, I plodded to the door. Quinn sat just outside, and his stricken expression said he had heard enough to not need an explanation. Silently, he pivoted and led the way across the hushed bullpen, and everyone in our path found an excuse to get out of his way. A lump of burning hatred lodged in my throat when I caught a glimpse of Nathan's triumphant expression. Then I locked my gaze on the exit and did my best to pretend my life wasn't crumbling to quicksand beneath my feet.

My legs gave out two blocks from the *Chronicle*. I plopped down on the curb in a shady spot between two parked carriages and rested my elbows on my drawn-up knees, my hands hanging limp in front of me. Quinn hunched beside me, his drooping wings spilling across the sidewalk. Miraculously, no hack journalists had thought to cover the building's back exit, and we had slunk away, unnoticed.

"I don't understand," Quinn said.

"That makes two of us." I scrubbed my palms across my closed eyes. "That's not true. I *do* understand, but I don't agree. What if Dahlia was just saying she would hire me back? What if, when the time comes, she changes her mind and decides I'm not good enough for the *Chronicle*?" Tears spilled onto my cheeks.

"Stupid Nathan." I punched my thigh, wishing it were my slimy coworker. I wanted so badly to blame someone else, and he was the obvious choice—for outing me, for slandering my reputation, for adding more suspicion on my parents. But I couldn't fault him for everything. "Stupid *me.* Why did I ever make that deal with Zipporah?" Bitterness choked my words. I had attained my dream job, and then I had screwed it up.

Quinn cupped a wing around my shoulders, scooting closer to me. "You're not stupid. You're curious and smart—"

"I walked into a harpy's nest because I thought it would make a great story. That's practically the definition of stupid."

"You're always thinking about how to write one-of-a-kind articles. That's the definition of a great journalist."

I tipped my head to rest it against Quinn's shoulder. He could have reminded me that he had warned me against following Grant up to Zipporah's nest all those weeks ago when this mess had started, but he hadn't. Quinn chose to see me in the best light, and I wanted more than anything to be worthy of his high opinion.

More tears dripped from my chin for failing to live up to everyone's expectations—Dahlia's, Quinn's, and my own. A knot of self-loathing lodged in my gut, and my brain heaped on the misery, reminding me of how utterly selfish I was acting. Here I was, crying over a temporary setback while my mom was being investigated by the FPD and dealing with the loss of the business she and Dad had built with their bare hands. If I were a better daughter, I wouldn't waste one mournful second over my own misfortunes and would instead be focusing on keeping my mom from being convicted of crimes she didn't commit.

"Listen to me." I dashed my tears away with a disgusted huff. "Yesterday I was moaning that my job was preventing me from tracking down the Airstrong thief. I should be thanking Dahlia for suspending me." My voice caught, but I forced myself to go on, as if by speaking the words, I could make them true. "Now I have all the time I need to decipher my seed's latest clue, help my mom, and come up with a clever way of surviving long enough so I can be rehired."

"What *are* we going to do about Zipporah?" Quinn crooked his head, his expression earnest and his eyes filled with faith that I would have an answer.

Blotting my cheeks with my shirt, I took a deep breath and sat up straighter. "We're going to put our journalistic skills to good use: It's time to do some research."

———

IN CASE ANY UNSCRUPULOUS GOSSIPMONGERS HAPPENED TO indulge in the rare art of fact-checking, I chose a seat at the back of the library, hidden behind rows of bookcases. Quinn caught up a few minutes later after stopping to talk with the library's resident gargoyle. Bernette's long-term residence over the information capital of the city had rubbed off on her: The gargoyle kept an ear tipped toward the street, listening for interesting conversations in the high-traffic courtyard below. Along with being Quinn's friend, she was a closely guarded source who had helped us out more than once in the past.

"What did Bernette say?" I asked Quinn, my fingers crossed for luck.

"No one's seen the spells, but there's a lot of excitement about the reward. Also, a lot of people suspect you or your parents took the spells. Bernette called them all mush-brains. She knows you're innocent."

I sighed and let my fingers relax. I appreciated the gargoyle's faith in me, but I would have been more grateful for a solid lead.

"What about you?" Quinn peered at the stacks of books on the low table in front of me. I had divided them by subject: thunderbirds, banned spells, and a month's worth of national newspapers.

"I'm just getting started. Want to divvy it up?"

"Sure." Quinn selected *Avian Predators of the Sea.* Holding the book open against the table with one large paw, he gingerly flipped through the pages with the tip of a claw until he reached the section on thunderbirds. He tugged the book closer to the edge of the table and began to read, his body freezing in place like a statue, only his eyes moving. I grabbed *Dangerous Birds of the Northern Hemisphere* and started reading. Five minutes later, the book had confirmed what I already knew—mainly, anyone with a grain of sense avoided thunderbirds at all costs.

"Did you know thunderbirds hunt in packs, or rather, in flocks?" Quinn asked. "This book says they're one of the only birds to do so."

"That's what this book says, too." It also included graphic details about thunderbirds' preferred method of gutting prey with their sharp beaks and formidable talons.

"They stun their prey with bolts of lightning?" Quinn's eyebrows rose as he read further.

"Yep." Why couldn't my everlasting seed have shown a magpie feather or maybe a hummingbird's? Or even the feather of a bird that lived close by. Thunderbirds lived exclusively near salt water, and the closest ocean was over a week's flight from Terra Haven.

I set *Dangerous Birds* aside and picked up *Meteorological Phenomenon Large and Small.*

"They hunt in storms." Quinn flipped a page. "That must be how they got their name."

"I think tossing around lightning makes thunder sounds,

too. Oh, wait. This book says they can also create thunderstorms. Let's see . . ." I skimmed the technical text about cold fronts, air currents, and vapor, slowing to read the pertinent details about thunderbirds. "Basically the shafts of their feathers contain water, their bodies heat it, and it evaporates, which creates the same conditions that are needed to make a cloud, more or less. Get enough thunderbirds together in one location, and they create a perpetual storm."

Quinn's brow furrowed. "How many does it take?"

"There's a footnote. The author estimates twenty birds, but she also says no one has ever gotten an accurate count at the precise moment of the formation of a storm."

"I hope we need to get near only *one*. Did you know a thunderbird's average wingspan is twelve to fifteen feet?"

I shook my head. I had imagined them smaller, closer to the size of an eagle than a harpy. "Maybe my seed won't require us to get near one at all. It could be pointing to some other thunderbird reference."

"Maybe."

Grimly, we both reached for another book. After rereading the same facts about thunderbirds, I switched to hunting through the newspapers for articles about recent thefts across the nation. A prized stallion, three dirigibles, a wyvern, assorted valuables, and bizarrely, a warehouse of smoked cheese wheels had gone missing in the last month, but none of the thefts shared similar characteristics with the Airstrong heists. It looked like whoever had targeted Airstrong hadn't branched out to any other crimes.

When I finished the last paper in the pile, I reluctantly opened the morning edition of the *Terra Haven Chronicle*. Nathan's smug expression flashed in my mind's eye, and the paper crinkled in my fist. His article in the evening edition had made my parents out to be criminals, and it was only the beginning of the investigation. Now that the thefts were public knowledge, readers would expect regular updates. I hated that a small part of me eagerly anticipated his next article, if only so I might glean an insight from it that he had overlooked. Memorizing every recorded fact about thunderbirds wasn't sparking inspiration. I needed a genuine lead.

With equal parts disappointment and relief, I examined the front page, finding only articles about the first summer solstice ritual held at the newly restored and reopened Focal Park. Nathan's byline ran beneath the top article. I tossed the section aside, determined not to give my jealousy more fuel. At least the celebratory events of yesterday had eclipsed my parents' troubles for the time being.

My interview with Adelaide ran in the middle of the entertainment section, taking up only half a column. But the size of the article and the placement weren't the most important factors. It was the quality of the writing that mattered. Rereading it, I was proud of my article. It had been published virtually unedited . . . except for the glaring change of my byline from "Kylie Grayson" to "Staff."

I resisted the urge to crumple the newspaper only because it would be offensively loud in the serene library. Against my better judgment, my fingers continued to flip through the paper, stopping on Lucas's article at the front of the society section.

I scowled at the picture of Zipporah and me that Nathan had so smugly shoved in my face earlier. The harpy didn't look half as terrifying in print as she did in real life. I, however, looked ten times as pathetic. Disgusted, I folded the paper so I couldn't see the image and read Lucas's article. He hadn't spared a detail, covering Zipporah's arrival, attack, and abduction; my mom's and Grant's rushed departures; Seradon and Raquel's flight; and quotes from the guests regarding my character and my return to high society. It concluded with, *Harriet Grayson was spotted in Terra Haven a few hours later, seemingly unharmed. Her dealings with the harpy remain a secret.*

My jaw clenched, and I forced it to relax. Lucas was a solid writer, and he hadn't slandered me the way Nathan might have. The quotes he had included varied from offensive to complimentary, and none of them had been spoken by Wetherill. But my appreciation for Lucas's objectivity withered when I spotted his second article printed directly beneath the first, in which he rehashed the "Airstrong scandal," disparaged my mom's business decisions, and speculated about the alliances being forged and broken—mostly broken—between full-spectrum families and my mom. Where the first article had been loaded with facts, this one relied on rampant conjecture to meet its word count.

"I can't believe the *Chronicle* printed this," I growled. It gave validity to all the outlandish rumors the gossip presses had been printing and added no real value to the overall story of the thefts. It was pure entertainment fluff . . . exactly what this section's readership wanted.

I thumbed through the rest of the society pages, stopping cold when my finger landed on a picture of Persephone. It had been taken at yesterday's party while guests were arriving. Persephone smiled charmingly at the photographer, her arm draped around the waist of two older gentlemen. But it wasn't the guests that drew my attention. It was the pair of pearl earrings Persephone wore. I didn't remember noticing those on her at the party, and they looked suspiciously like . . .

No. That's ridiculous.

I pulled the reward poster out of my bag and compared the sketch of the beguiling beads with the earrings in the photo. The newsprint blurred the delicate lines of the jewelry, but I was almost certain Persephone's pearls were marquise shaped. Just like the beguiling beads.

A chill ran down my spine. I was grasping. I had to be.

Because it couldn't be this easy.

Wouldn't I have noticed if Persephone had used magic to manipulate me? No, of course not. That was why the spell was prohibited.

I dove through my memories, reviewing my conversations with Persephone. What was the first thing she had said? We had talked about renovations, because the wing of her house I had stumbled upon had been so dilapidated—though in retrospect, the disrepair of those rooms seemed more from neglect than in preparation for a remodel. Then there was the dress. Last night as I was crawling into bed, I had marveled that Persephone had talked me into it. Accepting the hideous gown had felt like the polite thing to do, especially since my own clothing had been ripped and bloodstained—because of spook squirrels Persephone's weakened wards had allowed onto her property. Her flimsy explanation for the deadly varmints' presence had assuaged all my curiosity yesterday, but now I had a dozen follow-up questions I wished I would have asked. For instance, even a weakened ward should have prevented human predators from infiltrating her property. Plus, she claimed to have only weakened the wards for the day of the ritual, which shouldn't have been long enough for a pack of bloodthirsty rodents to make themselves at home. And what about the overgrown forest? Persephone had dismissed it as temporary neglect while she tended to household projects, but it would have taken years for the trees to become so overgrown. What about the bramble ward? She hadn't even bothered with an explanation, merely waved it aside as a—what had she called it?—a *bothersome* thing.

I couldn't believe I had been so easily distracted, and not just once, either; Persephone had repeatedly sidetracked me with feeble explanations and excuses, and I had gone along with each one of them.

I spun the newspaper and reward poster around for Quinn to examine. "Does it look like Persephone is wearing the beguiling beads to you?"

He squinted. "Maybe."

I tapped my finger against my chin. What if I was wrong? All I had to go on was a grainy photo and my own anomalous behavior. Neither were compelling enough to risk getting my mom's hopes up or poisoning an old friendship. It certainly wasn't enough to convince an FPD investigator to question a full-spectrum head of house.

I imagined the holes Investigator O'Hara would poke in my theory, and they were numerous. For starters, Persephone was an upstanding citizen of Terra Haven, without a criminal history. She didn't know enough about Airstrong's shipping practices to have pulled off such a complex heist. Even if she did, she wouldn't have possessed the insider knowledge necessary to know which crates the illegal spells were being shipped in, let alone the specific spells being shipped and how to replace each with an item of equal weight.

It made more sense that Persephone had purchased the earrings from the thief—or had received them as a gift.

Luther Wetherill, Persephone's new fiancé, might have had the necessary insider knowledge or the means of obtaining it. He would be the first to benefit from Airstrong getting bad press, too, which gave him a motive. He had a reputation of being cutthroat, as he had proven when he had jumped to disparage my parents when the firebirds had gone missing. But the difference between denigrating the competition and stealing from them was vast. Wetherill had no need to steal banned spells. He was far wealthier than my parents, so the promise of the spells' black-market worth wouldn't entice him. Plus, he had his own social and business reputation to maintain, and as a full spectrum, he protected his image more closely than his riches. As much as I wanted to fit Wetherill into the role of our thief, I couldn't allow my opinion of the jerk to cloud my thinking. Nor could I accuse Persephone of being an accomplice to a federal crime just because she had terrible taste in men.

Maybe if I talked with Persephone, I could learn something . . . No. That would be a disaster. So long as Persephone wore the beguiling beads—*if* the earrings were the beguiling beads—I wouldn't be able to trust a word out of her mouth.

Of course, for all I knew, Persephone *had* told the truth to every question I had asked. Full spectrums were known for their eccentricities. It could be desperation making me see a connection to the beads that didn't exist.

Yet, a familiar tingle tickled my fingertips, telling me I was on the cusp of a story. I could either talk myself out of following this lead or trust my instincts.

"I need more tangible proof than a single grainy photo."

"Where do we get that?" Quinn asked.

I blinked, startled from my reverie. "We get proof right here, if we're lucky."

I hustled to the help desk. Quinn trotted after me, his feet ringing on the stone floor. A trio of librarians stood behind the counter, and I beelined for Dione, a young woman with black hair, dark skin, and a bright smile.

"Kylie, I mean, Ms. Harriet Grayson, you look like you're

chasing a story," Dione said knowingly, having helped me with more than one research project in the past.

"Call me Kylie, please. And, yes. Though it's, ah, private."

"Of course. Come with me."

Dione led the way to an empty section of the library, her stride brisk, and when she stopped and faced us, her eyes were alight with interest. Gratitude swelled in my chest. Obviously Dione had read Nathan's article since she had addressed me by my real name, but it didn't appear to matter to her. Her usual friendliness and professionalism hadn't changed. I wanted to give her a hug but restrained myself.

"We're looking for information on the Kwan family, specifically Persephone. Friends, businesses, hobbies, her engagement . . ." I grimaced, anticipating sifting through stacks of gossip-filled articles. "Preferably truthful accountings, not rumors." Dione possessed a librarian's unique magic: an incredible memory. She would know which recent publications contained articles worth our time. With her curating our research material, we would shave hours of pointless hunting off our search.

"Got it. I'll bring what I find to your table."

"Thank you. Oh, and have you ever heard of Aurora Isle?" Adelaide had mentioned it right before Zipporah interrupted. If something in the Kwans' past had been a keystone moment in history, maybe it would be relevant. It was a stretch, but given the dearth of leads, I wasn't going to overlook a single possibility.

"I'll see what I can find."

Dione darted off with a smile, and Quinn and I returned to our table. I stacked the books we had abandoned to one side, then spread out the rest of the *Chronicle*'s society section. Together, we scoured the articles about the Kwan solstice ritual, searching for anomalous events that might support my theory. However, the most unusual event reported was everyone's delight and surprise over the unsurpassed success of the ritual.

"I guess her plan to make the ritual dramatic worked." I sat back, rubbing ink stains from my fingertips.

"It would have been fun to have participated. Yarra told me about past rituals. They sounded amazing."

"As amazing as besting a harpy in battle?" I winked to show Quinn I was teasing, and he grinned.

"Probably not."

Dione materialized beside me, her arms laden with reference materials. I swept the paper aside and helped her situate her findings on the table.

"These include recent mentions of Persephone, mostly of her engagement." Dione skimmed the top third off the pile and set them aside. She pointed to the remaining stack. "And these are publications that covered recent major full-spectrum events, though I can't be sure Persephone is mentioned. But I suggest starting here." She handed me an oversized book with a gold-embossed title: *Notable Spectrums of Terra Haven.* "Give me ten minutes, and I bet I can find something about that isle." She whisked away before I could thank her.

I flipped through the massive tome to the Kwan family tree. It spanned several pages, going back to the original settlers on the continent, long before Terra Haven had been founded. Not only were names, siblings, marriages, children, and birth and death dates listed for each family member, but most also included each individual's profession and elemental skills. A notation for full-spectrum-level powers marked every single name from the start . . . until Persephone's parents. The FSPP marker was also conspicuously missing from their daughter's information, too.

"Persephone isn't a full spectrum?" Quinn asked.

"She has to be." If even a hint of lower skill levels appeared among full-spectrum bloodlines, the high-society papers would have pounced. It was the kind of story they would fixate on for weeks, if not months or years. Yet I had never heard a whisper of Persephone or any Kwan being anything less than full spectrum.

Bending closer, I read the small print beneath Persephone's name. She had tested borderline full-spectrum strength in fire, air, and water, but not in wood and earth. Her scores ranked her as a more powerful elemental than 90 percent of the population—myself included—but not high enough to qualify for full-spectrum pentacle potential status.

I set the book down, stunned.

"Fascinating, isn't it?" Dione asked, returning with a handful of yellowing periodicals. "The Kwans aren't the first to keep their lower-scoring family members a secret. Most high-society family trees have at least one or two who slip below the official full-spectrum mark, but with the right breeding, they usually bounce back. I'm sure Persephone's children won't have a problem surpassing their mom's elemental talents, given who their father will be. Anyhow, these were all I could find on the isle. Let me know if you need help with anything else."

I thanked Dione and watched her walk away, not really seeing her. Maybe Persephone didn't have terrible taste in men. Maybe she had calculated taste. I should have realized she wouldn't marry for love but for the advantages her spouse could give her and her children. Persephone might not technically be a full spectrum, but she had been raised to think like one.

All of which was interesting—and sad—but not incriminating.

For the next hour and a half, Quinn and I numbed our brains on the gossip of high society. Persephone attended parties. Persephone attended pegasus races. Persephone shopped. Persephone went to the theater. Persephone didn't attend a party. Was there a rift between Persephone and the party's host? Persephone wore the same gown to an event as another woman. Was it the dressmaker's fault? Would the shop go out of business now that all full-spectrum women were boycotting its wares?

Just when I thought it couldn't get any worse, I reached the announcement date of Persephone's engagement. Every gossip magazine had a different take on the planned nuptials, and entire trees were wasted to print speculation about when and where the wedding would take place, what Persephone would wear, and how much money would go into the event. A headache lodged behind my eyes, and my stomach grumbled long before I reached the bottom of the stack of useless papers. Quinn flipped listlessly through his own pile. I was about to call off our fruitless hunt for anything useful among the unbounded drivel when I reached the tiny pile of aged papers. A grudging spark of curiosity pushed through my hunger pains. Dione hadn't been able to find much on Aurora Isle. It wouldn't take long to determine why Adelaide had mentioned the place, and then we could break for lunch. Maybe inspiration would strike once I was full.

I missed the reference to the isle the first time through the worn paper because I was focusing on the articles. It wasn't until the second pass that I spotted the ad embedded in the middle of the entertainment section. Spanning three quarters of a column and featuring twelve different fonts, it touted the healing properties of the spa and luxury retreat built on Aurora Isle.

"'Savor the curative properties of Aurora Lake's salt water, where good health is restored and prosperity follows you home,'" I read aloud. "Bold claims."

Flipping to the front of the paper, I noted the date. The edition was over seventy years old. The paper beneath it was even older and featured an article-like ad for the resort. Apparently, when healers failed, Aurora Isle could be counted on to cure the sick. The text detailed a story that read like a myth in which an ancient emperor from a faraway land had traveled to Aurora Isle to live out the last of his sickly days in the famously fair weather. Instead, he had recovered, thanks to the elixir-like properties of the salt lake. Restored of mind and body, the emperor had returned home to rule for decades longer, and his country enjoyed unprecedented abundance.

"They make this place sound like it could perform miracles," I said.

"It was owned by Judith and Monroe Kwan." Quinn used the pad of a paw to shift another yellowed paper in my direction. The pages crackled with age, and a delicate spell held the seams together.

I examined the faded picture of a couple standing in front of a fancy resort. AURORA ISLE, A NEW DAWN FOR HEART AND HEALTH, read the headline. I checked the Kwan family tree. Judith and Monroe were Persephone's great-great-grandparents.

"It says it was a healing center, and it's within a day's trip of Terra Haven." Quinn pointed to a crude map included with the article.

"How have I never heard of it?" I scrutinized the map, unable to pinpoint the location. Flipping to the next paper, this one a mere fifty years old, I found Aurora Isle mentioned in a small article buried near the bottom of the last page. "According to this, the resort closed due to an 'unfortunate change in the local climate that brought about longer and longer periods of rain.'"

A tingle shot through my fingers and up my spine. Salt water. Lots of rain. It sounded like the kind of place a thunderbird would live.

"Wait here." I rushed to the file drawers containing maps and grabbed one that showed major geographical landmarks around Terra Haven. Quinn nudged aside books to make room on our low table. Triangulating the approximate location based off the crude map in the dated newspaper, I traced my finger across the current map to an amoeba-shaped shaded dot.

"Dead Man's Swamp," Quinn read.

I double-checked the new map against the old, then darted through the bookshelves to the local geography section. I returned minutes later with *Terra Haven Traveler Beware*, fifth edition. The book was organized alphabetically and included a succinct entry on Dead Man's Swamp. About fifty years earlier, right around the time Aurora Isle closed its doors, the area was classified as hazardous due to the perpetual rainstorms that plagued the area, often accompanied by lightning and thunder. All train tracks, flight paths, roadways, and hiking trails were diverted in the name of public safety. A decade later, the region was given its new, ominous name.

"This is where your everlasting seed wants us to go, isn't it?" Quinn looked queasy.

"Nonstop thunderstorms over a salt lake." I danced in

place. "This is it. We have a connection between Persephone and thunderbirds."

Maybe I should have been scared, but I was too excited. We were one step closer to solving the Airstrong thefts. Finally, something was going right.

17

I forced myself to sit rather than sprint for the doors. I needed to be smart about this.

I couldn't confront Persephone on my own, not while—*if*—she possessed the beguiling beads. I didn't have the ability to detain or arrest her myself. Nor could I take my theory to Investigator O'Hara. An FPD investigator wouldn't arrest anyone based on my suspicions or my everlasting seed. But I knew in the marrow of my bones that I was on the right track: However improbable, Persephone had something to do with the thefts of the banned spells.

To prove it, I needed evidence, and for that, I needed help. Also, being the maligned subject of unfriendly press had recently taught me that if I wanted to prove Persephone's guilt and my parents' innocence beyond a doubt, I needed someone impartial to bear witness.

In other words, I needed Grant.

Unfortunately, I didn't know where he was. If I sent him a message, it could be tonight or even tomorrow before he saw it. The thought of waiting that long made me want to crawl out of my own skin with impatience. It looked like I was finally going to do what Grant had accused me of so often in the past: use a spell to track his whereabouts.

I told Quinn my plan, and we made quick work of returning our books to the circulation desk before jogging out of the library.

"This might take a minute," I said. I wasn't strong enough to craft a tracker that could pinpoint Grant from a long distance. Instead, I created twelve cruder reverse-tracking spells, releasing them as if counting off the hours on a clock. If a tracker encountered Grant's magical signature, it would return to guide me toward his location. Time and distance weakened the spell, so if Grant was outside the city, this wouldn't work. I prayed he would be close by.

"Now what?" Quinn asked when the last tracker disappeared over the library's roof.

"Now we wait."

Quinn lounged in the shade with a gargoyle's patience, drowsing, but I paced. We had a lead. Standing still was torture.

Time slowed. Traffic ebbed in and out of the library. Pigeons scuttled around the open pentagon in front of the building, nibbling up crumbs dropped by diners at the outdoor cafés. The sun shifted across the unblemished blue sky. It was an idyllic, peaceful afternoon, and every serene second that passed grated on my nerves.

Finally, a tracker returned. Sprinting down the steps, I scooped it out of the sky. Its subtle nudge pulled southward, and I pivoted to follow it. Quinn leapt to his feet and rushed to catch up.

We speed-walked from one street to the next, sweating in the hot sun. A bus would have been faster, but since I didn't know our destination, I couldn't rely on the bus's route to take us to the right location. I dearly wished I owned my own flying carpet or that I could rent one. However, considering how much I owed Josephine for the roof's repairs, I had to prioritize frugality.

The tracker guided us through downtown and into the residential neighborhoods beyond it. The buildings we passed grew gradually more dilapidated, the streets narrower, and the yards more run-down. I kept my eyes open for trouble. The city guard could never fully stamp out the gangs that claimed the fringes of the aptly named blight district, and criminal activity often bled outward to these blocks. Quinn stalked beside me, doing nothing in particular to look intimidating, but more than one person found a reason to cross to the opposite sidewalk.

I stopped several streets short of the actual blight. Leaning against the side of a hole-in-the-wall general store, I crafted a new tracker and released it. When it returned less than five minutes later, confirming Grant was in the blight, not somewhere beyond it, I settled in to wait. Grant had to be close, and he wouldn't welcome me showing up while he was battling the latest threat to the city.

"We're not that far from home," Quinn said, examining the nearby rooftops.

I glanced at the street signs. "About three blocks away," I agreed, surprised. I never had a need to come down this street. The *Chronicle* and all the decent restaurants and shops were in the opposite direction. I hadn't quite realized how bad the area was, and I silently apologized to Josephine. My landlady liked to claim she held back the blight, and I had often privately scoffed. Perhaps her boasts were more truthful than I realized.

"I hate waiting." I started to send the tracker out again to see if Grant was coming closer or moving farther away, but I stopped myself. I could afford a few minutes of patience.

After all, it wasn't as if we could dash off and arrest Persephone the moment I found Grant. We still needed proof.

I ran through the facts once more. I had a hard time picturing Persephone sneaking into an Airstrong warehouse and swapping out the banned and booster spells. She seemed too . . . shallow to pull off such a complicated heist. If not for my everlasting seed linking thunderbirds to the Kwan family, I might have dismissed my theory entirely.

"It's got to mean something that Persephone is connected with Dead Man's Swamp. But if she's our thief, what's her motive?" I paced the sidewalk, hoping movement would generate an answer.

Quinn sat, head swiveling back and forth to track me. "Money?"

"Maybe." The designated guest areas of Persephone's mansion had been predictably opulent, but elsewhere, the neglect had been striking, especially in the overgrown forest. If Persephone sold the stolen spells on the black market, the proceeds would go a long way toward fixing up her property.

Yet, if she was so cash-strapped, why had she hosted such an expensive event?

I mentally scoffed at myself for having momentarily forgotten the reason why full spectrums did anything: for appearances, of course. In high society, status was everything. Hosting the solstice ritual had transformed Persephone into the woman of the hour. The papers had raved about how well she had pulled off the party. No one would suspect the Kwans weren't as prosperous as Persephone pretended to be now.

"Her engagement," I blurted out. "Is it real, or did she use the beguiling beads to convince Wetherill to marry her?"

Quinn's brow furrowed; then he shook his head. "No, they were engaged before the first theft."

But what about after? Had Wetherill known of his fiancée's money problems before the engagement? Maybe Persephone had needed to use the beguiling beads to keep him from bolting when he realized he wasn't getting a full-spectrum bride.

I shoved my fingers through my hair, frustrated by my lack of answers. My pacing had drawn the attention of a thick-necked man and his knife-sharpening companion sitting on the porch of a house across the street. Two houses down, a pair of teens had emerged to throw balls of fire at metal cans propped up on a rickety railing. Resisting the urge to draw a ward around myself, I sat on the curb and flapped my shirt, trying to stimulate a breeze. How much longer was Grant going to take?

"Here." Quinn stretched a wing over my head, shielding me from the sun.

"Thank you."

Pulling out my notebook, I jotted down my thoughts, hoping that getting everything down on paper would inspire a fresh idea. It didn't.

"Whatever Grant's doing, it can't be as pressing as this discovery," I groused.

"He's a guardian of the city. I'm sure he's doing something important and probably dangerous."

My shoulders slumped, and I released a half-formed elemental message sphere. Quinn was right; Grant didn't need me distracting him. Leaning against Quinn's forelegs, I took a deep breath and let it out slowly. I could be patient. I could sit here, doing nothing, while the FPD investigator built a case against my mom. While Persephone plotted her next theft. While she hid the earrings or sold them and I never got the chance to prove my mom's innocence.

I ducked out of Quinn's shade and shoved to my feet with a frustrated growl.

"He's here," Quinn announced.

Grant jogged around the corner at the opposite end of the block. My stomach performed a tap dance and my pulse sped up. Sweat glistened across Grant's forehead. Dark smears that looked like tar or oil splattered his gray uniform. He scanned the buildings on either side of the street, his gaze jumping from person to person, shadow to shadow, and across the roofs, always vigilant for danger.

I waved. His eyes narrowed, and he slowed to a walk. Shifting his gaze over my shoulder, he made a subtle patting motion. I turned in time to see Seradon slip out of an alley farther up the street. She straightened from a crouch, exasperation replacing her cautious expression.

"The sooner you clear your debt with that trash bird, the better it will be for all of us," she said when she reached my side. Sweat, or perhaps water, plastered her short hair to her scalp and soaked the top of her uniform.

"What do you— Oh." The lessening of Grant's urgency once he saw me. Seradon's stealthy approach from a second angle. They must have thought I was in danger. "I didn't mean to alarm anyone. I just need to talk with Grant."

I glanced around, unsurprised that every porch on the street was now vacant, the occupants having found somewhere more important to be while FPD roamed past.

"Your mom and I had a nice talk on the way home yesterday."

Seradon's casual tone sent a frisson of alarm up my spine.

"She's under the impression that you're romantically interested in the captain," Seradon continued.

"She what?" I hissed. Grant was still half a block away. Close enough to hear if Seradon didn't keep her voice down.

"I assured her you were and that I thought it might be mutual. We were wondering how serious your relationship is and where you see it going."

"*We?*" I gaped at Seradon, shocked to hear my mom's words come out of her mouth.

Seradon laughed and slapped me on the back, jarring my mouth closed. "I'll give you some time to think about it."

"Gee, thanks." My words came out strangled. Grant had almost reached us, and his gaze missed nothing. His hearing likely hadn't, either. I willed my cheeks to cool and didn't meet his eyes.

Fortunately, the rest of his team rounded the far street corner, and I didn't have to pretend to be distracted. Winnigan, Marciano, and Velasquez escorted three scraggly men in null cuffs between them. The captured men looked like different versions of the same person, their brown hair all shaved close to their scalps, their bland beige clothes matching, their slumped postures identical. A net of wood-element bindings wove between the captives, herding them together, and Marciano walked with a hand clamped on one of the men's shoulders. The large wood elemental's uniform remained pristine. The same couldn't be said for Winnigan and Velasquez, who brought up the rear. Velasquez looked as if he had rolled in the oil that splattered Grant, his uniform more sticky tar than standard-issue gray. The same grime smeared half his face, but that didn't stop him from grinning. Winnigan, on the other hand, looked ready to kill someone. Her uniform clung to her skin as if she had gone for a swim fully clothed, and her hair hung in wet, lanky clumps, the right side a foot shorter than the left.

"You can hardly tell," Velasquez assured her, though his tone lacked earnestness.

Winnigan shot him a glare that would have drawn blood on a less sturdy individual. She spun a spell down her uniform, flinging a shocking amount of water out of the garment. Somehow, most of the flying droplets landed on Velasquez. He wiped off his face with the back of his hand, then flapped his shirt.

"Thank you. You're not still mad, are you?"

Winnigan snarled a curse. She fisted the shorn—no, *burnt*—half of her hair and shoved the melted mess into Velasquez's face. He danced aside, gagging.

"It stinks. It's ugly. And do you know how long it took to grow it this length? Years. And now I have to cut it." Winnigan leaned into the middle prisoner's personal space. He cringed away from the petite woman as she hissed, "I'm going to see that you suffer."

"They're already going to prison for life," Marciano rumbled.

"They're lucky they are, too."

The criminals scrunched their shoulders toward their ears, steps quickening. Velasquez dropped back, a grin flashing across his face. Winnigan spotted his amusement and punched him in the side. He grunted, rubbing his ribs, but his smirk didn't disappear.

My fingers tingled as I studied the three captives and the filthy squad. Whatever the men had done and whatever fight had taken place would definitely make a great article...

. . . For someone who still had a job at the *Chronicle.*

I stuffed my hands into my pockets. Clearing my parents' name was more important than reporting on these men's crimes, but that didn't take away the sting of remembering I had been suspended.

"Looks like more trouble just showed up." Velasquez glared at me as the group came to a halt.

Grant favored him with a raised eyebrow. "Escort our firebugs to the jail, Velasquez. Seradon, you're with him. Marciano and Winnigan, you're dismissed."

Velasquez scowled, and Seradon grimaced. Marciano handed the elemental binding to Seradon, then scooped Winnigan under his arm. Tossing me a wave, Seradon prodded the prisoners back into motion.

Grant waited until his team was out of earshot before turning to face me.

"You couldn't wait for another kiss, so you hunted me down?" he asked.

I blinked, speechless. The last thing I had expected to come out of Grant's mouth was a teasing comment. I had seen him joke before, but not often. His eyes, however, remained guarded.

I scrunched my nose. "I'm afraid my intentions were more serious. It has to do with the thefts."

"Ah."

Grant placed his hand on my lower back, guiding me in the opposite direction of his team, toward my home. Quinn fell in on Grant's other side. I didn't comment on the acrid combination of oil and smoke wafting from Grant's clothing. After all, I had smelled much worse in his company. Besides, despite the afternoon heat, the warmth of his palm seeping through the thin material of my shirt felt nice.

Why hadn't I said yes to his question? Would he have kissed me right there on the street? Was tracking him down for a kiss now an option? That was . . . intriguing.

"Kylie?"

Realizing he had caught me daydreaming, I blurted out the first thing that came to mind. "Are there thunderbirds in Dead Man's Swamp?"

I didn't need to spell out my reason for asking; Grant had seen my everlasting seed.

"Yes." His hand fell away from my back.

"Do the Kwans still own land up there?"

"I believe so."

I pulled the newspaper out of my bag and held up Persephone's picture. "I think she was wearing the beguiling beads yesterday."

Grant squinted at the grainy photo, his skepticism obvious. Before he could voice his doubts, I launched into a recounting of the state of the Kwan mansion and grounds, and how easily Persephone had explained it all away. "And the spook squirrels. Nobody, let alone the head of a full-spectrum family like Persephone, would ever allow those to invade their property. It's not just dangerous; it's the kind of elemental mismanagement guaranteed to tarnish a reputation. My editor at the *Chronicle* would have leapt at the story, as would any other paper in the city." I skipped mentioning that I had been suspended to make my point. "I should have been eager to take that story straight to Dahlia, but after talking to Persephone, I basically forgot about the spook squirrels."

"Your logic is that Persephone happens to be in possession of an illegal spell stolen from your parents because she convinced you not to follow up on a random story?"

I planted a fist on my hip. "When have you ever known me to give up on a story?"

Grant studied me, expressionless.

"I didn't plan on leaving Kylie's side during the party,"

Quinn said, "but Persephone convinced me to go up to the roof with Yarra."

"That's right!" He had been adamant about sticking to my side until Persephone had suggested he would be more comfortable on the roof.

Quinn twisted to peer up at Grant. "Yarra said something that reminded me of the interview; otherwise I don't know if I would have thought to come down. That's not like me."

Grant held his gaze before nodding slightly. "I've been replaying the party in my head and can't figure out why I let Persephone lead me away from Kylie." His frown settled on me. "The whole reason I showed up at that catered torture session was to protect you."

I winced to hear him put it so baldly—wishing he would have instead confessed to attending the party because he was infatuated with me—but a bubble of excitement squirmed through my midsection. Grant believed me. "It was the earrings. She's using the beguiling beads."

"Maybe. Persephone is a persuasive woman even without magic."

I knew Grant was playing devil's advocate, but a stab of jealousy made me snap, "Or she could have all the stolen spells."

"She's not a typical thief. It's more likely she was simply foolish enough to buy the beads off the black market."

"Either way, she would have information that could clear my parents."

Grant shook his head. "Persephone doesn't have any obvious motive. We have suspicions and a grainy picture. That's not enough to arrest her. We would need to catch her in possession of the beguiling beads, and I doubt she would be that dumb."

"She wore them at the party," Quinn said.

"No one suspected her. If O'Hara showed up at her doorstep now, she would know she was under investigation. It might spook her and ruin the chance of getting the proof you need to clear your parents."

"Exactly." I bounced on my toes, growing impatient with our circular conversation. "That's why we need to go to Aurora Isle."

"Where?"

"The island Persephone's ancestors owned that's now inside Dead Man's Swamp. We've got one suspect: Persephone. She owns property in the middle of a thunderbird habitat. My seed is pointing toward a thunderbird. That's too big of a coincidence. We need to go to the island. Somehow, this is all connected."

"We? No. *I* will look into it."

"You and your squad."

Grant ran his hand through his hair. His palm came away streaked with gritty oil. He made a disgusted noise and swiped a spell of water and fire across his hand, burning away the oil and leaving his skin clean. "You're not the only person in the city who needs protection. We have other assignments. I can't pull my whole team away for this."

"Not to retrieve four deadly spells?"

"Not to chase a half-formed theory."

I tossed my hands in the air, but I never got a chance to retort. Grant's hand shot in front of me, stopping me in my tracks. His other hand dropped to grip Quinn's wing, halting him, too. Peering through a wall of hedges at the corner, he whispered, "Are you expecting guests?"

I stood on my tiptoes to look, steadying myself on Grant's outstretched arm. It was like holding on to a steel bar. Between a gap in the hedges, I spotted the front walk of Josephine's Victorian. A familiar sandy-headed reporter slouched on the sidewalk curb: Xavier of the *Daily Elemental*. I grimaced. Craning my neck, I spotted two other reporters loitering against trees farther up the street.

"Nosy journalists." I dropped to my heels and retreated until the corner house hid me from view.

Grant backtracked with me, his eyes narrowed. "I think you stole my line. And my expression."

I smoothed my eyebrows and gave my hands a shake to loosen my fisted fingers. Quinn circled around me to rub his cheek against my thigh. It was a cat's move, designed to comfort. I petted him in return.

"They're all on the banned list, right?" I asked.

"Right." Quinn's expression brightened.

"Since when do you two dislike reporters as much as I do?" At my glare, Grant added, "Present company excluded."

"Since they started turning my life into entertainment."

"I've heard that can get tiresome." Humor glinted in Grant's eye, and it was the spark my temper needed to ignite.

"What I do is *nothing* like what those scandal vultures do. *Nothing.* They write *fictional* entertainment. According to what they printed, I'm in league with Zipporah *and* O'Hara to steal the banned spells, ostracized from my parents and also their secret weapon, and some speculate I already have the stolen spells in my possession. Oh, and Quinn is a *fashion accessory.*" I shared a disgusted look with my gargoyle friend. "I haven't read anything they published today, but I imagine by now they've got me using the beguiling beads on the mayor and you trapped in the snare and slice as part of some weird full-spectrum courtship. Quinn will have swallowed the truth hex, because they all believe he's a brainless sycophant, and my mom is obviously using the thief's key to rob all the wealthy clients who are taking their business elsewhere. Those people aren't reporters; they're menaces. Imbeciles. A blight on the respectability of the profession. They should be hiding in shame from the world, but instead they're harassing me."

I flung my hands up in exasperation. My fingers knocked into a ward, and I jerked them back. Grant had erected a soundproof ward around the three of us, and I had been so caught up in my rant, I hadn't noticed.

"You have a good imagination. Maybe you should write novels."

I glared at Grant.

"I'm in their articles?"

I shrugged. "I don't know. Probably. They were pestering me about our relationship."

"Huh."

"What?"

"No one has approached me about our relationship. Don't I get a say in our courtship rituals?"

"If you like, I can tell them you want to do an interview to set them straight." I almost wished I dared.

Grant's face turned stony. "Don't even try."

"Then maybe we should slip around them and head for the swamp."

"There will be no 'we.'"

"Of course there will. I'm not letting you go alone."

Grant snorted. "I can't decide if your tenacity is attractive or irksome."

"Irksome?" My voice spiked an octave. "Would you be fine with me going to the swamp alone while you twiddle your thumbs and waited to hear what I found?"

"I believe you think you're using logic, but you're forgetting I have combat training." Grant's smile held a hint of condescension.

"It's *my* parents who are the victims. I'm the one with the everlasting seed. I should go."

"Your strengths are sentence composition and proper grammar. Mine are melee weapons and elemental defense. Which do you think will be more useful against thunderbirds?"

Arrogant and insulting. "Fine. I have the brains, you have the brawn. All the more reason for me to go with you."

"For all three of us to go," Quinn interjected. "I have brains *and* brawn."

"Exactly," I said.

Grant opened his mouth, closed it, then finally said, "We'll go tomorrow. I'll pick you up at dawn."

I had been prepared for a much longer argument, and I regarded Grant with open suspicion. "Are you saying that, but you're really planning on leaving as soon as I'm out of sight?"

"Are you calling me a liar?" Grant's chest puffed up impressively.

I poked him in the stomach. "Don't get growly with me. I'm saying you're not above subterfuge."

"It takes at least four hours to reach the swamp." He enclosed my hand in a soft grip. "I'm not eager to confront thunderbirds in the dark. We'll go in the morning, when we're fresh."

My protest died when I realized he wasn't implying I needed rest; he did. The grime covering him had disguised his fatigue. If I hadn't made a habit of studying him, I might have missed it completely. While I had spent the day in the tranquil environment of the library, he had been battling arsonists in the blight.

"All right," I said.

"Until then, you stay put at your house."

That sounded dangerously close to an order. Normally, I would have argued on principle. I wasn't a member of his squad, and it was good for Grant to be reminded he wasn't captain of me. However, since I was getting my way, and since staying in tonight had already been my plan, I simply nodded.

"This is an information-gathering expedition only." Grant released my hand with a subtle caress. "Anything we find, we take straight to O'Hara."

I nodded.

"Don't tell anyone where we're going tomorrow or about your suspicions. Especially not your mom."

"Of course." As much as I wanted to tell my mom we might be close to finding Airstrong's thief, until we knew for sure, it wouldn't serve any purpose to get her hopes up.

"We don't want to chance tipping off Persephone if we happen to stumble onto useful information."

I gave Grant the flat look his choice of words deserved.

"Quinn, that goes for you, too," Grant said. "Gargoyles gossip."

"I won't tell anyone. Except my siblings. They can be trusted."

"I might tell Mika," I said. *If she'll talk to me.*

Grant crossed his arms, looking as if he was refraining from rolling his eyes. "No one else."

Quinn and I nodded.

"Don't get your hopes up too high," Grant added. "This is a long shot. You didn't ask your seed how to help your parents."

"I know, I know. I asked for the biggest story. Maybe helping my parents would be the biggest story of my career because it would be the one most important to me. Did you ever think of that?"

"Did you, when you framed your question for the everlasting tree?"

I studied the toe of my boot. "No."

Silence hung between us for a beat; then Grant asked, "Ready to go home?"

My gaze darted to his. I expected him to drive his point home or at least give me another lecture on safety. I appreciated when he didn't do either.

"Maybe we should part ways here," I said, thinking of the lurking reporters.

Grant waggled his eyebrows. "Are you asking for a kiss?"

"You keep bringing up kissing," Quinn said. "I think you like doing it more than Kylie."

Grant's eyes widened with surprise. I grinned.

"Is that true?" Grant asked.

"She hasn't mentioned kissing once," Quinn said before I could respond.

"Really? Not once?" A glint of something wicked lit Grant's eyes.

"Maybe it's not one of your strengths," I said, deadpan.

"Is that right?" Grant tugged me close, sealing his lips around my laugh.

I melted into his embrace, thrilled, for once, to be proven wrong.

18

Grant insisted on walking me to my door, and not even his impressive scowl scared off the reporters. I delighted in how much our silence irritated them, grinning foolishly when Grant used a blurred-air ward to prevent them from getting pictures of the two of us together. Quinn skipped the whole ordeal by flying to the roof. Though several journalists snapped shots of him, I doubted any achieved a crisp photo.

None of the sham journalists were brave enough to follow Grant when he left.

My good mood deflated with Grant's departure, and I struggled not to succumb to feeling like a prisoner in my own home. Being forced to keep all the curtains closed didn't help, nor did the house's new wards. Walking the halls felt like moving through fog, as if I should be able to see the eddies of the powerful protection spells Josephine had sunk into the foundation and tugged over the rafters. Only time would tell if the spells were strong enough to repel Zipporah.

I had the house to myself. Normally, I would work on an

article—either writing one up or developing a pitch for the next one. Barring that, I would go out and get a feel for what was happening in the city. It had been far too long since I checked in with my contacts. However, I had promised Grant I wouldn't leave, so I went up to my room. The roof had been repaired while I was out, and the construction crew had been kind enough to remove the pile of rubble from my bedroom, too. Everything was perfectly clean and back in order, leaving me with nothing to do.

Hoping to distract myself, I trotted down to the kitchen to bake a spicy mishmash casserole out of leftovers from the icebox. Josephine's favorite meals were ones that used up miscellaneous foods before they went bad. It wasn't a payment for the roof repairs, but it was the best I could do today. After cutting a slice off for myself, I nestled the bulk of the casserole in a spelled warming cozy. Because it needed to be said, I included a note.

I'm sorry for bringing my troubles home. K.

Normally, I would have perused a newspaper while I ate, but I couldn't face the *Chronicle*. Reading other people's articles—especially if they were about me or my family—would only depress and infuriate me. Instead, I took my plate to the roof and sat with Quinn. Neither of us spoke much, but the company was nice. We were both waiting—for tomorrow, for Zipporah to show up, for a brilliant insight on how to wrap up O'Hara's investigation. For the reporters to leave. They lingered on the sidewalk, but we were too far away and at a bad angle for them to get a worthwhile photograph. They tried to shout questions at me, but my neighbors yelled twice as loud for them to shut up. The crotchety old man across the street lobbed elemental water bombs to back up his threats, and after that, the drenched reporters lurked in sulky silence.

When Mika finally arrived home, I waited five excruciating minutes for her to settle in before climbing down from the roof and knocking on her door.

"Go away, Harriet," she barked. "I'm working."

I tried the handle. The door opened.

Oliver looked up from where he lay sprawled on Mika's bed. He stretched from end to end, his slender tail curled up neatly around his back feet. The rest of the room was sparse, with Mika's enormous worktable dominating the small apartment. She had shoved it against the bay windows, filling the square footage my bed occupied in my room. A rainbow of polished quartz stones lined the left side of the table, and a series of gargoyle-inspired figurines adorned the right. Ever since Mika had become Terra Haven's resident gargoyle healer, demand for her beautifully crafted figurines had skyrocketed, especially red Chinese dragon statues. Tiny carnelian likenesses of Oliver in flight, running, and curled in an impossible, perfect circle took up most of the space, but surprisingly, a few cheerful winged citrine lions stood in their midst.

Mika bent over an agate crystal, delicate bands of quartz-tuned earth element manipulating the purple, pink, and orange stone into an elongated blob. She pretended she didn't see me step into her room.

"I told you to call me Kylie."

"You told me a lot of things."

I muffled a sigh. I hadn't expected her to make this easy for me. "Have I said I'm sorry? I shouldn't have kept my identity a secret from you."

Mika turned the agate in her fingers, coaxing a long swan's neck from the blob.

"I only ever wanted to be your friend," I said.

The agate neck shattered, shooting splinters of quartz

across the table. Mika's shoulders hunched. I held my tongue.

"If you're waiting for me to fawn in awe, you're wasting your time." She used a curtain of hair to block her face from me, her delicate magic shaping a new swan's neck.

"Mika . . ."

A bird's head bubbled from the top of the neck, and Mika bent closer, her magic forming the beak with obnoxious meticulousness.

My fingers curled into fists. "You're right. I'm wasting my time." I stormed out of her room, across the balcony, and slammed my door. Wrapping a soundproof bubble around my mouth, I unleashed a scream of frustration.

Satisfied, I stomped back to Mika's room. She was waiting for me, her arms folded over her chest, her back turned to her work.

"I've known you for years," she said, not giving me a chance to speak, "and you didn't tell me who your parents are. You made me think we had a similar upbringing. You basically lied to me every day, and I trusted you the whole time. That was a lousy thing to do. You made me feel this big." She held her forefinger and thumb an inch apart.

"I'm sorry."

Her green eyes drilled into me. "Why did you do it?"

"When we first met, I was trying out the new me. I needed time to figure out who I was away from high society and out of my parents' shadows. But after I got to know you . . ." I played with the hem of my shirt, working the words out in my mind to make sure they came out right. "I didn't want to tell you because I didn't want you to look at me differently when you realized I came from money. I know you think most full spectrums are a waste of time and resources." I took a deep breath, then dove all the way in. "I didn't trust that your biases wouldn't taint our friendship. I was afraid you would stop seeing me as me, and you'd start seeing me as just another wealthy brat."

I forced myself to hold Mika's gaze. My friend could best Grant in an expressionless-mask contest. Nibbling my bottom lip, I stopped myself from adding anything further —or taking back what I had said. I had spoken the truth.

Finally, Mika's arms unfolded, and she relaxed against the chair.

"You were right." She held up a finger. "But only at first. After I got to know you, how could you believe I would dismiss your goofy sense of humor or your noble desire to change the world and see only an entitled snob?"

"Even entitled snobs can be insecure."

Mika scoffed, but the sound had no heat in it. I sank to the edge of the bed, and Oliver repositioned himself to lay his head on my lap. I stroked my fingers along his glossy forehead and down his spiked spine.

"I promise, no more secrets between us," I said. "I'll tell you anything you want to know."

"Why?"

"Why what?"

"Why give up the privileges of high society? Why live"— she gestured around the small room—"in relative poverty?"

"Fear. And hubris. I wanted to prove to myself that I could build my own career without my parents handing it to me. I didn't want to work at their company, either. I've always wanted to be a journalist—a *real* one, not someone who reports on the idiotic things full spectrums prioritize. I couldn't do that while living with my parents and socializing in their world."

I shook my head as I heard my own words. "Listen to me. Even when I thought I was being noble and brave, I was acting like a privileged snot. 'Oh, poor me. My parents have too much money and influence for me to act normal around them.' I guess there's no escaping your roots."

"If it helps, I never would have guessed you were from high society."

I chuffed a laugh. "It does. I think." I glanced out the window. From this angle, I couldn't tell if the reporters loitering on the sidewalk had left or not. "I didn't realize how much I would appreciate the anonymity. Being outed has been awful. I've got hack journalists stalking me, and half the writers at the *Chronicle* are acting like I swooped in on pegasus wings and stole all their best stories. Then there's Dahlia, who is—*was*—determined that I 'use every advantage,' which amounted to sending me to the Kwan solstice party."

Mika squinted at me. "You really didn't want to go to *the* high-society event of the season?"

"I would have preferred to get food poisoning. The whole party was awful. I wish I could have been here, with you guys. And not just because Zipporah tried to kill me. Everyone at the ritual was so pretentious. They refuse to believe anyone does anything for only one reason. You have to have layers of ulterior motives behind every action. I couldn't be there just to do an interview. I had to be there because I was making a statement about Airstrong. You want to hear one absurd claim that was circulating? Apparently I found the firebirds as a 'publicity stunt' for my parents, as if anyone with half a brain would go into Lunacy as a marketing ploy. Ugh, I don't miss that world at all." I realized I was chafing Oliver's short mane, and I forced my hand to still.

"Wait." Mika scooted to the edge of her chair. "Go back

to the part where the harpy almost killed you. You mean a second time?"

"Quinn didn't tell you last night? I thought he came to you for healing."

"He did. I healed his scratches from the spook squirrels, but he didn't mention the harpy." Scowling, Mika strode to the balcony door and called Quinn. He dropped from the roof to the balcony, then squeezed inside, not quite meeting Mika's eyes. "Why didn't you tell me you ran into the harpy yesterday? You better not start keeping secrets from me."

"I was tired." Quinn's voice dropped to a mumble as he added, "Plus, you would have been even madder at Kylie, and I didn't want you to wake her."

Mika's jaw worked as her glare bounced from Quinn to me, then back. I tried to convey my innocence with a look. I hadn't asked Quinn to keep silent about our encounter with Zipporah. It hadn't even occurred to me.

"Fine." Mika dropped into her seat with a huff. "How about one of you finally tell me why the harpy is after you."

"Because I'm an idiot," I confessed. I recounted my first meeting with Zipporah and my desperate deal that landed me in the harpy's debt. Mika didn't interrupt as I described the events leading up to Zipporah tossing me into Lunacy Labyrinth and the atrocious bloodstone she had sent me in search of. Quinn chimed in with his perspective, and we took turns explaining Zipporah's anger when we didn't have the bloodstone yesterday morning, and then her unexpected appearance at Persephone's. After Quinn described yesterday's battle, Mika wouldn't let us continue until she was certain his bizarre twisting of the elements hadn't caused any internal damage. Once she assured us Quinn was fine—which he had been affirming all along—Mika was rightfully horrified by Zipporah's latest demands.

"You can't let that harpy get her hands—claws, talons, whatever—on those spells."

"Giving her the spell isn't an option, even if my mom already told me to do it." I made a face.

"She's worried for you."

"I'm worried for her. The longer it takes to find the stolen spells, the worse it will be on her and Airstrong. It's a good thing we've got a lead."

"You do? Why didn't you start with that?"

"I forgot how much I had to catch you up on." I relayed the day's discoveries, and hearing it again fortified my resolve that we were on the right track.

"I thought you said Persephone was a family friend," Mika said when I wound down.

I shrugged. "I thought so, too."

"So you're going to Dead Man's Swamp? Just the two of you?"

"And Grant."

"Still, it sounds dangerous, to put it mildly."

My stomach flipped in agreement, but I pushed the anxiety down before it could form into a full thought. I had to go tomorrow. I couldn't let Grant go alone. He might not consider me useful in a dangerous environment, but my everlasting seed proved I was meant to be part of this expedition. I couldn't afford to let fear talk me out of it.

"It's not like I have anything else to do." I meant the words to come out flippant, but frustration tainted them. "Dahlia suspended me."

"What? Why?"

"She thinks me owing Zipporah is a conflict of interest and would look bad for the *Chronicle*."

"But—" Mika waved a hand at me. "You're one of her best journalists, and you're literally chasing *the* story of a lifetime. Didn't she learn anything after the firebird incident? First she forbade you from following up on the stolen birds; then it turned into the biggest story to hit the newsstands all month. Why would she doubt you again?"

I smiled inwardly, basking in Mika's indignation.

"How can I help?" Mika asked. "Want me to go talk with Dahlia?"

I shook my head. "Having your support means the world." I meant it. I was still anxious about tomorrow, worried about my parents' future, and bitter about my suspension, but having Mika on my side again was a huge step in the right direction.

"I was looking for a more actionable answer," Mika said. "Maybe Oliver and I should go with you tomorrow."

"I, ah, I doubt Grant would agree to that," I said, rather than voicing the adamant *no* that had been on the tip of my tongue. I didn't need Mika getting stubborn about accompanying us into thunderbird territory. "Besides, Grant, Quinn, and I are just going to pop in, look around, and pop back out." While dodging birds flinging lightning bolts as we navigated a swamp to an island no one had seen in half a century.

This idea was insane, but it was all I had.

"Have you packed?" Mika asked.

I shook my head, then allowed Mika to fuss, because it was the only way she could feel like she was helping. Oliver, Quinn, and I trailed after her across the connecting balcony to my apartment. The last purple highlights of the sunset illuminated the retreating backs of the reporters on the street below, and I breathed a sigh of relief. At least Dead Man's Swamp would be devoid of nosy muckrakers. The thought soothed my anxiety more than I thought it would.

Mika selected two outfits for me, both practical, one for

me to wear, one for me to pack. She wrapped my borrowed camera in a tight, waterproof leather pouch; folded my raincoat into a neat square; grabbed apples, hard cheese, and dried meat from the kitchen; and added chocolate from her own stash. When she was satisfied with the way each item was packed in my worn satchel, we worked together to weave a waterproof spell into the thick canvas.

I placed the bag by the door, then paced in the cramped space, unable to relax. Mika crawled onto my bed, and Oliver joined her. Quinn stretched out beside it, giving me more room. The initial thrill of discovering a possible lead had abated, and the reality of going to Dead Man's Swamp had settled in its place. I almost wished Grant had talked me out of going.

Almost.

Mika jumped to her feet, startling me. "I nearly forgot!" She dashed to her room and returned with a book. "This is for you from Ms. Flemming."

I accepted a copy of *Critical Moments in History* by Adelaide Flemming.

"Read the inscription," Mika said.

Flipping to the title page, I read the neat cursive note written in the white space:

Kylie,

Historians like myself wouldn't be able to do our research without dedicated custodians of facts like you. Your words and your articles shape history as it will be remembered. Be wise in how you wield your power, and thank you for immortalizing me in your beautiful article.

—Adelaide Flemming

I closed the book and hugged it to my chest, touched by her message. Yet again, I wished I had gotten to talk with Adelaide longer.

"I take it you went to her signing," I said.

"How could we not after reading your article?"

"Don't you mean 'Staff's' article?"

Mika waved aside my whining. "That piece was pure Kylie Grayson from start to finish. You have a distinctive style, Kylie, and you have a knack for making the reader feel what you feel. I'm not the only one who thinks so. You should have seen how many people were at the reading. The store ran out of copies of Ms. Flemming's book, and people were buying copies from other bookshops in town and rushing back to get them signed. I guarantee half those people wouldn't have shown up if not for your article. I mean, who thinks, 'It would be fun to listen to a history lecture in my free time'? You persuaded me and a whole bunch of other people to take a chance on Flemming, and I'm glad I did."

"Thanks." I hugged the book tighter. Despite my initial doubts about the interview, it had been exactly the kind of article I enjoyed writing: one that uplifted the reader, encouraged them to take a positive action, and made their lives better, even if only for a few hours. I also got a thrill knowing I had helped Adelaide's book become a bigger success in Terra Haven—partially because it felt wonderful to have proof my writing influenced other people but mostly because Adelaide deserved to have her book read by many people.

"How did Adelaide know you and I were friends?" I asked.

"It turns out we're the only two people she's ever met who are lucky enough to have gargoyle companions accompanying them." Mika gave Oliver a fond smile. "She asked if we knew each other. Then she insisted on gifting you her book. Oh, and she gave me this for you, Quinn." Mika held up a note written on thick ivory-colored stationery.

Quinn accepted the paper and unfolded it, reading it out loud. "'From one historian to another: Go for it.'"

Mika shot me a confused look. "What does that mean?"

"She thinks I should write a book about gargoyles and our history," Quinn said.

"A whole book?" Oliver asked.

"Would you?" Mika's eyes lit up.

"I'm thinking about it."

"That's wonderful! Let me know if I can help," Mika said.

"Me too," Oliver offered.

We speculated about the nature of Quinn's potential book for a while longer, but the physical and emotional strain of the past few days soon had me yawning. Mika decided that was her cue to depart, and she and Oliver returned to their room after wishing us both luck tomorrow. I took my time getting ready for bed. With the excitement of a lead—and the dread of chasing it into Dead Man's Swamp —bouncing through my thoughts, I was certain I wouldn't be able to sleep. But once I extinguished the lights and lay down, a sense of peace pervaded my body.

If something terrible happened to me tomorrow, at least I had made things right with Mika first.

19

I waited for Grant outside in the chilly predawn air. The house had been too stifling in its sleepy silence, and I hadn't wanted to risk waking Josephine by pacing on the creaky wooden floorboards in my room. Instead, I strode up and down the stone walkway between the sidewalk and porch steps, my gaze trained on the far end of the street.

It was too early for gossip journalists to be out hounding innocent citizens. It was too early for pretty much anyone to be out. Lamps and the glow of house wards softly illuminated the dark street, but no lights brightened any windows. Not even the birds were up yet. The only things awake were Quinn, myself, and my nerves.

I pivoted on the ball of my foot. So much could go wrong today, the least of which being that my theory might lead us on a wild cockatrice chase. Yet, if we returned empty-handed, I didn't have a clue where else to look for the stolen spells or the thief.

When Grant rounded the corner atop his flying carpet, my relief rivaled my trepidation. I trotted to the base of the porch steps to retrieve my bag, then rushed to the sidewalk, where Quinn already waited. Grant brought his carpet to a halt two feet above the sidewalk. The greasy substance that had marred his uniform yesterday was gone. The long-sleeve top and pants were spotless gray, and in the dim lighting, the elemental symbols woven into the fabric were all but invisible.

"Good morning," I said.

Grant grunted and tossed a bundle of gray fabric at me. I caught it reflexively and held it up to the light. The garment appeared strikingly similar to Grant's own. The tingle of spells woven into the fabric confirmed my suspicions.

"Did I miss the part where I got drafted into the FPD?" I asked.

"You're the focus of a harpy on a warpath, and we're headed to Dead Man's Swamp. You need all the protection you can get."

Pretending I hadn't hunched and scanned the sky at the mention of Zipporah, I asked, "Are you sure this isn't your way of making yourself feel like you're the boss of me?"

"Don't make me regret taking you, Kylie."

"I feel it's important to remind you that no matter what I'm wearing, I won't jump at your every command."

"Uh-huh."

I planted my hands on my hips. He pointed up the stairs.

"You're wasting daylight."

I stomped up the steps. "This doesn't mean I'm following your orders."

I closed the door on Grant's chuckle.

Four minutes later, we coasted through the sleepy streets of Terra Haven, with Quinn tracking us from the air. I enjoyed the temperature-moderating spell in my borrowed uniform and wished it fit better. The crisp breeze chilled my face and the strips of skin where the pants rode up above my ankles and the shirt cropped short of my wrists. Wherever Grant had found the clothes, it hadn't been from his closet. Given its lack of elemental designation on the collar, I guessed it was for trainees. I told myself it was better than swimming inside one of Grant's uniforms, but a small part of me would have enjoyed the intimacy of wearing his clothing.

I shook away the silly thought and focused on our surroundings. Grant's broad shoulders blocked most of my view. Instead of reenacting yesterday's cozy seating arrangement, Grant had instructed me to climb on behind him. I sat cross-legged, as did he, and the limited carpet space forced my shins against his backside. I kept a loose hold on his belt, afraid if I allowed my hands to rest anywhere else, they would go exploring when my thoughts drifted. I had hoped Grant would show up in a speedy FPD airship or, at the very least, with a gryphon. A carpet, while fast for city travel, wasn't the most speedy means of traversing the countryside.

When we left the city limits behind, Grant increased our speed, but he didn't top out the carpet's propulsion spell limits.

"Shouldn't we go faster?" I asked.

"No."

"Care to elaborate?" I allowed my exasperation to seep into my tone.

"Wearing myself out pushing the carpet isn't going to make that much difference in our travel time, only in my energy level when we get there."

His logic made sense, but it didn't assuage the anxiety driving my thoughts. The monotony, however, did. The sun rose. The hills rolled by. We passed small settlements and vast farms, and as the sun climbed the sky, we encountered a modicum of traffic, mostly in the form of wagons and horses. Gradually the landscape flattened into a long, tree-cloaked valley. Birds chirped and the wind hummed against my eardrums, but otherwise we rode in silence. Grant didn't tease me, and he didn't talk about kissing. He didn't talk about much of anything at all. Apparently, his desire to conserve energy extended to not engaging his vocal cords. I wondered if his thoughts were mired in regret for agreeing to this investigative trip, but I thought better of breaking the silence to ask.

I monitored the sky, as much to keep track of Quinn as to watch for Zipporah. Once, I spotted a large, winged creature in the distance. It could have been the harpy, but it could just as easily have been a gryphon or hippogryph. It didn't stop my heart from pounding in my chest and my fingers from digging into Grant's belt. When the creature disappeared over the horizon, I exhaled heavily and attempted to relax. I couldn't shake the dread of my next encounter with Zipporah. No matter today's outcome, I still didn't have a solution to appease the harpy.

Mounded white cumulonimbus clouds formed along the horizon and gradually grew to fill the sky as we flew closer. When the road curved to circumnavigate the swamp and its ever-present thunderstorm, we veered onto a smaller dirt trail. In places, rain had washed away the topsoil, revealing patches of broken cobblestones. At one time, this unnamed road had been a major thoroughfare. Now, weeds and weathered ruts clogged the little-used path. The levitation spell smoothed out the worst of the bumps, but I tightened my grip on Grant's belt anyway.

The summer heat that had dried the foothills around Terra Haven didn't appear to have touched this end of the valley. Baked yellow weeds transitioned to green meadows, flowering fields, and lush copses of thick-trunked birches and sycamores. Yet as attractive as the scenery was, the clouds captivated my attention. For an hour, they appeared suspended in the distance. Then, the first breezes reached us, carrying the delicious scent of rain and wet earth, and the puffy white tops of the clouds curved over us, seeming to lift to expose their blue-gray undersides.

Quinn dipped lower, flying above the treetops. His head swung back and forth, his curious gaze sweeping the terrain. I might have been worried about his stamina, but he had once kept pace with a gryphon for more than a full day. The modest speed of the carpet wouldn't strain him.

Thunder rumbled, its deep tones cutting through the rush of wind against my ears. Lightning flashed an erratic tempo in the dark clouds, the wild energy unmistakably powerful. My breath hitched when the clouds obscured the sun, casting a dense shadow across the landscape. I patted my chest, reassuring myself that my everlasting seed hung in a pouch against my breastbone. I had been scared to bring it and potentially lose it, and scared to leave it behind and potentially miss out on my one chance to evolve it. Ultimately, the fear of missing the story of a lifetime had won out. I triple-checked the knot holding the cord tied, then the security of the drawstring clamping the pouch closed.

A sharp gust buffeted the carpet. The slim platform bucked, and I bounced into the air, landing half off the side. Before I could do more than squeak in alarm, Grant's arm swung around and shoved me back in place.

"Hang on tighter," he ordered, drawing my arms around his waist.

I hugged him, hunched over my bag, my cheek pressed to his spine. Wind slapped us from behind, jolting the carpet forward before jerking it sideways. Grant powered the carpet back to the center of the road and fought to keep us there. He succeeded while we sailed through a thick grove of black ash, but the moment we cleared it, the wind assaulted us once more. Grant pulled to a stop. The carpet heaved beneath us, trying to dump us off the side as he deflated the levitation spell.

"We'll walk from here," he said when we came to a rest on the forest floor.

I climbed to my feet. My hips protested and my knees popped. I stretched, discreetly chafing my cheek to remove the imprint of Grant's shirt from my skin. Wind tugged at my hair, but it was no match for my spell-enhanced braids. I pivoted in a slow circle, taking in our surroundings. The trees had thinned, and between copses, I caught a glimpse of the cheery blue sky behind us. It beckoned, but I turned away.

Purple-black clouds hung ahead of us, streaks of dense gray stretching to the ground, promising a rainstorm in our future. Moisture already hung in the air. The atmosphere had taken on a charged, dangerous quality that reminded me of Grant's magical signature, crackling with immeasurable force. Lightning popped above us, deep in the clouds, brightening the charcoal expanse in a burst of diffuse white light. Three seconds later, thunder rolled across the landscape, vibrating in my chest. I sucked in an unsteady breath and let it out slowly.

Quinn dropped into the middle of the meadow, fighting the volatile wind currents that buffeted his heavy body. When he landed, he folded his wings tight and examined the foreboding clouds, determination radiating from every line of his body.

Grant rolled up the carpet and tied it to the back of his small pack. I fidgeted with the strap of my bag, adjusting its length unnecessarily while I mentally recited my reasons for marching into a place with the words *dead man* in its name.

"Are you sure you still want to do this?" Grant asked.

"No. But yes."

"You don't have to prove anything to me."

"It hadn't occurred to me that I did." I dropped my hands to my pockets, tucking them out of sight.

"So you're not trying to impress me?"

"Should I be?" I couldn't tell if he was teasing me or if I wanted him to be. "We should keep going, not waste time."

Grant gripped my bicep, bringing me to a halt.

"You don't need to worry about it," he said.

"About what?"

"Impressing me."

I shot him a suspicious look. "Because it's not possible?"

"Because you've already done it. Your determination, your loyalty, and your bravery are impressive."

Warmth kindled in my chest. Grant thought I was brave. And impressive. A cold, fat raindrop splashed my scalp, then another, but the rain couldn't dampen my inner glow.

"So you know I mean it when I say I wouldn't think any less of you if you waited here," Grant said.

"I can't."

"All right. Then you have to strip."

"What?" Had he just said what I thought he had said? And why weren't my feet moving as he reached for my top?

"The spells. They've all got to go." A twisted burst of all five elements spilled from Grant's fingers and spread through the fabric of my top. The subtle tingle of the uniform's protective spells died. His hand slid lower, to my hip, and the spells in my pants went inert.

Flustered and feeling dense, I asked, "Why?"

"Thunderbirds are drawn to shaped elements and active magic."

"Really?" My research hadn't mentioned that. Maybe it had been implied under the *stay far away from these birds* warnings.

"These small magics aren't likely to draw their attention, but I don't want to risk it." He yanked a gray duster from his pack and shrugged it on. The coat's long lines hung to his calves. Wind plucked at the hem, drawing it behind him like a cape before he got it buttoned. I itched to take a picture, but I couldn't chance unpacking my camera with so much moisture in the air. Nor did I think Grant would stand still and model for me if I asked.

While Grant strapped two long knives to his belt, I pulled on my raincoat. The initial drops had slackened to a fine mist that clung to my hair but hadn't yet penetrated my clothing, and I wanted to keep it that way.

"Do you still have my tracker on you?" Grant asked.

I lifted the hem of my shirt to reveal the badge clipped to my waistband. Grant took it and wiped away all traces of magic clinging to it.

"Why bother making me wear these if you knew I couldn't keep the spells?" I asked, plucking at my FPD uniform.

"In case Zipporah attacked while we were traveling. Plus, even without elemental enhancement, the fabric will likely keep you better protected than anything you had in your wardrobe." He gaze simmered under his brows. "And maybe I wanted to see how they would look on you."

Whoa. Pretending to be unaffected my his molten perusal, I managed a husky, "What about your uniform?"

"It's the same one I wore into Lunacy, and I haven't gotten around to replacing the spells in it. Don't forget to dismantle this." He made a sweeping motion around my head.

"Dismantle? It's twin braids, not an airship." I stripped the various weaves of air holding my flyaways in place. Two-thirds of my hair stayed secured by the braids; the other one-third instantly frizzed around my head. With a sigh, I tugged the braids loose, then pulled my hair into a simple ponytail that needed no magic to keep it out of my face. I supposed it was too much to ask that I look moderately cute on this expedition. And silly to care.

The waterproof spell on my bag was the last to go, but at least Mika and I had the forethought to wrap everything inside in individual waterproof cloths.

Grant offered me a standard-issue FPD trail ration bar. I'd had the misfortune of eating one in the past and shuddered at the memory.

"No thank you. Would you like some dried bison?"

Grant's eyes lit up, and he accepted a strip. While he chewed, he peered over my shoulder into my bag. "What else do you have in there?"

"Some apples, cheese, and chocolate."

"You brought a picnic to Dead Man's Swamp? I like your style."

Quinn took the lead, and we walked in silence, consuming our impromptu lunch on the move. I listened to my own chewing and the soft patter of raindrops on leaves. Frogs croaked in the distance, quieting as we neared. The drone of insects came and went with the breeze, and more than one many-legged creepy-crawly darted into the weeds in front of Quinn. Erratic wind flurries rubbed limbs against each other, adding creaks and groans to the swamp noises. It explained why the forest appeared unnaturally thinned: Only the hardiest of trees could withstand the constant winds; the rest broke and toppled.

It took me a while to realize the birds were missing. A normal swamp would have been teeming with avian wildlife, but the endless storm had rendered the region inhospitable to winged creatures.

"At least we know we won't run into Zipporah here," I said. As if to emphasize my point, lightning snapped far above us. Thunder broke in a deafening boom that rolled across the land. Rain pelted down, instantly soaking my scalp. I tipped my head and opened my mouth, drinking from the sky.

"I thought journalists were supposed to be cynics," Grant said.

I shrugged. "Truth is truth, no matter if you view it with a negative or positive outlook. I choose to be an optimist because it makes for a better life."

I didn't add that being positive kept me sane, especially lately. If I spent all my time dwelling on the problems in my life and the potential dooms bearing down on me, I wouldn't be able to get out of bed.

The deeper we trekked into the swamp, the darker it became, until I could have sworn it was closer to twilight than noon. Not even the lightning provided much in the way of illumination, since most of the flashes occurred high within the clouds. So long as we didn't disturb any thunderbirds, it would hopefully stay that way. As it was, the air vibrated with the charged tension of dispersed electricity, like a fully formed spell perpetually a hairsbreadth from being released. The sensation wormed into my skin, tensing my muscles and making me jump at every thunderclap.

The muddy road disappeared beneath standing puddles, most unavoidable. My feet squished inside my shoes with each step, and I tripped often, unable to see hidden obstacles. Eventually, the puddles spread outward, covering the ground in small pools of water that obscured the deteriorated path. Patches of mangroves, with their arching, invasive roots, made the trail even more treacherous.

Clinging to my positivity became increasingly difficult. Rain battered me, body and spirit, slicing through the gaps between my coat buttons, splashing up from each step, and beating down from above, eroding my resolve even as it stole my body heat. Between the runoff sluicing down my neck and beneath the collar of my borrowed uniform and the wicking of moisture up my soaked pants legs, I would have been hard-pressed to find an inch of dry skin on my body. I couldn't picture Persephone mincing through a single patch of mud, let alone making this same trek with the stolen spells. Even if she had, the storm would have washed all traces of Persephone's tracks away minutes after she passed.

An even more depressing thought occurred to me, and I tugged on Grant's sleeve for his attention.

"What about the thunderbirds?" I shouted.

"I haven't seen any."

I held firm to his coat when he started to turn away. "No. Thunderbirds and spells. You said they were drawn to magic."

Comprehension replaced Grant's frown, but he was forced to wait until the latest blast of thunder died down before he could speak. "There are ways to cloak magic."

"So this isn't a fool's errand?"

"What?"

I shook my head and released his arm. Grant gave me an awkward pat on the shoulder and pushed forward.

After Quinn tripped into a hole as deep as his foreleg, Grant acquired a long stick and took the lead. Our pace slowed to a plod as he tested the ground before each step. In his other hand, he carried a lantern and used its feeble light to keep us on track.

I longed to create a simple umbrella ward or a quick heating spell. I wouldn't have to sustain them, just hold them long enough to enjoy some relief. Or simply until feeling returned to my toes. However, Grant stoically endured the mud, the drizzle in his eyes, and the biting wind that alternated between slapping us with stinging droplets and buffeting our legs in an attempt to knock us down. Quinn walked without complaint, even when he sank up to his ankles in mud with each step. So when an urge to whine about wet socks or the weight of my soaked bag surfaced, I swallowed it. This was my mission. I needed and wanted to be here. Also, despite what Grant had said, I *did* want to impress him. I would suffer much more miserable conditions in silence before I gave him a reason to think I was ungrateful for his help. Or worse, a reason to see me as a burden.

My foot slipped out from under me, and I landed hard on my butt. Muddy water splashed around me, and pain slapped my backside. I shoved to my feet, but not before the cold water soaked through my pants and underwear. It wasn't the first time I had fallen, either. Flicking mud from my fingers, I stomped to catch up with Grant. Somehow, he hadn't fallen once. Beneath his long duster, he was probably toasty and dry. If this trip hadn't been my idea, I might have accused him of using this dreadful swamp to teach me another lesson in caution or humility or some such nonsense.

Quinn bumped his muzzle against my thigh. Mud

splattered his legs and the underside of his belly with each step, and the rain washed it from his slick quartz body almost as fast. At least the moisture wasn't bothering him.

He looked like he wanted to say something, but a boom of thunder broke before he could. Instead, he tilted the bend of his wing toward me, offering me a handhold. I grabbed it.

"Thank you," I shouted.

The next time I slipped, Quinn kept me upright. I gave him a tight smile.

We slogged behind Grant along a twisted course between the spidery roots of the mangroves for what felt like hours. If our guide were anyone other than Captain Grant Monaghan, I would have suspected we were lost and walking in circles. But Grant was too competent to allow insignificant obstacles like a landmark-free swamp, a disorienting thunderstorm, and a washed-out road prevent him from reaching his destination. For my part, I kept my head down and planted my feet in Grant's footprints. My grand contribution was keeping up.

When Grant jerked to a halt, I had to sidestep to avoid plowing into him. My knee knocked against Quinn's rock-hard mane. Pain flashed through my joint, then abated, numbed by the cold. Grant surveyed our surroundings with vigilant energy undiminished by the pouring rain. A handful of mangroves clustered on our left, while another trio swayed on our right. Between them was nothing but water. We had reached the lake.

Choppy waves topped with white foam seethed across its surface. In the dim lighting and ceaseless rain, I couldn't make out the opposite shore. My heart sank. When I had envisioned Aurora Lake and the isle, I had pictured a quaint body of water, perhaps an expansive pool given a more impressive name. This lake was massive.

A menacing shadow swooped through the sky above the water. I ducked instinctively, and Quinn hunkered low beside me. Grant didn't move.

The massive bird's wings spanned ten feet, but it twisted as agilely as a sparrow through the rain-choked air. Its head hung low, revealing an oversize glossy black eagle's beak. Blue-gray feathers coated the bird's sleek body, and its tail ended in a spray of navy-striped feathers that perfectly matched the markings on my everlasting seed.

I had never seen a thunderbird in person, only in pictures. I had never *wanted* to see a thunderbird up close. Every line of the bird's body screamed *predator*, including the wicked talons tucked close to its body. It soared through the downfall with grace and speed, anticipating the shifting winds with uncanny ease, at home in the inhospitable environment it had helped create.

A gust whipped my soaked ponytail across my cheek. The sting jolted me, and I tore my gaze from the thunderbird. The research books had all promised that where one thunderbird flew, more were guaranteed to be close by. I found them high above the lake, ominous slashes against the low-hanging clouds. Shielding my eyes against the driving rain, I counted five.

Grant seized my arm. I jumped, spinning to brace for an attack.

"Look." He pointed farther to the right, beyond the snarl of mangrove roots.

A crumbling stone causeway spanned the lake. Gryphon-size holes pockmarked the surface, and the pillars and abutments looked as if they had lost a battle with a leviathan. Saltwater waves frothed at the underside of the causeway, lapping at the eroded rocks. Blasts of wind swept miniature waterfalls from the causeway's surface, only to have the water replaced by crashing waves and rain. The whole expanse looked one well-placed lightning strike from crumbling into the lake.

A murky shape loomed atop the low railing at the causeway's entrance. Another lurked on the opposite side. More appeared to line the middle of the structure. I squinted at the closest one, staring until I was certain it was a statue, not a roosting thunderbird.

Lightning flashed low above the lake. Like an image captured on film, an imprint of a mounded shape topped with several ragged structures snapped across my peripheral vision. The island. Thunder clapped against my eardrums and spilled across the lake. I leaned forward, as if it would help me see better. The next jagged spear of lightning sparked before the echoes of the previous bolt's thunder faded. This time, I was facing the right direction, and the image that seared my vision made the hairs on my arms try to stand on end.

A dozen enormous thunderbirds squabbled in the air over the island. I surveyed our immediate surroundings, feeling exposed. The nearby spindly trees wouldn't provide shelter from much of anything, let alone electric aerial attacks. If the thunderbirds looked this way . . .

Grant had already doused the lantern. We stood in the shadows, and so long as we all stayed still, we would be safe.

I hoped.

Quinn's wing flexed beneath my white-knuckled grip. He studied me with worried eyes. I wondered if I looked as scared as I felt.

"What are they fighting over?" I asked Grant between thunderclaps.

"They're not fighting. Watch."

When the next flash lit the island, I saw its source: The lightning sprang from the open fist of a thunderbird's talons. The electricity shot a jagged line into the roof of a structure. The other birds congregated around the top of the island, sweeping and diving through the air. With the afterimage skewing my vision, I couldn't track their dim figures, but they appeared to all be focused on the same place. A nest?

Two birds spiraled straight up, so close together their wings would have touched if they hadn't been in complete synchronization. As one, they flipped and dove. Twin bolts burst from their clawed feet. The lightning cut irregular paths through the air. One jutted sideways; the other connected with the roof of the building. The structure held, thanks to the soft shimmer of a powerful ward.

I clutched Grant's arm, excitement surging through me. Thunderbirds hunted in packs. According to Grant, they were drawn to magic. He was right: They weren't fighting each other; they were working together to destroy something magical.

"Is that proof enough?" I yelled once the thunder died down.

"Maybe." Grant scrutinized the closest thunderbird as it swept across the lake's surface, plucking a fish from the water. "It could be a leftover—"

A crash of thunder cut off his words, but I got the gist. When Persephone's ancestors had abandoned the island, they might have placed a ward on the building. But that had been decades ago. If the thunderbirds had been living around this lake for even half that time, wouldn't they have destroyed old wards long ago?

"It's more likely that's where the stolen spells are hidden," I rushed to say between thunderclaps.

"Whatever it is, it needs to be investigated. Not by us. I need to bring my full squad. And O'Hara."

We were so close. It would take at least half a day to travel back to Terra Haven and another half day for the investigator and Grant's squad to make the return trip. That was only if O'Hara and Grant were prepared to take immediate action. They would likely wait until morning before returning. It could be a full twenty-four hours before anyone investigated the island. By then, the thunderbirds could have breached the ward and destroyed the spells.

Dread knotted in my stomach. If the spells were destroyed, I would never obtain the proof necessary to exonerate my parents.

If the spells were even stored on the island.

I had to believe they were. Why else would my everlasting seed have pointed us to this island, where a ward protected a forgotten ruin? My imagination still boggled when I attempted to picture Persephone traversing the wild swamp and outmaneuvering a flock of thunderbirds. Yet if she had done it once, she could do it again. What if she slipped in and retrieved the spells before O'Hara and Grant returned? If we left now, we risked the spells disappearing before we returned.

Yet if we charged across the causeway, we would likely die.

A series of lightning flashes exploded almost on top of each other, providing a strobing view of thunderbirds crisscrossing the air above the island, hurling their elemental weapons at the warded building. None of the lightning bolts were longer than a few feet, but they each had more than enough power to kill us. What defense could we possibly muster against their attacks if we couldn't use the elements?

I gave Grant a jerky nod to show I agreed with his plan.

Quinn tugged out of my grip, slinking several low steps toward the shore, his nose to the ground. I wanted to call him back, but he was too focused to notice, and the thunder was too loud to shout over. Carefully, he hooked a claw into the mud and came up with something long and stringy. My first thought was he had found a drowned animal, but the downpour sluiced the mud from the object, and I could make out the shaft of a feather. I took an excited step forward before Grant stopped me. Quinn transferred the rain-cleaned feather to his mouth and brought it back to us. I accepted it, minimizing my motions, mindful of attracting the thunderbirds' notice.

The feather spanned the length of my forearm, and the next lightning strike confirmed my hunch: It was a thunderbird feather. My free hand lifted to the seed hanging around my neck. The light of a firebird feather had evolved my seed the first time. Perhaps the second evolution would be similar, and my everlasting seed would need only to be close to a thunderbird's feather, not the thunderbird itself.

Mouthing a thank-you to Quinn, I tucked the feather into my bag. As much as I longed to pull out my seed and check right then, lingering was too dangerous. Straightening, I turned my back on the island and the thunderbirds, hoping I was making the right choice for myself *and* for my parents.

When I looked up, my eyes landed on a hydra.

Ice dove through my veins, and my knees locked even as my brain gibbered for me to run.

The hydra's massive front legs supported a body shaped like a bloated grizzly bear stuffed into a wyvern's skin. A second pair of legs flexed on either side of its sloped hind end, thinner and shorter than the front pair. Five spiked necks sprouted from the bulky hump above its forelegs, each column thicker than Grant's thigh and long enough to reach the top of a mangrove tree. Black scales swept from its multiple diamond-shaped heads down to its stubby tail, but the undersides of its rounded belly bore splotches of yellow, and bright yellow rings circled all ten eyes.

Each hydra head bobbed and weaved like a snake's. Narrow tongues flicked from mouths packed with ragged teeth. Two heads fixated on Quinn, whose wings had flared with alarm when he spotted the giant reptile. The other three heads divided their attention between Grant and me.

"Slowly," Grant said, his voice barely audible over the tail end of a thunderclap.

He fisted his hand in the back of my coat and guided me to the right, toward the closest tree. I reached for Quinn. He cautiously folded his wings, and together we inched toward cover. Two heads split their attention to either side of the hydra, but the remaining three continued to sniff in our direction.

Grant slipped off the edge of the road, his leg sinking to the knee in a puddle. I grabbed for his arm. Quinn's wings flared. All five hydra heads snapped to focus on us. The monster scuttled closer. Webbed, long-toed feet sank into the mud with each step, globs of muck flinging from its arched claws.

"Nobody move," Grant ordered.

We froze in place, Grant awkwardly splayed for balance and me with my arm floating between us. Quinn held his position with the innate skill of a gargoyle. The hydra slowed and stopped. Less than forty feet separated us, but it swung its heads back and forth like it couldn't see us. The tallest head jerked up, tracking the flight of a thunderbird above the lake.

That's it. Focus on the bird. You don't want us paltry humans and stony gargoyle. We all taste terrible.

Ever so slowly, Grant tested the ground closer to the tree with his long stick. Minutes ticked by while my heart tried to pound through my rib cage. Every direction Grant prodded, the stick sank even deeper in the water. The only solid land was the old road.

We couldn't risk swimming. For starters, it wasn't an option for Quinn. The passive magic that enabled gargoyles to fly did nothing to prevent them from sinking like the stones they were in deep water. Even if he hadn't been with us, swimming still would have been too dangerous for Grant and me. I knew exactly two facts about hydras: They lived near bodies of salt water and they were adept aquatic hunters. I had never expected to encounter one so far inland. Normally, hydras were predators only sailors and coastal residents had to defend against.

Grant eased back onto the road. Keeping himself between the hydra and me, he skulked to the opposite side of the road. Breathing too fast, I shifted with him, Quinn tucked against my side. The skin between my shoulder blades itched, and I twitched at every lightning strike. I kept picturing a thunderbird dive-bombing us, flinging deadly bolts at our backs while we were fixated on the hydra. I didn't dare turn to check, though, afraid I would be facing the wrong direction when Grant gave the order to run.

"Why hasn't it attacked?" I asked during a lull between booming thunders.

"Poor vision. They hunt by movement."

I clamped down on Quinn's wing. Slipping, falling, and giving away our location jumped to the top of my list of fears, pushing aside my worry about a thunderbird attack.

The hydra shuffled, heads swiveling, necks twisting until

it looked like it would tie itself in knots. The moment Grant poked into the water on the opposite side of the road, one head whipped forward to fixate on the moving stick.

Grant edged over another step. His stick slid deeper into the water. He stretched forward, then backward, searching for the ground. Abruptly, the mud beneath him gave way. Grant jumped, but not fast enough. The mudslide devoured the ground beneath his feet, taking Grant with it. Between one lightning flash and the next, he disappeared beneath the murky pond's surface.

"Grant!" Thunder drowned out my cry.

The hydra charged.

Quinn unleashed a lion's challenging roar and yanked free of my grip. Ten ebony hydra eyes locked on him. Snarling, Quinn surged forward, flinging mud with each powerful lunge. He was nearly as large as a flesh-and-blood lion, but even with his wings splayed, he looked tiny as he sprinted for the towering hydra.

"Quinn, stop!" Grant bellowed in a voice meant to be heard across battlefields—and over the peals of thunder.

Quinn didn't slow. Neither did the hydra. It bore down on Quinn with shocking speed, reaching him before I could do more than seize the elements. All five heads struck at once.

None connected.

A second before impact, a massive fist of air flung Quinn backward. He landed behind me, all four paws digging into the muddy ground as he slid to a halt.

"They spit poison," Grant yelled.

I gaped at Grant. Only his head was visible as he treaded water. Mud ran in rivulets down his forehead and rain splashed surface water into his eyes, but he had managed to redirect a couple hundred pounds of sprinting gargoyle with precise accuracy—all without drowning.

Deprived of its prey, the hydra screamed, five throats harmonizing in a grating roar, before plunging forward again.

Grant grabbed the nearest mandrake root and heaved himself out of the water. A river streamed from his pack and the rolled-up carpet tied to it. In a blur of impressive dexterity, Grant climbed the network of twisted roots. When he reached the trunk, he spun and leapt for the road, landing with a knife in each hand.

"Get him clean. Use mud," Grant barked, then rushed to meet the hydra.

Bursts of fire exploded in front of the hydra's heads—one, two, three, four, five. The downpour extinguished them almost immediately, but not before the hydra shrieked and skidded to a stop. Its heads swiveled and its teeth gnashed, biting at empty air. Grant dashed to the side, slicing an opening into the jaw of the lowest head. Blood and raindrops blasted away from Grant on a gust of air. He had used magic to deflect the poison.

I spun to Quinn. Pain pulled his mouth into a frightening snarl, and his breaths came in ragged pants.

"Roll, Quinn! Get muddy." I mimed my order, afraid he wouldn't hear me.

Quinn dropped and rolled, squirming against the soupy ground. I raced to him, landing on my knees and scooping handfuls of mud over his face and chest. The wind shifted and the rain intensified, washing the muck away even as I scooped more over his chest. Grit caught in the pockmarks marring Quinn's toes and forelegs, where the hydra's toxic spit had eaten into his quartz body.

Damn it! I should have stopped him. Gargoyles weren't indestructible.

Quinn used a wing to right himself and shook. Mud cascaded down his slick body.

"Better?" I asked.

He glanced over my shoulder. I had a second to read the determination in his eyes before he reared on his hind legs and launched skyward. I dove sideways, out of his way. Mud splashed into my mouth. Spitting it out, I scrambled to my feet.

My heart leapt to my throat when I spotted Grant. The hydra had him surrounded, heads snapping from alternating angles. He slashed a blade through the side of a neck, the dark spray of blood outlined in a lightning flash. The wounded neck retreated, replaced by two different heads striking at Grant's back and a third at his legs. Shields of air popped like miniature detonations in the hydra's faces, redirecting its toxic spray. Grant dodged and dropped into a roll to avoid a fourth mouth before springing to his feet. His knives never slowed, slicing and stabbing into any available flesh. The hydra had to be bleeding from a dozen cuts, but it showed no sign of letting up.

My feet burst into motion before my brain caught up; then I stumbled to a stop. I didn't have a weapon or Grant's reflexes. If I got close to the hydra, I would be more of a hindrance than a help.

Grant hammered the air around the hydra with fire, disorienting three of the heads. The other two shied back. I was close enough to hear the sizzle of extinguished flames during a rare lull between thunderclaps, yet I couldn't sense the elements being used. The air was so charged with diffused lightning that it had deadened my senses.

But not the thunderbirds'.

Any second now, they would notice the fireworks of elements being used here and investigate. My shoulders hunched in anticipation, but I didn't dare look away from the battle. Quinn fought the wild winds, beating his wings twice as hard as normal to gain altitude. Flashes of lightning highlighted him against the dark sky, the afterimage lending a shimmer around his bright body. It made him a beacon the hydra couldn't fail to miss.

"Higher, Quinn, higher," I urged.

The hydra whipped a head skyward, striking for Quinn's hind leg. I was prepared and slammed a ward in the hydra's way. Its blunt snout bashed into my elemental barrier. A reverberating gong of pain hammered inside my brain. The elements slipped from my grasp, but not before Quinn cleared the hydra's snapping jaws. The gargoyle folded his wings and dove toward the hydra's back, jaws agape.

Grant's magic shot over the hydra's heads and heaved Quinn aside before he connected. Quinn spun through the air, crashing into a mangrove's branches before plummeting. At the last second, his wings opened, and he landed with a jarring crash.

What had Grant been thinking?

The distraction cost him. Grant dodged an attack seconds too late, and a hydra head struck, engulfing his pack and carpet. The hydra yanked Grant into the air, the other heads snaking around to finish him off. I punched fists of air into their snouts. Each hit felt like slamming my head into concrete, but it made the beast pause. Grant slashed the straps of his pack, freeing himself. He fell, curling into an immediate roll.

Instead of escaping, he angled under the writhing necks toward the hydra's body. His knife jabbed toward the hydra's chest. It scuttled backward, too fast. A head dropped to rip into Grant's defenseless body. Grant flipped himself onto his back, crossed arms raised. Almost too fast to follow, he scissored his knives through the hydra's neck, slicing the head clean off. Air exploded upward, spraying a fan of blood away from Grant and knocking the decapitated head off the road into the water. Four throats keened the same note as the remaining heads flailed in a frenzy. Grant domed a shield over himself and rolled free. He should have run left to give himself breathing room, but he ducked right, scooping up his bag. He punched the rug free, then flung the lightened pack toward me. He barely finished the throw before jumping aside and slicing the jaw of a hydra head that bit the air where he had stood a second earlier.

The headless neck spontaneously severed from the hydra's chest, the long column toppling and narrowly missing Grant. A maelstrom of elements coalesced at the bloody stump, magic siphoning from the ether into the hydra in a tangible rush like nothing I had ever felt before in my life.

Quinn swooped in front of the hydra, drawing its attention. Grant shouted at Quinn. The wind stole his words, and I was too busy frantically blasting air in front of each hissing mouth to read Grant's lips. Like exhales into a wind funnel, the storm swallowed my small magics as fast as I created them. I strained to see if my deflecting tactics had prevented acid from landing on Quinn, but he dropped behind the hydra and out of sight.

The hydra's heads parted, providing an unwelcome view of the stump. The raw flesh writhed, gushing blood, the gory mass twisting and bulging as the hydra repositioned itself. My stomach flipped, bile splashing against the back of my throat, but I couldn't look away. Slowly, two black heads birthed from the wound. The necks lengthened a foot, two feet. Four sets of brand-new eyes opened. All four locked on Grant.

He redoubled his attack. With the hydra injured, he should have had the upper hand, but the monster didn't appear to feel pain. The writhing heads assaulted Grant with unrelenting viciousness. He had lost a knife—it protruded from the eye of the head farthest on the right. With only one blade left, Grant had to exert more energy to avoid being bitten, barely nicking the hydra when he was able to land a blow.

Magic funneled into the new necks, fueling their growth until they stretched as tall as the rest, though half as thin. Grant now had six jaws to defend against. He couldn't keep this up. We needed to escape.

I searched for Quinn. He dove through the rain behind the hydra, his descent silent beneath the boom of thunder, his body sheathed in a golden nimbus. My heart lodged in my windpipe when he raked his claws into the hydra's back. Three heads whipped around to decimate Quinn. He dodged, careening through the hydra's necks, pushed more by wind than his own wing flaps. He landed hard a body length in front of me, splattering me with mud. Without slowing, he bounded for the soft edge of the road and began digging with all four feet. Lightning flashed, illuminating his agonized expression.

"What's wrong?" I shouted.

"The blood. It burns!" Quinn submerged his feet in the goop he had churned up. I ran to him, bending to slap mud against his belly.

"Incoming!" Grant shoved me to the ground. His body curled protectively over me, and a ward of pure earth element domed all three of us seconds before a pair of thunderbirds arrowed through the trees. Electricity crackled close, lifting the hair on my arms. Two bolts launched from the thunderbirds' talons, blindingly bright in my peripheral vision. They struck for the hydra heads, both missing.

Grant cursed. "I should never—"

Thunder bludgeoned me like a physical punch, stealing my breath. The ward shimmered with a strange, sparkling glow. Grant mouthed a familiar curse, the sound lost beneath the ringing in my ears. He dropped the ward.

Two more thunderbirds swooped in from opposite sides, focused on the hydra. Another speared straight down. For a surreal, suspended second, I witnessed a glowing halo gather around the thunderbird's talon. Fire, water, and air elements churned inside the light, their pattern too complex to decipher. Then the thunderbird curled its foot into a fist, crushing the magic into a singular weapon. Lightning shot from the bird's talons.

The hydra whipped its heads out of the way, snapping time back to full speed. A skinny-necked head caught a mouthful of tail feathers and received a lightning blast down its throat. A shudder ran through the hydra, as if someone had tickled it. Three more bolts split the air around its weaving heads.

Thunder pounded relentlessly. Pain spiked through my head and the world spun in place. I clamped my hands over my ears, but it did little to muffle the concussive booms. Grant tugged me to my knees, pointing toward a stump farther up the road. It bounced in my vision. When I refocused on Grant, he shouted, and I read his lips.

"Run!"

Grant propelled me to my feet, holding tight to my bicep to keep me upright. I ran, each step hammering fresh agony through my head. Quinn dashed in front of us, his ears plastered to his scalp, mud spraying beneath his stone paws.

Massive thunderbirds careened above us, close enough to alter the wind currents. Battering waves of sound punched my rib cage. My breathing rasped from my lungs, hot and panicked. I couldn't hear any of it, just a high-pitched ringing. If not for his grip on my arm, I wouldn't have known Grant raced beside me.

I flung myself down behind the stump. Grant landed next to me. Quinn hunkered tight by our feet. The stump had once been a large tree, but not large enough to conceal the three of us.

Grant grabbed my face with both his hands, holding me when I would have turned to check the clash behind us. His mouth moved, but I couldn't read his lips in the dim lighting. He squeezed me tighter. I brought my hands up in protest.

White-hot agony drilled into my ears, melting my eardrums, igniting my brain. Screaming, I clamped down on Grant's wrists, trying to tear him away from me. Seconds later, the pain receded. I sobbed with relief and clung to Grant for support. A low-grade headache throbbed at the back of my head, but compared to the previous pain, it was almost pleasure.

"Your eardrums had ruptured. Sorry I'm not a trained healer."

I blinked rain and tears from my eyes and tried to nod. Grant shifted his grip to my shoulders. Thunder crashed close and fast, but a thick air buffer stood between us and the battle, deflecting the worst of the sound.

Even as I took a breath of relief, a thunderbird peeled from the hydra, diving for the magical barrier. The same static-like glow that had enveloped Grant's ward ghosted over the elemental wall, growing brighter as the enormous bird closed in on us. Grant collapsed the magic into a thick ball and threw it toward the hydra. Screeching, the thunder-bird banked to chase the wadded elements. They fizzled out seconds later, and the bird plunged back into the fray.

Grant scrunched lower and dropped a tight, soundproof ward around the three of us. Or rather, he crafted a ward that would have been soundproof anywhere other than in the middle of a frenzied flock of thunderbirds. It muffled the thunderous booms, giving them a pleasant, distant quality. It also cut through the wind and rain, cocooning us in a bubble of serenity.

"That won't distract them long," Grant said. "I never meant to cut off that blasted head, but maybe we can use this to our advantage."

We searched the storm-darkened swamp for an escape. Thunderbirds swarmed the air, diving again and again to pummel the hydra with lightning. The monstrous reptile appeared as unfazed by the birds' electric magic as it had been by my wards, absorbing countless lightning strikes without slowing—and without showing any sign of moving from the road.

We needed an alternate route out of the swamp, and quickly, before more thunderbirds noticed us. I considered and dismissed using the mandrake trees as a guide. Their roots grew in clumps above the water but didn't necessarily indicate solid ground. Nor could we make a bridge of sorts out of their gnarled roots. Even if I could have balanced atop the slick roots, the trees were too far apart to jump from one to the next. In between lay shadows and water, and only the stiller quality of the water's surface differentiated it from the lake behind me.

"We're too exposed here." Grant had somehow retrieved his pack before we had fled, and now he knotted the severed straps into a single loop, sliding it crosswise over his chest without pausing his examination of our surroundings. "We can't go back until the hydra is gone, and two others are about to join the fight."

He spoke so calmly, it took a beat before his words registered.

"What? Where?"

Grant pointed. The hydras swam through the swamp on our right, surging over half-buried hills and slipping back into the water. One had seven heads, the other only three, and both were smaller than the hydra Grant and Quinn had battled. In the gloom, I had mistaken their swaying necks for trees when I scanned the swamp. How many more hydras lurked in plain sight?

The seven-headed hydra clambered onto the road, lunging for the closest thunderbirds. An enormous bird carcass lay at the feet of the first hydra. Limp, it looked remarkably plain, just a huge blue-gray mass of feathers that would have blended in with the watery ground if not for the hydra head feasting on it. The other five heads continued to fight.

The third hydra joined the fray. It angled for the dead bird, attempting to steal it from the larger hydra. A flurry of reptilian fighting ensued, the heads whipping back and forth in a blur. When the hydras parted, the smaller one emerged with only two heads attached, the third hanging by a grisly string of flesh at the end of its long neck. Then the neck broke from the body, hit the edge of the road, and sank into the swamp. The wounded hydra shuffled backward. Elements whisked around us, rushing to the hydra's open neck wound. I looked away before the new heads emerged. Having witnessed that once was enough for a lifetime of nightmares.

"We don't have time to feel out another route—if one

exists," Grant said. "It'll take too long and leave us too vulnerable. We need shelter."

"We retreat?" Quinn asked.

"We retreat," Grant confirmed.

A rivulet of cold water trickled beneath my collar, tracing an ominous shiver down my spine. The only place we could retreat to was the island. Fewer thunderbirds clustered around the dubious structures, but the shoreline ruckus hadn't distracted them all. I still couldn't make out the building or what sort of magic prevented the thunderbirds from breaking through the roof, either. For all we knew, the ward would be equally impenetrable to us, too.

"Are you sure that qualifies as shelter?" I lifted trembling fingers to the pouch holding my everlasting seed, wondering not for the first time if it was trying to kill me.

"It's not ideal, but it's all we've got."

I squinted, scrutinizing the crumbling causeway for gaps, but the pounding in my head shattered my concentration. What had started out as a dull ache now felt like a pulsing fire. I clamped my hands down on my scalp, then released it just as quickly when something bit my fingers.

"Ow!" I examined my fingertips. They looked fine. I rolled my eyes up, as if it would enable me to see the back of my head.

"Release your magic," Grant ordered.

"I'm not holding any."

"Then why is your head glowing?"

Glowing? "It feels like my scalp is splitting."

Grant grabbed my shoulders and ducked my head between my knees. He cursed, and a second later, cool water and air magic washed through my hair, extinguishing the pain.

"What? What was it?" I asked, uncurling as much as our hiding place allowed.

"A tracker." Grant turned to monitor the thunderbird and hydra brawl.

"Whose? Yours?"

"Not mine."

Confusion knit my brow. "Why did it burn?"

"It's the thunderbirds. The air is so charged with their magic that spells attract an electric charge." He flicked his fingers toward the ward, which had taken on a faint glow. Sparks twinkled around the outside edge.

"Does it hurt?" I asked, hoping the space between his body and the spell meant he wasn't experiencing the same pain I had felt.

"It doesn't feel good."

That explained one mystery—two, if I counted the glow I had witnessed around Quinn. Gargoyle flight required passive magic. It hadn't been a trick of the light that had given him an aura when he had been attacking the hydra. But that didn't explain why a tracker had been hidden on me in the first place. Or who had done the hiding. It had been planted by someone skilled, otherwise Quinn, Grant, or I would have noticed it sooner. Had they needed to be close or had they embedded the magic from afar? And who would want to keep track of my whereabouts? Maybe Nathan. The jerk had followed me before to steal my stories. I wouldn't put it past him to have upgraded his stalking efforts. But did he have the kind of skill necessary to create such a subtle spell?

"Zipporah." I blurted the name out in a burst of insight. It had to have been her. How else had she found me at Persephone's?

"Likely," Grant agreed.

The screech of thunderbirds penetrated his ward. Five dove in unison for the largest hydra, lightning slinging from their feet. The air fragmented in thunderclaps, light strobing the scene into flashes of claws, teeth, and blood.

I pivoted to examine our escape route. The aged causeway looked even worse up close than it had from afar. Rubble from toppled decorative towers littered the water-slicked surface, and waves churned just below it. Even if the causeway was stable enough for us to navigate its entire length, we would be exposed, with nowhere to hide if the thunderbirds spotted us.

Grant locked his fist around my arm. "We're only going to get one shot. Are you ready?"

My stomach backflipped and dove for my toes. This was borderline suicidal, but what other choice did we have?

"I'm ready."

"Stick close," Grant said. "No sudden movements. We'll blend in with the shadows." His gaze fell on Quinn, and he frowned. The gargoyle's glossy citrine body shimmered like a lion-shaped glowball in every lightning flash.

"I can fly ahead—"

"No. Flying uses magic. The birds will swarm you. Just stay close."

"I'd rather have you by my side anyway," I said, resting my hand on Quinn's shoulder. He leaned into my touch, but worry pinched his expression.

"Kylie, use air to plug your ears and Quinn's," Grant instructed. "When it starts to hurt, release the magic, then form new plugs. Let's go before the birds remember we're here."

I stuffed dense air into my ear canals, then into Quinn's. We both gave Grant a nod to indicate we were ready. Grant released the ward. The sizzling elements collapsed against my soaked clothing, inflicting a cascade of pinching electric shocks. Quinn shuddered, shaking off the mild pain.

His quartz body might be hardier than mine, but he wasn't solid rock. He had stone muscles and innards and pain receptors that weren't immune to the crackling energy. If he suffered a lightning strike, he would survive, but the electric current would be agonizing. If he got struck repeatedly, it would be as fatal to him as a single strike would be to me.

Grant and I crouched as we jogged toward the causeway. Without the ward's protection, rain slapped my face, cold and sharp, and the next boom of thunder vibrated through my body. The air plugs cut the sound in half, but I already missed Grant's protective magic.

I expected thunderbirds to immediately peel away from the hydras and dive-bomb us. We were vulnerable and exposed, easy prey for the pickings.

"Not too fast," Grant said close to my ear. He tugged me back to a jog when I would have sprinted. "If you run, they'll give chase."

Quinn bumped my side, keeping close as the ground rose and we passed between the tall pillars flanking the causeway's entrance. On the left, a marble man of impeccable physique gazed out at the swamp, a benign smile fixed in place and a palm frond in one raised hand. Half the leaflets were broken from the frond. Claw gouges cut through the statue's stone hair, and its right arm and shoulder were missing. On the opposite pillar, only the knees, shins, and feet of another statue remained, the body pulverized against the stone walkway.

I couldn't resist glancing back. The thunderbirds circled the hydras, biting and clawing and electrocuting the nest of writhing heads. The hydras held their own, showing no sign of abandoning the road.

My toe met an immovable object. Pain jolted to my

ankle, and I floundered to catch my balance. Grant steadied me with a vise grip on my arm.

"Watch your step. Quinn, tighten ranks. Get behind us."

The causeway stretched wide enough for two horse-drawn carriages to pass, and we kept to the center. I squinted to pick out tripping hazards. As happy as I was to leave behind the thunderbirds, we also left behind the illumination of their lightning.

Wind picked up across the lake, unimpeded by trees. I leaned into it, ducking my head away from the stinging raindrops. Puddles lay inches deep across the stone surface, and each step splashed my pants and drenched my sodden boots. A low stone parapet ran along either side of the walkway, the knee-high railing providing no protection from the elements and nominal visual cover. Wind smashed a tall wave against the causeway, spraying my face. I spat out the briny salt water.

We swung wide around a ragged semicircle where the lake had consumed a chunk of the causeway. A wave sloshed over the remaining surface, obscuring our path. I slowed as the water ebbed, the rushing current tugging at my footing. Ripples in the receding water revealed broken stones and rubble. Carefully, we picked our way through.

My ears burned, the pain escalating fast. Hastily, I banished my air plugs and did the same for Quinn. Thunder assaulted my ears, pounding in rapid-fire booms. At least one hydra had fallen and writhed on the ground. A clump of thunderbirds swarmed it, their gray wings overlapping as they clawed the defenseless hydra's body. The other two hydras fought on.

I restuffed Quinn's ears, then mine, and faced forward.

We wove past crumbled sections and toppled statues of marble men and women, their arms snapped off, torsos cracked, and heads shattered. Among the remains, I caught glimpses of elemental symbols carved into the statues' hands and feet, stone vines twining along the parapet, and stumps of animal figures. At one point, this causeway must have been an impressive artistic welcoming to anyone attending the spa. I tried to picture it undamaged and bathed in sunshine, but my imagination failed me.

Grant slowed, and I stumbled to a stop next to him. The walkway disappeared into frothing waves, reappearing more than ten feet ahead of us. Only the parapet remained on the left, the low wall less than a foot and a half wide.

Jumping the gap was out of the question.

"Do we trust that?" I asked, pointing to the wave-eroded parapet.

"More than I trust swimming." Grant studied the thunderbirds circling the warded structure on the island, then the larger flock pummeling the hydras. Or maybe he was assessing all the lightning in the air. "I could levitate us, but I don't want to risk attracting attention if we can avoid it. Wait until I'm across, then follow."

With enviable agility, he traversed the slick capstones of the parapet, seemingly impervious to the wind buffeting him. When he reached the other side, I stepped onto the slender ledge. A spray of salt water slapped my face. I wiped the moisture from my eyes, the gesture futile in the downpour. Shoving wayward strands of hair out of my face, I shuffled forward. Water sluiced from the slender capstones into the churning lake, and dizzying flashes of lightning highlighted a strobe of waves on either side of my feet. A gust tore at my legs, and my foot slipped. I dropped to a crouch to catch my balance, my heart pounding in my chest.

If I fall, it's only water, I reminded myself. I could swim.

If I wasn't electrocuted first.

I forced myself to take the next teetering step, then another, hardly breathing until I jumped down beside Grant. I spun to monitor Quinn's progress. Even from a distance, he looked scared as he climbed atop the thin parapet. What was an obstacle to me would be death to him. Gargoyles couldn't swim. If he fell in, he would sink and drown.

No, he wouldn't. I would save him or Grant would.

The narrow capstones looked positively spindly beneath Quinn's lion paws. He spread his wings for balance and tiptoed forward, all four feet in an unnaturally tight line. Behind him, a trio of thunderbirds spun from the flock and arrowed toward us.

"Hurry, Quinn!" I called.

Static flicked the inside of my ears, hot and sharp. Grimacing, I released the elemental plugs on myself and Quinn.

"Hurry!" I shouted again before repacking dense air into our ear canals.

A repetitious three-tone whistle from the incoming thunderbirds sliced through the deeper crashes of rolling thunder. A faint reply sang from the island. I spun to check, my heart sinking when two thunderbirds launched from the devastated buildings, flying to meet the birds converging on us.

Quinn picked up speed, but he wasn't going fast enough. The edge of a capstone crumbled beneath his back paw, and his leg buckled. He scrambled for balance, then edged forward again, too slowly.

Grant heaved a bundle of water element out over the lake. The lead thunderbird peeled off to give chase. Grant tossed another, but the other thunderbirds didn't take the bait. Wings flapping in tandem, they split formation and swept wide to approach us from opposite sides. Half-formed lightning sparked on their talons.

Grant threw a spear of wood element at the bird on the right. The thunderbird twisted, avoiding the blow, but its momentum carried it past us before it could unleash its lightning. Deciding Grant's moratorium on large-scale magic was over, I drew deep on Quinn's enhancement. The elements thrummed in my grip.

"Quinn, duck!" I shouted, gesturing for him to get down.

Quinn hunkered down on his perch, and I flung a wood-element spear over his head at the thunderbird closing in on him. My magic wasn't as big as Grant's or as strong, and wind tore it aside. The thunderbird swept past Quinn without acknowledging him. Claws extended and sparking, it bore down on me.

I hurled a blast of wind at the bird. Magic and thunderbird collided, and I staggered in place, feeling like I had run headfirst into a wall. The thunderbird careened to the side, lightning spewing from its talons. It crackled horizontally above the lake, a short streak of deadly, blinding electricity igniting far too close. Thunder exploded, the concussive wave stealing my breath. The afterimage of the bolt blurred my vision, and the causeway tilted beneath my feet. I landed hard on one knee, my teeth snapping together. The coppery taste of blood flooded my mouth. I braced a hand on the drenched cobbles, gasping soundlessly.

Fire burned down my ear canals, and I flung our air plugs aside, replacing them just as fast. Successive, disorienting booms exploded around us as the thunderbirds unleashed their deadly strikes. Somehow, Grant retained his footing, and he launched a steady stream of elemental attacks at the thunderbirds. They ducked and wove, working in concert, avoiding his barrage even as they pressed closer. I couldn't tell if the birds were simply adroit hunters in their element, better equipped for this fight than Grant, or if fatigue had stolen the precision from Grant's assault. He was the captain of an FPD squad, a full spectrum, and battle trained, with the body of a warrior. It made it easy to forget he wasn't invincible. But he had already battled a hydra. Even Grant had his limits.

Quinn wobbled another dozen steps, then leapt for the causeway, coasting on his outspread wings. The nearest thunderbird pivoted and dove for him, screeching in outrage at the gargoyle's use of magic. I grabbed air and shoved it under the bird's wings, working with the wind to fling it aside. The thunderbird faltered, then flapped higher. Quinn touched down and bounded to my side.

Grant shouted something, his words lost beneath the thunder. Then he grabbed my arm and tugged me toward the island shore. Blinking to stabilize my vision, I broke into a sprint, Quinn on my heels. Lightning bombarded the air, illuminating our path in short bursts. My heart hammered in my chest, fear sharpening my coordination over the slippery, uneven stones. Grant ran blind, trusting me to guide us as he chucked elemental spears, driving the birds aside before their lightning could strike us.

Piles of rubble impeded our headlong dash, forcing us through zigzagging twists. Every obstacle that slowed us intensified my urgency. As long as we were trapped on the causeway, we would be vulnerable. If we hoped to survive, we needed to reach shelter.

"Jump!" Grant barked.

Nothing I could see lay in our path, but I didn't hesitate. I sprang as high as my trembling legs could muster. A platform of air materialized under my feet. I pitched forward, my knees buckling at the unexpected impact. Grant landed behind to me, locking me against his chest before I could fall. Quinn galloped beside us.

Chest heaving, I looked around frantically. Five thunderbirds had us surrounded, their glowing talons bearing down on us in a coordinated attack. I threw punches of air at their faces, my aim wild in my haste. Two elemental blasts connected, knocking the birds off their trajectory. They shook the blows off and circled back around. Grant tossed two others aside with calculated strikes. For a second, we had a reprieve.

Where was the fifth bird?

I tipped my head back. Rain splashed into my eyes, and I blinked it away. A cobalt shape plummeted out of the roiling clouds, coalescing into a diving thunderbird. I tried to scream a warning to Grant, but rain hit the back of my throat on my inhale. Sputtering, I pointed frantically.

"Quinn, here," Grant shouted, extending the platform on our right.

Quinn landed beside me, smashing into my thigh. The elemental platform dipped, and I clutched Quinn's wing for balance, throwing rapid-fire air punches at the diving thunderbird. None of my efforts slowed it. Cupping its wings, the thunderbird brought its sparking feet forward to strike—

Our platform jetted forward. My head knocked against Grant's hard chest. I bent my knees, struggling for equilibrium. Behind us, frighteningly close, lightning split the air.

"Link!" Grant bellowed a fraction of a second before the deafening blast of thunder punched us.

I grabbed a balance of all five elements and thrust the bundle at Grant. He seized it and plunged my magic into his. His power swamped me, encasing me in a riveting mix of volatile energy and unyielding control. A dizzying rush of elements surged through me, and I held fast to my mental balance as Grant used me—and Quinn—to augment his own impressive powers. Swifter than I would have been able to follow without the link, he wove wood and earth into a perfect sphere around us.

Lightning struck the barrier with a crack. Electricity fizzled around the ward in a hot wave that stole my breath. The hairs on my arms and neck attempted to stand on end despite being soaked. Another strike hit the ward, then another. Thunder assailed us. My vision blurred, my heartbeat faltering, then catching between the pounding assaults. The ward crackled with an electric glow, the buildup of the thunderbirds' magic sparking around the elemental sphere. Grant shielded me from the burning pain, but I could feel the strain it put on him. I yearned to contribute, to drive the thunderbirds back, but doing so would require drawing on magic Grant needed to maintain the ward.

Waterlogged cobbles of the causeway flashed past beneath us. Lightning sparked in the air, dancing across the standing water. If Grant dropped us, we would all be electrocuted.

Hold on, Grant.

The earplugs began to burn, and I dispersed the magic. Drawing cautiously on the elements, I replaced them, doing my best not to distract Grant.

The platform dipped toward the causeway, the sudden drop sending my stomach into my throat.

"Get ready to run," Grant shouted. His ward blasted outward. The thunderbirds scattered, repelled by a flurry of elemental spikes that chased the dispersed magic. "Now!"

Grant shoved me, and I stumbled into a run, my arms flailing for balance when I hit the ground sooner than I expected. He caught me a stride later, his feet clipping mine, spurring me faster. Quinn tripped, skidding on one foreleg.

"Quinn!" I twisted in Grant's grip, a useless hand flung out to help Quinn. Grant ruthlessly propelled me onward. Over my shoulder, I watched Quinn scramble to his feet and leap after us. He caught up in two massive bounds.

I spun forward. The stones sloshed in foaming peaks in front of us. I stared at the bouncing surface, my brain taking a moment to process that I was looking at the lake, not a wind-frothed puddle atop rock.

"The bridge is missing," I shouted.

"I see it." Grant didn't slow.

The thunderbirds swept closer. A fisted talon sparkled in my periphery. I pushed more speed from my burning thighs, eyeing the gap.

"I can't make it," I panted.

"Get ready." Grant's hand constricted on my bicep. "Jump!"

I flung myself over the water. A platform of air materialized beneath me—beneath all of us. It sagged, swaying and rocking above the waves. I pitched into Quinn, bending in half to keep my balance. Through the link, I felt Grant fight for control as the waves pummeled the levitation spell from below. Then we were across the gap, and the cobblestones were beneath us once more. I tensed to run, but Grant snapped an elemental bubble around us in time to deflect a barrage of lightning bolts. Each hit rang through the link like a sledgehammer blow. Even insulated inside Grant's magic, the battering spiked pain through my head. It must have been excruciating for Grant, but he held the ward unwaveringly and propelled the platform forward with renewed speed.

The causeway finally, *finally* gave way to solid land. Or semisolid land. A shallow waterfall cascaded down a broken stone incline, and rivulets of perpetual runoff sculpted the mud into dense veins on either side. Grant steered us straight up the slope.

The old resort sprawled atop the hill. At one time, it must have been beautiful, but in the strobing light, the broken structures and gaping windows now resembled a troll's gruesome grin. We blasted past twin semicircles of charred stumps cupping the entrance, enclosing a cracked, overflowing fountain adorned with a trio of headless herons. The warded section hunkered to the left, but Grant kept our flight path locked on the closest building. Heat condensed inside the ward, radiating inward from the electric charge sizzling around the barrier. I could no longer distinguish individual thunderclaps; they exploded so rapidly, the world had turned into one ceaseless roar. Agony cleaved my head, drilling through my earplugs, and my heart fluttered to catch its own rhythm between waves of sound. A spike of searing pain leaked through the link before Grant reasserted control, and I gasped, locking my knees so I didn't crumple.

We shot through an open doorway too fast. The ward clipped the frame in an explosion of wooden splinters, and Grant flung the spell aside. Sparks arced through the air, racing in short, charged dashes across leaf-strewn puddles on the tiled floor before extinguishing. We careened through a dilapidated foyer, dodging broken furniture and cracked earthen pots to reach a dry patch of shredded carpet at the back of the room.

"Brace yourself," Grant barked a second before the platform dissipated and our link evaporated.

Electricity snapped against my waterlogged pants, biting my flesh. I hit the ground on numb feet and slammed into the wall. Grant smacked to a halt on my left. Quinn crashed into the wall on my right, shaking the whole building.

Chunks of plaster exploded around his impact, and dust rained from the ceiling.

I spun to check behind us. A flurry of blue-gray wings and ebony talons obscured the broken windows and doorway. The door swayed, the last hinge holding it snapping. The slab of wood crashed to the ground, spraying grimy water, and the thunderbirds launched into the air with angry shrieks.

I waited for them to return. The entrance was more than wide enough for the birds to fit through if they walked. But the windows remained vacant, the doorway gaping open on a view of the angry lake and the long, eroded causeway.

Despair sank into my gut. We had reached our destination, but would we ever escape?

22

I lifted the collar of my jacket, breathing through the soggy fabric until the dust settled. Quinn righted himself, looking dazed but otherwise unharmed. Gingerly, I tested one ankle, then the other, twinges of discomfort confirming I had landed badly. My wrist hurt from impact with the wall, and I shook it out.

A faded fresco adorned the ceiling, more than half of it missing, the rest of it ruined by dirty water stains. Puddles marred the floor, trickling toward the entrance, where wind drove rain through the broken panes and splintered doorway. For now, though, we were sheltered. No lightning could reach us, and the walls muted the thunder. Persephone's ancestors might be horrified to see the current condition of their once-majestic resort, but in that moment, it felt like a slice of paradise.

Beside me, Grant remained bent in half, one hand braced on the wall. Water dripped from his forehead to combine with the puddle growing around our feet.

"Are you all right?" I reached for him, his uncharacteristic lack of vigilance setting off internal alarm bells.

He shook his head. "How do you talk me into these predicaments?"

"I believe coming here was your idea."

He shot me an incredulous look.

"Here," I clarified, pointing at our feet. "I was ready to leave the swamp, remember?"

"Remind me what your grand plan was for sneaking past a clutch of hydras."

"Mostly waiting for them to die first."

"Ah."

"Having a roof over my head is nice." I nibbled my bottom lip, then blurted out the question I was almost too afraid to ask. "Are we going to be able to leave?"

"Not a chance."

"What?" Quinn shoved his face into Grant's. "But—"

"Not without my team."

"You can get a message through that?" I flung a hand out to indicate the storm, not liking Grant's defeated tone.

He snorted and finally straightened, his eyes squinted with pain. "I had a feeling this trip might not be the easy reconnaissance mission you imagined. Which is why Seradon knows to mobilize the squad and rescue us when we don't return."

I sagged against the wall. A rescue was on the way. We wouldn't die here.

"They won't be coming for another twenty-four hours, though. I need to get you both to a more secure place to wait it out."

Thunderclaps no longer exploded on top of each other. Actual blissful stretches of quiet existed between sky-sundering booms. We had found a dry patch free of the driving rain, and we appeared to have been forgotten by the thunderbirds. I was loathe to move. But before I could argue against leaving this haven, a thunderbird struck the roof. The walls shook, fresh dust cascading from cracks in the plaster. Something heavy hit the floor above us, and the structure moaned ominously. The birds took up a raucous cry like oversize crows arguing over a scrap of food. Lightning brightened the world for a split second, highlighting the heavy downpour and our dilapidated surroundings, including the sagging support beams we had blasted past on the way in.

"Lead on, fearless captain," I said.

Grant gave me a mock salute and strode toward an inner door. He made it three steps before his knees dipped. He caught himself, swayed unsteadily, and braced a hand against the wall. Dread spiked down my spine.

"Grant?" I darted to his side. Ragged rips perforated his coat, visible on either side of his pack. The fabric lay matted against his back, and more than shadows darkened the material. Blood? I had seen the hydra bite him, but he hadn't reacted. I had assumed the monster's poisonous, deadly teeth had caught only the carpet and pack, not his flesh.

"How bad is it? What can I do?" I reached for his coat, but Grant pushed my hand aside. "Don't play tough. Tell me how to help you."

"I will. But neither of us is using magic until we're inside that ward."

In the storm's abysmal lighting, I had missed more than the cuts on his back. Grant's face had lost its color, and pain pinched white around his lips. His free hand fisted at his side, his body stiff.

I didn't waste time arguing. Sliding an arm around his waist below the bite marks, I held him, acutely aware that if he collapsed, I wouldn't be strong enough to carry him.

"I'm not an invalid," Grant grumbled, but I had to brace my thighs when he leaned his weight against me.

Quinn rushed to lead the way, casting a worried glance over his shoulder at Grant. We bypassed a grand staircase that led to a soggy pile of rubble. Mud and leaves caked the ruined maroon carpet, and a carved wooden banister that had once been a work of art now lay in pieces, warped and cracked. The next room had fared no better. We skirted an enormous crystal chandelier, our footsteps scattering sparkling shards into a pile of broken chairs. Massive arched windows lined one wall, a smattering of panes clinging to the frames. Beyond them, the storm continued to rage, as did the thunderbirds. From inside, I couldn't tell if they were agitated by our movements or by the warded building, and I wasn't eager to step outside and find out.

Grant hobbled on stiff legs, his jaw clenched and his breaths escaping in ragged wheezes. I clutched him tighter, anxiety gnawing at my thoughts. I needed Grant conscious to tell me how to save him from the hydra's poison. We needed to be somewhere safe from the thunderbirds' retaliation when I used the elements, too. But with each step, Grant leaned more of his weight on me, and I feared we wouldn't make it to the ward—and that even if we did, it wouldn't let us inside.

The rooms blurred into a surreal blend of wealth and ruin. Slimy, waterlogged carpets squelched underfoot in the same rooms where gold-inlaid carvings adorned wall sconces; leaping jade pegasus statues lay broken on either side of a demolished stage, the heavy curtains reduced to a moldy heap; and a burbling river spilled down turquoise-tiled steps, seeping from an otherwise impassible doorway, the entire second floor having collapsed into the room.

The hallway we had been following dead-ended at a

husk of an old ballroom, the far walls reduced to spindly frames and half the ceiling missing. Beyond it, the ward beckoned. At some point, the thunderbirds had managed to start a fire in the midst of their storm. Or maybe a series of smaller fires had whittled away twenty feet of structure between the main resort and the warded building. Rain pelted the ash and mud, puddling around downed beams and the collapsed remains of the tiled roof.

Lightning ripped through the sky, searing my vision. Thunder punched my eardrums. I stuffed fresh air plugs into my ear canals and Quinn's. After a moment's hesitation, I shoved the small elemental sound dampeners into Grant's ears, too. I had experienced a mere echo of the pain Grant had endured from the thunderbirds' electric assault during our chaotic flight. His mental pathways had to be pulverized and tender.

"We should be able to walk through." Grant indicated the ward with a feeble gesture.

"Should?" Metal-tuned earth composed most of the elemental dome, with a fair amount of fire and air rounding out the complex net. Nothing about it looked as if it had been designed to obstruct humans, but hidden traps could lurk beneath the surface. "Do you recognize the magical signature?"

Grant shook his head.

The ward couldn't have been in place long. The unassuming building it protected bore the same signs of storm damage as the rest of the resort. The only difference was the building was made of stone, not stucco, and most of its roof remained intact.

Two thunderbirds dove into view, spewing lightning from their talons in a coordinated strike on the ward. The barrier absorbed and dispersed the energy, sending it into the ground. Thunder pounded through my diaphragm, rattling my vision.

"Quinn, I need you to verify we can get through the ward," Grant said.

"He can't go out there," I protested.

Grant waited until fresh thunder abated, swaying on his widespread feet. "He can if he walks."

"They didn't pay attention to me on the bridge until I flew." Quinn's tone sounded reasonable, but his head hung low, his shoulder blades hunched with anxiety.

"But—"

Quinn might have the greatest chance of surviving a wayward—or intentional—lightning strike, but he wasn't invincible.

"Kylie." Grant said my name like a plea. We hadn't been moving faster than a walk, but he was panting as if we had run, his breaths shallow and his skin cast in a sickly pallor.

"If they attack, I can make it back here," Quinn said.

I wanted to protest, to keep Quinn safe, but ultimately, it wasn't my choice. Quinn could decide for himself the risks he was willing to take, and I knew he was as concerned as I was about Grant.

"Be careful," I said uselessly.

Quinn stalked to the edge of the shabby hallway. Lightning high in the atmosphere set him aglow, imprinting his brave outline on my retinas. With his belly to the ground, Quinn slunk into the open. No birds dove to attack; no lightning speared through the sky to strike his vulnerable back. My toes curled inside my boots, and my free hand fisted around the strap of my bag. *Hurry, hurry, hurry,* I urged, the word repeating like a prayer.

Piles of blackened rubble forced Quinn along a serpentine route. He kept a measured step when I wanted him to run. Slow and steady meant he was less likely to attract the thunderbirds' attention, but lingering too long in the open could get him noticed, too.

Grant's hand squeezed my shoulder when Quinn reached the ward. The gargoyle lifted a quartz paw and tentatively tapped the elements. His paw slid through the ward, but he yanked it free, leaping straight backward with feline grace and speed. Then he surged forward, bursting through the ward.

The darkness beyond swallowed him.

I held my breath, my body straining toward Quinn. *Come on. Where are you?*

Quinn reappeared just inside the doorway, his face shockingly bright in the next lightning flash. Electricity cascaded down the ward. Quinn retreated a step, then motioned for us to follow him.

I drew in a deep breath. "Ready?"

Grant took a hobbling step. He tried to hide his wince, but this close, it was impossible for him to keep his pain from me. Together, we crept to the edge of the ceiling. Wind flicked drips from the overhang into my face, and the air carried the acrid tang of ash. My heart pounded in my throat as thunderbirds swooped less than ten feet above us. Countless more circled high in the storm clouds, but I was more concerned with those that continued to bombard the ward. Unable to land on the elemental dome's slick surface, the birds took turns strafing past, hurling lightning with impunity. We didn't have the luxury of creeping across as Quinn had. If one of those bolts hit the wet ground, we would be fried. We would have to time it just right.

A trio of thunderbirds flung bolts at the ward, then retreated. Thunder clashed, deafening.

"Go, go, go!" Grant yelled.

We burst out of the shelter. Wind drove rain into my face, stealing my breath and stinging my eyes. I tucked my head down and held fast to Grant. He jogged clumsily, lacking his usual grace. I did my best to bear his weight as I guided us around obstacles, our feet sliding on wet boards buried in the slick mud.

A thunderbird unleashed a shrill, repetitious squawk, and the others took up the cry. We had been spotted. I clamped my fingers around Grant's waistband and urged him to run faster. He struggled to comply, his ragged gasps audible despite my earplugs and the birds' screams.

We hit the ward at full speed. Its magic clamped down on me, burrowing white-hot jabs into my skin. The pain coalesced over my heart, beneath the pouch containing my everlasting seed. Or maybe it tunneled into my actual heart, the skittering electric energy diving into my core to kill me.

Then we were through the barrier, stumbling to a halt, limbs weak with relief. I glanced back in time to see lightning spray against the ward and flash across the demolished landscape. Thunder followed instantaneously, but it sounded as if it were a mile distant, not right outside the open doorway. We were safe.

"Kylie," Grant wheezed. He tried to take a step, but his legs gave out. His eyes rolled into the back of his head, and he crumpled lifelessly in my grip.

My knees buckled under Grant's weight. We fell together, but I managed to twist and catch Grant's arm, preventing him from cracking his face against the stone floor. I landed hard on my side, half under his dead weight.

"Kylie!" Quinn shoved a paw under Grant's shoulder, lifting him gently.

I willed Grant to open his eyes, but they remained closed, his face abnormally slack. I banished the earplugs from all our ears. A steady drip of water splashed deeper in the room, audible over the muffled booms of thunder. Grant's breath rasped laboriously. I checked his pulse. It fluttered weakly beneath my fingertips.

"Help me get him onto his side."

With Quinn's assistance, I rolled Grant partially onto his side and squirmed out from under him. My bag dragged on the stones, catching on a crack. I shrugged out of the strap and knelt over Grant, my hands hovering above his body. Fear paralyzed me. We were trapped on a remote island in the middle of a flock of thunderbirds with no means of returning to Terra Haven. Grant was injured and unconscious. He was supposed to be the strong one, the one in charge. The one with all the answers.

"What would Grant do?" I asked myself, trying to stem my rising panic.

Fire element leapt to my bidding, forming a bright glowball over us. No painful tingle assaulted my magic, and I allowed myself an exhale of relief. The ward not only kept out the thunderbirds, but it cocooned us from the electric-charged atmosphere, too.

"Grant. Grant, wake up." I brushed wet hair from his feverish forehead. "Come on. I need you to tell me what to do."

He groaned when I gave his shoulder a shake, but his eyes didn't open.

"You're not ever going to hear me say that again," I said, not paying attention to the words coming out of my mouth. I wracked my brain for the proper course of action to treat a venomous bite. Cleaning the wound and negating the poison were paramount. I scrambled around to Grant's back, tugging my glowball after me. His pack and coat obscured the hydra's bite, and removing the pack while he half lay on it wasn't going to work. I seized Grant's knife and hacked through the jury-rigged strap Grant had tied together before our dash. The bag dropped to the ground, and I tossed it aside.

"Quinn, hold him steady."

Quinn straddled Grant's thighs, using his legs to hold Grant on his side. He stretched a wing forward to brace against Grant's chest, keeping Grant from flopping onto his face.

"Perfect. Thank you."

Blood soaked Grant's coat, staining the brown leather

black. I unbuttoned it, then tugged a flap aside, but I couldn't shove the garment high enough for a good view of Grant's back with him lying on it. Once more, I employed the knife, sawing through the leather coat, then the thick weave of his uniform. The hydra's lethal blood had corroded the blade's edge, making the task more arduous—and increasing my worry for Grant. If the hydra's poison could eat pockets in metal, what sort of damage was it doing to Grant's insides?

Employing muscle, I ripped the last five inches of his shirt asunder, then spread the flaps wide. Jagged puncture wounds ran in twin tracks down either side of Grant's back, with several cuts crisscrossing between his shoulder blades. All the wounds were shallow. Under normal circumstances, a simple binding to stop the bleeding would have been enough to tide Grant over until we reached a healer, but with poison already in his bloodstream, I needed to figure out something—fast.

"You couldn't wait"—Grant's breath hitched—"to get me naked?"

"Grant! What do I do? What spell should I use?" I had a knack for tweaking spells into new uses, but no matter how I twisted my knowledge of rumor scouts or wards or any of the dozens of spells I had memorized, I couldn't fathom a way to combine the elements to counter the poison in Grant's bloodstream.

Grant lifted an arm. His knuckles grazed Quinn's chest and fell to the ground. His voice came out weak. "My bag. Cure."

I dove for his pack and yanked out its contents, lining them up beside me. I had brought jerky and chocolate, and he had brought the antidote to hydra poison? Every time I thought I was getting a handle on the dangerous twists my life threw at me, Grant showed me how much more I had to learn.

"What am I looking for?" I assessed my options: two knives, a cannister of energy-boosting tablets, five ration bars, a compass, a thin canvas, null cuffs, and three vials in a leather pouch. "Wait, I found them. Which vial is the antivenin?"

Grant shook his head. "My seed. Inner pouch."

My fingers shook as I unsnapped the pack's inner pocket and pulled out his everlasting seed. It had started as a beautiful opalescent sphere, but after we rescued the firebirds, it had evolved into a porous, misshapen beige blob that resembled a pumice stone.

"This will heal you?" I tested the seed with a gentle elemental probe. Earth enhancements layered every porous surface of the spongelike interior and exterior, the magic adding a parched, sandy texture to the stone. "Are you going to ingest it? Do I need to grind it up?"

"Lay me flat."

Quinn eased Grant onto his stomach. Grant didn't make a sound with the position change. When he was prone, he turned his face toward me and let out a slow breath through clenched teeth. I tried not to let my worry show on my face, but I could feel how wide my eyes were. I wasn't fooling anyone.

"We need to link," Grant said.

"Are you sure?" After the magical beating he had taken, touching the elements would surely hurt him.

"Trust me."

Wordlessly, I collected the tiniest balance of elements I could hold, hoping a light touch would spare him pain. He accepted my bundle, and fire ignited in my head. I bit down on a moan before it could escape. It wasn't my pain. It was his, burning into his magic through mental pathways that had been electrocuted one time too many. Ten times too many.

Quinn circled Grant's head to sit next to me, and I leaned a shoulder against him, taking comfort in his enhancement and the echo of his enhancement inside Grant's magic, but mostly in his solid presence. Together, we would save Grant. I wasn't in this alone.

Grant had closed his eyes, and he spoke without opening them. "Watch closely."

Through the link and with my eyes, I studied the spell Grant created. Using fire, air, and water, he wove a delicate siphon, leaving the tip open, the ends of the elements fluttering like lace. I swallowed hard. We weren't creating a cure; we were building a spell to draw the poison out of his body. I didn't need a healer's training to recognize we were venturing into dangerous, exploratory territory, but Grant wouldn't be chancing this if we had a better option.

"Got it?" Grant asked. His eyes bore into me, his iron determination shining in their brown depths.

I nodded. The spell was complicated but doable.

"Now you," he said.

He let the spell unravel, then inverted the link, handing control over to me. I fumbled it. He groaned when I yanked magic through him to stabilize my control.

"Sorry."

His magic rested inside me, a nugget of energy sitting at the back of my mind, not quite at the source where my access to the elements originated, but somehow within it. We had linked in the past, but never with me in command of our combined energy. I didn't do more than hold the link secure, but I could feel the strength and potential power in my grasp. It was like tapping into a gargoyle instead of passively receiving a gargoyle's boost.

In any other situation, I might have relished wielding so much raw power. Yet, instead of drawing on it, I did my best to insulate Grant and avoid using his magic while I carefully replicated the siphon spell. The moment I stabilized the siphon, Grant spoke.

"Good. Cover the tip with a filter that mimics my magical signature."

Even if Grant hadn't been hurt, he wouldn't have been able to do that himself. A person's magical signature defined their connection to and strength with the elements, but it was more than that. It was a person's identity and personality translated through magic. Forming a collection of elements to match one's own personal signature was akin to drawing a self-portrait having never looked in a mirror. In other words, impossible.

Concentrating intently, I built a net composed of a micro-version of the sensual storm that resonated in Grant's signature: the wild winds of a hurricane tempered by the kinetic force of a cresting wave and heated by the warmth of a constrained inferno, the energy braced by stabilizing beams of wood and grounded with anchors of earth. When it was complete, I carefully hooked the filter to the siphon's filigree edges.

"Attach the spell to the seed," Grant instructed through gritted teeth.

I winced in sympathy, realizing that the strain of holding two separate, intricate spells had required me to draw on our link. I tried to ease back to only my own magic, and the spells trembled.

"Kylie," Grant grated. "Use me."

I brought the seed and spells together, and the seed's

magic clutched at the siphon with an almost physical hunger. Following Grant's rasped instructions, I set the seed smack in the middle of his largest wound, the siphon drilling down into the raw opening. Angry red streaks radiated from the puncture marks. Blood oozed down his sides, sluggish and dark. I didn't know if that meant the poison was coagulating in his veins or if he had already lost too much blood. Neither grim scenario seemed preferable.

"Whatever happens," Grant said, "don't stop until the siphon runs clean. Don't hold back."

"I won't." I gave his elbow a squeeze and activated the siphon.

The elements clamped down on Grant's wound like a leech, swallowing his blood. The force of the suction startled me, and I nearly lost my grip on the filter. Black liquid gushed into the siphon. It hit the porous seed and disappeared into its cavities, the parched-sand elements lining the pumice absorbing the liquid faster than a sponge would have soaked up water.

I tugged the glowball closer. The substance flooding the seed wasn't blood, or at least it was no longer regular, healthy blood. That, I could feel pulsing against the filter, Grant's magical signature working like a thin skin to cap the wound while allowing tainted particles to pass through. The muck filtering into the siphon was everything else—all the poison and polluted fluid that Grant's body desperately needed to expel.

It was a genius solution given our limited healing options, and I might have been more excited to see it work if not for the rictus of pain that transformed Grant's face into a stranger's.

"Faster," he panted. "Expand the spell."

I dug my fingernails into my palms. I didn't want to, but I

forced myself to comply. Diving into the magic, I widened the funnel and filter. Blood pounded against the enlarged opening, virtually heaving toxins into the siphon, healing Grant three times as fast. But increasing the spell required me to draw heavily on my link with Grant. The white-hot echo of Grant's pain seared through my brain, the abuse to his battered elemental muscles flaring through the link. I gritted my teeth. I could take the pain, but Grant had already been through enough. It wasn't fair to hurt him further.

The tendons in Grant's neck stood taut, and his spine bowed, his chest curving upward from the floor. His hand clamped down on my ankle with grinding force. I laid my hand atop his, wishing I could offer him greater comfort than a simple touch, but I was afraid if I did more—even spoke—I would lose my concentration, and the spells would unravel.

The pumice darkened as if it were being slowly dipped in tar, until the every last trace of beige vanished. Still, more poison rushed past the elemental filter. What if the seed wasn't big enough? The siphon spell only worked because of the seed's complementary magic. If the seed reached its saturation point too soon, I wouldn't be strong enough to add a third complex spell to replace it. As it was, my mental muscles screamed for relief. I panted shallowly, eyes fixated on the seed without seeing it, straining to hold the spells together.

When the stream of toxins slowed, I could have cried in relief. I narrowed the siphon, and despite Grant's agony, I didn't release the magic until the siphon ran clean for a count of ten. With a pinch of air, I plucked the poison-choked seed from Grant's back and set it aside.

Grant slumped flat, his hand on my ankle going slack

and our link breaking. I checked his breathing and pulse. Both were weak but steady.

Inhaling deep into my lungs, I collapsed against Quinn.

"Do you think that was enough?" he asked.

"It has to be." The seed was saturated, and even if it wasn't, I wouldn't be able to re-create those spells while Grant remained unconscious. "How are you doing?"

Quinn shook his head. Lifting a paw, he examined the pockmarks marring his claws and the pads of his feet where the hydra's acidic blood had eaten into his stone flesh. "It stings, but it's not too bad."

"I wish I could do something."

"It's no big deal. Really," he added when I snorted.

Quinn had been known to downplay his injuries. At least these appeared minor, though they probably ached plenty.

"Look." Quinn sat straighter, jostling me.

Grant's everlasting seed shimmered, swirling with wild elemental energy. Liquid black and white tendrils snaked out of the pumice and dove for Grant's wrist. In a blink, they encircled his wrist. Magic spun faster, spiraling the black and white threads together and cinching the whole bracelet tight to Grant's skin. Five disks blossomed out of the threads, twisting into interlocked teardrops, each flat circle half black and half white.

The seed's magic faded.

I placed a shaky hand on Grant's arm, tentatively testing the bracelet for hydra venom. It was clean. Somehow, the everlasting seed had neutralized the poison. I tested the bracelet. I couldn't fit a finger between it and Grant's skin. He wouldn't be able to remove the seed until it evolved.

"Is that metal?" Quinn delicately tapped a claw against the bracelet. The connection elicited a clear, high *clink*.

"I don't know of any white metal." The white lines and teardrops glistened with pearlescent undertones reminiscent of his seed's original shape.

"What do you think it means?" Quinn asked.

"I wish I knew."

It might help if I knew Grant's question. Twice now, his seed had changed while he was with me. Had he asked about me? That seemed unlikely, especially since both of his seed's transmutations could also be linked to life-threatening dangers. He had probably asked how he could save the most lives or something noble like that.

A shiver wracked my body, and I abandoned my ruminations. Assembling a basic air-and-fire heat spell took abnormal concentration. I set it to work down Grant's clothes, then my own. I almost stopped there, savoring the euphoria of being dry, but if I paused, exhaustion would cripple me, and Grant needed more tending. After drying the damp stones where we sat and around the edges of Grant—drying the floor beneath him proved impossible without disturbing him—I finished sawing the hazardous material from his coat and shirt. I tossed both aside; then I cleansed my fingers and Grant's back with yet another spell. My magic responded sluggishly, fatigue weighting it, and even Quinn's enhancement couldn't lend speed to the process.

Without water soaking my clothes, the humid heat of the perpetual storm warmed my skin. Nevertheless, I tugged the canvas over Grant, hoping additional warmth would help his body recover faster. His color already looked better.

Quinn lifted his seed from his chest to examine the copper-laced green surface. "It didn't change."

"That doesn't mean you weren't tremendously helpful—

with the hydra and with healing Grant." I tugged my pouch free of my shirt and dumped my seed into my palm.

"Nothing?" Quinn asked.

"Nothing." It still resembled a peach pit painted like a firebird feather. When I had raced through the building's ward, I thought it might have evolved, but the fiery pain that had clamped down on my chest must have been courtesy of the lightning-dispersing spell. Disappointed, I tucked the seed away.

Quinn curled on his side, close to Grant, resting his head on his paws. I sagged against him, pillowing my head on his wing. My jaw cracked in a yawn. I should have been investigating the room and verifying the stolen spells were here. Grant had almost died. Might still die. *No.* I couldn't think that way. But after everything we had risked to prove my theory, I should have been busy examining every nook and cranny.

And I would . . . as soon as I could muster the strength to stand. I couldn't remember the last time I had been this tired. Faint alarm pinged through me. Was it this place? Was the spell sapping my energy? After a second's thought, I shook my head. I had traversed a swamp, fought hydras, sprinted down the world's longest causeway while surrendering more magic to Grant in our link than I typically used in a month, and then performed a complicated healing spell. It would have exhausted anyone.

Another yawned filled my vision with tears. They leaked down my cheeks as I locked my gaze on Grant, willing him to recover quickly. His breathing had evened out, and I found myself mimicking his rhythm. In, out. In . . . out . . .

———

THE SOUND OF A GROAN WOKE ME. I JERKED UPRIGHT, SWIPING drool from the corner of my mouth. Grant sat with the canvas blanket pooled around his waist, his arm wrapped around his chest to prod the wounds on his back.

"Grant." His name came out husky with relief. I wanted to leap across the space separating us and wrap my arms around him, but I held myself in check.

He was conscious. *Alive.* My heart sang with happiness.

Dark circles shadowed his eyes, but they didn't detract from the intensity of his stare when his gaze met mine. I dropped my eyes, my emotions too close to the surface, too raw and intimate.

Grant had tossed the remnants of his shirt aside, leaving his chest and arms bare to my scrutiny. Strictly for a health assessment, of course. Now would be an inappropriate time to ogle the flex of his abdominal muscles or the firm curve of his biceps. Instead, I concentrated on the network of pink creases bisecting his tanned skin, providing a map of the stones he had sprawled on. He couldn't have been conscious long if their imprint still remained.

I cleared my throat. "How do you feel?"

"Like I was trampled by a khalkotauroi, but alive. You keep impressing me, Kylie."

My cheeks heated, and I had to clear my throat again. "How did you know your seed was designed for hydra poison?"

"I didn't. Not until the hydra bit me, and even then, it was a guess."

I jerked my head up to check his expression. "You didn't know if it would work?"

He shrugged.

"But what if . . . ?"

"It worked. We don't need to think about what-ifs." He lifted his arm, showing me his new bracelet. "My seed?"

I nodded. "How does it feel?"

"Tight. Did you put it on me?"

"Nope. That was all the everlasting tree's magic."

He flexed his fist, rotated his wrist, and stretched his hand. The bracelet didn't budge, but it didn't impede his movements. Apparently satisfied, he glanced around the room. "Are the stolen spells here?"

"You didn't check while I was still asleep?"

"You're giving me a lot of credit." Grant cautiously flexed, testing the limits of his back. "I've been conscious about two minutes, and it took all my energy just to sit up. If you want to hand me one of those bars and the canister of Quick Boost, I might be able to do something as impressive as stand in another half hour."

I scooted the pile of supplies closer to Grant, then took a bar for myself. It tasted atrocious, both bitter and dry. I chased it with a Quick Boost and plenty of water to swish the brackish taste from my mouth. Both the bar and tablet had been specially formulated to restore elemental and physical energy—flavor hadn't been factored into the equation.

I finished before Grant, who ate his bar with methodical concentration, as if chewing required thought and effort. He must have been feeling even weaker than he let on. Considering what he had been through, I shouldn't have been surprised. When my gaze dipped to skim down Grant's body again, I forced myself to my feet.

"I'm going to look around," I announced. It would be a far more productive use of my time than constantly reminding myself not to stare at Grant's chest. It wasn't as if I hadn't seen it before or that I was so juvenile as to be unable to focus when in the room with a half-nude man.

Mentally rolling my eyes at myself, I pulled my hair from its ragged ponytail and tugged it back into place with a liberal use of untangling spells. After sliding the water jug closer to Grant, I turned to face the bulk of the room.

I shot glowballs into the room's corners and nooks, illuminating our sanctuary. Windows marched down the wall facing the lake, providing a view of the frothing waves and raging storm beyond the ward. The glass panes lay in shards beneath the empty window frames. Uniform openings to the sky had also been cut into the roof. I puzzled over the architectural choice until I remembered this had once been a sun-drenched island. What had allowed in welcoming light and warmth years earlier now opened the room to flooding—or it would have if the ward hadn't blocked the downpour. A blinding flash of lightning crackled against the ward and pulsed down the dome, highlighting the swift path of a thunderbird overhead. I flinched and reminded myself we were safe. Until we had to leave.

"Watch for traps," Grant said, showing no sign of standing.

I nodded and walked deeper into the room. My footsteps echoed in distorted hisses that set my arm hairs on end. I gave Quinn a grateful pat when he rose to follow me.

A pentagon-shaped pool dominated the center of the room, ringed by five pillars carved to resemble trees. Moldy water filled it to the brim, but between the flotsam of leaves and bugs littering the slimy surface, I could make out a checker-tiled bottom. Smaller soaking tubs lined the back wall, recessed into individual grottoes and overtaken by a host of green and pink algae. Glints of color and patterns came to life in the warm glow of my lights, hinting at mosaics adorning the walls beneath layers of mold and moss. Dozens of grimy male and female relief sculptures protruded from the walls, their demure poses deformed by erosion and muck.

This was the main attraction: Aurora Isle's fabled exquisite spa touted to have healed emperors, even if it looked like a nightmare now.

"The ward can't have been up long," I said.

Grant grunted in agreement. "A multi-anchor shield under constant assault? It hasn't been here more than four days." He swallowed a Quick Boost before continuing. "Maybe seven, if it took the birds time to notice it. I didn't see a nest, so they might normally congregate at the other end of the lake."

Naturally he had thought to look for thunderbird nests while we were running for our lives. I had been too preoccupied with my fear of dying.

Grant gazed at the ward through a skylight. "Unless the spell gets reinforced soon, whatever is holding it together will crack."

I whirled to face him, almost knocking a knee against Quinn's chin. "Should I be doing something about that?" The last thing we needed was to be facing off against thunderbirds while Grant couldn't even stand.

"Not yet. Save your strength." He unwrapped a third bar and took a bite, chewing slowly.

"What *is* generating this ward?" Even a full spectrum couldn't have anchored a spell this big and walked away, definitely not if it had been in place for days. I had been too relieved by its presence to question the spell's mechanics earlier, but since we relied on it for shelter, it seemed prudent to learn more.

"Did you see the metal rods when we ran in?" Grant asked.

I glanced out the doorway. A finger-length glint of silver poked out from the mud, visible only because another wave of dancing static cascaded down the dome and funneled into the rod.

"Those ring the building every three feet or so," Grant said, following my line of sight. "The spell runs through them. Putting it all together probably burned through a booster or three, especially if this was done by one person."

"Boosters like those stolen from Airstrong." I pivoted to resume my search.

My knee slammed into an invisible object. The illusion spell cloaking it flickered, revealing a glimpse of a box, some cloth, and a falling flash of white.

If I hadn't been so tired, I might have been smart enough to jump away from the disguised table and its contents. Instead, my hand shot forward of its own free will to catch the falling item.

"Kylie, don't—" Grant shouted.

Too late. My fingers had already curled around a six-sided bone star. A coil of razor-sharp magic burrowed into my wrist, spasming my hand into a fist. The illusion spell shattered. I stared down at an overturned crate topped with the stolen snare and slice, its lethal magic looping around my wrist and the baleful truth hex fused to my palm.

Terror tunneled my vision. I was a dead woman.

24

Magic seared my wrist like a friction burn, twisting tighter when I straightened. I gasped and struggled to open my fingers. When they didn't obey, I reached to unbend them with my free hand. If I could pry my rigid fingers open, maybe—

"Don't move," Grant barked. "Don't touch the elements. Quinn, stop where you are."

I froze, though every fiber of my being protested. My fingers shook around the truth hex. A snare and slice was inescapable. Wasn't that what Grant had told me? It could hold a centaur herd if they got tangled in its magic. If that were true, no amount of flailing would liberate me. Logic wasn't helping, though. My muscles sang with the need to squirm, to struggle, to grab hold of my trapped wrist with my free hand and tug until the snare unleashed me—

"Easy, Kylie. Stay as still as possible."

Grant's steps wobbled as he approached, and my panic ratcheted higher. Until today, I would have said Grant could protect me from any danger, but the venom had ravaged his strength. He could barely walk. How was he going to counter a banned spell?

Quinn waited for Grant to reach him, then followed on his heels as Grant circled me. Apprehension radiated from both of them, though Grant did a better job of hiding it.

"I can't believe how stupid I am. I should have been more careful," I babbled.

"You're going to be all right," Grant said.

No, you're not, whispered my subconscious.

"What can I do?" I asked.

"Right now, nothing." Grant pointed to the air between my hand and the crate. "Do you see that nasty elemental tether attached to your wrist?"

"I can see it *and* feel it."

"Do you see the other end, where it meets that snarl of elements woven into the snare?"

I studied the cloth, at first seeing only the elemental symbols sewn into its surface and the two objects lying on it. One was a fingernail-size silver-parsley-leaf booster charm embedded with healing enhancements. The other was a miniature umbrella hardly big enough for a house cat. Elemental symbols adorned the shaft and curved handle in a perfect three-dimensional replica of the thief's key sketch on the reward poster. All that was missing were the beguiling beads. We had found the thief's stash, but what should have been a triumph would become a tragedy if we couldn't figure out a safe way to release me from the snare and slice's wicked magic.

I traced the coil of elements attached to my wrist back to the source, and my breath caught. The snare's magic writhed around the base of the cable, menace emanating from the cluster of seething layers.

"I can see only about three layers deep, but this thing is

dangerous. Deadly." Grant halted five feet away, pressing a hand to Quinn's muzzle to stop the gargoyle, too. "If you move or lose touch with what you're holding, it will kill you. I'm not sure what will happen if you try to use the elements, but it won't be pretty."

Foolish girl. Why can't you ever use caution? my inner critic whispered.

"We'll figure out how to free you," Quinn promised.

I don't want you to die.

A frisson of alarm pinged through my gut. That hadn't been my thought. It was almost as if it had been Quinn's.

The truth hex thrummed in my grip. Grant had said it revealed the truth to whoever held it—and drove them mad in the process. I swallowed hard, my throat painfully dry.

"Soon, right?" I asked. "You'll get me out of this soon?"

"It's going to take time. I'm not exactly at full strength."

I wouldn't risk your life trying to free you on my own, even if I were fresh, the hex translated.

I let out a shaky breath. I could see how someone might consider it a boon to have blunt honesty piped straight into one's thoughts. I could also see it driving me mad if I was forced to hold the hex too long.

"So long as I don't move, the snare won't do anything more to me?"

"I need to get word to my squad," Grant said, sidestepping the question. "And to O'Hara."

"How?"

Grant turned to Quinn.

"No." I shifted, and pain jolted up my arm. "I can wait. Didn't you say your squad would be twenty-four hours behind us? We've been here awhile, right? They can't be far off."

"Unless they've been waylaid by an assignment in Terra Haven. I can't take that chance."

Your life may depend on speed.

"I'll go," Quinn said.

Grant knelt in front of him, turning Quinn's face away from me. "Do you remember our exact path through the swamp?"

Quinn nodded.

"No," I repeated, louder. Quinn had exceptional recall of landmarks, but even he couldn't be expected to have memorized the winding path buried in water and mud through the featureless swamp after having traversed it only once.

Grant ignored me.

"So long as you don't fly, the thunderbirds shouldn't bother you."

"What about the gaps in the bridge?" I demanded. "He'll have to fly. And the hydras. It's too dangerous. Quinn, I can't let you do this for me."

"I'll keep my jumps short and avoid the hydras."

"Go straight to the guard station at the gate," Grant instructed. "They can get word to my squad and the investigator. They might need you to show them the way back, so wait for them before you return."

Don't rush back here and get yourself killed. It's dangerous enough sending you out alone.

Tears welled in my eyes, blurring my vision. Why hadn't I been more careful?

"I'll be back soon." Quinn held his head high, his chest puffed with resolve, and his promise rang in his words.

I would run to the end of the earth and back for you.

"Good luck," Grant said.

Hurry.

"Be safe." A tear spilled onto my cheek. I swiped it away

with my free hand. I flinched at the thoughtless move, but the snare didn't retaliate. I tried to take heart. So long as I kept my trapped wrist stable, I had a marginal amount of freedom.

Quinn slipped out a side door and slunk to the edge of the ward, pausing to glance over his shoulder at me. I raised a hand, wanting to call him back but unable to force the words out. He was doing this for me. I should be grateful—I *was* grateful—but a much larger part of me was terrified this would be the last time I saw my friend.

Quinn fanned his feathers in a fluttering wave, then leapt through the ward. A whimper slid from my throat, and I cut it off.

"He's strong, fast, and smart. He'll be fine," Grant said.

I wish I didn't have to rely on a half-grown, untrained gargoyle, but he's all we have.

I nodded and blotted tears from my chin.

Quinn skulked down the mud slope leading to the causeway, using the limited cover to disguise his movements. I lost sight of him as he neared the bottom of the hill, and I counted the seconds until he reappeared farther away, at the base of the causeway. He ran at a flat-out gallop, wings clamped to his sides. My heart lodged in my throat, and I frantically scanned the skies, searching for thunderbirds chasing him. None appeared.

Sheets of rain drove across the lake, obscuring Quinn's progress. Waves of light crackling across the ward distorted the view further, and I strained to keep Quinn in sight. He dashed down the center of the causeway to the first gap. I held my breath as he leapt into the air. At the apex of his jump, his wings snapped open, beat once, and drove him down to the other side. In less than four seconds, his feet touched down on the cobblestones, and he tucked his wings tight. The thunderbirds likely hadn't had a chance to sense his magic.

"That's my clever gargoyle." I yearned to rush to the window when the wall blocked my view of Quinn's progress. *Be safe. Please be safe,* I prayed.

And fast, a more selfish impulse urged. My wrist already ached from the snare's grip. I mentally raced alongside Quinn, calculating how long it would take him to reach help. Navigating the causeway would be quick, but what about the water-saturated mud road on the other side? No matter how good his memory, he would have to slow to make sure he stayed on firm ground. He would need to take breaks, too. He had incredible aerial stamina, but he wasn't used to running for miles. At best, he would leave the thunderbirds' territory within the hour, and it would be even longer until the winds died down enough to make flying safe. Once clear of the storms, he wouldn't need to rely on roads, and he could fly straight to Terra Haven. He was far speedier than the carpet Grant and I had rode in on. Still, it would be hours before he reached Terra Haven.

Once there, finding the squad would take time, especially if they were already engaged in an assignment. Returning would take even longer . . .

Could I stand still for six hours? Ten? Already an unpleasant heat radiated through the rigid muscles in my arm and down my back from holding myself immobile. I tried to alleviate the stiffness by shifting my feet and earned a fresh stab of pain.

Grant circled me, examining the snare from a safe distance. His steps had steadied, but I caught a glimpse of his back. Leaping to his feet had opened several punctures, and blood soaked the hem of his pants.

"How do you feel?" I asked.

"I'll live."

I should be in a healer hall right now.

I agreed with the hex's translation. I wouldn't have minded being in a healer hall, either. Of course, healers had no cure for the guilt eating at me. Grant had almost died because he was helping me—and he was still suffering. Quinn was all alone in a hydra-infested swamp, running on injured feet, because he was an extraordinary friend. And what had I done? I had stupidly, idiotically, *moronically* gotten myself snared in the very spell I had been searching for. Velasquez was right: I was a menace to everyone close to me.

Tears filled my vision, and I tipped my head back, refusing to let them fall. Wallowing wouldn't help. I couldn't change the past. I couldn't mend all of Grant's wounds, or Quinn's. I couldn't chase after Quinn as I so desperately wanted to. I could only be here, in this moment, with the man I was falling in love with and the truth hex in my hand.

"Do you believe my parents are innocent now?" I asked, pleased when my voice didn't sound as close to tears as I felt.

Grant shot a suspicious look at my fist. "Is it working? Does it tell you if I'm lying?"

Are you going to use it against me?

"I know when you're telling me the truth." He had known what I was holding all along, which explained why he was being more evasive than normal.

"Yes."

I frowned. "Yes to what?"

"I think your parents are innocent."

No translation followed, and I managed a fleeting smile. "Did you always?"

"No. The more you use the hex, the worse its effects on you will get."

I waited for a translation, expecting the hex to deny Grant's claim. Its voice remained silent.

"I don't think it's doing anything bad to me."

"You've been rubbing your head like it hurts. And how does your hand feel?"

You're not thinking straight.

I frowned. How could he think that? I was being logical and calm. That didn't mean the emotional and physical stress couldn't give me a headache. And my hand hurt because one of the hex's six points was gouging a tendon. If I could adjust my fingers, I would.

I lifted my chin. "I'm fine, but sure—"

A light glinted across Grant's chest, like the reflection of the sun off a gold coin. I glanced up, then behind me, hunting for the source. When I checked Grant's chest again, the light had disappeared.

"Uh, sure, let's stand around in silence." I had intended the comment to come out tart, but instead it sounded like a question.

Where had that reflection originated from? The dimly lit spa didn't possess a direct light source. I had lost control of my glowballs in the surprise of being trapped by the snare, and Grant hadn't created any to replace them. All ambient lighting radiated from the electrified ward, sporadically enhanced by lightning flashes. The only reflection in the room was a soft shimmer above the pool, where its tranquil surface refracted the sparkling light filtering through the openings in the roof.

I checked the snare's magic. The elemental snarl was more prominent than before, as if it were gaining strength. The cord binding my wrist looked thicker—

Teeth sprang out of the snare's magic and bit down on my wrist. I stifled an instinctive flinch. The bizarre image disappeared with my next blink. I stared at my hand. I hadn't experienced any fresh pain, so what had just happened?

"Kylie?" Grant studied my expression, worry clouding his eyes.

"This is really bad, isn't it?"

"Yes."

"I was hoping for a bit more reassurance."

Grant's gaze didn't waver. "I'm not leaving your side."

I'll do whatever it takes to ensure you survive.

I was too afraid to ask if it would be enough.

An hour passed in excruciating tension. My worry for Quinn swelled between waves of physical discomfort, the cycle broken only by sharp jolts of the snare's punishing magic when I inadvertently twitched my trapped wrist. The whole time, my pulse pounded a painful drumbeat against the dull prongs of the truth hex, never letting me forget what I held.

If I could have distracted myself with conversation, every second might not have felt as if it oozed past on the back of a molasses slug. But Grant wouldn't talk. He insisted that speaking activated the hex's magic, unnecessarily endangering me. When I had argued, he had shaken his head and refused to engage. Which was why when his voice broke the silence, I startled hard enough to spark the snare's vindictive magic.

"There's someone out there."

"Quinn?" Despite the ache thumping in my feet and calves, it hadn't been long enough for Quinn to make it to Terra Haven, let alone all the way back. Unless— "Is he hurt? Do you need to—"

"No." Grant backed away from the window, deeper into the shadows. "It's Persephone Kwan."

My stomach dove for my toes. "Alone?"

"Yes."

This is terrible timing, the truth hex translated.

"It's not terrible; it's perfect."

Grant shot me a wary glance, and I realized I had responded to the interpretation of his words, not what he had spoken aloud. I rushed on before he thought too much about it.

"The investigator is on his way"—or he would be once Quinn found him—"and he can arrest Persephone here, in front of all this proof of her guilt." That sounded like a great plan, if incredibly simplified. We would have to detain her and wait, and I would still be trapped in the snare. But it was a start.

"Before you snap your front-page photo, you might want to ask yourself: How did she know we were here?"

Think it through.

"Could she have sensed the snare when I tripped it?"

"Maybe, but to get here this fast, she must have already been on her way. Either it's coincidental that she decided to come out here the same day we did—"

If it looks suspicious, it's suspicious, the truth hex whispered.

"—or she was tracking us and knew right where to look."

I should have spotted that spell.

I didn't need the hex to follow Grant's logic. "You think she planted the tracker on me?"

"Maybe. It makes as much sense as Zipporah. If Persephone was worried about your investigative skills, she would have wanted to keep track of your whereabouts. The moment we veered into the swamp, she knew you were onto her."

She might have set this whole island up as a trap for you.

"Wait—the earrings! Quinn!" Pain ripped into my arm, cutting my lunge short. "What if she saw him and did something to him?"

"Quinn knows about the earrings and to be wary of Persephone. If he saw her, he would have hidden."

If Quinn is dead, it's too late to do anything about it now.

I gasped, my free hand flying up to cover my mouth. Persephone was a thief, and she had used illegal spells to manipulate others, but was she also capable of murder? I remembered how easily I had gone along with everything Persephone had said, clueless to the magical compulsion puppeting me. If Quinn had been caught by Persephone during his race through the swamp, he would have helplessly obeyed any order she gave him. All she had to do was instruct him to walk into a pond where the water was deeper than his head ...

"You don't think she ... ?" I couldn't finish the question. It was rhetorical anyway. The hex's translation had confirmed Grant's thoughts.

I refused to believe it. Quinn couldn't be dead. Grant might be brutally practical, but I needed to believe Quinn had escaped Persephone's notice. If I contemplated the alternative, I wouldn't be able to function.

"How is Persephone getting past the thunderbirds?"

Grant stepped to the side, giving me an unobstructed view of the pulsing ward outside the broken window, and beyond it, sheets of rain driving sideways across the causeway. Persephone was impossible to miss, standing atop a floating white carpet, a weatherproof bubble encasing her. An occasional thunderbird swooped past her, but none hurled lightning, and the electric glow outlining Persephone's ward didn't seem to trouble her.

"How is that possible?"

"It has to be her magical signature. Have you ever linked with her?"

I shook my head.

"I never realized how close her magic feels to a thunderbird's. It looks like she found a way to exploit it."

I should have made the connection sooner.

"Are you saying it's a coincidence that Persephone can come to this island unharmed? Or are you saying she's the reason this sunny island became a haven for thunderbirds?"

Grant stooped to gather his supplies, stuffing them into his pack. "Does it matter?"

You can worry about getting her backstory after we survive this fiasco.

"It might," I said, feeling like I was arguing with two people instead of one. My headache pounded in rhythm with the pain pulsing in my palm, fighting for dominance.

"The swamp was here first, then Persephone's something-odd-great-grandparents worked their magic to bend the environment to their bidding." Grant carried our packs into the shadows while he talked, returning to my side with null bands in his hand. "If I had to guess, I'd say Persephone's ancestors had magical signatures a lot like hers, and it enabled them to chase away the native thunderbirds and keep them out. The swamp became a lake, and the sunny Aurora Isle became a profitable resort for the Kwan family. But the family's elemental strength has been fading with each generation, and Persephone's grandparents couldn't maintain the magic. The sunny island reverted to its natural climate. I don't know if the thunderbirds returned to reclaim their territory unprompted or if Persephone had something to do with it, only that the thunderbirds aren't reacting to her magic, and she's not reacting to their electric effect on the elements. If she's working alone, it explains how she set this all up."

"So you know she's not a full spectrum?" I asked while the hex babbled about Grant's low opinion of people who took it upon themselves to alter weather patterns and animal habitats for their profit.

"Knowing the dirty secrets of full-spectrum families is part of my job."

It's a large waste of time, until it's not.

Persephone sailed off the causeway and veered straight for our location.

"I'm going to lock her in place with a net, then slap these on her." Grant held up his null cuffs. "Once they're in place, the beguiling beads won't work. This should be over fast."

One way or the other.

I flinched at the hex's translation. Grant hadn't had long enough to recover from being fried by the thunderbirds. Using the elements would be excruciating, and he wouldn't be operating at full strength. However, voicing my doubts wouldn't change our predicament or Grant's mind.

"Be careful." I wished I could link with Grant, or better yet, that I wasn't trapped and could capture Persephone myself. I despised being so helpless.

"Whatever happens, don't move, and don't touch the elements," Grant said.

Stay alive long enough for me to save you.

25

Grant stuffed thick air into his ears, then mine, cutting off all sound except the pounding of my own heart. Striding across the room, he pressed his back to the wall by the doorway and waited to spring his trap.

My breaths came too fast. Persephone would spot me the moment she entered the room, if she didn't see me through a window first. I fought an almost unbearable urge to squirm, acutely aware of my vulnerability.

I jumped involuntarily when Persephone floated past the far window. Magic sharp as fishing wire burned into my wrist, so tight it would have cut off circulation if it had possessed physical form. I hunched, holding my breath to contain my whimper.

Persephone glided through the ward, and her protective sphere melted as she entered the dome's coverage. Her pristine white carpet floated inches above the muddy ground, shockingly bright. She looked as if she had dressed to go shopping. Buckskin breeches clung to her slender legs, and the scoop neck of her maroon silk top revealed a jeweled charm dangling from a golden chain. Despite her flight through Dead Man's Swamp and the thunderbirds' storm, not a strand of hair had escaped her high bun. The beguiling beads dangled like pearls from her ears. Her audacity escalated my tension. Persephone wasn't trying to hide her thievery or her use of an illegal spell.

As her carpet crossed the threshold, a glowball sprang into existence in the middle of the room. I flinched from the sudden light. Persephone shouted something I couldn't hear and flung a ward between us, but it melted when she took in my rigid stance and my arm locked in the snare's magic. Her alarm transitioned to cool amusement. My heart pounded like a chased rabbit in my chest, and I held her gaze as if my life depended on it, desperate not to give away Grant's location behind her with even a flicker of my eyes. My toes scrunched in my boots, doing little to relieve the tension quivering through my body.

Persephone stepped to the ground. Her mouth moved, her expression mocking. When she was three steps from her carpet, Grant struck, seizing Persephone's arm even as he ensnared her in a net of air. Persephone screamed. Grant snapped a null cuff around her wrist and lunged for her other arm. He was slow, his speed robbed by the hydra's poison, his magic weakened by the thunderbirds. Before he could capture her free hand, Persephone smashed a mace of earth into Grant's net, shattering it. The backlash must have felt like an ax to the head, and Grant stumbled. Persephone drove a spike of earth into Grant's ear canal. His head snapped sideways, and the air plugs in my ears vanished.

"Stop!" Persephone barked.

Grant swayed in his tracks, confusion plowing lines across his forehead. Blood trickled from his ear. He lifted a hesitant hand toward Persephone's free arm, then let it drop.

Persephone straightened warily, standing as far away from Grant as his grip on her would allow.

"You don't want to restrain me, Captain. I'm here to clean up this mess." She gestured to the thunderbirds above us. "I need your help."

The hex's translation was short and precise. *I control you.*

"Don't listen to her, Grant," I yelled. "Cuff her. Quick!"

"Captain, you're hurting me," Persephone said, ignoring me. "Please let me go. I need both hands free."

You're my puppet now.

Grant stared at his hand fisted around her delicate wrist as if he couldn't figure out what he was seeing.

"Grant, look at me. *Grant!*" I screamed his name, but it was as if he were deaf to my voice.

"I'll comply with whatever you decide." Persephone sounded so calm and reasonable, and even with the hex gouging into my palm, I wanted to believe her. She smiled up at Grant, the picture of sweet innocence. For a split second, her expression twisted in malicious delight, then she was all sweetness again. I blinked and shook my head. No one could change expressions that fast.

Grant released her, removed the null cuff, and dropped it to the ground. My stomach flipped, nausea and fear battling it out in my gut. Grant had no defenses left against the beguiling beads' power—and I had run out of allies. Persephone shook out her hand; then she patted Grant on his naked chest. Her hand lingered. I bit back a growl.

"I appreciate your warm welcome, Captain, and your choice of attire."

If only my fiancé looked like you.

"Now be a dear and stand there quietly admiring me while I think." She straightened her disheveled clothes and patted her hair, brushing aside ebony strands that had escaped her bun. The bright light of her glowball emphasized the shadows beneath her eyes, and the frizz of hair hanging around her face lent her a haggard air that hadn't existed when she had sailed into the room. The strain of using a manipulation spell must be catching up with her. She no longer appeared effortlessly confident. When her eyes narrowed on me, I shivered. Gone was the friendly, mothering person who had greeted me at the solstice party. In her place stood a calculating woman with a malevolent glint in her gaze.

"Framing Charlotte was a good idea, but this is positively inspired. Her own heroic daughter found responsible for the company's downfall? Her daughter's lover dying in the process? The newspapers will lap this up."

"What are you talking about?" I glanced at Grant, hoping he would say something, move, do *anything* to help, but he merely stared at Persephone's profile, a soft, besotted smile curving his lips. It made me want to scream, but it wouldn't do any good.

Persephone paced closer. "You don't know? You're here. I thought that meant you had it all figured out." *You stupid, nosy twit.* "You already did the hard part for me. Everyone at my party saw how you've got the captain hooked." *It's unfair that he's interested in someone as plain and weak as you.* "He's so besotted with you, you've got him leashed to your whims. With his skills and your access, it was easy to steal the banned spells." Persephone held a hand over her open mouth, feigning shock.

Aren't I so clever? the hex translated.

"That's absurd. No one would believe . . ." My voice warbled and died when wolverine claws flexed from Persephone's fingertips, each drenched in blood. Clearly, it was an illusion, and an impressive one, but why? And who was generating it? Persephone wasn't using magic—other than the power of the beguiling beads. Grant hadn't touched the elements. The only other magic active in the room was the snare and slice.

And the truth hex.

Could it do more than whisper in my head? Its magic revealed truth, and people could lie with their bodies as easily as their words. But no one had mentioned the hex could project images into the user's mind. No one had said it would work by inserting a voice into my thoughts, either. I was in uncharted territory.

Persephone twisted her features into a mimicry of sympathy, but when she laid a possessive hand on Grant, the illusionary claws sank into his flesh as if she would rip his heart from his chest.

"It's awful when love doesn't stand the test of time, or in this case, the test of sharing the proceeds of ridiculously expensive illegal spells." Persephone tipped her head up to look at Grant. "Your falling-out with young Harriet will be quite tragic." *It will be no less than she deserves for dating above her station.*

"Can you see how the snare is put together, Captain?"

"Of course."

"Could you unravel it?"

"Maybe."

Persephone made a sad moue at me. "Well, we'll never find out. Be a dear, Captain, and give the whole thing a jolt. Put your impressive power into it."

I couldn't breathe. She had just ordered Grant to murder me. And he was already gathering the elements.

"That will kill me. Grant, please don't do it." My heart fluttered in my throat. Even under the beguiling beads' influence, he had to know the snare would perceive any magical strike as an attack. It would lash out, violently.

But Grant wasn't in control of himself. I knew firsthand how subtle the beads' magic could work. Persephone had convinced me to overlook being attacked on her property, and I hadn't even noticed the manipulation. She had done it without giving me a direct order, too. The beguiling beads' powers would be amplified in a command. Grant wouldn't be able to resist. I desperately didn't want to die, and if Grant killed me, he would never forgive himself. Words rushed from my mouth.

"Persephone, wait. I'll do whatever you want. Just don't make Grant do this. The snare could backfire and kill him, too. You don't want that."

Persephone shrugged. "Better him than me."

I wanted to close my eyes, but I couldn't look away from Grant. His brown eyes bore into mine, power and pain roiling in their depths. His hands fisted at his sides, but he didn't lash out.

"I'm sorry," I whispered, apologizing for dragging him into this mess, for being stupid enough to get caught in the snare, for being able to do nothing while he was forced to murder me.

For the relationship we had only just begun and the future we would never have.

Illusionary golden light glowed inside Grant's chest, growing brighter until it shone like a warm sun.

"What are you waiting for? Kill her!"

Grant's throat flushed, the darkening red tide creeping toward his jaw. Thick veins swelled in his neck, throbbing visibly. His jaw muscle flexed and held as the flush crested his cheeks and climbed higher. His eyes never wavered from mine.

Hope unfurled inside me. Grant was fighting Persephone's order. Telling him to kill me had been too much, too far outside Grant's nature. It had given him the kernel of awareness he needed to fight the beads' compulsion. It was a battle between Grant's iron will and the beads' unlimited magic. Eventually, the beads' power would overwhelm him, unless he passed out first. Maybe that was his goal, because he didn't appear to be breathing.

Persephone slapped Grant's cheek. His hand shot up to grab her wrist, his bracelet glinting in the light.

"That's enough. Stand down and breathe," she ordered. *You're a disgrace to full spectrums everywhere.*

Grant relaxed and drew a deep breath. His gaze transferred to Persephone, and his expression slackened as his color returned to normal. He made no attempt to restrain her further. I held my breath, hoping he had somehow shaken off the beads' influence and was biding his time for the right moment.

Persephone lashed out with a scalpel of air, fire, and water, puncturing the ward next to the window. "Oops. Looks like we need a hero"—*fool*, the hex whispered—"to save us. Go fix the ward, Captain, and keep us safe." *There's more than one way to get you to kill yourself.* "Oh, but first." She grabbed Grant's arm before he could move, leaning close to whisper, "It's going to be an impossible task, as weak as you are."

Die trying.

My hope for Grant to be faking his compliance died when he rushed to the window. Persephone had given him a task he would have done without prompting, and his defiance vanished.

His face a mask of concentration, Grant wove the elements into a patch that resonated with the ward and set it across the rift. The two spells melded, mending the ward . . . until Grant's magic unraveled. The rift split, and rain splattered against the stone windowsill. Grant shook his head, his brow furrowed in confusion. Then he constructed another patch. It unraveled faster than the first.

Persephone clapped with amusement. "Keep it up, Captain."

A thunderbird dove for the opening, scraping a claw along its edge. Lightning flared from its fist, bouncing harmlessly across the ward when it missed its mark. Grant ducked away from the talon's sharp tip and drew his knife. Fresh blood trickled from the cuts on his back.

"Don't hurt the birds," Persephone ordered.

Grant slapped the side of his blade against a monstrous black beak that thrust through the opening. The bird retreated, and he shoved a fresh seal over the gap. For a second, it held. When it unraveled, Grant's hands fisted in frustration before he dodged another thunderbird attack. The pain of using the elements must have been excruciating, but that didn't stop Grant from attempting again and again to patch the ward, just as his physical wounds didn't stop him from battling the thunderbirds drawn to the ward's weak spot. Yet, no matter how hard he fought, he couldn't break the beguiling beads' power. Persephone had doomed Grant to a slow, painful death, one I couldn't bear to watch.

"Think about what you're doing, Persephone," I pleaded. "Grant is an FPD captain. If anything happens to him, the government will hunt you down. But right now, you haven't done anything terrible. Take off the earrings and turn yourself in. I'm sure we can convince—"

"Silence," she barked.

I wanted to shrink away from the madness in her gaze, but I forced myself to maintain eye contact. If I could keep her attention focused on me, maybe Grant would be able to shake off the beguiling beads' influence. Their compulsion didn't last forever. Quinn had remembered to come down from the roof at Persephone's party. Maybe Grant just needed time. Meanwhile, I wracked my brain for a means of nullifying Persephone without activating the snare's torturous magic. Right now, all I had were words.

"Persephone, I thought we were friends. Why are you doing this?"

Persephone whipped to face me. Her gaze dropped to the snare, then my fist. "You always were too smart for your own good, but holding that truth hex won't help you. Its magic is too passive."

"It's helping me see the truth, and that's all I really want. To understand. Why did you steal the spells? What do you have against my mom?"

"I'm balancing things out. There's a certain order to the world, and I'm fixing it." *I'm putting myself back on top.* "It's not fair that Charlotte rose so high while I sacrificed so much. She's not a full spectrum. None of her ancestors are. She shouldn't even be part of high society. She's a commoner. I'm a Kwan. I descended from the country's first full spectrums. Yet I've had to barter, beg, and *borrow* to protect my family name."

Me, me, me, the hex whispered.

I almost told her she was insane—or reminded her *she* wasn't a full spectrum—but I didn't want to antagonize her into doing something rash. Something *more* rash. "What about your fiancé? You don't need to destroy my family. Luther Wetherill has plenty of money. You won't have to ask for anything once you're married."

"Do you think he would marry me if he realized I'm a pauper? When I sell the spells, I'll be able to enter our alliance with dignity. Besides, with Airstrong out of the competition, Luther's business will bring in even more money. My children will live the lives they deserve." *They'll have the life I should have had. They'll never have to debase themselves to anyone.*

"Luther loves you for you, not your estate or your wealth. Everyone could see it at the party." The lie bubbled out, carried on the sincerity of my wish to save Grant and myself. Wetherill loved himself. He loved his power and his wealth. I hadn't seen him look twice at his fiancée at the party. Interestingly, the truth hex didn't whisper a correction for my lie, either.

"He loves me for me?" Persephone giggled, the sound brittle. Her laughter grew to a cackle, but mirth never reached her eyes. How long had she been wearing the beads? How much of her delusion was fueled by the beads' influence and how much was her own warped mental state? After all, she had concocted the scheme to steal the illegal spells and, apparently, to frame my mom for it *before* she had started using the beads.

An inky void bored through Persephone's stomach, the edges spinning hypnotically. Shadows hollowed her eyes and cheeks, until a thin-skinned skeleton stared back at me. Agony lit a fire around my wrist and spiked to my armpit, halting my instinctive retreat.

Lightning hammered the ward, the blast of thunder resonating through the spa. I jerked, earning another whip of pain from the snare. A thunderbird foot slashed through the torn ward, clipping Grant's shoulder. The force of the blow knocked him against the rock wall. The second slash would have decapitated him, but he dropped to a crouch and kicked off the wall, rolling beneath the deadly talon. Before he sprang to his feet, Grant blasted air through the ward, shoving the bird aside. Another took its place, the jagged edge of the rift giving the bird purchase on the otherwise slick dome. Grant flung a patch into place, punching the bird out of the way.

Persephone observed Grant's struggle with a smile as sharp as Zipporah's curving her lips, a light more cruel shining from her eyes. Sweat gleamed on Grant's torso and ran down his temples. Fresh blood tracked down his back. That he could function at all after having just recovered from a hydra bite was a miracle. I wasn't sure how much longer he could fight or how many more knocks he could take before his compromised reflexes enabled a thunderbird to land a fatal blow. I needed to think of something fast.

"Your plan will never work," I said, trying to draw Persephone's attention. Grant held an elemental patch across the opening rather than knitting the rift closed. Holding magic had to be an exquisite strain, but it also prevented the whole patch from unraveling. I hoped it meant he was fighting off Persephone's compulsion, and I didn't want her to notice.

"Because you'll stop me?" she asked, bored.

"Because it's stupid."

She whirled to face me. "I'm brilliant!"

"No, you're not. You need to sell the spells for money, and you need to frame me for it, but you can't do both. You have to deactivate the snare. You can't leave me trapped *and* get away with the spells."

Persephone glanced from the crate to me, and when her gaze lifted to mine, a murderer stared back at me. "I never said I needed you alive."

26

Persephone circled me, tapping her chin musingly. "I can't touch you. The snare might grab me. I also can't risk its backlash if I hit you with magic." *I'm too important to die. No one will miss you.* "If I pull the knot of fire there . . . No, that will incinerate you. I need something that will kill you but leave your body identifiable. Wouldn't that be dreadful—all this work and then no way to prove you're you."

I bent my legs, testing my chances of grabbing Persephone and trapping her in the snare with me if she got close enough. Hot magic seared my wrist, blistering my veins, and I froze. Gritting my teeth, I reached for the elements. The snare fired two spears of wood element into my arm, piercing my forearm and elbow. Agony clenched my tendons, severing my grip on the elements.

Kill the girl, rule the world; kill the girl, rule the world, the hex babbled, translating Persephone's mutters. She sidled closer to the crate, squinting at the snare's magic. Behind me, Grant grunted in pain, his breaths rasping audibly across the room. I didn't need to check to know he fought on borrowed time.

Persephone shaped a spell and pushed it toward the snare. A wild bundle of elements shot from the dark cloth and hooked onto Persephone's magic. She yelped and flung the spell into the air. The snare popped and crackled, devouring her magic. The lash holding me quivered, gnawing on my wrist with needlelike elemental teeth. I breathed shallowly until the pain passed, hiding my reaction, afraid Persephone would notice how easily she could torture me. But she was too busy crafting a new spell to pay attention to me. I wanted to cry. She didn't care about tormenting me; she wanted me dead, and she wouldn't stop until she achieved her goal. So long as I was caught in the snare, I was helpless. I couldn't fight. I couldn't use the elements. I couldn't run.

The fingers of my free hand trembled as I contemplated the only option left to me: the thief's key.

It was a ward breaker credited with being able to crack any ward, no matter how complex. Theoretically, I could use it to break the snare and slice. But activating the thief's key was phenomenally risky. The snare thrummed with power. If I used the key on it, I would be forced to absorb all the snare's magic. I would be gambling that I could hold more magic than the outlawed ward. If I was wrong, the thief's key would permanently burn out my ability to touch the elements—if it didn't kill me first.

Yet, if I waited, Persephone would certainly kill Grant and me both.

I snatched up the thief's key. Persephone gasped, backpedaling fast. The snare's magic cinched down on my wrist, a hundred thorny spikes embedding themselves into my flesh. Before the magic locked my arm in place, I jabbed the tip of the umbrella into the snarl of magic at the center of the snare and slice. Grabbing tendrils of all five elements, I shoved them into the umbrella's slender shaft.

Punishing whips of magic lashed out from the snare, stinging up my arms, but it was too late to change my mind: I had already activated the thief's key. The umbrella's leather panels unfurled, revealing elemental symbols burned into the undersides. Magic spun through the spokes, sinking into random symbols without my prompting. The last element clicked into place, and magic surged from the snare into me with all the delicacy of a mace. I screamed as it set fire to my brain.

Persephone laughed. "You stupid girl. You'll kill yourself for sure." *I couldn't have done it better myself.*

The onslaught of elements ceased, and I sagged between my trapped arms, panting. A layer of explosive earth unraveled from the snare, disintegrating into harmless particulates. It was working: the thief's key had disarmed the first of the snare's traps. I blinked blearily at the remaining snarl of deadly spells, fearing Persephone might be right. How many more could I disband before the snare's magic became too much and I was forced to stop?

My stomach lurched when the elements cycled unprompted through the ward breaker's leather panels, forming a new pattern. Alarmed, I tried to withdraw my magic. A wallop of elements shot from the snare through the thief's key, bludgeoning me. My panic skyrocketed.

Persephone studied me, her eyes glistening in the sunken depths of her skull. With the hex's cadaverous illusion overlaying her features, her sympathetic smile appeared all the more ghastly.

"Don't fight it, Harriet. Let the magic take you. It'll be

better that way." *Watching you struggle is distressing. The sooner you die, the better.*

A chain of elemental knives dematerialized. Magic spun through the umbrella's panels, clicking into place before I could gasp my next breath. The snare's magic slammed into me, drowning me. The spell for a massive fireball dissolved. The onslaught of magic slackened, the pain receding in a slow tide. I grabbed for the runaway magic as it shifted through the thief's key, only peripherally aware of the snare's painful punishment when I manipulated the elements. If I didn't slow this down, I wouldn't survive.

My magic skimmed the umbrella panels as if sliding across ice. Nothing penetrated the key's spell. When the cycling elements locked into place across the leather panels, I desperately slapped counter-elements atop them. The thief's key wrenched my magic into the spell, morphing the elements to fuel what I was trying to slow. A fresh torrent of magic sent razors slicing through my mind. My thoughts splintered as raw elements consumed me. Then the torment paused. I didn't waste time trying to catch my breath or fighting the thief's key. I used the precious reprieve to shove excess elemental energy from me in a burst of unrefined air. It should have unleashed a hurricane inside the spa. Instead, the magic imploded, and the thief's key absorbed it. A backlash of magic hammered my senses, blending with the snare's stinging counterstrike. The next layer of siphoned magic slammed so close behind it, I couldn't catch my breath. The world dimmed, closing in around me, until all that remained was pain. It flickered, slackened, then redoubled. Persephone faded from my awareness, unimportant. Grant . . . I couldn't hear him over my own screams.

White-hot needles drove through my brain. Pain dipped, then pulsed even higher. The thief's key shoved more magic into me until the very elements stretched inside me, swelling beneath my skin. *Pulse.* Magic dove inward, pulverizing my muscles, shattering my bones. Every nerve seethed, split, and exploded in a nonstop assault of agony. *Pulse.* I couldn't see, couldn't hear. I existed in a cyclone of consuming misery, teetering on the precipice of burnout.

My limbs convulsed, then locked in rigor. The room canted, the floor sweeping upward. *I'm falling,* I realized, the thought a thousand miles away. I was too brittle, too swollen with magic. The impact would shatter me. *Please, let me die,* I begged. *Please end this pain.*

Disappointment tasted like blood when the stones cushioned my fall.

The thief's key slid from my numb fingers. I floated, disassociated from my throbbing body and wheezing lungs.

"Impossible," Persephone breathed. *I couldn't have done that.*

My heart pounded as if it were attempting to crack through my rib cage, but I couldn't feel my feet or fingers. I needed to move, to rise, to escape, but all I managed was a spasmodic twitch.

The snare didn't react.

I tested it again, flopping a hand over my stomach. The truth hex clutched in my numb fist punched my stomach, but the snare remained inert. It had worked! I couldn't see the surface of the deadly ward from where I lay, but I didn't need to. The thief's key had broken it. I had done it.

"Why won't you die?"

I rolled my head toward Persephone. She hunched several feet away, her withered body bent, her beautiful features desiccated and gaunt. An empty vortex spun in her stomach. With a growl, she flung a skeletal hand at me, hurling lightning at my chest. A tiny voice in the back of my head screamed for me to *move*. My body didn't comply.

Persephone's spell split, exploding into ice and fire. The fire engulfed her, and she doused it with a screech. The arctic blast pitched me across the floor, snapping me out of my stupor.

A slender ray of hope lit my thoughts, giving me strength to push myself to my hands and knees. The last time a spell had failed so spectacularly had been when Quinn had warped the elements for Zipporah.

I looked for my beloved gargoyle companion but didn't spot him. Good. So long as Persephone wore the beguiling beads, he needed to stay out of hearing range.

Persephone flung another lightning bolt. It curved into the floor, blasting a jagged line through the rocks straight into the main pool. Electrified water and stinging shrapnel spewed across the room, chased by a disorienting concussion of thunder. The crisp scent of ozone filled the air. I staggered to my feet, rocking on unstable legs. My ankles felt as if they had been fused with granite, my calves carved from marble.

"Stand still, Harriet," Persephone ordered. *Let me kill you.*

I tightened my fingers around the truth hex, grateful for its whispers. So long as I held it, the beguiling beads' manipulative magic couldn't affect me.

Persephone thickened air into a sword only to have it jerk skyward and devolve into a wind spout against the ceiling. She cursed and re-formed the spell.

My first step landed heavy; the next almost pitched me on my face. Persephone fought the elements, her ice pick fracturing into a rain shower, her wooden cage splintering, her lightning exploding into sparks. With each failed spell, she backed up another step, her wild eyes locked on me.

"You can't do this. You have to die. Don't move. That's an order, Harriet!"

I'm better than you. You should be dead already. I'm in control. I'm the one with all the power.

Lumbering into a charge, I bore down on Persephone. She grabbed for me, her illusionary claws slashing through my arms, her fingers grasping at my shirt. I rammed into her, knocking us both to the ground. Persephone landed beneath me and fought, clawing and kicking. A punch landed like a boulder in my side. Nails raked my neck. I didn't attempt to block her or fight back. I wanted only one thing: the beguiling beads.

Persephone tried to dislodge me, and I used her grip on me to secure her arm beneath my knee; then I put my full weight on it. She screamed. Her free hand slammed into my cheek, making my ears ring. My fingers closed on one clip-on earring, and I yanked it free.

Persephone grabbed for my hand. "Give it back! I need it to survive."

I flung the earring across the room. Her inhuman shriek echoed through the spa. She twisted, her neck kinked to track the glimmer of the beguiling bead as it rolled into a groove between two stones. She flailed, no longer fighting me as much as attempting to propel herself after the bead. I ripped the other earring from her ear and threw it in the opposite direction. Persephone's entire body spasmed, bucking me to the floor beside her.

Quinn burst through an empty window. I might have cried from relief if I hadn't been awestruck. He landed on paws twice the size of my head, the rest of his body proportionally giant, with his chest spanning ten feet and his forehead brushing the ceiling. When he unfurled his wings, they spanned the room. A sun beat in Quinn's chest, the pulse of his heart a blinding glow that radiated through his massive citrine body. My wrist slipped, and I fell to my elbow, gaping in shock.

"Kylie! She's getting away." Quinn bounded across the room, his quartz paws ringing on the stone floors, and planted himself in front of Persephone. Somehow, he squeezed his colossal bulk into a space half its size. He bowed low, his enormous jaws opening as he shouted my name again.

I peered down his cavernous throat and saw . . . his face? The puzzle snapped together. The giant suit was another hex illusion. Just as Persephone's true nature was a hollow, vacuous shell of a person, Quinn was larger than life, a true champion with a heart of pure gold.

Persephone had rolled to her hands and knees, her glassy eyes fixed on the closest beguiling bead halfway across the room. Quinn fanned his wings in front of her, caging her in, but he seemed hesitant to touch her. I had no such qualms. I lurched to all fours and slammed my shoulder against Persephone's hip, knocking her onto her side. Another shove pushed her facedown.

"Paw here," I ordered, pointing to Persephone's back.

Quinn delicately settled a paw atop her, his expression crinkling with concern. His foot appeared to span Persephone's torso and part of her thighs, but I patted through the illusion until I found the solid gargoyle leg beneath. I leaned my weight against it.

"Hold her down."

"Let me go!" Persephone scraped for purchase, her fingers clawing into the stone seams.

"Hard," I said when Quinn allowed her to slither an inch.

"What's wrong with Grant?" Quinn asked.

Grant stood at the rift, locked in a magical compulsion, knitting the elements as fast as they unraveled, never quite finishing the repair. Thunderbirds flocked around his magic, pecking and clawing at it. A golden nimbus of agonizing energy ate at Grant's magic, but he didn't let up.

"Persephone spelled him."

Quinn shoved his foot into Persephone's back, pinning her in place. She screamed half-coherent threats of our deaths garbled among orders for us to release her and kill ourselves. The hex translated it all the same: *I need. I need. I need.*

I staggered to retrieve the null cuffs. Persephone fought me when I bound her wrists behind her back, but the moment the cuffs snapped in place, she went limp.

Quinn lifted his foot. Persephone curled into a ball, sobbing.

"Watch her, please." She didn't appear capable of doing anything dangerous, but I didn't want to chance both of us turning our backs on her. If Persephone escaped, I would never forgive myself.

I dragged myself to my feet again. My legs sagged, exhaustion stealing my strength. Curling up on the floor sounded divine, but not quite yet.

On stumbling steps, I crossed the room.

"Grant, it's over."

"Don't come closer," he warned, weariness flattening his voice. "I can't hold them off much longer." The indomitable captain swayed on his feet, sweat and blood dripping from his body. His face had lost all color, casting his lips and skin in the same ashen pallor.

"You can fix the ward now. You just have to finish it."

"I can't. It's too much for one person."

The defeat in his voice cut to my heart. I had assumed

that removing the beguiling beads from Persephone would break their spell, but it was stronger than I realized. Hoping I was doing the right thing, I uncurled my fingers enough to expose the truth hex clutched in my palm.

"You have to see the truth, Grant." I pressed the hex against his bare chest, my hand disappearing into the center of the golden illusion. It was the same glowing hue that radiated from Quinn, the embodiment of honor and loyalty.

Grant stilled, his magic holding solid above us.

"See?" I whispered. "Your magic is enough. You can fix the ward. We're safe now."

His chest swelled against my palm, and his magic faltered. Then, in a single powerful pulse, he closed the rift and sealed the ward. The thunderbirds scrabbled for purchase, flapping off into the storm, their lightning striking harmlessly against the solid elemental barrier.

Grant dropped his arms around me and tugged me closer. I sagged against him, breathing in the scent of sweat, mud, and ozone clinging to his skin.

"We did it." I failed to pack enthusiasm into my words, but that didn't make my sentiment any less heartfelt.

Grant flinched. He leaned back to put space between us, dropping his chin to examine his chest. His hand slid up to cover mine where I pressed the hex over his heart.

"Thank you," he said.

I love you.

My eyes widened at the hex's translation. "What?" I croaked.

As if he were afraid I would shatter, Grant carefully circled my wrist with his fingers and lifted my palm away from his chest.

"Drop the hex, Kylie." *This isn't right.*

"No. I need it." I heard the echo of Persephone's cries in

my words, but I wasn't anything like her. Persephone was insane. She had worn the beguiling beads too long and they had warped her.

I tipped my chin up, looking Grant in the eye. "I do need it. It's the truth, and the truth is what makes me a good journalist. The hex will make it so I'll always know the truth." See? I was sane and rational. Logical.

I tried to tug my hand free, but Grant's gentle grip was deceptively strong.

"You're an accomplished journalist, and you didn't need the hex to get where you're at. You don't need it now." *Trust your instincts.*

"I got fired. Did I tell you that?"

Grant shook his head, but no sympathy softened his expression.

"Don't you understand? This"—I rattled my fist in his grip—"could get me my job back."

"How much does it hurt to hold it? How much does it hurt each time its magic interprets the truth?"

"Hurt me?" I crinkled my nose, unsure where he was going with this new tangent.

"You're bleeding. You've been cradling your arm like it's broken. You're rubbing your chest like it hurts." *It's eating you up.*

I dropped my free hand from my chest, puzzled by its actions. Grant held my other hand higher, forcing me to look at it. Two blunt tips of the six-sided hex were embedded in my palm, and blood smeared the bone star and ran down the outside of my forearm, garishly bright against my pale skin. Tension distended the tendons in my arm. Despite my hand being partially open, my fingers curled like claws, every knuckle and nail bed white.

The sight pushed aside a fog of numbness, awakening a

piercing ache in my elbow and a humming sting engulfing my arm. Pain snapped against my breastbone with each heartbeat.

"Let it go," Grant said.

If I did, I would never have this same conviction of truth again. I would never know if a person's words hid a lie. I would be vulnerable to being taken advantage of and tricked.

"It's all right. I'm here," Grant said. *You're safe with me,* the hex whispered.

Slowly, I tilted my hand and uncurled my fingers. The hex slid from my flesh and dropped to the stone floor, bouncing once. The light in Grant's chest winked out, revealing my bloody handprint smeared across his pectoral muscle. Across the room, Quinn shrank to his normal size.

Tears blurred my vision. I wanted to pick the truth hex back up. I *craved* the certainty of its voice even as my arm pulsed with fading pain.

"It's going to be all right. Help is here." Grant looped an arm around my waist, steadying me when I swayed toward the truth hex.

A flurry of people dressed in FPD uniforms burst into the spa, entering from multiple angles and ringing the room. An elemental net snapped between them, filling the room with a massive nullification field.

A blanket of nothing wrapped my head, cutting me off from the elements, shrinking the world down to my basic senses. I must have made a noise, because Grant squeezed my hip.

"It's temporary," he murmured.

I nodded. Hot tears spilled down my cheeks, and I didn't try to explain the jumble of emotions rolling through me. I had come perilously close to being permanently nullified, to forever being a shell of a person unable to touch even the tiniest bit of magic. And yet, in this moment, having a buffer between my overtaxed body and the elements was a gift.

"Let me through," bellowed a familiar voice. Persephone's fiancé, Luther Wetherill, shoved past a slender FPD agent standing at the far door and flung a hand in my direction. "Now do you believe me when I say the Grayson girl is guilty?"

I opened my mouth to defend myself, but my teeth clicked together as Nathan slithered through the doorway on Wetherill's heels. The senior journalist gaped at the room and Persephone handcuffed on the floor. Then he spotted my haggard appearance. A smirk curled the corner of his mouth, and he snapped a picture on a fancy new camera.

Since when did the FPD allow reporters to tag along on dangerous missions?

I suspected the answer tied in with the equally suspicious presence of Luther Wetherill, my parents' chief business rival.

"Glad you could make it, O'Hara," Grant said, ignoring Wetherill's bluster and directing his comment to the dark-skinned FPD man with a silver goatee and a short-cropped gray hair standing next to him.

"I do enjoy a good thunderstorm." O'Hara swept the room with a practiced eye, taking in the null cuffs on Persephone and the banned spells scattered haphazardly across the floor, then Grant's half-naked state and his supportive hold on my waist. When the investigator's critical gaze shifted to me, I swiped the tears from my face and attempted to stand straighter.

"You have an inventive interpretation of surveillance, Monaghan," O'Hara said, not breaking eye contact with me.

"Just doing my part to assist your investigation."

O'Hara snorted.

Quinn abandoned Persephone and bounded to my side, giving me a welcome excuse to blink and drop my gaze. I ran my fingers across Quinn's forehead, and he rubbed his cheek against my thigh before planting himself practically atop my foot. With Grant on one side and Quinn on the other, I felt as if I were wedged between two pillars.

O'Hara pointed a finger at Quinn. "I told you to stay with us."

"You were going too slow."

"We could have used your help with the hydra."

Quinn shook his head. "Kylie needed me more."

O'Hara's eyes bored into me again, his expression unreadable.

"Grant and I would be dead if Quinn hadn't shown up when he did." The words came out more belligerently than I intended, but the investigator's challenging stare—and his offhand reprimand of Quinn—made me defensive.

Persephone struggled to sit up, her low moan drawing everyone's attention. Her hair hung frazzled around her face, and her cheeks were blotchy from crying. Without the truth hex showing me her true nature, her distressed appearance gave her a fragile, vulnerable beauty. Her bottom lip trembled. "Luther?"

"What did Harriet drag you into?" Wetherill asked, his face softening into pitying lines.

I bristled.

"Sir, this is an unstable environment," O'Hara said, deftly stepping into Wetherill's path when he started forward. "Please remain here while we conduct our investigation."

Indignation sharpened Wetherill's features. "That's my fiancée and the full-spectrum head of the Kwan estate. I won't stand for her to be treated like this. Now, get rid of this nonsense." Wetherill batted his hand through the air as if he could wave away the FPD team's nullification net. "I'm not a criminal. You can't strip me of my elemental rights, and I won't let you—"

A shadow moved past the window; then the largest centaur I had ever seen bent through the doorway and tapped Wetherill on his shoulder. "Excuse me," he rumbled.

Wetherill sucked in a breath and puffed out his chest, redirecting his indignation. The centaur took a stride into the room, crowding Wetherill. Another step, and the centaur straightened his human torso. Given the option of being trampled or stepping aside, Wetherill wisely joined Nathan, who cowered against the wall.

When the centaur stepped fully into the room, the spa shrank around him. Black from the crown of his bald head to the tip of his long tail and massive hooves, the centaur's equine body rivaled that of the Clydesdales used to pull logging wagons, and his human torso stretched proportionally large. If he had been fully human, he still would have dwarfed Grant. Next to him, Wetherill looked like a child.

I almost missed the willowy woman who darted inside after him. Khaki pants stacked with pockets encased her slender legs, and a matching multipocketed vest swallowed her torso. A gold FPD logo adorned the back of her vest, partially obscured by her thick, chestnut braid. The centaur's only concession to a uniform was a black armband with a matching gold FPD logo.

"That's Jax and Harper," Quinn whispered, his eyes glowing with awe as he watched the colossal centaur. "They are fearless, and Harper has all kinds of neat things in her pockets."

Harper strode past O'Hara. Persephone, Grant, and I each received an impassive once-over before her gaze bounced from prohibited spell to prohibited spell.

"O'Hara, clear the air. We need to get these spells bagged." Harper beelined for the snare and slice. She didn't seem to notice the tension in the room as she withdrew a canvas pouch from one of her many pockets and shook it open. Jax joined her next to the crate, his hooves ringing against the stones.

The null net dissipated. I took a second look at Harper. She couldn't have been older than me, yet she commanded the investigator with self-assured authority. I had never seen a gold-level FPD warrior before, but it must have signified a high rank.

"That's better." Wetherill straightened his vest. He had come dressed for a business meeting in charcoal slacks and a matching vest, his shirt beneath a crisp white. Since he had brought along his own pet journalist, maybe he had dressed with a photo opportunity in mind. He certainly spoke as if he were onstage. "I may not be an investigator, but it's obvious this is no coincidence. First the stolen fire-birds, and now Harriet Grayson and her consort are found in possession of yet more stolen items from Airstrong? What are you waiting for? Arrest them."

My *consort*? I peeked at Grant out of the corner of my eye. His captain's mask was firmly in place, his pallor aiding in concealing his thoughts.

O'Hara's nostrils flared before he, too, adopted an impassive expression. "You're right; you're not an investigator. A moment of your patience, if you will, while we get this sorted out."

"I've been patient enough."

"Mr. Wetherill, if you insist on delaying us—"

"I insist you stand aside—"

O'Hara popped a soundproof ward around Wetherill, caging him against the wall with Nathan as if he were an annoyance, not one of the most powerful men in Terra Haven. Wetherill's mouth snapped shut, but the mottled red of his face conveyed his fury. O'Hara turned his back on the full spectrum and addressed his squad.

"Phelps, McGrath, fortify the perimeter ward. Anderson, see to Ms. Kwan, but keep the null cuffs on her. Xinh, see to Ms. Grayson."

I didn't like the way O'Hara had worded his instructions, as if I required the same degree of suspicion as Persephone.

Two men slipped outside, staying beneath the dome as they jogged around the spa in opposite directions. A stout woman knelt next to Persephone and began a clinical examination of her wounds. That made Xinh the slender man Wetherill had blustered past earlier. He had friendly features and at least one recent Asian ancestor in his family tree.

"Null cuffs?" Xinh asked O'Hara as he crossed the room.

"Not yet." O'Hara canted his head toward the back of the spa. "Monaghan, a word."

"Can you stand?" Grant asked me.

I tore my glare from O'Hara. "Shouldn't I be asking that of you? You're the one who got bitten by a hydra."

Xinh's eyes darted to Grant, his eyebrows lifting fractionally.

"Kylie already did all the hard work," Grant said, waving aside Xinh's concern.

Grant gave my hip one last squeeze, then followed the investigator into the shadows. I reached for Quinn, trepidation fluttering in my stomach. I shouldn't have anything to fear from O'Hara and his team, but his *not yet* response to Xinh's question about null cuffs made me nervous, as did his arrival with Wetherill in tow. Wetherill had every reason to want to clear his fiancée's name, and no reason to help me. Despite his cavalier use of a ward to cage Wetherill, the investigator would place more importance on the word of a respected full-spectrum businessman than he would on anything I said.

Xinh scrutinized Grant's back as Grant walked away. The gashes oozed blood, but it ran clean red. He needed a healer to stop the bleeding and patch him up, but he wasn't in danger of dying of poison. A burst of pride brought a small smile to my lips.

Xinh nodded to himself, apparently deciding Grant would survive without his intervention, then turned to me. "Where are you hurt, Ms. Grayson?"

The water symbol on his uniform's collar likely meant he would be a more skilled healer than Grant, but I shook my head to decline his offer. I wanted answers more than healing, and the investigator and Grant were already too far away and speaking too quietly for me to eavesdrop on their conversation.

"Why is Wetherill here? And Nathan, the reporter?" Despite myself, my gaze flicked toward the men. Wetherill had gotten his expression under control and stood with his arms crossed, looking every inch the irritated full spectrum. Nathan hung back, keeping out of Wetherill's line of sight. Cowering like the slug he was. Only his eyes betrayed his pompous joy. When he saw me looking, he allowed himself a smug smile that screamed, *I have a front-page story. Nanny-nanny-nu-nu.*

"Why are *you* here?" Xinh countered, drawing my attention back to him. He gave me a disarming smile.

"I'm here to clear my parents' names." I eyed the truth hex. It lay several feet beyond Quinn, within easy reach. What would be the harm of holding it a few minutes longer? I could pick it up long enough to determine if Xinh's friendly demeanor could be trusted. And maybe hold it until I was certain that I could trust O'Hara and that he believed my parents were innocent. It also would be invaluable in determining the reason behind Wetherill's presence—

"That looks painful. May I?" Xinh reached for my injured hand.

I uncurled my fist, disturbed to realized I had been squeezing my nails around the cuts the truth hex had left in my palm, driving fresh pain up my arm.

"I, uh—"

"Who has been using these spells?" Harper demanded.

O'Hara jerked his head up from his quiet conversation with Grant. "Which ones?"

"All of them." Jax divided a suspicious look between Persephone, Grant, and me.

"Persephone wore the beguiling beads," Grant said, speaking around a mouthful of ration bar. O'Hara had healed the wounds on his back, and fresh pink scars replaced the jagged teeth marks. His color looked better, too.

A knot of worry inside me unraveled, and exhaustion swooped in to replace it. I swayed on my feet. Xinh transferred his grip to my elbow, bracing me.

"The snare was—" Grant cut himself off when O'Hara lifted a hand.

The investigator swung around to pin Wetherill with a withering glare. The caged full spectrum jabbed O'Hara's ward with a splinter of wood element. The magical prod hit again and again, fast as a woodpecker drilling a hole, with a force that looked just this side of painful. If he had wanted to, Wetherill could have broken the ward, but he apparently possessed enough sense to avoid openly defying a member of the FPD—though not enough sense to avoid antagonizing him.

O'Hara let the ward drop, leaving a shining line across the floor in its place. "Do not cross that line or attempt to interfere again, Mr. Wetherill. My patience is thin."

Fury flashed across Wetherill's haughty features before he masked it. I guessed not many people dared to talk so bluntly to him.

"Did Kwan also use these?" Harper demanded, indifferent to Wetherill's posturing.

"No," Grant said.

An irrational part of me wanted Grant to rush to my side, sweep me into his arms, and explain everything to O'Hara for me, but he appeared content to shadow the investigator for a closer examination of the inert thief's key and snare. Clasping his hands loosely behind his back, Grant gave me a subtle nod. It was a respectful acknowledgment of my ability to speak for myself. I attempted to appreciate his vote of confidence and not feel betrayed.

I cleared my throat. "That was me."

"You?" O'Hara's question held equal parts surprise and suspicion.

The enormous centaur spun on his haunches and thundered across the room. His massive black chest and flashing, shovel-size hooves filled my vision, and alarm jangled through my fatigued limbs. Xinh slid aside, leaving me exposed. Jax crashed to a halt in front of me. I locked my knees and craned my head back to meet his eyes, swallowing hard.

"Which one?" Intensity blazed in the centaur's obsidian gaze.

I struggled to corral a thought. My eyes bounced from Jax's fists, each as large as my head, to his bare human torso stacked with as much muscle as Grant and Velasquez combined. Words eluded me.

Harper jogged around Jax. With relief, I transferred my gaze to her.

"Obviously the truth hex," she said, assessing me with cool detachment.

"And the snare and slice and thief's key," I said, pleased to have found my voice.

"All three?" Jax asked. He and Harper shared a look I couldn't interpret.

"The snare was hidden, and I accidentally tripped into it. The truth hex fell and I caught it." I grimaced to admit my foolishness. "Then I had to use the thief's key to break the snare when Persephone attacked."

Harper's thin eyebrows danced upward. She snatched my uninjured hand from where it rested on Quinn's wing. I swayed, and Quinn pressed his shoulder against my hip to steady me. Harper didn't seem to notice. She scraped my skin with a lath of elements.

"You're lucky to be alive," she said.

"I didn't want to—"

Harper yanked my other wrist to her face, studying my cut palm. Her lips flattened. She wrenched my arm higher, jerking me onto my toes as she displayed my palm for Jax.

"Oh, that's no good," the centaur said.

"What?" This conversation would be so much easier to follow if I were holding the truth hex. It could have already whispered the true meaning behind Jax's terse questions and Harper's cryptic comments. I tugged on my arm, and Harper let me relax, but she didn't let go.

Jax bent and laid a huge hand gently against my back, effectively caging me between his muscular arm and Harper.

"This is going to sting," he warned. "Hold still."

"Wait, what?"

Harper spun a spell together, too fast for me to track, inverted the elements, stretched the jumble into the shape of a pair of scissors, and plunged the tip into the cut on my hand. I cried out as the sharp blades sliced through my palm, cutting in a tight circle. Harper held my hand rigid when I would have jerked away, and Jax prevented me from escaping backward. When Harper pulled her elemental scissors from my flesh, something dark and wriggling came with them. I gasped and leaned closer, trying to examine it through tear-blurred vision. Harper jerked it away from me. In a flash, she folded the scissors into a new shape, enveloping the seething bundle and snuffing it out of existence.

I took a deep breath, my chest rising lighter than before, as if Harper had lifted a weight from my body. I tasted the salt in the air, smelled the comforting warmth of Jax's body and the soft jasmine scent of Harper's hair. The details of the room clarified as if a fog had been removed from my vision.

"The truth hex was still linked to you," Jax said before I could form the question. "Harper just broke its connection. After a proper healing, you'll be hearty and whole again."

"Allow me." Xinh slipped an arm around my waist, supporting me, and lifted my cut palm.

I looked past him, at Grant. He hadn't moved when Jax had galloped across the room, and he hadn't interceded or assisted when Harper had worked magic on me, but he looked as if he wanted to shove Xinh from my side now. Did he mistrust O'Hara's people? I arched an eyebrow in silent question. Grant's gaze flicked to Xinh's hand on my ribs, and his jaw clenched before he smoothed his face. A spurt of wholly inappropriate delight bubbled in my stomach: He was jealous.

Cool magic soothed across my palm, drawing my attention inward as muscle and flesh stitched together beneath Xinh's masterful touch. In seconds, the cut painlessly disappeared without a scar, leaving me with a bloody palm and the tingle of freshly knit flesh. The room spun when I glanced up too fast. The minor healing had sapped my depleted energy. Nevertheless, I stepped out of Xinh's supporting hold, opting to lean against Quinn instead.

Jax backed up a step, then bent a knee to lower himself to talk to Quinn. "You did well, little gargoyle. Hexes can get nasty if they're allowed to fester. Ms. Grayson is lucky you rushed us."

Quinn's chest swelled with pride, his eyes wide with adoration for the enormous centaur. "Thank you for coming."

Harper cleared her throat and held out a canvas bag. Jax stepped away to assist her with tucking the hazardous truth hex inside. The bone star disappeared, and I let out a shaky exhale. I no longer craved its creepy whispers to help me translate the world—though I couldn't help but wonder what the people in the room would have looked like through the hex's symbolic illusions. Specifically Wetherill.

"Ms. Grayson, explain how you came to be here," O'Hara said.

I waited to speak until Jax and Harper had crossed to the far side of the room to collect a beguiling bead so I didn't have to compete with the ringing of the centaur's hoofbeats. Then I started at the beginning—the solstice ceremony—describing how Persephone had used the beguiling beads on me and the rest of the guests, and how I hadn't recognized the mental manipulation until I saw Persephone wearing the beads in the paper the next day.

"I also saw that picture in the *Chronicle*," Wetherill interrupted. "Having nothing to hide, I took it directly to the investigator. Yet you somehow ended up here, with the spells in your possession."

Persephone stirred for the first time, her brows drawing together in confusion as she studied her fiancé.

"I researched the Kwans, wanting more than a grainy picture as proof before I accused anyone of such a heinous crime," I said. "That's when I learned about the Kwans' defunct Aurora Isle and suspected this would be the perfect place to store stolen spells." I decided against mentioning my everlasting seed's help in connecting the dots, not wanting to sidetrack the investigator. More important, I didn't want to bring up my seed in front of Nathan, who was lapping up every word spoken as fodder for his story. I tried to summon anger that, once again, Nathan was stealing a story that should have been mine, but I couldn't muster more than minor frustration. I had a bigger goal here than advancing my career: I had my parents' freedom and reputations to protect.

I explained our intention of returning to Terra Haven and notifying O'Hara once we saw the warded building, and how the hydras and thunderbirds had prevented us. I rushed through my description of healing Grant, figuring that was his story to tell if he wanted. By the time I got to my fight with Persephone, my throat was dry. I kept my recounting succinct, trying to stick to the facts and not flavor my words with my opinions or emotions. O'Hara listened, his expression unchanging and unreadable.

"Are we supposed to believe Persephone did all this by herself?" Wetherill demanded when I wound down.

"She was wearing the beguiling beads," O'Hara said. "You came to me yourself, saying you feared Ms. Kwan was trying to set you up."

"I would never," Persephone protested, her voice barely above a whisper. She pulled her gaze from the pouch where Harper had sealed the beguiling beads, shaking her head as if to clear her thoughts—or perhaps in denial of Wetherill's accusation.

"It pained my heart to even think it, but yes, I thought my fiancée—my *ex*-fiancée—might be trying to trap me."

Persephone gasped at his casual sundering of their relationship.

"But Persephone as a mastermind?" Wetherill spared her a pitying glance. "She doesn't have the skills or knowledge to steal from Airstrong."

As much as I hated to agree with anything Wetherill said, he made a good point about Persephone. She had worn the beguiling beads at a public, photographed event. It was an amateur mistake incongruous with the cunning the thief had exhibited.

"But Harriet knows all about her parents' business," Wetherill said, turning away from Persephone's tears. "By her own admission, she used three of the illegal spells almost as if she had prior training with them. And her fanciful story? Well, she's a writer, after all."

"I had nothing to do with the thefts," I protested.

"We're supposed to take you at your word?" Wetherill sneered. "You, a woman disowned by her own family, cut off from their support and living in poverty? It's not hard to see why you would lash out the way you did to make your parents pay. It's heartbreaking that you dragged Persephone into this."

I ground my teeth, swallowing another knee-jerk denial. Getting into a shouting match wouldn't convince O'Hara of my family's innocence. But it was galling to watch Nathan take notes of every word spoken. How much of Wetherill's unfounded claims would be reported as facts in tomorrow's *Chronicle*?

Forcing the worry aside, I focused on O'Hara. "I enjoy a healthy relationship with my parents, and it was *my* choice to live on my own, one they both supported. Persephone, however, admitted to me that she's broke, her family is destitute, and she feared her *adoring*"—I sank sarcasm into the word—"fiancé wouldn't marry her if he found out."

"That's preposterous," Wetherill scoffed. "You and your mother must have planted the idea in Persephone's head."

"It was Charlotte Grayson." Persephone's thready voice strengthened as she spoke. "I thought she was a good friend, a best friend." She glanced around, blinking rapidly as if waking from a dream. Her feverish gaze latched on to Wetherill, and her voice turned pleading. "Charlotte gave me these spells. She said they were gifts. I had no idea they were stolen."

"Or banned?" I checked O'Hara to see if he was buying Persephone's accusations, but his stoic expression gave me no clue. "Sir, until the solstice ceremony, neither I nor my mom had seen Persephone in years. I had no influence over her actions, and my mom had no opportunity or motive to give her a gift of any sort, let alone deadly spells."

"Says the girl who's been in hiding for years." Wetherill tsked. "People who are engaged in aboveboard activities do not attempt to conceal their identities."

"You're right, it's suspicious why I wanted to escape high-society dramatics and live more authentically, isn't it?" I snapped, my temper getting the better of me.

A ghost of a smile curved O'Hara's lips.

"I can speak to Ms. Grayson's character," Grant said.

"I bet you can," Wetherill muttered just loud enough for it to carry.

"I will vouch she's no thief. It must be shock and grief over his lost future with the woman he loves that is causing Mr. Wetherill to speak so ill of an honest woman."

Grant was far more diplomatic than I would have been. He had given Wetherill a way to save face and gracefully bow out of the argument. Unfortunately, his words inflamed Wetherill. With a flush suffusing his face, he waggled a finger at Grant, then at O'Hara.

"I trust you're too smart to take the word of a man who is obviously infatuated with the Airstrong heiress. He's clearly thinking with his di—"

"*Enough*, Luther," O'Hara snapped. "I respect Grant's judgment and trust his word. Besides, he informed me yesterday of Ms. Grayson's suspicions and his plans to investigate this island today. We've encountered no evidence to contradict their accounting of the events, right, Harper?"

The slender woman glanced up from a pouch she had been securing with a thick knot of elements. "Grayson's signature is on the three spells she said she used, the snare was broken in a manner consistent with the use of a thief's key, and the beads were coated with Kwan's magic signature."

Wetherill's jaw jutted stubbornly, but O'Hara had already turned his back.

"Persephone Kwan," he said, "you are charged with multiple counts of mental manipulation, possession of banned spells, and grand theft."

"It wasn't me. It wasn't my idea. It was Charlotte. She's behind it all. Charlotte Grayson is the thief." Persephone struggled to her knees, but the FPD woman standing beside her clamped a hand on her shoulder, preventing her from rising.

O'Hara gently placed a recording spell across Persephone's mouth and layered it with a soundproof ward. Her lips continued to move, contorting with rage, but no sound made it past the ward. O'Hara shook his head, but he appeared contemplative, not dismissive.

"Do you believe my parents are innocent now?" I asked.

"Possibly."

"But—"

"You have walked a thin line with the law, Ms. Grayson. I'm willing to overlook your use of three illegal spells due the circumstances. Do not make me regret my leniency."

My teeth clicked shut. I wanted O'Hara to declare my parents free of suspicion, but I would have to trust he would see reason after he had time to process everything.

In the meantime, I focused on the most important victory: Grant, Quinn, and I had survived.

EPILOGUE

O'Hara and his squad escorted us safely past the thunderbirds on Aurora Isle and through the hydra-infested swamp. We flew atop their carpets—all except Jax, who galloped alongside, easily keeping up. Quinn rode with Harper, and I slumped against Grant on a separate carpet. The entire convoy traveled in an impenetrable protective ward powered by O'Hara's squad, Jax, Harper, and Wetherill. Persephone's earlier animation had faded, and she sat limp in front of O'Hara, hands cuffed behind her back, her eyes glassy and unmoving. Wetherill ignored her, too busy dictating to Nathan while the sycophant jotted down notes. The story Nathan was going to submit to the *Chronicle* might as well have had *Luther Wetherill* in the byline. I couldn't bring myself to care. My head pounded, and dozens of aches and scrapes pinched my body, trapping me in a limbo of exhaustion and discomfort.

We sailed out of Dead Man's Swamp into the jaws of a mob. Dozens of reporters swarmed us, their glowballs preceding them, fracturing the darkness in a chaotic flurry of lights and shadows. Rather than bypass them, O'Hara brought our caravan to a halt. I wanted to cry when Grant urged me to my feet. Reporters engulfed us, their barrage of questions hammering me like physical blows, the snaps of flashes from cameras thrust into my face spiking pain through my brain. Grant wrapped a protective arm around me, and I curled into his chest, closing my eyes tight to fight off nausea.

Then Seradon was there, elbowing her way through the reporters, the rest of Grant's squad in tow. They scooped me up as if I were one of their own and whisked me to their waiting open-top air sled, the tall bodies of Velasquez, Marciano, and Grant boxing me in like a human ward. I caught glimpses of O'Hara and his squad striding in the opposite direction toward a wyvern-drawn sleigh, Persephone stumbling in their midst. Jax and Harper disappeared behind a cloak of shadows, slipping away unnoticed.

When Marciano slammed a soundproof ward around us, the reporters threw their hands up in disgust, then rushed to pester the investigator and Wetherill. Before Wetherill finished building his elemental soapbox and spotlight, Velasquez steered our cramped sled toward the road, and we sped into the night.

I sat squished between Grant and Seradon on a seat meant for two normal-size people. Grant's shoulder dug into my back, and Seradon's knee knocked against mine. Letting my head fall back against Grant's chest, I tracked Quinn's moonlit form circling above us and only half listened to Grant fill his team in on our adventure. After a minute, Winnigan's soft hand settled on my scalp, and cool magic slid into my skull. The pounding pain of my headache receded. I tried to thank her, but my eyelids were too heavy, and sleep tugged me under before I got out an intelligible syllable.

I woke at the steps to Blackwell-Zakrzewska Clinic rather than at Josephine's. No one listened to my protests as Grant carried me into the healing hall's lobby, and Seradon tossed me a cheerful wave as she and the rest of the squad departed.

"I need to go home. Quinn needs healing. He's been brave, but the hydra hurt him. He shouldn't have to suffer—"

"He flew ahead when we reached the city, but only after we promised to bring you here," Grant said.

"Oh." I rubbed my bleary eyes. "Well, we're here, and now we can go. Really, all I need is a bed and forty-eight hours of sleep."

"You and me both," Grant agreed, but he didn't put me down until a healer directed us to a room.

I endured a few minutes of basic healing followed by several hours of prodding and subtle synaptic rehabilitation to repair the damage done by the thief's key. It wasn't often a patient survived interacting with three banned spells simultaneously, and I had the misfortune of being the subject of an impromptu lecture on rare healing techniques, with every apprentice and healer in Terra Haven trampling through my room to gawk at me.

Grant underwent healing as well, though his was more routine. His scrapes and bruises as well as the strain of elemental overuse and the damage inflicted by the thunderbirds' electrifying powers didn't warrant more than a steady healer hand. My pesky audience didn't give him a second glance. Grant also finished a lot earlier than me, but I found him waiting in the lobby when they finally released me.

"Ready to go home?" he asked.

"You have no idea."

The glow of false dawn brightened the horizon as we

coasted through the silent streets of Terra Haven on a two-person flying carpet. One of Grant's squadmates must have loaned it to him since Grant's had been lost in the swamp. I gave silent thanks for that sacrificed rug. It had inadvertently protected Grant's back, and without it, the hydra's bite would have certainly killed him.

Closing my eyes, I savored the cool breeze on my face, Grant's warm arms wrapped around me, and the blissful absence of pain.

When we reached Josephine's, light shone from my windows, so the lack of gargoyles on the roof didn't alarm me. I stood with a groan and collected my battered bag from Grant's carpet. He sprang to his feet beside me, annoyingly perky after our ordeal.

"What are you doing?" I asked when he rolled up the carpet and tucked it under one arm.

"Seeing you to your door."

I eyed the five-foot expanse of stone and stairs leading up to the Victorian's entrance. "I think I can make it on my own."

"Probably." Grant slid his arm around my waist.

He felt so good against me, warm and safe and solid. I forgot why I was arguing with him, and I didn't protest when he let himself inside and escorted me up the internal stairs, too.

Warm lamplight illuminated my room in a soft glow. Mika, Oliver, and Quinn were sprawled on the floor around my low table. A pile of clear-crystal marbles lay in front of Mika, where she lounged against Oliver in her pajamas, a blanket wrapped around her shoulders. Quinn sported new clear patches on his paws and chest where Mika had mended his wounds. My heart swelled with gratitude for

Mika's care of Quinn and for having people who cared about me to come home to.

Mika sprang to her feet when the door cracked open, and she rushed to squeeze me in a tight hug. "Oliver and I were so worried. Quinn told us everything that happened, and it sounds terrifying. I can't believe you found your parents' stolen shipments. I mean, I can, because you always get your story, but the snare and slice? Persephone and the beguiling beads? Hydras? Thunderbirds? If Quinn were anyone else, I would say he was either exaggerating or making it all up." She examined my bedraggled, borrowed FPD uniform, my snarled hair pulled into a ponytail, and finally my face. "I had to see for myself that you were all right."

"I'm fine. Tired, but fine."

"I bet. I'm wrung out just hearing about everything you went through. Come." She took my bag and directed me to my bed. I gratefully sank onto its cushioned surface, and Mika sat beside me.

Reaching for Quinn, I ran a hand across his forehead and over his stone mane. He gave me a lolling smile, his eyes closing in contentment.

"I'm fine, too," Grant said.

Mika snorted. "Well, of course you are. You're—" She waved a hand to indicate his muscular frame.

Somewhere between the swamp and leaving the healer hall, he had acquired a change of clothes, and his current gray uniform appeared freshly laundered and armored with protective spells. He once again looked like an FPD captain, but I preferred it when he had been topless.

"I'm what?" Grant asked. "Too handsome to die? Too clever?"

"Too formidable," Mika said.

Grant grinned. Rather than take his leave, as I expected, he settled on my love seat and rested an arm along the backrest. His knees poked up higher than his hips, and the small couch looked more like a delicate chair with him in it. I cocked my head and studied him, trying to divine his intentions. He smiled back. A zing went through my stomach.

"These arrived not too long ago, both by special courier," Mika said, handing me two envelopes. "Luckily, Oliver intercepted them, and no one woke Ms. Zuberrie."

"You're the best, Oliver. Thank you." Being jerked out of bed in the wee hours of the morning wouldn't have done anything to improve Josephine's disposition toward me.

My stomach flipped when I caught sight of my boss's sharp scrawl on the first envelope. The other was addressed to *Harriet Grayson and Quinn the Gargoyle* and stamped with the FPD's seal.

"What are you waiting for?" Mika asked. "They have to be important if they were sent out this early."

I handed Quinn the FPD envelope, steeled myself with a deep breath, then ripped open Dahlia's letter. A single piece of paper was folded inside, a short note scribbled in the upper margin:

Let me know if there are any inaccuracies. —D

I skimmed the typed text below it, then reread it more slowly.

"What is it?" Quinn asked.

Everyone was staring at me. "It's Nathan's article about the stolen spells, the one that's going to be printed tomorrow—today." He must have written it during his flight back to Terra Haven and typed it while I was being healed. The printers would be scrambling to fit it into the morning edition.

"Of all the reporters . . ." Mika shook her head. "How bad is it?"

"About what I expected." The article didn't include any outright fallacies, but it did a good job of insinuating I might not be innocent, citing the suspicious coincidence of my presence at yet another location where stolen Airstrong shipments were recovered. Nathan made Wetherill out to be the hero, crediting him with steering the FPD to the island. While Nathan accurately reported on the stolen spells' recovery, the FPD's involvement, Persephone's arrest, and even Jax's and Harper's actions, he somehow failed to mention that I had battled with Persephone and that it had been me who had wrested the beguiling beads from her control and secured her in null cuffs. Instead, Grant received passing mention as the "FPD captain working with Investigator O'Hara," and I was "discovered in the company of Persephone" when the FPD arrived.

"It's probably better than anything else that's going to be printed," I said, recalling the horde of reporters who had been waiting outside the swamp. The hack journalists would likely have me training thunderbirds as avian assassins to coerce O'Hara into declaring my parents innocent or some such nonsense in the morning editions of their gossip rags.

My fingers twitched to make editorial notes atop Nathan's article—just enough to eradicate his unsavory innuendos. However, I stopped myself before I reached for a pen. The changes I wanted to make were cosmetic, not factual. Nathan had reported on the events as he saw them, and I couldn't change his personal biases. Nor had Dahlia asked me to. She had requested a fact check, nothing more. Perhaps this was another test. Maybe she wanted to see if I could separate my personal life and interests from my professional duties.

I set the paper aside and sat on my hands.

"What's that one?" I asked Quinn.

Using a freshly healed, clear-crystal claw, Quinn sliced open the top of his envelope. A check fell to the floor. It was made out to me and Quinn, and the amount made my jaw drop. Mika picked it up, holding the check reverently between her thumb and forefinger, as if afraid it would spontaneously combust if she breathed too hard.

Quinn unfolded the paper that came with the check, revealing official FPD letterhead.

"It says this is the reward for finding the stolen spells," Quinn said.

He glanced up, his expression as nonplussed as mine. I had forgotten about the reward. It had never been part of my motivation in finding the illegal spells. I had only wanted to clear my parents' names.

"Did you do this?" I asked Grant.

"Wasn't me. That's Jax and Harper's department."

I examined the check, my eyes lingering on the amount. It was the full promised reward. "This should be made out to you, Grant. We wouldn't have gotten close to the spells if not for you."

"Employees are ineligible to collect FPD-issued rewards. Besides, I didn't find the spells; you did."

"When I blundered into them?"

"When you made the connection between Persephone and that cursed isle."

Mika carefully set the check on the table. "What are you going to do with the money?"

With that amount, I could replace my broken camera instead of borrowing one from the *Chronicle*. I could afford my own flying carpet and never have to rent or borrow one again. I could buy a whole new wardrobe or—

"I'll pay Josephine back for the roof," I said, cutting the fantasies short.

"The repairs couldn't have cost *that* much," Mika protested.

"Well, the other half is Quinn's."

"Mine?" Quinn's eyes widened.

"Is there anything you want to buy?" I asked.

"I don't know." Quinn glanced to Oliver, then back at the check. "I've never had any money before."

"I'm sure you'll think of something," Grant said.

A lull settled over the room as we all contemplated the check, and I did my best not to let my thoughts drift back to Nathan's article.

"Yarra," Quinn blurted out.

"What?" Grant asked.

"Yarra. She lives at the Kwan estate. But now that we know Persephone is a terrible person and going to jail, she'll need a new home."

"She's the gargoyle you told me you met?" Oliver asked.

Quinn nodded. "She said no one else stays at the estate anymore, just her and Persephone."

"That sounds lonely."

Mika stroked Oliver's neck, the amethyst hexagons on the back of her hand glinting in the lamplight. "Let's invite her to come stay with us. We can help her figure out her next step."

"She'd like that," Quinn said.

Grant shifted, and the love seat's frame creaked ominously. "If you don't mind, Mika, I'd like to speak to Kylie in private."

"Sure thing." Mika pushed to her feet, but I grabbed her hand to stop her from leaving.

"She can stay. I don't keep secrets from Mika."

"You might not, but I do," Grant said.

Mika's smile turned into a grin. "I can take a hint." She winked, then yawned wide enough to crack her jaw.

An excited tingle shivered through my chest. Did Grant want to get me alone for a kiss? I tried to read his expression through my lashes, but he had picked up Nathan's article, and the paper hid the lower half of his face.

Oliver trundled across the balcony and through the door to Mika's room. Mika followed, closing the door behind them after Grant invited Quinn to stay with us.

My lips twisted down before I schooled my expression. Apparently, kissing *wasn't* on Grant's mind. He set aside Nathan's article and closed the balcony door with a push of air before dropping a soundproof ward around the room. Anxiety roiled in my stomach.

"You know Zipporah isn't going away, right?" he asked.

"Yeah. After she hears the spells she wanted are back in the hands of the FPD, she's going to be furious. I don't know how long I'll be able to avoid her."

"That's part of the problem. You've been on the defense. You've been reacting, and that put you in a position of weakness. You need to be proactive. You can't afford to have her show up whenever and wherever she wants."

"I know." She had already cost me my reputation and my job. Not to mention that each time she popped into my life, I barely survived and my friends got hurt.

"You need to settle this debt with her."

"How?"

"You and I are going to visit the harpy."

"We are?" I squeaked.

"Every paper in the city is going to have this story on the front page." Grant rattled Nathan's article. "You need to talk with Zipporah before she demolishes your roof again. We'd go now, but you and I both need sleep."

My stomach knotted, but I nodded. Grant leaned back in the love seat. I waited for him to drop his soundproof ward. He didn't.

"That's not what you wanted to talk to me about in private, though, is it?" I hazarded.

"I'm not convinced that Persephone planted the tracker on you."

I frowned, needing a moment to catch up with his subject change. "You said yourself that she had to have known I was in the swamp with how close she was behind us. The only way she could have known was if she was tracking me."

"Or she didn't know we were there at all. She could have been coming to collect the spells for another reason. I keep thinking about Zipporah showing up at the solstice gathering. How did she know where to find you?"

"She could have been spying on me or paid someone to spy on me."

"But she flew to your exact location. She didn't bother with the ballroom; she dropped into the courtyard outside the library, where you happened to be. Unless this fictitious spy was also at the party, it's an awfully big coincidence that she knew right where to look for you."

"Maybe she smelled us?" Quinn guessed.

"If she were a cerberus, I might agree." Grant shook his head. "Either way, I'm teaching you how to detect foreign spells later. You shouldn't be vulnerable like that again."

"All right."

I waited. Grant's expression remained troubled, but he

didn't speak. It wasn't like him to be hesitant. "Grant, you're making me nervous. Get to the reason you sent Mika away."

"I spoke with O'Hara while you were being healed." Grant ran a hand through his hair. "Persephone has made a lot of wild claims since her arrest, but she insists your mom gave each spell to her."

"That's a bald-faced lie."

"It's more likely she obtained the beguiling beads first, and they enabled her to manipulate employees into giving her access to the rest. But even that would have required an accomplice to identify when banned spells were being transported."

I slouched as his words sank in. "O'Hara isn't ready to dismiss my parents as suspects."

"No, he's not."

"Even after everything we uncovered?" Quinn asked.

"There's no solid evidence against Kylie's parents, but there's also no solid evidence exonerating them. Which is why I'm wondering . . ." Grant braced his elbows on his knees, his gaze steady on my face. "Your seed has led you into the thick of your parents' problems—twice. Did it evolve while we were on the island? Did it give you a new clue?"

I closed my fist around the pouch holding my seed. It still hung from a cord around my neck. I had checked the seed at the spa while the FPD had wrapped up their investigation of the premises. It hadn't changed, but that had been in natural light. I hadn't had the firebird feather with me, and so long as Nathan had been spying on me, I hadn't dared to pull out the thunderbird feather I had tucked inside my bag, either.

I hesitated to do so now, too. My zeal for uncovering the story of a lifetime had diminished in light of my parents' troubles. I had thought my question for the everlasting tree would lead me on a noble quest, and I had never once considered that a huge story could also have unprecedented fallout—and the people harmed by the coverage might be my parents. If only I had worded my question to the everlasting tree better! I hadn't even thought to specify that *I* would get to be the person to write the story.

Following my seed had also landed me in two of the region's most dangerous locales. I had nearly died both times, as had Grant and Quinn. Maybe I didn't want to know where the everlasting tree's magic would lead me next.

Yet, even as I entertained the thought, I knew it was a lie. The potential reward outweighed the risks. In chasing my seed's clues, I had harmed my parents' reputations, but I had ultimately helped them. If evolving my seed gave me a chance of clearing my parents' names once and for all, I had to try.

Besides, if I didn't, curiosity would corrode my sanity more surely than the truth hex had.

"What was your question for the everlasting tree?" I asked, stalling.

"It's private." Grant twisted his arm, examining the bracelet with a frown.

"It's something about me. I deserve to know."

Genuine surprise lit Grant's features. "What makes you say that?"

"I was present both times it evolved. This last time, I was even the one to apply magic to your seed."

"That's interesting logic."

I waited. Grant waited more patiently.

"You're not going to tell me?" I planted my hands on my hips.

"Not yet."

I engaged him in another staring match, throwing my hands up in exasperation when my eyes started watering. "Fine. Douse the lights."

It took less energy to walk across the room and pick up my bag than it would have to use the elements to float it to me. I settled on the floor on the far side of the table. Grant slid off the love seat to the floor, and Quinn nestled up against the third side. No one spoke as I pushed aside the check and laid my seed and the firebird feather on the table.

I rummaged through my bag, pulling out a damp thunderbird feather. At first, I thought it had been sitting in a puddle at the bottom of the bag, but a closer examination revealed a sheen of mist coating the feather's surface. When I wiped a swath away, the moisture reappeared, seeping outward from the barbs.

Holding a feather in each hand, I cupped them around my seed. The golden-and-copper shimmer of the seed changed in the firebird feather's light to the stormy blue-gray of the thunderbird feather, the navy zigzag markings on the seed perfectly mimicking those at the feather's tip.

I held my breath, waiting for the seed's next evolution. Nothing happened.

How was this possible? After everything we had gone through, I had been certain I was on the right path. Defeat welled thick in my throat, choking me.

A drop of water coalesced on the tip of the thunderbird feather and splashed onto the seed. Liquid amber washed across the seed, smoothing its grooves and pits. Lighter yellows licked beneath the surface, shifting and shimmering as if the seed were a molten lump of polished coal.

Quinn leaned closer, his eyes glowing in the twin light of the firebird feather and the seed. "Is that . . . ?"

"A phoenix egg," I finished, my voice hushed. I wasn't

entirely shocked that my seed had taken on yet another bird-related shape, but did it have to be a *phoenix*?

My hand trembled as I tapped the seed, afraid it would burn my fingertip. Phoenix eggs were notoriously volatile and would explode when the birds hatched—or if the eggs were mishandled. The detonation of a single phoenix egg wouldn't just demolish my apartment; it would level the whole Victorian.

The egg—the *seed*—was cool to the touch and smooth as glass. Barely breathing, I flipped it over. An FPD logo and serial number were stamped on the back in ebony against the seed's shifting, fiery core.

"I was afraid of this," Grant said.

I met his grim expression. "What's that supposed to mean?"

"O'Hara held back one detail of the Airstrong thefts: Among the stolen FPD items was a shipment of phoenix eggs. A complete clutch. Your mom never mentioned it to you, did she?"

I shook my head, horrified. Losing one phoenix egg would have been bad, but an entire clutch in the wrong person's hands could be catastrophic. If Airstrong's security on the illegal spells had been strict, it should have been impenetrable on phoenix eggs.

"You can't think . . . My parents would never . . ." If O'Hara decided my parents were guilty of trafficking in phoenix eggs, they wouldn't just go to jail; they would be imprisoned for life. Possibly hanged.

The room swam in my vision. My seed might as well have had an Airstrong logo printed next to the FPD's. My parents' troubles were far from over.

"Persephone has babbled a lot of nonsense," Grant said, "but she never once mentioned phoenix eggs."

"Which is why O'Hara hasn't taken his sights off my parents."

Grant nodded.

Slumping, I set aside the feathers. The seed reverted to its original shape—grooves, pits, firebird markings, and all. I wasn't sure why it didn't hold its transformations like Quinn's and Grant's seeds had, but that mystery paled in light of my new concerns.

"Is anyone looking into Persephone's ex-fiancé?" I asked.

"Wetherill? He's on my suspect list."

"Mine too," Quinn said.

"He seemed awfully determined to make me look guilty," I said.

"I noticed," Grant growled.

A kernel of heat loosened the coil of dread binding my midsection. I had Grant on my side. Grant and Quinn. I would need them, because going up against someone as cunning, elementally powerful, and wealthy as Luther Wetherill would be as dangerous as hunting phoenix eggs— and I would be doing both.

"Any chance I can convince you to let me pursue this on my own?" Grant asked.

I shook my head. "You're going to need my help. Besides, you heard Mika: I always get my story."

COMPLETE THE SPELLBINDING TRILOGY

The story of a lifetime is almost in reach, but can Kylie unravel the clues of her seed before her life—and her parents' lives—goes up in flames?

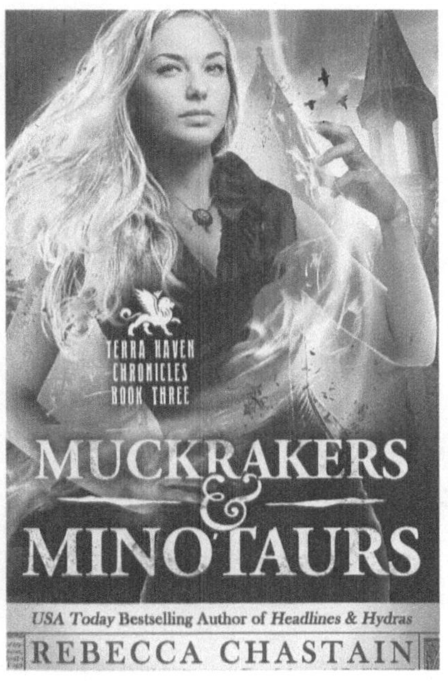

READ *MUCKRAKERS & MINOTAURS* TODAY!

ABOUT THE AUTHOR

REBECCA CHASTAIN is the *USA Today* bestselling author of the Madison Fox urban fantasy series and the Gargoyle Guardian Chronicles fantasy trilogy, among other works. Inside her novels, you'll find spellbinding adventures packed with supernatural creatures, thrilling action, heartwarming characters (human and otherwise), and more than a little humor. She lives in Northern California with her wonderful husband.

Visit RebeccaChastain.com for updates, extras, and so much more!

facebook.com/rebeccachastainnovels

twitter.com/Author_Rebecca

instagram.com/chastain.rebecca